blaze of misery

EMBER GLEN | BOOK TWO

BRYNN FORD

<u>More from the Author</u>
www.brynnford.com
brynnfordauthor@gmail.com

content warning

This is a dark romance series involving many triggering elements which may be upsetting for some readers. A complete list of tropes and triggers can be found on the author's website.
www.brynnford.com/triggers

series note

Blaze of Misery is book two of three in the Ember Glen trilogy. It is not a standalone; the books must be read in order.
Books one and two end on cliffhangers.

reading order

EMBER GLEN
Spark of Madness
Blaze of Misery
Embers of Mercy

playlist

Seven Devils by Florence + The Machine
Black Hole Sun by Soundgarden
In Flames by Digital Daggers
Love and War by Fleurie
Take Me to Church by Hozier
Can You Feel My Heart by MOTHICA
Lost My Mind by Alice Kristiansen
Just Found Heaven by Daughtry
London by Starbenders
Heaven or Hell by Digital Daggers
Can't Help Falling in Love (DARK) by Tommee Profitt ft. brooke
A Little Wicked by Valerie Broussard
Battlefield by SVRCINA
Fallout by UNSECRET & Neoni
Solitude (Felsmann + Tiley Reinterpretation) by M83

For all the women condemned by the rules of men…
Lift your chin, raise your voice,
and give them hell.

chapter one
ARLO

I CALL FOR the desecration of Mercy's flesh with four echoing words. "Let the trial begin."

I expect there to be some pause, a moment's delay or hesitation before the same level of debauchery as a night of service falls upon Mercy while she's strung up in the foyer of the Homestead. But there is no delay. My brothers in God have waited for this moment to punish a true sinner, and it's evident they do not intend to waste a moment of their seven hours of torture.

An invisible fist curls around my heart, squeezing with a vice-like grip as I watch them descend upon her. I try to ignore the way that fist tugs through my chest—as if it comes from Mercy's outstretched hand, trying to drag me toward her…except her arms are solidly secured behind her back. She couldn't reach out to me if she wanted to.

Does she want to?

Or has she lost all faith in me?

Air leaves my lungs as Killian slips his palm around the back of her head. My eyes widen as his fingers tangle with her hair, tightening his grip. He jerks her head back, and Mercy cries out with a sharp, grating sound. I fight the urge to shove to my feet.

"Open your mouth," Killian demands, and her hesitation is clear.

Of course, she doesn't open for him. She holds on to the last fraying thread of her defiance as he pulls out his cock. I already feel the anger of my false possession brewing.

Mercy is mine.

She's mine, though she doesn't belong to me. She belongs to God, and we are nothing more than the men who help make our women godly.

She sinned.

She earned these trials as her punishment—her chance at redemption for her soul. Yet I'm starting to wonder how this trial proves anything at all.

I can see Mercy's throat bob as she swallows the last dregs of her refusal, then opens her mouth to meet Killian's demand.

"Good," he says, then presses his cock between her parted lips.

My body tenses and jumps at her whimper, and I nearly leap from my seat with the urge to tear him from her, to slam my fist against his jaw, and punish *him* for making her taste him. Sucking in a heavy breath, I force myself to lean back in my chair, fingers interlocking as my palms come to rest at the back of my head. I lift my eyes toward the ceiling as I work to gather my composure.

Regardless of her suffering—regardless of my *own* suffering—I can't stop this.

I *won't* stop this.

It's better they focus their efforts on Mercy than Delle. Mercy's strong; she has experienced every sexual act imaginable in her years of service, and though she's never served multiple men at once, she can do this. I have to let her—not like there's a choice in the matter.

Still, the sound of her gagging as he forces himself to the back of her throat is challenging to ignore. I drop my hands to my lap, bringing my head down to level. The way he's moved in front of her to alter his angle blocks my view of her eyes.

I want her eyes fixed on me.

I want her to remember that I'm here, that I'll take care of her.

I want her to remember the way I touched her before the trial began and encouraged her to find pleasure here, any way she can.

Ryker strips naked, then steps in close against her backside. His hand slides down her lower back, over her ass, and he reaches between her legs from behind. Mercy's muscles jerk against the tension in her bindings as he roughly rubs his hand over her cunt.

I shove to my feet before I can take another breath and stomp across the tile. I come to a stop in front of her, close enough that she can see me while my brothers remove their clothing, preparing to defile her. Her watering eyes meet mine, and I've never seen such despair in her gray-blue gaze. It slices right through me—it pummels me with her aching, twists me with her anger.

Ryker's hand is moving, collecting her wetness, dragging a trail of it backward along her crack. My jaw sets with the primal need to fight him away from the prey I've claimed. Mercy yelps as Ryker's fingers play at her back entrance, and Killian pulls out of her mouth long enough to dip and grip her chin, forcing her eyes to meet his.

Killian leans close, his nose touching hers. "I hope his cock rips your insides apart." His voice is a venomous hiss.

A devious grin spreads across Ryker's cheeks as he tosses his head back to shake the dark blond hair from his eyes. Ryker lines up and thrusts, pushing inside her forcefully. Her screams intrude my ears the same way Ryker intrudes her body, and I feel her pain in the deepest parts of my soul.

Killian slaps his hand over her mouth to silence her as a tear slips down her porcelain cheek. A pained shudder ripples through me, and it causes every nerve ending to pulse with raging pain against the rigidity I must maintain to avoid interference. Mercy's expression scrunches and strains as Ryker fucks her ass with brutal force and a relentless pace.

She wasn't ready for that.

I should have had the fucking foresight to prepare that part of her body for this. I should have spread her wetness there myself, should have stretched her, played with her, loosened her up.

I failed, and now he's fucking her, and she's hurting.

It's my fault she's hurting.

Hardly five minutes have passed and it's the most torturous five minutes of my life.

How can she endure seven hours of this?

How can I?

I have to make it better.

Stepping closer, I reach out, seeking to touch between her legs and draw her back into pleasure, but her eyes snap to mine with fury. She practically growls against Killian's hand with a feral sound that halts me—it sounds like a strangled, "No."

Killian moves his hand, as if he's interested in knowing what she has to say.

Her face is puckered with rage, and she spits the words at me with fury. "Don't you fucking touch me!"

Led by her command, I yank my hand away, and I immediately know it was a mistake. Regardless of the fact that I feel things for this woman that I'm not allowed to feel—regardless of my odd compassion for her as a sinner enduring this trial—I must continue to demonstrate my authority, lest my own sins be found out.

I'm a sinner, too.

Perhaps I should be strung up beside her.

I shake my head to snap myself back to the authority I must represent. I step forward, moving in close, and before she can give my brothers the satisfaction of her angry words again, I bring my fingers to her pussy and slip them inside her. She gasps, jerking her head back. I can sense her protest as she opens her mouth, but Killian halts her words by shoving his cock between her lips again.

The weight of the world settles painfully on my shoulders.

I need to be seen as a willing participant in her trial.

I can't stop this.

I can't stop them.

I want nothing more than to end this, to end it *now* and take her back to the caves where I can hide her away from this world, where I can hold her in the darkness and bring her comfort. The only comfort I can bring her now is pleasure, and though I hadn't intended to let her come so early in the trial—though I know she has so much yet to endure—I can't help myself. I can't bear the sight of her eyes squeezed shut in misery.

Ryker and Killian fuck her from both ends with a shared rhythm that almost seems intentional—a rhythm that ensures she always feels one of them buried deep inside her without reprieve.

Though my breath catches in my lungs and my eyes burn hot, I do the only thing I can. I gently stroke my fingers inside her, coaxing her into pleasure. Her eyes snap open and her stare locks on mine, though her mouth is filled with *him*—Killian, a man I've always viewed as my brother in God, though at the moment, he looks like a fucking demon.

Maybe he's possessed by her demons the same way I am. The thought stirs jealousy in my gut. I prefer that her demons possess me, and me alone. And though it should be because I'd want to spare my brothers of the sin she inspires, it's not for that reason at all—it's because I want to be the *only* man Mercy's demons invade with thoughts of depravity.

I *am* the only man who gives her pleasure, and I intend for it to remain that way.

"Come for me, Mercy," a strangled voice demands, and it takes me moments to realize it was my own.

I sense Killian's eyes on me as I bring my thumb down over her clit, rubbing relentlessly as I stroke inside her.

The scent of her arousal swirls in the air around us, each stroke of my fingers kicking up a little bit more of her lustful aroma. It intoxicates me with desire, hardening my cock.

I hear them moving, rutting, groaning as they use her. I sense Killian's oncoming release in the way he holds her head and angles his hips, fucking her mouth faster and harder. The anger inside me has nowhere to go, so it shoots down my arm, spurring my fingers to work harder, faster, more intentionally.

"Sinner, you're going to make me come so quickly." Killian chuckles. "*Fuck.* I'm going to come all over your face, and then I can take my time to really show you what a sinner deserves."

My arm jerks involuntarily at his words and my fingers spear too harshly into Mercy. She whimpers as he pulls out of her mouth, wraps his hand around his cock, and strokes in quick, short jerks.

"Stop..." she pleads, but her eyes aren't on him...they're on me.

chapter two

Mercy

STOP, STOP, STOP, please *stop*.

I'm filled and tense, my muscles cramping and twitching as I fight the building climax Arlo tries to draw from me.

I don't want it.

I don't want his touch in this moment because it doesn't feel good. Though my inner walls clench around his fingers and a tingling pressure beneath his circling thumb tells of an onrushing orgasm, there's nothing pleasurable about it.

I feel like my insides are being ripped to shreds by Ryker, and every involuntary spasm inside my pussy makes me clench against him painfully. I've been fucked there before, but not like this—never with such relentless pounding, never so dry and unprepared. Men don't care if they hurt us in service; they only care if they enjoy themselves. The way Ryker pounds inside me makes his intention clear—he doesn't care about his own pleasure.

He only wants to hurt me.

And Killian, with the hatred in his eyes, the way he shoved his cock so deep, blocking my throat where I couldn't breathe…Now he strokes his cock, and I have the misfortune of spying the spot of pre-cum beading from the tip.

I want to scream, but I've already given them too much of my voice. I gave Arlo my voice, yelled at him to stop, yet he hadn't. His fingers remain inside me, and I never could have imagined his touch ever feeling so horrible. I don't want to tell him to stop again because it hurts enough that he hasn't already. It hurts that my gaze holds his, that our eyes are locked and he sees my pain, yet his fingers remain.

Ryker's cock swells inside me, adding pressure to the burning pain that scrapes along my insides. Killian devolves to vile thrusts against his hand and vulgar panting as he approaches his climax.

With a deep thrust, Ryker hisses and spills inside me. Killian jerks himself to orgasm, intentionally aiming and splashing his cum across my cheeks, and I pinch my eyes shut against the pulsing release. Arlo pulls his hand away—*finally*—as though he was only waiting for his brothers to finish.

He's right there, yet I feel so far from him.

Ryker pulls out from behind me, and I sense Killian's foreboding presence move away. I try to take a deep breath, to relish a moment of emptied relief before they start again. But the moment I inhale, another cock touches between my legs—a quick brush across my slickened cunt before slamming inside me. The jolting pressure forces my eyes open to see Wesley standing before me, angled between my legs, cock buried deep.

Will the next seven hours be so relentless?

How much time has passed? Minutes? Seconds?

My head rolls, seeking a place to rest in dejected exhaustion, but it only rolls aimlessly. Strung up the way I am—angled sidelong to the sunburst tile beneath my swaying body—my neck strains in all directions. I let it drop and hang sideways, gravity tugging it toward the floor. It stretches tightly through the side of my neck, causing my hair to drop over my face, sticking to the fluid Killian sprayed across my cheeks. I shut my eyes in disgust.

Then a hand slips along the side of my face to cup my cheek, easing the strain through my neck as my heavy head is lifted. My heart flutters, and for a moment, I believe it's Arlo's touch returned to comfort me…but when I open my eyes, I see that it's not.

It's Killian. He lifts his other hand to gather his cum from my cheek and swipes it across my lips with his fingers. He presses at the seam with his fingertips and urges me to open. I jerk my head toward the ceiling to try to shake free from his grasp, but he curls his fingers, tangling them into my hair, gripping the strands tightly to hold me in place.

"Open, Mercy Madness. This is what your sin tastes like." He bares his teeth with the righteous indignation that burns within him…it burns within me, too.

"Only a demon would have cum that tastes like sin," I say without thinking, my need to insult him overtaking any sense of reason.

His eyes flash with fury, and he rushes to push the sticky substance into my mouth while I'm still speaking, forcing his coated fingers between my lips. I whimper against the intrusion, and as the repulsive taste of him rubs across my tongue, I clamp my mouth shut, snapping his fingers between my teeth.

Killian curses, jerking his hand back as fury and madness overtake me. I throw every ounce of hatred into the force of it as I spit out his vile fluid. I take pride in watching it spew against his cheek, causing him to flinch as it lands.

Momentarily, I feel satisfied.

And then the satisfaction is gone, replaced by sudden, overwhelming fear.

I can't run from this. I can't fight. I can't hide…and I'm alone.

I'm alone.

Where's Arlo?

I can't feel the pulse of him nearby, and I mourn the loss of it. Without him near, I am entirely, utterly alone in this.

My breath catches as Killian's temper flares, dreadful intent glaring at me through his raging eyes. Fear grips me as sadness replaces my anger, my heart pounding out a steady, pulsing rhythm that begs for Arlo to return.

Come back.

Come back.

Come back.

Killian grips my chin with one hand, digging the fingers of the other deeper into my hair to jerk my head back. He comes forward in a rush, pressing his lips to mine, opening his mouth against mine, then biting my bottom lip, hard. He tugs at it, stretching the skin beneath my lip as his teeth sink sharply without care. He releases, and when my lip springs back into place, I taste blood…all while Wesley fucks me.

I'm weak.

All I can think about is the insistent pounding behind my ribcage, my fervent need to not be alone in this, my unexplainable need for Arlo.

Come back.

Come back.

Tears flow, sobs wrack my lungs, and I cry.

I'm horrified by my reaction. I'm showing so much weakness when I'm meant to show strength, to meet their disgrace with my grace, just as I have for years in service. Yet, I can't stop the tears that fall.

Arlo made me weak.

I close my eyes, uninterested in seeing Killian's pleased reaction to my pain, but I can hear him chuckling, feel his hand pinch my chin and angle my head higher.

"That's perfect. You're giving us exactly what we hoped for. Let every tear fall from your wretched soul and purge it of the liquid sin that runs through your veins. Perhaps if you cry enough, there will be absolution for you yet."

Absolution.

They could etch the word into my skin, and still, it would never find me.

There is no absolution for my soul. There is no God so worthy of worship that He would create a ritual such as this for one of His daughters to reach it. So if this is God's will—if the one they worship does exist—then I dissent.

Killian moves and Owen appears before me, naked and seeking my mouth while Park comes around behind me. His hand disappears between my cheeks to find the spot Ryker had already desecrated.

With sorrow and outrage and a weakened, broken soul, I silently beg for Arlo with the painful pounding of my heart.

Come back.

I can't survive this without his presence.

chapter three

Mercy

I'M DRAINED AND dry. There isn't a single ounce of liquid left inside this body. After three hours of use, my tear ducts have dried up, my cunt is raw and sore, and the hole behind is scratched and stretched and throbbing. Of course, they were prepared for that to be the case, and have resorted to the use of slickening oils to ensure their comfort. It makes no difference to me—it all hurts, regardless.

Five men have come on me or within me—most of them have done both within the first few hours. Arlo hadn't left, like I thought he had, but maybe worse than him leaving is the fact that he sat in the armchair across the room this entire time…tense and watching. Like he was waiting for something, but I don't know what.

While Ryker finishes fucking me—coming with a groan and a deep thrust inside my pussy—I scan the room. My lax, drooping head tugs an ache through my neck as it hangs sideways, gravity pulling it toward the floor. My hair sweeps across my face and some strands stick to the sweat, filth, and bodily liquids drying on my cheeks. Ryker pulls out and steps away, releasing me. Left alone in my bindings, my body slowly turns.

I think I'm a dying star, the lonely twin of the sun painted on the tiles beneath me. I'm forever dangling, gravity pulling me toward her—it feels as though I'll never reach, as though I'll remain tethered and reaching forever. I'm burnt out, my energy draining, and all I want is to fall upon the sun beneath me and burn in her light, to drop from these ropes that bind me and burn to ashes as I fall through the fire.

For moments, I spin alone, stillness finding me for the first time since the trial began.

Am I still in the trial?

Or am I strung up in hell?

A gradually turning image of Arlo comes into view as I spin toward him. My gaze catches sight of him as he moves to rise from his seat. I don't feel anything about him as he crosses the foyer, heading in my direction. I blink slowly, my vision strained from dryness now that all my tears have been shed. He's a step closer with every blink, and I wish I felt something for that. I wish I felt comforted, that I felt some relief as he moves closer.

But I only feel alone.

He turns my body to face away from him, and his hands tug at my bindings, lightly brushing against my skin as he handles the rope. I think he's untying the knots that keep my right knee bent, loosening them, untangling them.

It must be break time.

I'm allotted two breaks during this trial—ten minutes granted as a reprieve from my misery before I'll be bound and trussed up, used and abused all over again.

Arlo pulls the ropes free from my bent leg, and my foot drops toward the floor. My muscles are tired and weak, and I think my toes would've jammed against the tile if Arlo's hand wasn't there to guide it down. My foot feels heavy, numb and tingling all at once. I don't have to put weight on it yet since the rest of the roping still holds me up, but I press down through that leg all the same, feeling relief to put pressure on my tingling toes.

Arlo moves to my drawn-out left leg, which is held straight and holds knots that keep me suspended. He loosens those knots, then gently lowers my leg to the floor. He reaches above to pull and slacken the line while shifting a hand to curve around my hip. He presses me down, encouraging me to kneel.

My body slumps, and I sit back on my heels, bending at the waist and curling forward. My head drops low in shame and exhaustion. Then his fingers graze my flesh as he undoes the knots at my back. He doesn't say a word as he unties me, freeing me from the binding that traps me in this hell on Earth.

Once my arms are freed from behind my back, they drop weakly to my sides. I hadn't realized how exhausted I'd grown when the ropes held me up, but now I feel so tired and overwhelmed, beyond ready to be done with this.

Arlo swoops his arms beneath me and scoops me up from the floor. I don't have the strength to throw my arms around his neck, so I just let them dangle, one landing across my stomach as he carries me down the hall, away from this torture.

I think for a moment that I'll be haunted by the sounds of grunting, rutting men forever. I hear the muffled sound of it along the way, but then I realize the sound isn't haunting my mind; it's coming from behind the closed door where Delle is enduring her trial alone. I quickly force her from my thoughts because I feel so broken right now that I don't have the capacity for compassion. In this moment, I'm struggling to simply exist.

I pretend not to hear it as Arlo carries me past Delle's trial room, taking me farther down the hall, then through a door into a bedroom. He takes me across the carpeted floor to a bathroom at the back. It's too bright here—much like the all-white bathroom in my suite.

Are we in my bathroom?

No, he didn't go upstairs.

He crosses the room and bends while holding me, reaching out and carefully dipping to lift the lid over the toilet with one hand. Then he lowers me, setting me down and pressing on my shoulder until I relent and drop to sit on the toilet. I don't even have the energy to feel shame as my bladder empties.

There is no privacy left for me—no common decency, no shame. I'm reduced to a soulless body and desecrated flesh, just as they had intended.

I hear the faucet running and slowly turn my drooping head to look over at Arlo. He's standing at the sink, palms pressed against the countertop, leaning forward with his head hung.

"You're nearly halfway done," he mutters, and I can hardly hear him over the running water. "You've come this far, Mercy, and I know you can get through this."

"It's not as though I have a choice." I can hear how weak and weary my voice is—it doesn't even sound like me.

His eyes turn to glance at me beneath his lashes, and then he straightens, clearing his throat, reaching down to pull open one of the cabinet drawers. He pulls out a white washcloth and soaks it beneath the flow of water. He turns off the faucet, wrings out the cloth, and moves in front of me, crouching to his haunches. He lifts the damp cloth to my face and, with gentleness, starts wiping the dried cum and sweat that smears my cheeks.

I watch as he does this, wondering what thoughts plague him from behind his tortured blue eyes. I see hurt there, and I see pain. Sadly, I don't know whether the pain is for me or whether it's from controlling his impulses while watching the debauchery as his brothers fucked me. Part of me wonders if he hasn't taken a turn with me yet because he's edging his release, biding his time.

I watch the muscles in his neck work as he swallows. "Theo and I will need to fuck you before this is over."

I scoff because the statement is pointless. I'm well aware of that fact, and it only bothers me more to be reminded of it. Honestly, I don't know how I'll shut off my feelings about Arlo when he takes his turn with me in front of the others. They can do whatever they want to me and bring me shame, but the idea of Arlo using me along with them hurts me more than I can say.

I don't know if he'll be kind and gentle, like he's being now. He hurt me when he fucked me in the cavern—when he ignored me as I told him it hurt. With all the Control present and encouraging this depravity, I don't know how Arlo will behave. I know he feels strongly for me. I know he's claimed me, and I let him. I worry he'll lose control and hurt me again, though I suppose I can't hurt much more than I do now.

He folds the washcloth and brings it to my hair, wrapping it around a matted strand and dragging it through. "Where do you want me to…" he trails off, feigning more careful inspection of the strand of hair.

"What?"

"When I have to take my turn…when Theo has to take his…"

"Are you asking which hole I'd like you to fuck me in?"

He puffs out a breath through his nose, his nostrils flaring as he closes his eyes. "Yes." He slowly opens his eyes, meeting my stare. "It's the only choice I can give you, but at least I can give you that."

I turn my head, looking off at the white wall. "I don't care."

"Yes, you do. Tell me."

I look at him squarely. "No. *No.* You're not going to put that on me. You're not going to make me choose how you hurt me."

"I won't hurt you, Mercy, I'll be—"

"Gentle? Soft? Sweet?" I shake my head. "No. There is no way for you to make this any easier on me. Everyone in the village will be watching; the Control and the Elders will be watching you. You can't be anything less than brutal in your participation, and you know that. You and Theo both." I feel hot tears well behind my eyes, and I'm surprised since I didn't think I had any left. "Is Delle…? Is she okay?"

I'd somehow managed to forget about her in the other room.

I feel guilty for forgetting, but I feel glad for it, too. The burden of carrying worry for her is too much when I can't even carry myself.

Arlo grabs my hand and pulls me to stand with him, lowering the washcloth between us. He reaches between my legs to wipe me clean, and I'm too tired to care, too weary to stop him and do it myself. He owes me care, anyway. I'm his ward; it's his job to take care of me.

Let him cleanse me.

I wish he could cleanse the filth of this trial from my mind.

"I've done everything I can to keep them focused on you and away from her," he says. "But I haven't seen her yet. Theo's still with her."

My weak knees wobble and I slap my palms to his biceps, digging my fingers into his skin to steady myself. He tosses the washcloth toward the floor and brings his arms around me, pulling me to lean against his chest while he holds me up. I turn my cheek and press my ear over his pounding heart. I close my eyes and listen, focus on the steady rhythm.

"You have to fuck her, too," I whisper.

I'm met with silence. He doesn't admit that he must, but he doesn't deny it, either. He says nothing at all, and at least the silence feels honest.

"I'm sorry, Mercy. For all of it. For everything."

"I'm so tired," I mutter.

His hand strokes down the back of my head. "I know. It's nearly done, and when it is, you can rest."

"Can I?" I chuckle humorlessly against his chest.

"Of course," he replies too gently, his voice too soft.

"I won't have rest until I'm dead, Warden Rainn. I don't think you quite understand what's going on here." Silence lassoes around us through a pause. "Maybe I'll get lucky and the next trial will end me quickly."

His heartbeat hastens as his grip on me tightens. Though we're standing still, he seems to stumble, as though something I said had bodily pushed him back. He keeps moving, walking backward and dragging me with him, until his back hits the white-tiled wall, and he hugs me closer.

Air rushes out of him, blowing warmth over the top of my head as he weakens and slumps, slipping down the wall, taking me with him to the floor. Sitting, he pulls me onto his lap and cradles me like the small broken thing I feel like I am right now.

He presses a kiss to the side of my head, holds me tight, and I'm truthfully surprised that I find warmth and comfort in his arms. I'm surprised that I'm not repulsed by any touch right now. All I wanted was to be free and as far from the touch of another as possible.

Yet…I feel nearly peaceful here in his lap. I think it's his anxiety, which pulses through his racing heart, that serves to calm me. His heart beats fast, but steady, soothing. For the moment, I let him take my burden, let his anxiety build so I can find peace in the rhythm of it, and finally rest. I close my eyes and focus on the beat of his heart, letting it lull me into a sense of calmness.

"We only have a few minutes," he mutters, his lips moving against my hair. "Tell me what you need from me before it all starts again."

Slowly, I raise my head, pressing myself away from his chest so I can look up at him. "I need you to check on Delle."

He tucks my hair behind my ear. "I'll check on Delle, but that's not what I asked. What do *you* need? I guarantee you, she's in much better shape than you are."

My eyes search his face and I'm struck by his expression—the twitch of his cheeks through the tension he holds in his jaw, the softness of his eyes, the odd downward slope at the corners of his lips in sorrow. I have the urge to kiss those corners with a strange hope that it would force them to curl up again, to cause him to smile so I can see the long dimples in his cheeks.

"I need you to be the last."

His brow furrows, waiting for me to say more.

"I need you to be the man who ends the trial. You need to be the last memory of this awful day."

His chest sinks as he sighs and his eyes fall shut. He presses his forehead to mine. "I'll try."

I lift my arms and wrap them around his neck, holding him to me, suddenly fearful of our separation.

"Why are you sad for me?" I ask, closing my eyes. "I'm a sinner and this is my penance. I deserve this, don't I?" I throw his words back at him, asking out of frustration for his emotion, but also out of curiosity about the frown and the gentleness I hadn't expected from him.

"I don't know...I don't know what to think right now."

"Don't tell me what you think. Tell me what you feel."

"I feel conflicted. I don't know what else to say."

"Do you still think I deserve this?"

He goes quiet, and I let him. I let him sit with the thought, watching as he brews over it. If I have to endure this, then he should be forced to endure the conflict within him as he draws a final conclusion about what I do and don't deserve.

If he says that I truly deserve it, then I want him to writhe in the contempt he must hold for me as a sinner. If he says that I don't, then I want him to bask in the revelation and sit with the dissonance that could make him understand me.

I'm desperate for him to understand me.

But after a minute passes and he still hasn't spoken, I start to pull my hands away, dragging them down his shoulders. His hands shoot up to snatch my wrists and he pulls them back up, latching them around the back of his neck again. My lips part to let air rush through as I suddenly feel breathless.

"You don't deserve this. You don't deserve it, Mercy."

I tighten my arms around him, pulling closer to hug him, and the way he hugs me back is *everything*. What I feel in his embrace is everything I ever wanted, all wrapped up and tied with a bow. It's warmth and tenderness, shared heartache and fear, adoration and… love.

The way he holds me almost feels like love, but I know it's not—it could never be.

I'm a sinner condemned, and he's only my warden.

chapter four
ARLO

THE TEN-MINUTE BREAK ends quickly, and I'm forced
to bring Mercy back to the foyer. She kneels on the center of the
hard tile sun, sitting back on her heels with her head dropped low
in exhaustion.

Standing behind her, I sift a length of rope through my hands
as I stare down at the seven lines my brothers and I sliced into the
back of her neck to mark her for these trials. I consider how to bind
and suspend her, wanting to avoid irritating the red, raw markings
left on her skin from the first part of the day, but I don't think it can
be avoided.

She's endured three of her seven hours, and another four remain.
My hands tremble as I anxiously snake the rope between them. I've
never felt so sick in my life. I'm fighting the pain of watching her
endure atrocious acts performed by my brothers in God, but I'm also
fighting my feelings for her.

I'm fighting my *lust* for her.

Even from the way she waits there now, naked and kneeling,
submitting to her trial with such grace and dignity…

It's fucking beautiful.

Horrifying and beautiful.

Her pain hurts me, yet the sight of her, the smell of her, the
anticipation of tasting her hurts me, too.

All I want is to take her away from here, wrap her in warmth, move inside her with care and passion and tender attention to make up for all the pain they've caused her...the pain *I've* caused her. Because I've hurt Mercy, too. I fucked her raw, strung up in the caves when I prepared her for this trial, moved inside her past her point of protest.

I won't ever fuck her like that again.

That's a promise I know I can't keep.

A door down the hall clicks open, and Theo and Delle appear in the hallway. His arm is around her shoulders, helping her hold a robe over her body. He turns to walk her back to the room where she's been used, bringing her back from her break. I promised Mercy I'd check on Delle, and none of my brothers have returned yet to continue their defilement of Mercy.

"Theo," I call out to him, dropping the rope and heading in their direction.

He stops to look at me, meeting my eyes with a look that reveals him to be as shaken and pained as I feel. I quickly cover the short distance between us and approach him. He turns himself and Delle—who looks shaken, sad, but not broken—to face me.

"How is she?" I ask.

He shakes his head. "Not good, but I imagine better than Mercy. They've been unusually gentle with her, which I imagine means—"

"They've been brutal with Mercy." I know I shouldn't have said that within Delle's earshot when she whimpers.

"When do we switch?" Theo asks.

It's inevitable that Theo and I will need to switch places at some point. It's our duty to engage with both Delle and Mercy—just as our brothers have done—during this trial. But only one of them is being filmed and watched in the foyer.

I have no intention of laying a finger on Delle—I still can't help but see her as I once saw my own sister—and duty or not, this is one I cannot carry through with her. It's unsettling to think of neglecting my duty, but the thought of touching Delle fills me with something like disgust.

It will be yet another sin to add to my growing list, though I know God will forgive me...

But why will he forgive me and not them?

I glance over my shoulder at Mercy.

Is she justified in questioning our faith?

"Perhaps now would be the best time." I turn back to face Theo. "We can switch again after the next break."

"Okay," Theo agrees. "But let me bind Delle first."

I nod. It's fine with me; I don't wish to touch her.

The sound of raucous laughter and the padding of footsteps behind draws my attention away. I turn to see Killian and Ryker enter the foyer. Killian is finishing off a mug of ale, tipping it all the way back before slamming it down on the side table behind the camera...but his other hand isn't empty. He turns a kitchen knife in his palm.

"Go and bind her," I rush to tell Theo as I turn away from him. I charge down the hall as I watch Killian and Ryker approach Mercy from afar, and I shout to them, "It's Service of the Flesh; no blood is meant to be drawn."

My heart hammers as I watch Killian tap the tip of the blade beneath Mercy's chin, forcing her to lift her head and look at him with wild fear in her eyes.

Killian glances at me with pure glee. "I understand the trial, brother. I have no intention of drawing blood."

Rushing into the foyer, I shove his hand and the knife away from Mercy, then I step between them. "Then what is your intent with that? To spark fear?"

"My intent is to find my own personal satisfaction. That is the point of sexual service, is it not?" He turns the knife in his palm. "Shoving the knife's handle into her cunt will satisfy me immensely, so why don't you go ahead and get her back into position so we can carry out the trial?"

I can feel my face contort in rage; heavy, heated breaths slipping in and out through my flaring nostrils in a rush. I'm so livid at the mere thought of him touching her anywhere with any part of that fucking kitchen knife that I can't hold back. Unable—unwilling, perhaps—to hide my fury, my palms land on his chest and I shove him back.

He stumbles backward, tilting sideways and catching himself against the side table that holds the camera. The table legs screech as they skid across the tile floor. The camera shakes, then falls sideways, bouncing off the tabletop before crashing to the floor. The light remains on, so I know it's still recording, but I imagine it's only filming our feet.

"You use your cock for satisfaction," I tell him, "not an object."

He rights himself, slowly bringing his gaze to meet mine. "You would dare put hands on me to spare that *sinner?* What's come over you?"

"Nothing's come over me," I falter, searching my soul for a way to calm my nerves, to correct this misstep that could reveal my sinful thoughts about Mercy. "Sinner or not, I will uphold the integrity of this trial."

"And the integrity of this trial will be upheld with our sexual satisfaction. This," he holds up the knife, "will satisfy me. You have your ropes, and I have my objects. We each have our own sexual impulses, brother. Now step aside."

I hear the sudden scuffle of movement behind me, followed by Mercy's soft whimper. In the blink of an eye, I've forgotten about Killian and his knife. Whipping around, I see Ryker yank Mercy down to the floor, covering her body with his. His hand is around her throat, and worse than anything, he's kissing her. His lips are on hers and it's all I can see.

Those lips are mine.

Her kiss belongs to me.

Killian drops the knife as I charge across the room. It clatters against the tile and slides across the floor toward Ryker, racing me to meet Mercy at her side. With his hands free, Killian grabs my shoulders and jerks me back in my rush to get to Mercy.

My eyes widen as I watch Ryker with his mouth on hers, and I struggle not to fight, trying not to tear myself from Killian's grip, rush to her, throw Ryker to the ground and beat him senseless.

Mercy's eyes are squeezed closed, creating wrinkles across her forehead and creases at the corners of her eyes. Her lips are pursed shut as she turns her head, trying to fight the kiss he forces. It's as though I can feel my ribs break, one after the other, cracking under the strain of trying to contain my pounding heart.

"Watch," Killian says to me quietly. "Watch and remember who she is...*what* she is. She's a sinner and she deserves this. I'm afraid her demons are coming for you, too. Let us help you, brother."

Dear God, what's happening to me?

I feel for her, I want her...Sometimes I think I need her, and I shouldn't. I worry God has forsaken me, letting the demons that plague her claw into my soul. But the deeper they dig and the stronger I feel them, the truer their influence feels.

I'm conflicted.

I'm afflicted.

I don't know how much longer I can fight it.

Ryker's fingers curl tighter, squeezing her throat as he sits up, straddling her waist. Her hands fly to his wrist, gripping, pulling, swatting, and her lips and eyes part wide as she fights for air. If Killian didn't grip me right now, my hands would be around Ryker's throat, squeezing just as tightly as he squeezes hers.

I know my brother is trying to help me. I know he's trying to save me from sin.

But what if I no longer want to be saved?

What if I want to be a sinner?

"I know it's difficult," Killian says as Ryker reaches to grab the knife on the floor.

If he knows it's difficult, then he knows I feel for her. If he knows I feel for her, then he may prevent me from caring for her when she needs it the most. As much as it pains me to watch this unfold, I know that I must. I must stand here and allow it to happen, even though it's shredding my soul.

I didn't know my soul could ache this way.

I shrug him off and take a step forward. "It's not difficult. I only want to ensure the rules are followed."

He moves around and strides past me toward Ryker, who holds out the knife for him. "And they are being followed. It won't hurt her." He takes the knife from Ryker. "Maybe she'll even enjoy it."

They both laugh, and I force myself to curl the corners of my lips in a fake grin because I'm failing miserably at keeping my feelings for her unknown. Ryker grabs Mercy's hands, lifting them above her head, bending over her to press her wrists to the tile floor. He raises onto his knees and Killian moves between her legs.

Mercy shakes her head frantically and kicks her legs—which is the very reason she was supposed to be bound. Each kick and thrash could make this more dangerous for her. She could cut herself on the blade as Killian moves it toward her, as he kneels between her legs, and nudges his knee against the inside of her thigh to spread them.

"You can't...Don't...No!" Mercy stammers, eyes wide, trying to lift herself against Ryker's weight pinning her down at the waist.

I told her not to give them her words.

Her words only add to their pleasure, making them more eager.

I should cover her mouth. I try to take a step forward. I try to move to her to do just that, but I can't. I can't figure out how to move if it's not to save her from this torment. I can't figure out how to bring myself to her presence, to look into her bewitching eyes and cover her mouth to keep her quiet while my brothers fuck her with the handle of a kitchen knife.

My stomach lurches without warning, some sudden sickness coming over me, and I double over, turning swiftly to grip the table beside me as my breaths turn to heavy panting that work to keep me from retching.

"If you don't hold still, you'll cut yourself, sinner." Killian's tone is so ordinary and plain, as if he's performing a procedure she had agreed upon.

"Warden…Warden Rainn…" she whimpers.

Self-hatred boils in my gut, adding to my nausea.

I squeeze my eyes shut and try not to listen.

"There you go, keep those legs open for me, nice and wide," I hear Killian say.

Tears flood my eyes and I fight to keep them back. I don't remember the last time I cried, the last time I felt pain so deep as this, the last time I felt so truly and completely out of control…

I feel out of my mind.

I raise my head, turning to look, and I instantly regret it. My gaze lands on the scene at the precise moment that Killian presses the handle of the blade against her slit and plunges it inside her. Her body twitches beneath Ryker, though she fights to keep still. And while I know I'll regret it even more, I look at her face. She watches me, her head turned toward me, tears streaking across her face and tumbling toward the floor.

She looks broken.

She looks hurt.

She looks angry…with me.

"Starlight." I don't know why the word slips from my lips, but the utterance brightens her sad eyes for a fraction of a moment.

Even in this darkest hour of her defilement, she shines brighter than all the stars in the sky. She lies there, broken, on the tiled pattern of the sun, and it's her presence that gives it light…light that breaks through the dark shadows of space that hold her down, that try to break her and take that light away.

And how dare they try to take that light away?

I rise and charge, some reckless fury overtaking me. There's a piece of me that wants to protect that light at any cost, *at all costs*, because the parts of Mercy that are good and pure—uncorrupted by the demons and sin—reside within that light. And if they take that from her, then they'll surely ruin her.

I reach for Killian's shoulder, but before I touch, two heavy hands grip the back of my shirt and yank me back. I stumble, but right myself quickly, whirling around and coming face to face with Theo.

"Go," he says. "Go to Delle." He comes in closer, lowering his voice. "You can't be here for this. Don't let her lose you to this, brother."

I blink, taking far too many moments to tear myself from my rage, but as his words sink in, I hear them. I understand. And as painful as the truth is, I know he's right.

I cannot be called out for my sins here; I cannot show my feelings for Mercy here. I must save that for behind closed doors so I can be with her until the end.

Theo turns me, shoves my back, and pushes me toward the hall. With my brother's insistence, I'm able to walk away, but Mercy's gravity tugs at me with each heavy step.

chapter five
Mercy

"I SWEAR ON all things holy, Killian Cole, if you don't let me down for a break *right* now, I will *piss* all over your godforsaken face." I hardly recognize the sound of my voice—it's filled with such fury and contempt.

"Do it and you'll regret it, Mercy Madness."

Theo has me bound and suspended in a way that's similar to how Arlo had me in the caves—suspended facedown, my front parallel to the floor with my arms pinned behind my back. My knees are bent and spread, and my height is adjusted so Killian's face is aligned with my pussy while he kneels behind me.

Killian takes his time clipping clothespins around my slit. I've counted five so far, and he's taking his damn time placing a sixth. He started fifteen minutes ago when I asked for my second break, but he insisted this "wouldn't take long" and decided to prolong my torture, simply because he could. My whole body trembles around the pinching pain between my legs, and my bladder is so full, I'm about to burst.

"Just one more," he says as if it's soothing to hear, "then I'll let you down for your last little break, sinner."

"If she pisses on you, you're cleaning it up," Theo says from where he's sitting in the armchair across the room.

I wish he'd be more insistent. He's supposed to take care of me in Arlo's stead, but I've been begging for a break for the last fifteen minutes. I honestly don't know if I'll make it to the bathroom after they untie me, but I'm determined not to humiliate myself further—though I would find a sick sense of satisfaction if Killian got too close and I drenched his face.

"I swear I'm going to—"

Killian cuts me off with the placement of a final clothespin, pinched right onto my clit. The nip of it screams through me, my sensitive, raw, overused flesh roaring against the sharp new pain. I purse my lips, holding my cry inside, refusing to give him another shriek of pain or scream of protest.

"There," he says with finality, and I hear his hands slap against his thighs before he pushes to his feet and moves around me. I lift my head so I can glare at him as he approaches my side. "You can let her down now, Theo. I can always start over after her break."

I'm so furious that if I wasn't bound, I fear I might launch myself at him. I felt broken and sad earlier in the day, but the sadness has given way to anger, and I embrace it.

"You're disgusting," I spit the words at Killian as Theo and Owen work together to bring me down to my feet.

"Slinging insults is rather undignified," Killian sniffs, doing nothing to help me down. "And there is no one in this room more vile than you, sinner. I'm so disgusted that I have to touch you for this trial."

"You could've fooled me." I'm standing on trembling legs as Theo and Owen work to untie the knots that wrap around my torso and legs.

Killian gives me a sneer that's filled with pure evil. I hold his stare, unwilling to back down from him.

I dare you to touch me once my arms are free.

He sighs, as if he's bored all of a sudden, and looks away. "I suppose I'll take a break for a while, too. Can't steal all the fun from my brothers."

"For someone so disgusted by me, you have spent an awful amount of hours between my legs." I look him up and down with hatred.

He grins, and I hate it. "You're always good for a laugh, sinner."

I let out a breath of relief as he strides past, and I look over my shoulder to watch him jog up the staircase and disappear from sight. Now if I can just empty my bladder, I can take one full damn breath.

"Please, hurry." I rush them along.

The ropes have been pulled free from my waist and legs, but the ones that keep my arms behind my back remain. They keep my forearms pressed together, drawing straight lines across the middle of my back.

The pressure on my bladder is immense, and I can feel the release about to happen. I bounce through my legs, desperate to get to the toilet. "I can't wait. Just let me go…" My feet are already moving, stepping away from them. "Can I go?"

"Okay, just go," Theo says.

With his utterance of permission to take my second break from this trial, I run down the hall with the dangling ends of the rope flying behind my back.

I turn into the bedroom Arlo had brought me into before and head for the bathroom. I lower myself to the toilet, taking care to keep the dangling rope ends out of the way, and pee more forcefully than I ever have in my life. The relief is wonderful, but as the fluid drains from my body, so does the momentary relief.

Embarrassment floods me as I realize the clothespins are still clipped—some of them, anyway. One has fallen into the toilet, and I must have lost three others on the way here. Somehow, two still remain, pinching so much flesh that their grip stays strong.

"Mercy?" I look up at the open doorway when I hear Arlo call my name. "I'm coming in," he warns, but God, I don't need him to see me this way.

"Don't," I yell back. "Don't come in."

I don't want him to see me right now, but I actually need help. My arms are still bound at my back, and I can't cleanse myself or remove the clothespins. The humiliation of it overwhelms me with such a rush that tears flood my eyes and sobs threaten to break free from my chest.

He moves into the open doorway, and the moment I see him, I drop my gaze, letting my head fall forward. "I had to go…I couldn't wait," I whisper, and it's even more humiliating explaining myself.

Arlo appears in front of me, crouching to his haunches, tapping beneath my chin to lift my head. I can't look him in the eye.

"Just take a breath," he says. "I'll take care of you."

I want to find comfort in his words, but annoyance greets me instead. It's not annoyance for him so much as the fact that I need to be cared for right now at all. He and his brothers did this to me. They declared my self-preservation a sin, forced me into these Trials of Dissension, and here I sit, embarrassed and agitated because of them—and because of *him*, too.

Anger twists my expression as I look at him, watching his eyes skim over my body. He inspects me like I'm a possession, some porcelain doll he loaned as a toy to his brothers that he expects to find chipped or cracked from their play. Maybe I am chipped and cracked…I feel fragile in my anger.

Somehow, he spots the clothespins and grips my elbows, pulling me up to stand as he rises. My fury simmers as he reaches between my legs and pinches them off, as if it's the most normal thing in the world.

He lets go of me, and I stand, waiting as he wets a washcloth under the faucet. Outrage quakes my bones as I watch him return to me, reaching down to wipe between my legs. He cleanses me instead of freeing my arms and letting me do it myself, and I've never felt so low.

I don't tell him that, though. I'm tired of speaking, tired of shouting about my rage and rights into a void. So I let him do it, silently taking note of his ignorance of my shame so I can let the anger build within me.

"You left me," I mutter, and I'm surprised that the words came out.

"What?" He finishes with the washcloth and tosses it to the floor, stepping closer, as though he's going to pull me into his arms. "What do you need from me?"

I twist my body away, staring off at the wall. "I don't need anything from you," I reply sourly.

"What did they do to you?" He gently touches my cheek, but I whip my head in his direction, meeting his eyes with heat and forcing his hand to drop. "I'm back now. I'll be with you through the end."

"Fine."

"It's almost over now, Mercy. There's only an hour left."

"Then I suppose it's your turn to have your way with me."

His jaw clenches and his gaze travels down my body, then back up again. "You know it has to be done."

"Then fuck me how you did in the cave," I tell him. "Fuck me hard and wild; take what you want from me without giving it back."

His eyes harden as he stares back at me, nostrils flaring as indignation rises through his features.

Good.

He should feel as indignant as I do.

"Is that really what you want from me, Mercy? You want me to use you like my brothers had?" He steps closer and I step back, turning my body and backing away from him.

We move until my spine hits the wall, and he closes in on me, pinning me as he aligns his body to my curves. "It's what you're meant to do."

"And I'm meant to enjoy it, but there's only one thing that gives me anything resembling satisfaction these days… " His fingers find my stomach, tracing a path up my side that makes me flinch as he tickles the soft flesh. The flinch sends a jolt of electricity straight through me. "Do you know what that thing is, starlight?"

Starlight.

Wildflowers and starlight.

Arlo had told me that my hair smelled like wildflowers, and that it was the color of starlight.

He had uttered the nickname I've come to know as Ryker held me down and Killian pushed the handle of a knife inside me. He'd whispered, "*Starlight,*" and the sound of it cut through the noise of the traumatic moment, just long enough to give me a beat of peace, a bit of hope to cling to…

I realize I'm panting, pressed between Arlo's body and the wall.

"Wh…what?" I finally ask.

His palms press to the wall on either side of my head and he leans in close, brushing his lips over the shell of my ear. "Watching you come undone."

"Don't…" I whisper. "Don't do that. I'm so *angry.* Just let me be angry," I whimper. "Please don't take that from me…"

His hands drop from the wall to the small of my back, dragging me against him as a heavy breath rushes out of me. "You want to be angry?"

I nod, though I feel warmer in his hold, my body feeling pliant and relaxed from the simple touch of him.

"Is rage what you need to hold on to while I do this to you?" I hear him swallow as he hugs me closer. "Is that what will help you through?"

Though being in his arms inexplicably calms me, it's not as though I can stand here forever, letting him hold me this way. There's still time left in my trial—time that Arlo will have to use to fuck me in front of the entirety of Ember Glen—and though part of me wants to succumb to the calm and let him take me into bliss, the stronger part of me knows that shared rage will help us both.

Fury will help us get through this. It will help him to hurt me, and it will help me to endure the hurt. It will keep suspicions of our forbidden feelings for each other at bay. Anger will save us both.

I nod with my cheek against his chest.

"Okay," he concedes. "Then in five minutes, you'll be angry with me. I'll give you a reason to be. But until then, you'll let me hold you."

He bends abruptly, sweeps an arm beneath my legs and swoops me off my feet. He carries me easily through the open bathroom door, across the room, and lowers to sit in an armchair across from the bed. He sits me sideways across his lap, rolling me toward him and hugging me close to his chest.

There's a moment when I panic as the ropes still binding my arms tighten with our movement, the immobility frightening me, but as still and quiet moments pass, the fear lessens. I can hear the beating of his heart as I settle against his chest, and the beats lull me into calmness.

He calms me, though I'm still simmering with anger.

I shut my eyes and drift into darkness.

Sleep.

I blink and feel as though I've been forcefully dragged from a days' long slumber. Last I knew, I was resting my head against Arlo's chest, listening to the sound of his beating heart, and suddenly, his hand pinches my chin. His fingers dig painfully into my jaw as he twists my head up so I can meet his eyes. I must have nodded off, but the trial is still on. I'm still on Arlo's lap in the chair in the bedroom. I had a moment's peace as I fell into sleep far too quickly, and he's dragged me from it five minutes later.

He had to…I still have to finish my trial.

He bends over me, touching his forehead to mine and staring so deeply into my soul that I think the blue flames in his eyes could burn it to ashes. "It's time to get angry with me, starlight."

I don't know why, but the abrupt shift into his intensity does something inside me. My stomach twists, my belly clenches, and my pulse thumps faster. I feel a tug of desire through my core, as if it were just me and him, alone in a room, and I've given him permission to take control of me.

Maybe it would be easier if I did.

And that's why I need to get angry.

If I'm angry, it will mask everything else I'm feeling. It will take the shame away from the inexplicable desire that exists within me. It will make it feel okay for him to take me and use me in the brutal way they are all expecting. Anger will give us both permission to let go and give into what we've wanted from each other all along—pure, unhindered carnality without judgment, without shame, without fear of being found. We have a certain kind of permission right now that we'll never find again.

My voice comes out as a breathy whisper. "Then make me angry."

The blue flames in his eyes dance across my face before landing on my lips. There's a beat of hesitation and I plead with my eyes for him to push the limit…to walk right up to that thin line between authority and abuse and step across it.

"Make me—" I start again, but he cuts me off with a kiss.

His lips land on mine and push with bruising force while he digs his fingers into my face beneath my cheekbones. I jerk in my bindings, trying to pull away from him, but at the same time, I force my tongue between his teeth, sweeping inside his mouth, eliciting a groan that vibrates all the way down to my toes.

I get one lick, one taste of his fever before he pulls back and ends the kiss. With a flick of his hand, he pushes my head sideways before shifting his arms around me. He grabs my wrists in one large hand where they touch the middle of my back, then he hoists me up as he stands, jerking me around to get my feet on the floor. Shoving from behind, he marches me forward, reaching around me to open the bedroom door before he pushes me roughly into the hallway.

He keeps pushing, moving me down the hall to the foyer. Ryker and Wesley are there waiting, chatting side by side. Ryker is seated in the armchair Arlo had occupied for much of the first part of the trial. They both turn their heads as I walk in, watching as Arlo takes me to the center of the sun.

As if I were truly standing on the surface of a burning ball floating through the heavens, I feel like my blood is rising to a boil inside me.

"Time for another round," Ryker says, pushing to his feet. "Get her strung up and the three of us can all have another go at her."

"No," Arlo snarls. "You've had your turn; now it's my time." He puts his hand on top of my head and forces me down to my knees.

"If we're all up and ready, we should fuck her together for the sake of the trial—"

Arlo's head whips over his shoulder to look at Ryker behind him, and though I can't see Arlo's eyes, I know he's staring his brother down with fury. "I'll fuck her well enough for all seven of us, now *back the fuck off.*"

My stomach flutters and flips at the way he claims me, and it doesn't make any sense.

Ryker lifts his palms in surrender and takes a step back before lowering to the seat again. When Arlo turns his attention to me, everything sinks inside, a heavy rush of heat dripping down my insides.

I've had enough today.

I've had more than enough.

Enough touching, rubbing, grating, grinding, and fucking to

last me a lifetime.

Yet, on my knees here for Arlo Rainn, looking up into his eyes filled with affection and true desire for me, I cannot deny the way I want him. I'm willing to take more for him—not just willing, but strangely eager.

He removes his clothes as I look up at him, dropping his shirt to the floor and showing me his bare chest, strong and chiseled and undeniably masculine.

He unbuckles, unzips, shoves his pants and black underwear down his legs, then rises to grip his cock, already standing proud and threatening. He strokes as he looks down at me. The connection between us is daunting, all-consuming, and the longer he holds me with his eyes, the more the world around us fades into the background.

His hand lands on the top of my head and slides down the back. He curls his fingers into my hair and grips me, jerking my chin toward the sky. "I almost wish I hadn't cut off your hair. I could've braided it with rope and tied it to the ceiling." My mouth drops open on a sigh, and he bends over me. "Is that open for me?"

Yes.

I try to close my mouth, but he grips my chin with his free hand, pinching my cheeks like he did in the bedroom. "You're going to take every inch of me inside your mouth, draw all of me past these pretty lips of yours. Do you understand, sinner?" He forces my head to nod in his grip, and though I feel my pussy clench for the way Arlo so greedily wants me, the anger of our forced scenario remains. That anger heats me, boiling me with frantic energy that flows to my cunt as easily as it does through the rest of my body.

The way he angers me is erotic and chaotic, draining in a way that makes me thirst for him.

I jerk my head to the side to try to free myself from his grip, just to convince myself that I did try to fight it, but heaven knows I have no real desire to fight this.

His grip on my chin loosens, but doesn't relent as he turns my head back in his direction. Stepping closer, he lets go of my chin to grip his cock, rubbing the tip over my lips as his fingers sink into my hair. He twists and tangles the strands at the back of my head. He gives a sharp tug at my hair, and with a yelp, I part my lips, letting him press his hips forward and slip along my tongue. He sinks in deep, but not deep enough to gag me, just enough to pause and let out a breath of relief, as though he's been waiting for this moment all day.

He has.

Nervous energy tickles beneath my skin as the rush of ire floods me. I swallow anxiously and it makes him shudder. He groans and my eyes drift shut to the sound of it, to the pleasure that having him inside me brings. His taste isn't vile like the others. Though I imagine no one's cock tastes particularly good, I also don't know how else to describe it.

Arlo's cock tastes like it belongs inside me.

Firming up his grip on my hair, he slowly presses deeper, fulfilling his promise to bury every inch of himself inside me. I gag and splutter as he sinks, and when he's all the way in, he loosens his grip on my hair and his palm strokes down the side of my head.

"That's perfect, Mercy," he whispers.

My eyes fill with tears from his invasion, and I open them to blink up at him as salty tears slip from the corners. The way he looks at me is strained as he moves inside me, hardly pumping with tiny strokes, moving just enough to allow some relief of the pressure at the back of my throat.

More.

I want more of him.

He fills me in every sense, taking up all the space in my mouth, but also in my mind. With Arlo, the world doesn't exist, the pain doesn't exist. With Arlo, I don't have to think about what comes next or what came before. All that exists are him and me and this time we have together to be completely unhinged and bare, sharing our debauchery with each other unashamedly in this Service of the Flesh.

This trial requires his indulgence, and I will let this man indulge with me in all the ways that please him…because his pleasure is linked to mine. I'll never understand that, but I don't need to understand to know that it's true.

He rocks his hips, pumping slow and long over my tongue. He leisurely fucks my mouth, and my arousal grows with each stroke. He strokes until he's shuddering, and his hips start moving faster, frantically thrusting out of rhythm. Then he slams to a sudden stop, gagging me as his cock nudges against the back of my throat. He holds still as his body trembles.

I prepare to feel the splash of him down my throat, and I'm ready to swallow everything he gives me, but he doesn't come. He keeps himself there on the edge, trembling with his eyes pinched shut. I'm surprised his expression doesn't show frustration; it shows bliss.

Pure bliss finds him on the precipice of release, and he keeps himself there.

Then, without warning, he pulls out, and I cough around his absence, feeling saliva coat my lips and drip down my chin. He grips my hair again and arches me back, leaning down over me, so close that the tips of our noses touch. I gasp for air as his fingers touch my chin, rubbing across it to gather the spit from my skin and swirl it around my lips before pressing his fingers into my mouth. Instantly, I close my lips around them and suck lightly.

I find myself in some wanton headspace where this filth feels good.

I'm too lost in this, making it too obvious that I want him.

I need to feel angry again.

I bite down on his fingers, sinking my teeth into them.

"Fuck," he cries out, pulling his fingers from my mouth.

I gaze up at him, chest heaving, and lick my lips. His mouth twitches to fight the curl of a knowing smile—a grin that tells of the way he wants me roughly.

I harden my eyes, having to hide my expression of taunting, aching, pure lust. "It would be a failure on your part to underestimate me, Warden Rainn."

To anyone else, it sounds like a threat, but he knows what I'm telling him. He knows I can take what he gives me—and I want him to give it all to me.

He drops his hand from the back of my head to grip my bound wrists behind my back. Closing his grip around them tightly, he twists me around and shoves me forward so harshly that I shriek with the unexpected motion. Still on my knees, he shoves me face-first to the floor. I squeeze my eyes shut as the floor rises quickly to meet me. I can feel my breath bounce off the tile and hit my face as I come to a sudden stop.

From there, he lowers me slowly, pressing me down until my turned cheek touches tile and my shoulders are on the floor. I struggle, but with my arms behind me, I can't push myself up.

His hands land on my hips and lift, raising my bottom high. I can feel him slide closer, his legs nudging my knees apart, his thumbs circling over my cheeks. I feel like I can't breathe, waiting for him to fill me, because for the first time, I actually want it.

How can I want it?

It doesn't matter why…only that I do.

"Please," I whimper.

He groans in response, his hips jutting forward to rub his hardness against me. His hands flatten to my lower back and slowly slip along either side of my spine, fingers climbing over my bound forearms. I shudder at his touch, panting in need. His hands keep moving, skimming over my shoulder blades, up my neck, tangling through my hair. He lets go as he folds over me, placing one palm on the floor above my head to brace himself. He reaches back to tuck my hair behind my ear so he can look at the side of my face. He presses a kiss to my cheek before moving his lips against my ear, whispering so softly.

"You're going to come for me, starlight. I will make you come so hard that you'll scream, make it feel so good that it makes you cry, because I want them to see your tears. I want them to think I'm the most brutal thing that's happened to you all day, but you and I both know I'm the best."

He is the best.

He's simultaneously the best and worst thing that's ever happened to me. I loathe how much I love the feel of him against me.

I don't respond, but I don't need to. He can see my response in the way I squirm beneath him. He can hear it in my pleading whimpers. He can taste it as he draws his tongue along the line of my jaw, all the way back to my ear, causing me to shiver.

He snaps upright, his weight leaving me all at once. His hand lands harshly on my hip and his fingers dig into my flesh. I feel the tip of his cock rub through my folds, dragging wetness as he moves behind me.

He presses inside me, easing his tip little by little. Then, with a groan, he slams inside me, pushing so hard and fast that I cry out. He lets out an audible breath of relief that sounds absolutely indecent. His hand slips from my hip, up the side of my waist, tickling my skin and making me flinch. He pulls out and slams in again, shoving me forward along the tile, my body lurching forward as my sweaty skin sticks to it.

"Sweet sin," he mutters as he slowly starts to fuck me, holding on to me with one hand around the smallest part of my waist.

A guttural moan claws its way past my lips as I try to choke it down. He made no false promises—he will have me screaming from this sensation that consumes me.

He leans over me again, one palm landing on my cheek and pressing down, squashing my face against the tile. "You make sin feel so good…so fucking good," he grits through his teeth as he fucks me harder, faster, deeper.

He continues this way, thrusting into me steadily. I know I won't come like this, but it feels so good, nonetheless. I feel so full, so complete. I wonder how he's going to get me there, but he answers me without a word.

His hand moves from my cheek, and I feel him grip the knots that bind my arms behind my back. He lifts me harshly from the floor, bringing me upright while he's still deep inside me. I gasp as he arches me back against him, my head falling back onto his shoulder.

My eyes instantly drift shut at the feel of his lips brushing my cheek. He brings both arms around me, one reaching all the way across the middle of my waist to hold me in place against him, the other covering my breast, squeezing lightly.

He doesn't speak as he draws his fingers back to play with my nipple, rolling, tugging, squeezing, pinching. It all sends jolts of pleasure straight through me, making me tremble in his hold.

He doesn't say a word, but it feels like an entire conversation transpires between us as he works me up. We engage in an unspoken discussion of desire and need, of want and appreciation, of chaos and corruption. When his hand falls away from my breast and slips down my stomach, dipping low between my legs, I open my eyes and drop my head to watch.

I want to see the way he touches me.

He presses in and moves two fingers over my clit, rubbing back and forth in a quick but easy cadence that beckons me to the edge. I pant, watching his hand move, feeling his body rock slowly, his cock thumping steadily against the perfect spot inside me, over and over again.

"You're gonna scream for me," he says, and I find myself nodding, knowing it's true. He's taking me there so hard, so fast, with more knowledge of my body than I have for myself…like he was always meant to touch me.

And then I slip…He leans us forward together, adjusting the angle he hits inside me to perfection. He fucks me harder, with a steady pounding rhythm that has me clenching around him in time to match it. My clit sparks and pulses, ready to catch fire.

"Warden Rainn…" I huff out a breath and take another before I explode.

An orgasm rips through me so powerfully, so fully, that I scream, sounding a primal release from the way I feel it tingle out from my center, rushing through me in waves of pleasure.

"Sweet fucking sin," he grits.

I'm still coming as he pushes me down to the floor again, my face on the tile, his hand around the side of my neck, pressing down.

His force strengthens as his pace slows, thrusting so hard and deep that I imagine I can feel him in my stomach. His hand drifts away from my neck, finding my arms and holding tight to use them as an anchor. He pulls back on them so hard that my chest lifts from the ground while he fucks me harder, my breasts rubbing against the tile with each thrust.

I'm still pulsing around him with aftershocks from my climax. I keep expecting him to come, but he doesn't. He just groans, grinds his teeth, and keeps fucking me. It's like he's trying to drag this out for as long as he can.

Of course he is.

That's exactly what he's doing. He's filling the last of my time, so I don't have to endure his brothers again.

My chest feels a lightening flutter at the understanding.

He leaves me all at once, and I whimper at the loss of his pounding warmth, but he finds me just as quickly as he left. He grips beneath my elbows and hoists me from the floor, planting me on my feet. He turns me to face him as my legs tremble beneath me. His palms cup my cheeks as he bends to kiss me hard and fast, his tongue sweeping around my mouth as deeply and sensually as his cock was buried inside me.

I kiss him back.

But then I think I shouldn't because this isn't something I'm supposed to enjoy.

But I do enjoy it.

I enjoy it so, so much.

Our bodies move together as he walks me backward, stopping when my heel hits the marble. He releases me from the consuming kiss, and I realize we're at the staircase—the marble my heel had hit was from the bottom step.

His eyebrows lift. "Up."

Locking eyes with him, I step backward onto the first step.

"Higher."

Another step backward and up. Then another, and another, and another. He stops me there, telling me to sit, and I do. As soon as my bottom hits the marble beneath me, he crawls up the steps between my legs. My knees spread for him naturally. His sight is set on my pussy and he descends, kissing me there as feverishly as he kissed my lips.

Unable to contain the way I love this—the way I *want* it, the way I *need* it—my head falls back on a moan.

I need him so much.

He licks and laps, settling to consume me for what feels like forever, but he doesn't make me come. He groans and pulls away, climbing onto his knees beneath me. He positions himself between my legs and grips my hips to hold my ass on the edge of the step where I'm perched.

"Hold still," he warns.

I spread my fingers, trying to wrap them around the edge of the step to hold on to. Arlo thrusts, sinking deep inside me with a groan that shakes the world around us…at least, it feels that way. I feel him burrowed inside my soul, and I don't think he'll ever leave.

Never.

"This," he mutters, breathing heavily as he picks up his pace, "this is what you get, sinner." He swallows hard, reaching out to lasso his hand around the back of my neck, curling me forward so he can place his forehead against mine. His hips jerk madly as he tries to hold back, but he's too close to the edge to hold out much longer. "This is…what you get for sinning."

His eyes flutter shut, and when they open again—half-hooded—he locks onto my stare. His eyes tell me so much and so little all at once. He's so restrained, but his self-control is waning. I want to push him over the edge.

"What do I get?" I whisper, quiet enough that only he can hear. "Show me what I get, what I deserve."

I think I've lost myself because I know I shouldn't be engaging in this kind of talk with him. I shouldn't be finding satisfaction in pretending I'm the sinner they say I am, that I deserve to be sexually destroyed by these terrible men in charge of Ember Glen—that I *want* him to sexually destroy me. I know I shouldn't hold his gaze. I know I should cry or thrash or detach so completely that I'm not aware of what's happening. But I can't do any of that with Arlo, and that's why this hurts me so much.

It hurts, because I know that if what I feel between us is real, then it will only last for moments. With one breath or the next, my life will be done, and what we do or don't have between us won't matter.

But it matters right now.

"Stop fighting it…please," I quietly plead with him.

As if all he needed was my permission, he ruts chaotically, frantically pumping himself to orgasm. I feel him swell, feel him rub along my sore inner walls, and within moments, he spills inside me with a primal roar.

And then he's still.

We're both still.

Though bliss finds us for a few precious moments, it fades away so quickly. Out rushes the unexplainable connection between us, and in rushes reality.

chapter six

ARLO

I FILLED UP the last hour of her trial.

I filled *her* up for the last hour of her trial.

Killian came back and tried to take her from me, but I didn't let him. I told him, as well as Ryker and Wesley, that the rest of her trial was mine, and I made sure no one touched her but me until the time was called.

All my brothers have returned to the foyer and we've brought Mercy and Delle to stand before the camera, both wearing black silk robes, my brothers and I fully dressed. Wesley just announced the successful completion of their first trial and completes the final ceremonial prayer.

"*Malo mori quam foedari,*" Wesley says.

Mercy lets out a groan in agitation, dramatically covering her ears with both her hands as my brothers repeat, "*Malo mori quam foedari.*"

And just like that, it's over, and seemingly everything returns to normal. We disperse, and Mercy is among the first to march away, charging toward the staircase. I watch her knees wobble as she takes a single step, pausing and reaching out for the railing at the bottom of the staircase. The bindings have worn her muscles, and she's endured so much today. I go to her, ready to sweep her into my arms, but the moment my hand touches the small of her back, she flings her arm, whipping her head to the side.

"Don't touch me," she hisses. "Let me walk."

"Let me help you."

She doesn't respond. She stubbornly takes a step, then another, slowly climbing the staircase on weary muscles. I follow behind her, ensuring she doesn't tumble backward down the steps.

It feels like it takes an eternity watching her climb the stairs in her soreness and exhaustion, but she finally reaches the landing. I let her continue down the hall for several paces before my frustration at her stubbornness takes hold of me.

"This is ridiculous, Mercy." I close in and dip behind her, sweeping her off her feet, scooping her up into my arms.

She lets out a yelp. "I said—"

"Shut up," I hiss. "Just shut up for once and let me help you."

I feel her tension as her arms fling to latch around my neck. She's prepared to fight me because that's what she does. She fights. But this time she doesn't. Her tension lessens with each step, and her weight sinks into my hold as she slowly gives in.

I carry her down the hall and manage to get her bedroom door open without setting her down. I turn sideways to carry her over the threshold.

"I can walk," she says, though it's a perfectly pointless statement now that we're in her room.

I kick her door shut behind me and take her straight to the bathroom. "I know you can."

I lower her feet to the tile floor, but keep my arm around her waist, tugging her close to my side, holding her up as I bend to flip on the faucet of her bathtub. I hold my hand beneath the water, adjusting the temperature to a perfect warmth before engaging the drain block and letting the tub fill.

"I need to use the toilet," she says quietly. I start to lead her in that direction, but she halts me. "Give me a minute, *please*. I just want to be alone."

I don't want to leave her alone. I don't want to remove my arm from her waist. I don't want to step away from her for a second. I've never felt so insistently needed, even though she tells me she doesn't need me.

"Please, Arlo…Just let me have one moment of privacy."

I sigh, gradually dragging my arm across her waist until it drops free. She bends to grip the edge of the tub, letting out a breath of what seems to be relief.

Was my touch bothersome?

Was I too rough during the last hour?

A lump rises in my throat and I swallow against it, taking a step back. "I'll give you a few minutes, but I'll be back. I'll bring food."

"Go. Please—" Her voice cracks, and I know she's fighting to hold herself together, waiting for me to leave before she falls apart.

I don't want to leave her to fall apart alone. But I can't deny her the space she needs after what she's been through. I take a step back, then another, watching her fingers as she tightens her grip on the tub rim. Though it feels like the tether that binds us is made with unbreakable twine, I somehow manage to snap myself free from it to turn and walk away—because she asked for me to.

"Arlo," she calls, and I stop, whirling around to face her. She hasn't moved. "Give me fifteen minutes, but please…come back."

Her plea slices right through me, cutting a hole that immediately fills with need for Mercy—need to be near her, the need to touch her, to care for her. I'm so needy for this woman, and it's frightening.

It's wrong.

I'm not sure how much longer I can care that it's wrong.

"I'll come back. I promise." I leave before I lose the ability to pull away.

I rush downstairs to the kitchen and grab a plate I'd made for her and set aside earlier, knowing she'd be hungry after the trial. I filled it with fruits, cheese, and crackers—quick eats that didn't require time to be heated or cooked. She can start with this, and I'll make her something else myself if she's still hungry.

I bring the plate and a glass of water back upstairs, taking it into my room because she asked me for fifteen minutes, and that's what she'll get. But I don't know how to kill the small amount of time that seems like hours before returning to her.

I pace for a few minutes, crossing back and forth along the end of my bed, but as I walk, the need to be close to her claws away at my insides, scratching at my soul, and the itch is unbearable. Yet, she asked me for fifteen minutes, and I want to honor her request and grant her that time. She's earned that time alone. She deserves it.

She deserves it more than anyone.

What she's endured today is something that no man in Ember Glen could ever endure—and certainly not with the dignity and grace Mercy had showed. She championed her way through an arduous trial, passed it, and walked away from it on her own two goddamn feet.

I walk over to my desk and I lower into my chair. I unlock the drawer and pull out my journal, uncoil the leather twine and open to a blank page. I lift my pen, and the moment it touches the paper, it begins to move with the flow of poetry in my mind.

Your demons become mine,
creeping slowly through the flow of our touch.

A touch is all it takes,
and your sins bind to my heart.

Your sins pulse with the rhythm of my prayers,
prayers I repeat for the pardon of your soul.

Your soul calls to mine,

seeking light in the darkest time.

But the light in me is gone,
gone with the secrets I've asked you to keep.

You keep without contempt, endure without hope, need without fear,
yet I am not dignified in the same.

I hold contempt—contempt for the madness you've brewed within me.

I hold hope—hope that the madness will never fade.

I hold fear—fear that the madness will be snuffed out with your life.

Your life will be taken.
Your light will be extinguished.
Your madness will fade into history…
but it will never be snuffed from my memory.

I pray my memory will be enough to sustain…to endure a lifetime
without your madness.

I slam the pen down and slap the journal shut. Panting, I huff
with agitation at the disjointed and nonsensical scribbled words—a
brash display of my confusion and misunderstanding of our world,
our God, the truths that are proving to be lies.

Yet, after what I witnessed today, my world feels…wrong.

And the only thing that feels right is Mercy Madness.

I bind the journal with the leather strap and return it to the
drawer, taking notice of Mercy's mother's journal locked in there
with it. I've considered reading it on several occasions, but I haven't
brought myself to do it yet. I'm afraid of what I'll find; I'm afraid
that I'll learn too much about Mercy's mother and the influence

she had over shaping Mercy into becoming the rebellious, stubborn, blasphemous woman I can't seem to get out of my mind. I'm afraid it will grant me too much sympathy for the woman meant to die at the end of the trials—the woman I feel too much for, the woman I'll have to let go of one day.

I shove the drawer shut and lock it, rising so fast that my chair tumbles backward. I ignore it, stepping around it, rushing toward the fireplace with the intent of grabbing a candle and burning myself to gain some sense of self-control. My eyes brush past the clock on the mantelpiece, and I quickly realize that more than fifteen minutes have passed.

I stop everything and charge for the door, opening it and stepping out into the hallway before I realize I've left the plate and water behind. I rush back in to grab both, then quickly let myself into Mercy's room. I drop the plate and water glass too heavily on the table between the armchairs. The plate clangs, and the water sloshes from the top of the glass, but I don't care. All I care about is returning to her side because I promised her I would.

I enter the stark white bathroom, but I don't see her. At first, all I notice is the bathtub full of water. It takes me a few seconds to see the nearly white strands of her short hair floating up and around her head.

She's sunk beneath the surface of the cooling water.

I panic as I rush to the tub, feeling the same fear I felt the first night she was here—when she'd dunked herself beneath the waterline, and I thought she must be trying to drown herself. I had pulled her out, and she'd told me she only wanted a moment's peace. The recollection does something to calm my nerves as I approach, as I see she's pinching her nostrils closed with one hand and her eyes are open, slowly blinking beneath the rippling water.

I know she's not trying to drown herself.

I feel the peace settling in the room, as if she's taken all of today's negative energy beneath the surface to drown it. Still, I'm ready to grab her and yank her out if she spends another ten seconds down there.

I lower to my knees, looking over the edge at her slowly blinking eyes. Her irises blend so seamlessly with the water—the same silvery blue reflected from the light against the white backdrop of the porcelain tub. Her head turns a little, and I notice the slight dip of her eyebrows as she recognizes my presence above her.

Gradually, she rises, her starlight tresses—darkened by the water—stick to her cheeks as her head moves above the waterline. Bringing her hand away from her face, she takes in a deep breath, pinching her eyes shut to squeeze the water from them. She pushes her hair up her forehead, smoothing it away from her face.

I watch the muscles in her throat work as she swallows, shifting to sit with her spine against the back edge of the tub. She casts her gaze to the top of the rippling water. "I was starting to think you'd forgotten about me."

I shake my head, reaching out to brush my knuckle across her cheek and wipe away the stray droplets of water. "If you think that's possible, then you obviously haven't been paying attention."

She turns her head to look at me and several silent beats pass. The silence pounds loudly in my mind with the echoing beat of my heart taking in the sight of an angel. She looks as though she's emerged from the heavens—bare, clean, refreshed, and renewed. A small smile even touches her cheeks, and I think it's enough to brighten the room.

Then the smile fades, as does her attention. Her head turns and her stare fixes on the faucet near her feet.

"Are you hungry?"

She shakes her head. "No." She pauses. "Yes. But I don't want to eat right now."

"What do you want?"

She shrugs, and the movement of her shoulder pushes the water, causing a ripple to fan out across the tub. "I just want you to hold me."

Her eyes turn to meet mine, and they track with such misery that it makes my fists clench. I rise to my feet and rush to remove my clothes, keeping my eyes on her to watch for protest as I prepare to climb into the tub with her. If she does protest, I don't see it in her eyes.

I strip to my underwear—deciding it would be best to leave them on—and reach down to place my hand at the base of her neck. I nudge her forward and climb in to sit behind her. I spread my legs around her hips before gripping her waist, tugging her back to rest between them.

She holds herself up, tense and rigid. Her fingers grip the edges of the tub, and I see the subtle movement of her chest as she takes in quick, shallow breaths.

What has this trial done to her?

How much did I hurt her during that final hour?

Eventually, her back rounds as her tension releases. Her grip on the tub slowly loosens, and soon, she lets go. When she does, I ease her back, sliding her against me. I snake my hands across her stomach to wrap my arms around her.

Minutes pass, and I hardly breathe until she's let herself lay fully against me, until she's calmed enough to let her head fall back onto my shoulder, and she's closed her eyes to rest.

Finally, she can rest.

There's a beautiful silence surrounding us where the only sound is the light movement of the water when one of us shifts or moves an arm. It's peaceful, at least for me, and I hope it is for her, as well.

"Did it upset you?" she asks after a few minutes, interrupting the silence.

"What?"

"Watching your brothers use me…Did it upset you?"

I sigh, taking a moment to figure out how to frame my response. "It made me feel a lot of things, Mercy."

"I asked if it *upset* you."

"Yes, it upset me. Of course, it upset me. But that's not the only thing it made me feel."

A stagnant beat hangs in the air, and when she speaks, her voice trembles, as if she doesn't really want to ask the question. "Did you find enjoyment in watching me that way?"

"Not in the way you think."

She shoots up and spins, her body easily turning to face me in the water, which splashes over the edges. "In what way, then? Tell me. Don't attempt to give me comfort without honesty."

I stay put, though my hands twitch to grab her and my arms ache to wrap around her again. "I've always enjoyed watching, and hearing, which shouldn't surprise you. On nights of service, I often sit and watch before indulging." I lift my arms from the water and lay them along the edges of the tub, afraid I'll grab her if I don't do something else with them. "I did enjoy seeing you bound and strung up, but I don't think that should come as a surprise to you. You know how beautiful you are to me in bondage."

She shakes her head subtly, slowly, sadness creeping in around the edges.

"I was excited by the sight of you, Mercy. But it devastated me to watch them hurt you." I look down at the settling water between us. "I nearly lost control when I saw Killian come out with that knife."

I hear her blow out a breath, see it skim across the surface of the water as a ripple disturbing the stillness.

"It wasn't the first time he did that to me," she says. "He used me in service before he was selected to be one of the Control." Her eyes drop to the water. "You know he always brings a knife to service."

I sit up, ignoring the water sloshing over the edges of the tub, splashing onto the floor, and touch my knuckle to her chin, lifting her face and forcing her to meet my eyes. "He's put the handle of a knife inside you before?"

She nods, her eyes gazing off in the distance rather than at me.

There's the dissonance again, the broken chords of conflict inside my mind. I'm angry that Killian has done this to her—and not just today, but during nights of service. I'm sad that she's had to endure that at all, let alone more than once.

But I shouldn't feel angry or sad about it.

I shouldn't feel anything about it at all.

It's Killian's Impulse, and she is a servant—*was* a servant. It was her duty to serve the Impulse then, and it was her penance to serve it today. It's something she and I both should take pride in.

Yet, I don't.

It feels…wrong.

Why does it all feel so wrong?

"Mercy, look at me," I demand, desperate for her gaze.

She turns her eyes to look at me, though they flicker around my face, never settling. I slide closer as I slip my fingers along her jaw, taking my palm around to the back of her head to hold her there. I press my forehead to hers and she's forced to meet my eyes.

"You can tell me how you feel," I tell her.

"No, I can't. I can't trust you. Not fully."

That hits like a lightning strike through my chest.

"You can trust me, Mercy. I promise you can."

"Don't make me promises you can't keep. I can't trust you, Warden Rainn. At the end of the day, you're the Control. Your duty is to care for me until I die…and I *will* die. When I'm gone, you'll have to go on with your life as before, and you have to protect yourself to ensure that happens. I'm disposable to you, and I always will be." Her palms touch my chest, resting delicately as she speaks.

"I can never fully trust you not to take my secrets and betray me should it help you maintain your station."

Our bodies slip toward one another, slowly moving together without reason or control.

I have no control over myself with her.

"I could say the same about you," I tell her softly. "You could betray me with our secrets, with the sins I've committed with you."

Her hands slip over my shoulders and around my neck, bodies still drifting together, as if the water itself knows that nothing can keep space between us.

"I won't," she whispers.

"Why?"

Her eyes drift shut. "You know why."

"Tell me."

"Because I need you." She slips closer. "Because thoughts of the trials and death and hellfire fill my mind until I think of you."

I sink one hand beneath her knee, tugging her leg forward along the side of my hip. Naturally, she brings the other forward, too, until her body wraps around mine, straddling me in the tub. One of my hands remains at the back of her head, keeping our foreheads touching, while the other slips around her back to hold her close.

"When you enter my mind, everything else slips away," she confesses, and my heart pounds. "When I think about you, I can't think about anything else, and it's freeing."

Sweet sin.

My breathing grows heavy, but not with lust. My lungs demand more air because her confession has sucked them hollow.

"Mercy…" I have no other words. No response I can think of could ever express the overwhelming storm of emotions sweeping through me.

She lets out a sigh, as if the confession alone is freeing, and sinks into my arms, slipping hers all the way around and hugging me tightly. I hold her closer, burying my face against her neck and inhaling her scent deeply. Even in the bath, the faint aroma of wildflowers in the meadow lingers in her hair.

Wildflowers and starlight.

An image comes to mind of Mercy laid out on a raised platform, her starlight hair spread out around her head like a halo, and the scent of wildflowers surrounding her because they lie around her lifeless body at her funeral.

Will her hair still smell like wildflowers when she's dead?

Will it still shine like starlight?

A shudder rips through my chest, a lump rises in my throat, and warm tears—something I haven't felt in ages—burn behind my eyes.

My arms close tighter around her, and I press a kiss to the crook of her neck before settling into her embrace.

My thoughts are consumed by you, too, sweet Mercy.

I just can't bring myself to say the words out loud.

chapter seven

Mercy

I HAD FALLEN asleep in my bed with Arlo at my side, but I was alone when I woke. The other side of the bed had been neatly made while I slept, and there'd been no trace that he'd ever been there in the first place. I must have slept heavily because I found a tray of breakfast foods left on the table between the armchairs—he left and came back and left again, all while I peacefully slumbered.

Exhausted and overwhelmed, I pull on the long black silk robe I'd worn back to the room after the trial yesterday, and sit quietly in one of the chairs, leisurely chewing my way through a slice of toast and jam from the tray. I consider remaining in my room all day. I also consider going back to sleep because then I can avoid thinking about the trial I endured yesterday…or what's to come in the next.

But my mind flashes through the images of debauchery, the use and abuse that stretched on for so many hours. My body aches from the bindings and being suspended for so long. Spots of my skin are red and rubbed raw, and my muscles are sore from being held in a single position for hours on end.

I can manage the physical aches and pains that remind me of the trial, but I can't handle the way they make me think of Arlo and how he cared for me last night. The emotional awareness of it is daunting. He'd tended to the rope burns, massaged my aching muscles, and put me to bed. The admissions I made to him replay in my mind, and it brings me anxiety. I'd told him that he fills my thoughts, and how those thoughts of him bring me peace. I'd admitted my need for him…yet he'd said nothing in return.

He'd said nothing, that's true, but he had tightened his arms around me…he had held me closer, nuzzled his face against my neck, kissed my cheek, and gave me a kind of affection I've never known. Though a mother and father could hug their child and kiss her cheek, though a dear friend might pull you close and offer you comfort in their embrace, the moment I shared with Arlo was nothing like that…

Nothing like that, at all.

It was so much more.

Thinking of it makes my heart race, and I don't think I can handle that right now. I don't want to think about him. I don't want to think about anyone but myself. I only want to rest, but a knock at the door derails that plan.

"Mercy?" comes a sweet voice from the other side.

Delle.

I feel immediate regret for being so selfish and not going to her earlier. I rise from my seat and rush to the door, flinging it open. Delle stands on the other side, fully dressed in a burgundy silk gown that hugs her comfortably, a matching silk belt wrapped around her waist and tied in a bow at her side.

The sight of her is nothing short of surprising. I'm surprised by the color in her cheeks and the care she's taken to groom and dress today—I didn't have the energy to care for myself, but I'm glad to see her looking so well after the torture of yesterday. I reach for her, and pull her straight into a hug.

"How are you?" I ask. "Are you okay?"

"I'm okay," she says quietly.

I step aside and motion for her to come in, letting her move past me before shutting the door behind us. She sits in one of the armchairs, and I sit beside her.

As I look over at Delle, I see that her gaze is downcast and I can feel the anxiety rippling out of her in waves. Though she sits there quietly, I know there's a reason she came to me, so I remain silent and give her some space to gather her thoughts. If she wants to talk, she will. And if she doesn't, then we'll just be quiet together.

A few moments later she lifts her head and turns toward me. "You've served every month for four years, right?"

I nod.

"How…how did you do it, Mercy? How did you survive it for so long?"

I feel my forehead crease in consideration of her question, because truthfully, I don't know the answer. "I just…I just did what I had to do."

"Yesterday was…" She shakes her head and sighs. "I just feel like less of a person today than I was before."

My eyes press shut to hide the silent tears that gather for her, though I know they're not only for her. The tears also come for the person I was before I began service at sixteen. I was an entirely different person then, and I had to become someone new when I started serving. I feel like someone I don't even recognize now, knowing that my death is coming and my actions no longer matter.

"You're no less of a person, Delle. Please hear me when I tell you that. But I do understand what you mean. They took things from you that you weren't willing to give and that…that changes you."

"But in a way, I was willing, wasn't I?"

I tilt my head, regarding her with a curious expression, unsure of what she's saying, waiting for her to say more.

"I can't help but feel like I have no reason to feel this way—this sick to my stomach, this sad." She looks over at me and tears gloss over her hazel eyes. "I *chose* the trials. I *chose* to participate yesterday."

In the span of a breath, I'm out of my seat and on my knees in front of her. I don't reach out to touch her as I would have before yesterday—I don't know if she wants to be touched at all right now.

I let out a sigh. "You said it yourself, Delle. It was never a choice for you at all. You endure the three trials, or you serve every month for the rest of your days. They made it impossible to choose any life other than the one you were given. They made it impossible for you to ever truly be free."

Her tears flow as she drops her face in her hands. I remain quiet as she sobs, as she lets the pain from yesterday flow out of her with each broken breath. I stay still and silent as my own tears, so eager to fall, prick behind my eyes. I sniff and draw in a deep breath to try to hold them in just a little bit longer.

I can cry for myself once she's gone.

"Why are we the only ones?"

"The only ones?"

"Who see the truth? Who see the madness of everything in Ember Glen?" she asks.

I shift to sit on the carpet, bringing my knees to the side in a fawn position, then adjust my robe. "I don't think we're the only ones. After all, there have been trials in the past; others before us have chosen to dissent." I turn my gaze away as I drift through my mind, staring off at the door. "And I imagine there will be others long after we're gone."

"It shouldn't be this way. We should be free to choose how we live, who gets to touch us and who doesn't—"

"Who we love…" I interrupt unintentionally. I blink and turn my head, giving her my attention again. "It shouldn't be this way, but it is."

"Why can't we change it? I want to change it so badly, Mercy. I want change so much, but I don't know how that could ever be. I feel more powerless than ever." She sniffles, dragging the back of her arm beneath her nose. Then she chuckles through her tears. "Why haven't you hugged me yet? You always force-hug me whenever I cry like this."

I shake my head to draw myself from my thoughts, and give her a smile. "I'm so sorry." I rise onto my knees and hold out my arms, drawing her into a hug. "I didn't know whether you wanted to be touched."

"I don't," she breathes, wrapping her arms around me tightly, like a young child clinging to her mother for comfort, "but a hug from you doesn't count."

I let her cling to me for as long as she needs. I find comfort in her hold as much as she finds comfort in mine. "Do you want to talk about what happened to you yesterday?"

"No," she says, gently pulling back. "I want to forget it ever happened." Her brow furrows, and her eyes turn away. "Except, there was something about yesterday I did want to tell you about."

"What is it?"

"Theo…and Arlo." Her eyes meet mine. "I think it's meant to be a secret, but neither of them used me yesterday."

I blink, taking a moment to make sure I understand exactly what she's saying. "Do you mean that neither of them participated? That neither of them sought sexual service from you?"

"Theo only touched me to knot the ropes. And Arlo…"

"What did Arlo do?" My heart stalls as I wait for her response.

She chuckles. "He talked to me about his sister."

"What? He didn't touch you?"

"Only once to adjust the ropes when they were hurting me. But otherwise, no. He…he did remove his clothes, all except for his underwear, but just for a short time when we were first alone in the room. He said it would make it look like he'd just finished with me if he were putting them back on while the others came in to use me. Theo did the same thing." Her cheeks flush pink at the mention of Theo.

I'm surprised at this news…relieved. Incredibly relieved. I feel a heavy weight that I didn't know existed lift from my shoulders. I don't know whether I thought Arlo would actually use her. He was supposed to use her. In fact, by not engaging, he's failed in his duty—and Theo as well.

They willingly neglected their duty…but why?

"I don't understand." I shake my head, looking away in my confusion.

"I'm not sure I understand it, either. But Mercy, I think it's supposed to be a secret."

My eyes snap to hers. "It *is* a secret, Delle. They were both supposed to use you. If anyone else were to find out, they could be punished for it." I reach out to touch her hand. "Promise me you won't tell anyone else."

"I won't tell." She swallows visibly. "I don't want Theo to get in trouble."

"We could all be in trouble if someone finds out. I fear what you might be made to endure should it be found out that you didn't complete your first trial."

"That I didn't—" Her eyes widen with panic. "*What?*"

"The trial was to serve the sexual needs of the seven members of the Control over the course of seven hours. You endured the seven hours, but if Arlo and Theo didn't use you, then you only served five of the Control. It means…it means that, technically, you didn't complete the trial."

Her hand comes up to cover her mouth in shock. I reach up to grip her wrist and gently tug it away, clutching her hand in mine.

"You have nothing to worry about, Delle. I promise you this doesn't matter. As far as it concerns anyone else, you completed your trial. Like you said, this is a secret. And I promise, I won't tell a soul; and neither will Arlo or Theo. They could be punished for neglecting their duty. They won't tell."

"But why didn't they—"

A loud knock interrupts our conversation. I give Delle a quick, reassuring smile and a pat on the hand before climbing to my feet and crossing the room. I pull open the door to find Arlo standing on the other side, and the mere sight of him kicks my heart into a flurry. He glances over my shoulder to see Delle behind me, and my head naturally turns to follow his stare. When I turn back to face him, I catch his eyes darting to look me up and down, and it sends an odd thrill shuddering down my spine.

Then his head turns, and he looks down the hall. "Theo, she's here," he says, then looks at me again. "I need you to get dressed."

"Why?"

"The Control want to speak with you…the *both* of you."

Theo appears in the hall just behind Arlo, and I see his cheeks twitch to hide a smile as he spots Delle walking up behind me.

"What could they possibly want from us today?" I huff.

"It won't take long," Arlo replies. "Get dressed."

He steps over the threshold, nudging into my space, and I suck in a breath as he reaches past me. Our eyes meet and he holds my stare for a tense moment. I'm not sure exactly what he's doing, but he's far too close given our witnesses. Then I realize he's reaching past me to grab the doorknob. I take a step back to let him pull the door shut as he leaves too quickly. I miss him immediately, and that's difficult for me to admit to myself.

"Do you think the Control knows about Arlo and Theo? Is that why they want to see us?" Delle asks, and I turn around to find her with wide, panicked eyes.

I shake my head as I cross to the wardrobe and pull it open. "No. If the Control knew, they wouldn't send our wardens to fetch us."

"Then what do they want from us? I don't want to see them today."

"Whatever this is about, I can tell you that what they truly want from us is a reaction. Otherwise, they wouldn't waste their time to call us before them just to deliver their messages."

And knowing myself, I'm certain they'll get a reaction from me because I refuse to keep my mouth shut any longer.

ARLO AND THEO have brought us into the dim courtroom. The spotlight shining down over the black, semi-circular table casts an eerie glow to the room, outlining the silhouettes of the Control who sit behind it in shadows.

Delle and I stand on the opposite side of the table beneath a second spotlight, which is so bright that it drenches us in heat. The three Elders are projected onto a large white screen at our backs, and it makes me feel uneasy to be so completely surrounded by the authority of Ember Glen.

"How are you feeling today, sinner?" Killian regards me with disdain.

I grit my teeth. "I'm fine. How are you?"

He scoffs, dropping his pen to the table, sitting back and crossing his arms. "I've already taken three showers today trying to scrub the filth of you from my pores."

"Well, I only took one bath last night, and I feel clean enough. Though perhaps I'm more efficient in cleansing than you are. Do the boys' teachers instruct them on how to bathe? I'm certain there was an entire unit on cleanliness and hygiene taught when I was a girl."

Arlo leans forward into the light. "Enough, Mercy," he scolds sharply, though I believe I see a hint of humor dance across his cheeks. He looks over at Killian on his left. "Would you just tell them so we can get on with our day?"

Killian doesn't look at Arlo. "Fine." He remains still, with his arms crossed, his glare focused on me. "We asked you both here to deliver this news. It's been collectively decided that neither of you will serve during the next full moon in two nights' time. I think we all agree that we've had enough filth from you." He only looks at me when he says it.

"This isn't news," I tell him, confused. "We were told from the beginning that we were sinners, no longer servants. By definition, you deemed us unfit to serve since our participation in the Trials of Dissension was decided."

Owen leans forward, tossing his head to throw back a strand of nearly black hair that had fallen over his forehead. His dark eyebrows dip toward his nose to frame his blue eyes, which always seem to cast a deliberate gaze.

He clasps his hands on the table. "It's the decision we expected to make, but we hadn't made it official until just now. We felt it most prudent to wait until after the first trial."

There's a pause, as if they're waiting for us to respond. Surprisingly, I have nothing to say to this, so I finally break the silence.

"Will that be all, then?"

"There's just one more thing." Ryker locks his fingers behind his head over his wavy, dark blond hair as he stretches back. "We're going to broadcast a special viewing of this month's purge. A live stream of the event, just for the two of you." He looks only at me, never a glance spared at Delle because none of their taunting is meant for her.

"You're both going to sit and watch it together," Killian says. "You'll view the sisterhood you left behind as they serve the men of Ember Glen with honor and pride. And since neither of you will be serving, your former sisters will have all the more work to do, won't they?" He leans forward. "You're going to watch every minute of it in your shame."

I feel bold, and speak likewise. "Presumptuous of you to assume I'll feel shame for it."

I will feel shame, but not in the way he wants me to. I'll feel shame that I can't help them; I'll feel shame that I'm powerless to save them from their fate.

Killian's expression melts into anger, his brown eyes darkening to black as his palms slam against the table. He shoves to his feet, his chair teetering. "I've never been more disgusted by a woman in my life—"

"You were hardly disgusted yesterday, Killian. I remember the pride in your cock as you shoved it into my mouth."

His chair topples to the slate-tiled floor as he shoves back and jerks sideways. He rushes around the table—behind the backs of his brothers—to get to me. I push Delle behind me, and take a step back as he advances.

Arlo leaps up, spinning and sprinting to catch him before he clears the side of the table. Arlo grabs above Killian's elbows and yanks him backward, effectively halting him. "You lose yourself to rage and we have all lost, brother."

I feel the corners of my lips snarl at Arlo's words—the way he calls him *brother*, the way he makes it sound as though they're in this together.

Because they are.

I think I'd almost forgotten that he wasn't one of them.

Killian's jaw is tense, eyes narrowed in anger, wild fury pulsing from him across the room and punching straight through me. Yet gradually, he relents and turns to face Arlo. Killian blows out a heavy breath, conceding his struggle.

"You're right," Killian says to his brother. "She's not worth it. I mustn't let the Impulse overcome me with the night of our purge so close." He straightens, brushing his hand down the front of his blazer to smooth it as he strides back to his seat.

"Right," Arlo says to him, though his eyes rise to meet mine. "Release is coming with the full moon."

My throat suddenly feels dry, and I swallow before clearing it.

"As we were saying," Killian says as he and Arlo return to their seats, "you'll both watch the service as it's streamed. Of course, we can't place cameras throughout the entire forest, but they will be placed at camp where most of the activities will be taking place."

"What's the purpose?" Delle asks from behind me, her voice meek, though striking all the same.

A swell of pride rises through my chest at the sound of her voice, though it's quickly followed by fear. I turn my head over my shoulder to look at her, and she begs me without words not to silence her, not to speak over her with my urge to protect her. Though my eyes narrow in consideration and worry, she moves around me, steps forward, and faces the Control on her own.

"Why should we watch our sisters suffer by your actions?" Delle's voice grows louder with each word. "I watched them suffer at the last service, and I suffered myself. I endured my trial yesterday. I'm already condemned for choosing to participate in the Trials of Dissension. So again, I ask, what is the purpose?"

I want to pull her back behind me so I can protect her, but more than that, I want to applaud her. I want to cheer for her. I step in closer behind her and stand silently, giving her the power of my support as she finds her voice.

"We don't owe two sinners an explanation for our decisions," Owen says calmly.

"Is that because you don't *have* an explanation?" Delle asks with a tilt of her head.

Her fingers curl at her sides and it draws notice to the trembling of her hand. She trembles, yet she still speaks, and I don't believe I've ever been more impressed by someone in all my life.

Killian chuckles darkly, and Ryker's face brightens with glee for the drama unfolding before him. Wesley looks over at Owen with furrowed brow, confusion wrinkling his forehead, as if he, too, wonders about the explanation.

"I'll say it again and more clearly this time." Owen speaks with crisp precision, emphasizing his words. "We don't owe two sinners an explanation for our decisions."

Delle straightens, pulling her shoulders back. "Is it written in the Impulse Edict? In the documentation of past trials? That participants should be subjected to witness service rather than focus their energy preparing for their own trials? I've chosen not to serve, so why must I be subjected to witness those in service?"

Killian slaps a palm on the table, the noise of it startling everyone in the room. Delle's right foot moves, as if she's going to step back. I move closer to halt her, pressing my hand to the small of her back to help her hold her stance with courage.

Killian leans forward. "You cannot *choose* not to serve. What you've *chosen* is to be a sinner. You've chosen to dissent, to defy God, to defile the values of Ember Glen in your participation in the Trials of Dissension."

Delle's head dips, but only for a moment before she lifts her chin again. "The only choice I was ever given was whether to continue my existence with a certain future in service, or to participate in the trials. I will not feel shame for making a choice for myself when I was presented with an option for the first time in my life."

I take in the most satisfying breath of my life, drawing in her strength and grace, breathing out my pride and gratitude that I've found a truly kindred spirit in Delle.

"Enough of this." Wesley waves his hand, looking to his brothers. "We've said our piece and they've said theirs. I think we're all exhausted enough from yesterday."

"Agreed," Park says from beside Wesley. "They know they'll be watching the service. Let's get on with our day."

"We might've spared the drama," Theo grumbles as he turns his head of messy blond hair in the direction of Killian, "if only we'd been allowed to deliver the message to our wards directly, rather than dragging them here."

Some voice in the back of my mind urges me to pay attention to these interactions, to take note of the way these men react to each other—and to us—in these heated moments.

Arlo stands abruptly, drawing my full attention. "I'm calling this meeting," he says with command, leaning on his palms on the table, and stirring heat in my belly. "Mercy and Delle just completed their first trial, and they need to rest to find more favorable moods. All we've accomplished here is creating a space for them to argue needlessly with decisions that have already been made."

"Well said." Wesley stands, smoothing down his waistcoat. "Owen and I need to deliver evaluation times to some of the domestics for their children today, anyway. We have a rather large group of girls to rule on this season."

A heavy weight drops into my gut. When the girls of Ember Glen turn five, they're brought before the Control for this evaluation and ruling. Each of them will be told their future fate that day, assigned to their lifelong role in Ember Glen as either a domestic or a servant. My hand floats up to rub over my heart as anger and discomfort ripple through me at the realization that Wesley and Owen will be making those decisions soon.

"Actually," a voice from the large screen behind us booms, startling me and Delle as we both jump and whirl around—I'd nearly forgotten the Elders were here. "We need Owen to remain behind," Lawrence says. "As well as Killian and Arlo."

My head whips over my shoulder to glance at Arlo, and I find his eyes are already on me, so I turn away just as quickly, afraid someone will notice.

"We need to speak to the three of you," Lawrence says.

"I'll join you then, Wesley," Park offers.

Delle and I turn back to face the Control as they rise from their seats, breaking into side conversations as they move toward the door.

Theo turns to Arlo and says something quietly to him. They both nod before Theo steps away, moving quickly toward me and Delle.

"Come on," he says, "I'll return you both to your rooms."

He grabs a hold of Delle's elbow and drags her forward, but my gaze is drawn back to Arlo. Our eyes meet and he holds my stare. I don't know the intention of the look he gives me because I find some uncertainty there, as though he's not entirely sure why he's been called to speak to the Elders.

Worry grips me as I recognize the uncertainty that he feels. I suppose I relied on that certainty to some degree before—his confidence and command, the way he can take control and I can trust him…

Trust him?

I don't think I've ever trusted him.

Or perhaps I always have, and I'm only realizing it now.

His head inclines toward the door, indicating I should go. I don't want to go; I don't want to leave him. Admittedly, I'm feeling nervous over him being called out by the Elders.

"Get moving, sinner, or I'll drag you out myself," Ryker says as he brushes past me, turning and walking backward, waiting for me to move.

I glance over at Arlo one last time, but he's already turned away, lowered into his seat, his eyes downcast to the table where he taps his pen incessantly with a gloved hand.

"Mercy," I hear Theo call for me from the hallway.

I drag myself away, though the desire to remain with Arlo is strong. I pull myself from the overwhelming urge to sit at his side, to hold his hand, to offer him the comfort of my presence. It's an urge I'm surprised I have for him, but I suppose I shouldn't be. There's compassion in my heart for him as real as there is for everyone else I care about. Yet the strength of the compassion I have for him is bewildering, overwhelming, consuming every inch of my damned soul.

It grows stronger with each passing moment, and I fear it will be the thing that breaks me.

chapter eight

ARLO

MY MIND IS lost, entrenched in thoughts of Mercy Madness, which never seem to cease—thoughts that overcome reason and threaten to swallow me whole.

Something dangerous has begun to shift within me since the trial, since her admission in the bathtub as I cared for her after. She told me that when I enter her mind, thoughts of me filled her up and freed her from the burdening fear of what's to come.

And how desperate I am to fill her up in every sense.

It's not a sin to lust after a servant, especially knowing you can use her in service under the next full moon. But it is a sin to lust after someone you can never have—a domestic, or worse, a sinner on trial.

I don't know where God is in these moments where my attention is lost. He's failing me when she's brought to stand before me, when my eyes see nothing but her starlight hair and silvery blue eyes, when my ears hear no other sound but her voice, when my nose detects no scent beyond the heady aroma of wildflowers and the sweet musk of her arousal.

I can always smell her delicious scent, even from across the room, even when her scent couldn't possibly be heavy enough to float across the space between us so strongly. It's a phantom scent which haunts me so divinely. It's as though her demons—which possess me now as fully as they possess her—manipulate my senses to the point of drawing obsession.

I'm becoming *obsessed* with her.

Worse than the obsession itself is the way I enjoy it—the manner in which I intentionally indulge myself by letting the wicked thoughts of her simmer to a slow boil inside my mind.

I had to force myself to lower to my seat in the courtroom. I had to force myself to grab my pen with my gloved hand, and I'd begun to tap it against the table to distract myself from the sight of her.

I focus on the incessant *tap, tap, tap* against the dark wood, letting the sound flood my mind. She needs to leave. I need her to leave the courtroom before I lose control entirely and chase her to her bedroom.

Drape her in rope and bind her to the bed.

Sweet sin, after all she's been through, I need to leave her alone.

The flicker of a small orange flame against a dark background enters my mind, and I close my eyes to focus on it. I imagine removing my gloves and lowering my palm over the flame, which dances atop a candle in my imagination. I imagine burning my skin, letting the fire sizzle and tear through my flesh to bring me the distraction of pain against my impure thoughts.

Eventually, the courtroom door slams shut, forcefully yanking me back to reality. I slam my tapping pen to the table and raise my head to find Killian lowering in the seat to my left, and Owen already seated on the other side of Killian. Lawrence, Edgar, and Clyde remain on the large white screen before us.

"I suppose you're wondering why we wanted to speak to the three of you alone," Clyde begins.

I nod, as do my brothers.

"I assure you the news we have to share with you is good." He smiles, and it begs my curiosity. "This is to remain confidential, as the decision will not be final until the next Shift."

There's a transition of power every twenty-five years in Ember

Glen, called the Shift. The last Shift occurred two years ago when my brothers and I became the current group comprising the Control. At the same time, Lawrence, Edgar, and Clyde—who were members of the Control before us—had been officially declared the new Elders. The other four men from their cohort retired from their time served as members of the Control, sent to live blissfully-ever-after in the Land of Kings—a place where it's said the Impulse doesn't exist.

And since the next Shift won't occur for another twenty-three years, I'm confused about the fact that they're speaking to us now about a decision to be made later—more than two decades into the future.

"It goes without saying that this information cannot be shared," Edgar continues the conversation. "We need your confirmation that the information we're about to share with you will not leave this courtroom. You will not discuss it with each other, and certainly not with your brothers. This is crucial."

"Of course, you have our word," Owen says before stealing a glance at me and Killian. He looks as confused as I feel.

"You have my word," Killian says.

I turn my gaze to the Elders. "And you have mine, as well."

"Good." Clyde nods. "I'm pleased to share that you three are slated to become the next generation of Elders in Ember Glen."

My eyes widen in surprise, and my heart stops for a moment. I've just heard words that I've longed to hear for so much of my life. I dreamed of becoming one of the Elders, of becoming one of the highest and most respected leaders in Ember Glen. It's a true honor granted to so few; and only the most devout of men would ever even dream of achieving it.

Joy touches my cheeks as my lips curl into a grin, yet…my smile quickly falters. Excitement for this news that I'd only ever hoped to receive stutters and slips from my grasp.

"Really?" Owen asks with a pleased chuckle. "The three of us?"

"Yes," Edgar confirms. "We began making our observations as soon as your term began. When you're each at your best, we feel the three of you would make for a well-balanced combination of personalities to replace us when the time comes."

"This is an honor to be considered," I say slowly, cautious with my words, "but how can you make such a decision so early on in our term? The next Shift won't occur for another twenty-three years."

"That question leads us to our next point of conversation," Lawrence says slowly. "At your best, the three of you are perfectly suited to take on these roles later in your lives. But at your worst… our support for this may change."

"What do you mean?" I ask.

Clyde's eyes shift on the large screen to look over at Owen. "Owen, you're a strong leader on your best days. Others look to you easily for guidance and to bring calm reflection to stressful situations. Yet, too often, you retain your silence and allow yourself to be overlooked. You allow those with stronger voices to take charge when the situation at hand calls for the composed leadership skills you naturally possess.

"Killian, you're passionate about upholding the values of Ember Glen and are strong in representing the best interests of this community. But your passion often gets the best of you, spurring your Impulse in such a way that it may lead you to misbehavior if you aren't careful. Sin hunts you in your passionate rage, and it will find you if you aren't mindful of your reactions."

Their large eyes on the screen turn to me. "Which leads us to you, Arlo… You possess a more ideal blend of their two best qualities as a strong leader and a passionate believer. Yet we've begun to see a wavering in you, hints of ambiguity where there should be none. We've all had our moments of weakness, our own misunderstandings of God. As you come to understand Him better, and the plan He has for your future, we believe your moments of ambivalence will simply become a regretful part of your youth."

"Blended together," Clyde continues. "The best qualities of each of you will balance well to lead the community of Ember Glen, both while you remain in your term as the Control, and in the future, when you should be confirmed as the Elders of this community."

To be one of the Elders…

I'd often envisioned myself as one of the figureheads on the screen—a man with true power over his community, authority to ensure our Edict is upheld. To be privileged with the honor of accessing the Impulse Edict, to be able to learn of all the laws and history of our land, would be nothing short of incredible.

It's everything I've ever wanted.

Killian and Owen are grinning gleefully from ear-to-ear, and my lips twitch to smile the same. But something holds me back, dampens my pride, floods me with an odd feeling I can't quite name…

Guilt? Shame?

Heartache?

"And now that you know this," Edgar says, "we must discuss the Trials of Dissension. The manner in which the final two trials are carried out will have a major bearing on how we perceive your fit moving forward. At this moment, you are the three we envision as destined to become the next set of Elders. But God's will is always changing, and He may change that destiny should He see fit. You each hold the power to impress Him…or to change His mind entirely."

"You *must* regain control of Ember Glen," Clyde adds with urgency. "We sense there may be whispers among the servants. They have such great shame for Mercy Madness and Delle Carter for the choices they've made; but Mercy's ungodly wiles have bewitched those girls, making them believe she had been a compassionate and caring sister when she served along with them. They cared for her, and they express some sadness for her situation. We cannot fault them for being so weak-minded, but it is our job as the authority of Ember Glen to make them see the truth and bring them closer to God.

"We *cannot allow* their empathy, as such feelings lead to indignation, which gives way to rage, which strikes the match of rebellion. Establish your power and set them right. Your power will be found in brutality through the final two trials. You must ensure the masses know what rebellion would lead to."

"Of course." Killian nods, serious intent gleaming in his overeager eyes. "We will ensure that Delle and Mercy face punishment equal to their crimes."

"Will you?" Lawrence asks. "Because I found the first trial to be rather unimpressive."

Owen's eyes narrow as he tilts his head. "Oh?"

"Keeping Delle off camera, tucked away in a separate room? No one in the village witnessed what she faced, and she *chose* to participate, even when she didn't have to," Lawrence explains.

Killian clears his voice. "I can see how it was a misguided notion. We'll choose more wisely for the next trials."

"Of course you will," Edgar says. "After all, your future depends upon it."

Killian looks over at me, quirking an eyebrow. "Our future depends on it. Of course." He turns back to the Elders on screen. "We'll do our very best."

"Absolutely," Owen echoes.

I nod, though my mind twists and turns, swooping through a field of visions which clutter my thoughts—visions of Mercy, of wildflowers and starlight, and the softness of her touch.

"Arlo?" Owen questions, and it snaps me from the reverie.

I clear my throat. "Of course. Our very best," I confirm, though I'm not sure I believe myself.

chapter nine
ARLO

"ARE YOU COMING?" Owen asks.

Killian pushes open the courtroom door, breezing out into the hallway like a king. I'm sure he feels even more like a king now than before with his over-inflated ego—he's the last man who should've been given prior knowledge of the fact that we're slated to become the next generation of Elders.

I give Owen a tight smile and nod. "I'll be out soon."

I remain in my seat as he leaves, the room empty and the projector off. I lean back in my chair as I try to sort out how I feel about this news, contemplating what this all means for my future. There is a part of me that's thrilled, honored, excited for my future and the good fortune it holds for me. But those feelings are muddied by Mercy's presence in my mind, and the understanding that I have a future—bright with power and prestige—while she has none.

My fingers grip the armrests as I tilt back in my chair, lifting my chin skyward and looking up above me. I avert my gaze from the spotlight that hangs directly above the seat to my left, wondering if it always felt this warm to sit beneath its glow.

The dissonance in my soul has never reverberated with such intensity. This is what I wanted. It's what I've always wanted—to be shortlisted as a future Elder is an honor of the highest degree. But all I can see in my mind is a future where Mercy doesn't exist, and it pangs in my chest.

Worse than the thought of a future after her death is the means by which the Elders asked for us to achieve it. They want brutality in the trials to make an example of the sinners. To achieve the future I've always wanted requires me to ensure Mercy's brutal demise.

"Fuck," I mutter to the ceiling.

"Warden Rainn?" I sit up with a rush when I hear her call my name, the door creaking as it slowly opens.

Starlight shines in through the opening as her head peeks through, turning to search for me. I shove to my feet too quickly and my chair slips back along the floor with a screech.

"What are you doing here?" I ask.

"Everyone has left the courtroom except for you."

"And?" I snap unintentionally as unease waves through me, crashing like a breaking ocean tide.

"If you want to be left alone, just say so." She steps back, turning to leave.

"Mercy," I call after her as I dash for the door.

I fling it wide just as she turns, and I step into the hallway to grab her wrist. I drag her back, pulling her inside the courtroom with me. She whirls around when I release her, stepping backward as I pull the door shut behind us.

And then I stand there—silent and conflicted—looking at her as though an answer to a question I don't know to ask might burst from between her lips. The longer I stand and stare, the more the world fades away, the more space she takes up in my mind, forcing out the discordant harmonies that sing through my combating thoughts to make space for her perfect melody.

It's what I've come to feel more and more whenever I'm alone in Mercy's presence. And *sweet sin*, how it twists me when she looks at me like that, with that expression which reflects a perfect mixture of compassion and curiosity.

"Are you okay?" she asks, and with the slight tilt of her head and narrowing of her eyes, I can see she truly wants to know.

"No," I tell her honestly. "I don't think that I am."

"Did the Elders tell you something upsetting?"

I shake my head as I stride deeper into the courtroom, brushing past her side and shuddering with the vibration of her energy as I move away from her toward the table. "I'm not sure whether upsetting is the right word for it." My fingers come down to graze the tabletop as I walk along the curve of it.

"If you'd like to share, I'm sure I could help you find the appropriate word to match your feelings."

I chuckle, stopping at the center point of the table and turning back to look at her. She stands with her arms crossed, one hip jutted out to the side beneath the red flowing gown she wears so well—long sleeves that are cuffed at the ends, a deep V-neck with the point resting on her cleavage, cinched at the waist and flowing down around her like a crimson waterfall.

"Do you think I can tell you what they told me?" I lean, sitting against the edge.

"I think you can do whatever you want to with little risk of consequence."

"Oh?" I raise my eyebrows.

"Do I need to remind you of the sins you've committed with me?"

I swallow, my jaw tensing. "I don't need a reminder, Mercy Madness. I'm reminded of our sins every time I close my eyes."

She looks down at the floor, averting her gaze.

"Look at me."

Her eyes snap back to me in a flash. "Don't tell me what to do."

"Why are you here? Why did you wait for me?"

Her hands drop to her sides as she shrugs. "Honestly, I don't know, Arlo. I don't know anything anymore."

"Says the woman who knows everything…"

"Are we back to that?"

"Back to what?"

"Your self-righteous snark—"

"*My* self-righteous snark?" I laugh. "And what about yours?"

"*Mine?*"

"I've never known a person more self-righteous and snarkier than you."

"Then perhaps no one has shown you a mirror."

I can't help the grin that cuts across my face. "Perhaps you can guide me to one."

"Perhaps I will." She tries to remain stoic, but I don't miss the twitch of her cheek as she fights a smile.

Dear God, let her give me that smile.

My grin broadens as it slowly creeps through. My fingers curl around the edge of the table on either side of my hips, the leather of my gloves creaking with the tension, and I drop my head to gaze at the gray floor. If I look at her for too long, I might lose control of myself and take her right here in the courtroom.

"I received news from the Elders."

She's quiet for a moment before she asks, "What news?"

"I'm not supposed to tell anyone." I glance up to find her a step closer, and it kickstarts my heart.

"You could tell me."

"Could I?"

Could I tell her?

"Have I given up your secrets yet?"

"You haven't."

She takes a step closer, dropping her arms to her sides—an opening, an invitation that unwittingly tugs at my heartstrings. "Are you still worried that I will? After what I confessed…"

"After you told me that you need me?"

Sweet sin.

Hearing the words come out of my mouth is jarring enough, but it draws the memory of holding her in the bathtub after her trial, hearing them from her while she held me. I swallow hard against the rising lump in my throat.

"No, I'm not worried, though I know I should be." Confusion wrinkles my brow. "I *know* I should be worried, Mercy. I should be terrified of the sins we've committed together, and I don't know why I'm not."

"Maybe it's because we both know I'm going to die. Because you know it wouldn't serve me to tell anyone the things we've done in secret." Her head drops as her gaze lands on the floor. "Because we'd both like to have more secret moments with each other before the end."

"Come here," I demand.

I tighten my grip on the table's edge to keep myself from moving—I want her to come to me. Even when I desperately need her near, I want to see her move; I want to know she *chose* to come to me.

I want to know she chooses me.

She hesitates, but then she glides across the floor like an angel on a cloud—a dark angel in a flowing crimson gown who stains the purity with her divinely indecent sway. Each step loosens my grip on the table, easing bit by bit with each shared breath between us. And each moment where space remains between the gravity of our bodies becomes more painful than the last. Her gliding steps aren't quick enough to sate my boiling need for her.

I reach out and clamp my gloved palm around the side of her waist once she's within reaching distance, and I forcefully drag her against me. Our bodies collide with shared heat and the instant relief of finally connecting. One of her hands grips the open collar of my button-down shirt while the other drops to my waist, fingers locking on the chain that links from one button of my waistcoat to its pocket at the side.

We lock eyes, staring at each other with a soul-deep gaze that has tremors of need rippling through me. And at the same moment, we let go, wrapping our arms around each other, embracing as intimately as we did in the bathtub last night. We share an exhale in relief as we shift together, her curves gliding against me until we align perfectly, locking together like two puzzle pieces. She nuzzles her face into the crook of my neck as I slide my hand up her spine, cradling the back of her head in my palm as we strengthen our hold on each other.

"I wish it didn't have to be like this," she whispers.

"I wish for so many things when I look at you, Mercy."

"Tell me."

My fingers curl, sinking into her hair as I turn my face to press kisses to her cheek with my blasphemous lips. "I wish to understand what I feel for you and why I feel it...why my thoughts are so conflicted. Has God forsaken me to make me want you the way I do? What is this that I feel for you?"

She sighs with contentment as her hands move across my back, stroking me. "Connection."

"It's more than that."

"Lust."

"If that were all, my need for you would have been satisfied when I filled you yesterday during the trial."

She breathes out slowly, and I swear I feel her shudder. "This is something more than connection and lust for you?"

"I don't know what it is, but it's *more*, Mercy. Of course, it's more."

Her tension gives way and she sinks, her body relaxing in my arms. I rise from the table to hold the weight of her, relishing the way she relents to me. Holding her this way is divine, but my body begs for her unholiness.

I grip her hips and spin us both around, rushing her backward until her ass hits the table's edge. Her hands find my biceps and grab hold as she arches back to look at me. Our eyes meet, and her silvery blue irises flicker as they search mine beneath the glow of the spotlight over the table.

"I know it's more," she whispers. "But even that's not enough to save me, is it?"

Mercy's fate is sealed.

She is destined to die.

And there's not a damn thing in the world I can do to save her. Yet the admission that she feels something more with me—and her expression of sad acceptance—feels like a rope being drawn around my heart, a knot being tied and pulled until the beating muscle stops altogether.

I bring my hands to her face, cupping her cheeks. "Mercy, you sin—"

"Don't tell me I've sinned," she says on a rushed exhale. "Don't say I'm a sinner. We both know my sins have nothing to do with this."

Confusion creeps through my mind. "What do you mean?"

"It's about power, Arlo. It's about control. It has nothing to do with my sins, because if it did, then you'd be condemned, too."

"I *would* be condemned if anyone found out—"

"And they won't because you're allowed to sin in secret."

"Well, that's a ridiculous argument. By that logic, anyone in Ember Glen could sin in secret."

"Yes," she chuckles humorlessly, "that's exactly my point. How many men do you think are sinning in secret? And if they're found out, how many have been brought to judgment for their sins in comparison to the number of women?"

"Women bring temptation."

"Yes, of course," she rolls her eyes, "and it's a woman's fault that a man chooses to act on that temptation." Her voice twists with sardonic anger and my indignation rises to meet hers.

"It's the fault of the Impulse, Mercy. It's why we purge; it's why there are servants to satisfy those temptations on a single night so all the others can be free from the horrors brought by sex and violence."

Her hands slap against my wrists and she shoves them away from her face, forcing me to step back. "We meet those horrors monthly in service. We are *not* free from them."

"Servants sacrifice such that others—"

"Such that *men* can indulge themselves without consequence."

"And so that domestics can be free from fear, free from threats of violence, and—"

"Entirely devoid of passion of any kind? Is that what you were going to say? What kind of life do they live with nothing to fear? With no sense of urgency? Without sense of their own mortality?" She raises her hands, and though I'm expecting her to shove me away, she doesn't. Instead, they land on my chest with a half-hearted thud and remain there, drawing my breaths quicker and heavier. "Without fear, there is no drive, there is no passion, no desire..."

I step forward, crushing her to the table's edge, laying my palms on either side of her hips on the dark wood. I bend over her deeply, forcing her back to arch as my body kisses hers.

"Do you fear me, then?" I ask. "Is that what this is? Does your passion and desire for me come from your fear of me?"

"Yes," she blurts without hesitation.

Conflict swirls within my soul. I want to prove that she has no reason to fear me; equally, I want to give her something to fear, if for no reason other than to draw out her passion for me.

Heat rises within me, suffocating my lungs, making it so difficult to breathe that I pant for air. Her lips part as I stare her down. The arch in her back deepens as she places a palm on the tabletop behind her, leaning against it and jutting her hips forward. I bring one of my hands from the table to her lower back, encouraging the alignment of her body with mine.

I dip my head to bring my lips only a breath away from hers. "Do you fear me now?"

We both know what I'm really asking.

Do you desire me now?

Do you have passion for me now, in this moment?

She bobs her head with a jerky nod.

I rub the tip of my nose across hers. "Then I suppose I fear you, too, Mercy Madness."

Leaning all her weight on one hand, she lifts the other to touch my cheek, and I sigh, letting my head fall into her palm as she caresses my skin with her brushing thumb.

"I see your disbelief and the way it plagues you," she whispers. "It hurts me so much that you won't let go, that you let the conflict in your mind gnaw away at your soul. My heart wouldn't be drawn to you so intensely if it didn't know the truth hiding in yours. I just wish you could see it, too. I wish you would let yourself see me as something other than the temporary conflict that plagues you." Her eyes move about my face, studying me with such intensity that I feel burning through my skin. "Call me foolish because I must be to say this, but…I won't betray you, Arlo. I don't think I ever could, even if I wanted to. I'll take all of your secrets to the grave with me."

My eyes fall shut at the odd sense of shame I feel for her admission, because I can feel her shame for saying it rippling from her the same.

"Why?" I ask.

"I don't wish my fate upon anyone, least of all you."

"Perhaps I'd deserve it."

"It's not my judgment to make."

I drop my forehead to touch hers while she continues to brush her thumb over my cheek. "Is it God's?" The question feels strange to ask—blasphemous—but it's genuine.

"I don't know," she says. "But I know it's not mine."

I touch my lips to hers. "I haven't earned your tireless compassion."

"So earn it now. Tell me your secrets."

I kiss her softly, chastely, humming against her lips, which part gradually against mine. It's a soft, subtle movement that coaxes my tongue to slip between them. A moan vibrates through her throat as I taste her slowly, languidly swirling my tongue with hers as I shift my feet to press in closer, harder.

The kiss deepens and simmers, heating steadily, bubbling to a boil. Her hand on my cheek slips, fingers reaching for my hair and tangling through it, her grip tightening at the back of my head. Every inch of my frame is fastened to hers, our legs tangling through her long skirt as they shift beneath us, our bodies molded in mirroring arches as she curves back and I bend with her.

I'm so securely bound to the need for our bodies to exist as one that I nearly collapse on her when she turns her face away, unexpectedly breaking free from the kiss. My lips burn as though she's torn them cleanly from my face. My palm splays across the small of her back to secure my hold on her, afraid she'll squirm away from me.

Though she keeps her head turned sideways, avoiding my eyes, both her palms find my cheeks to cup them in her hold. I don't know whether she's holding me to keep me from stealing another kiss or if she's trying to hold herself away from the temptation of stealing one from me.

"Someone might see us," she pants.

"I nearly don't care."

It's dangerous for me not to care. It worries me about the state of my mind and how she's changing it, how her demons have dug in so deep that they may never climb out. But that's the thing about demons…they make you feel so good, so unbelievably alive, that you forget the higher power you follow, along with your morals and beliefs. They take it all away and make sinning feel like finding God, like dropping into paradise, like nothing could ever feel better than committing these moral offenses.

The demons are winning.

I'll soon be forever lost to these sinful delights, and my soul begs me to give into it.

chapter ten

ARLO

"STARLIGHT, I—"

"I know about Delle."

I know Mercy's only trying to change the subject, trying to break free from the sexual tension that refuses to let us go. She can try all she wants, but she can't deny how she trembles as those two syllables shake through her.

Starlight.

It's the word I use to claim her.

She turns her face to meet my gaze squarely, tightening her grip on my cheeks to hold me in place. My eyes fall to her perfectly parted pink lips, my mind stuck on the taste of them and struggling to focus on her words. I lurch for them, trying to push past the grip of her palms to steal another kiss, but she jerks her head back.

She won't let me taste her—and it's killing me—but the way she studies my features, then settles her gaze on my lips with restrained longing sends a pleasant thrill through my body.

"I know you and Theo didn't participate in Delle's trial."

The mention of the trial drags me back to reality. "How do you know that?"

"Delle told me." Her hands lower, slipping down the sides of my neck, coming to a stop over my chest, gripping my collar. "She told me this morning and I…"

"What?"

"I want to know why. I want to know how you justified it to yourself," she demands.

The sincere curiosity in her gaze implores me to speak the truth. She's given me no reason to think I shouldn't trust her with yet another secret.

"I could see her as my sister." I lick my suddenly dry lips, struck by the sobering memory of seeing Delle on display, ready for use by my brothers in God. I pull back, straightening, though I remain close with my arm around her. "I couldn't bring myself to touch her that way."

"It was your duty, and you neglected it." I hate the way she says it, with self-satisfied righteousness, but I can't deny she's right.

I sigh. "Perhaps it was, and perhaps I did."

"If they found out she didn't truly complete the first trial, would they make her repeat it?"

"No," I tell her firmly, with lifted brows, "because they won't find out."

"You're going to lie to your brothers?"

My head jerks to the side. "Are you trying to bait me into an argument?"

"I'm only asking, Arlo."

"Delle completed her trial, and that's the truth as far as anyone can see it."

"That's something I needed to know; something I needed to hear from you." She sighs in a manner of reverie. "I think there must be some goodness within you after all, Arlo Rainn."

"You think there's *some goodness* within me?" Anger shades my mind with gray clouds that threaten to storm between us as I release her and step back. "What did you think of me before? Did you think there was something wrong with me?"

Mercy pushes off the table, stepping toward me. She opens her mouth to speak, but I don't allow it. I close the distance between us, meeting her chest to chest, glaring down at her with ferocity.

"Did you think I was a bad person? Did you think *I* was the sinner?"

She doesn't back down, staring up at me with a ferocity that matches mine. "Yes. Yes, I thought you were a bad person. Yes, I thought there was something wrong with you. And, according to the Edict, you *are* the sinner. You lusted after me. You fucked me outside of service. You—"

"For God's sake, Mercy, shut your beautiful fucking mouth."

I grip her hips and spin her, turning her to face the table. I grip the back of her neck, pushing down to bend her over the edge. She slaps her palms against the hard wood, trying to press up, but I fold over her, pinning her heavily with my weight resting on her back.

She turns her cheek to press against the surface as I apply pressure to the back of her neck. "Let me up."

"You don't want me to." I reach between our bodies and press my hand to the back of her thigh, dragging my fingers slowly up toward the curve of her ass.

Her body jerks beneath me as she tries to rise. "Don't..." she whispers half-heartedly.

"Don't, what? Don't touch you? Don't prove you right in thinking I'm a sinner, the same as you?"

I'm suddenly panting as my fingers grapple with her skirt, lifting it up enough to slip my hand beneath and find her underwear taut across her cheek. She whimpers as I play with the hem, slowly nudging the fabric to bunch toward her crack.

"Someone might walk in..."

"Is that your *only* protest, starlight? That someone might walk in?" I tear my glove from my hand and land my bare palm against her exposed cheek with a light smack before caressing her skin. "Give me a more compelling reason to let you up, and I will."

Sweet sin.

One moment, I'm furious with her, and the next, I'm lost in my lust for the feel of her skin against mine.

She's quiet for a moment, still as my fingers draw along the lines and curves of her flesh. The longer her silence stews, the more pliant we become, both slowly submitting to the dominant gravity between us. The more I want her, the more my need grows. The more I need her, the more my convictions splinter. And the wedge is so deep, they threaten to shatter spectacularly.

"I don't have one..." she finally says, and my fucking cock twitches to sink inside her.

I dip my head to kiss the side of her face, her hair spread haphazardly across her cheek, soft against my lips. "I need you to give me a reason," I whisper with a trembling voice. "I beg of you, Mercy. Give me one reason to let you up before I lose control... before I lose everything."

"I'm..." Her panting hesitation reaches inside me, grabs hold of my heart, and tears it out from between my ribs.

My hips move, grinding against her ass, my cock throbbing to find some relief. My pounding heart beats wildly in her phantom grip, waiting for her to decide if she's going to encourage this or give me a fucking damn good reason to stop.

When she finally speaks, her voice is quiet, but sure. "Yesterday I was fucked for seven hours by six men I don't want, and one who I do. And though I always want you, Arlo..." She pauses, and her admission lingers, the weight of it heavy, anchoring to my lust and sinking it right down to the ground. "I always want you, but I need to heal. If you start, I'll make you finish, and it will hurt for me."

I drop my forehead to her shoulder, feeling suddenly defeated, though I can't quite sort out which battle I feel I've lost—the battle with my lust for her, the battle with my growing feelings for her, or the battle in my mind with God.

All I know is the thought of hurting her makes my chest ache, makes my spine tremor with rage— yet I'm meant to hurt her so much worse before the end of the trials.

"I wish I could erase the pain of yesterday." I stroke my palm once more down the curve of her ass, and mustering all my strength, I rise and step back.

She remains bent over the table for moments after I've left her, half of her dress hiked up, tucked into the side of her underwear, leaving her cheek exposed. And those boots—those fucking servants' boots she still wears make it so much harder to resist the ache to fill her.

With a huff, she rises all at once, tugging her dress down with a sharp hand before whirling around to face me with pinkened cheeks. "You can't. No one can. Just like you can't erase the years of pain I've experienced in service."

My instinct is to argue, to remind her that her pain in service doesn't matter, so long as she's done her duty for the men of Ember Glen. But a niggling voice inside my mind halts me, silences that instinctive voice that only concerns itself with rules and laws and godliness. She's becoming the gray that muddles my mind in the slivers between the black and white.

"Is that what service is like for you? Like your trial yesterday?"

I don't know why I asked, but I'm suddenly curious to know. I felt her pain yesterday—her moments of fear, her moments of resignation. I felt it all as though I were living it with her because of this odd connection between us. Her head ticks to the side as her expression flickers in curiosity. Perhaps she noticed the way I quelled my instinctive voice, too.

"Sometimes, yes. Sometimes it's more violent and less sexual, and sometimes it's the opposite. But focusing on one man, as opposed to several, is easier." She blinks her eyes shut, her head lowering. "Not easier, but different."

"Yesterday felt different?"

"Yes." She looks up at me. "But mostly because of you."

"What did I do?"

She shakes her head, leaning back against the table's edge, bringing her hands in front of her and wringing them nervously. "It's not about what you did, Arlo."

"Then what was it?" I fold my arms over my chest.

"It's because…it's because of the connection I feel with you." She looks down at her twisting fingers. "Having your presence and feeling it's absence are both profound."

Profound.

My arms feel heavy, and I drop them to my sides. "Mercy, I… Your presence is profound for me, too. And I imagine…" I pause to gather my words, "I imagine your absence will be, as well."

"So you think you'll miss me when I'm gone?"

Sweet sin.

Will I miss her?

Some unseen force moves me and deciphering whether it's divine or demonic in nature is pointless. It's powerful, and it barrels through me, pushing me closer to her, overwhelming me with poetic words I know I'll need to write later.

I tap my knuckle beneath her chin to lift her head. "Would the sky miss the stars? Would heaven miss an angel? Would the wildflowers in the meadow miss the rain?" My eyes skim the features of her face as I speak, finding more beauty with each line I trace. I grip her face as I step closer, aligning to her body, tilting to rest my forehead against hers.

"If God does exist," she whispers, "then He's a cruel maker to bring us together this way."

I should revolt from her words, but oddly, I feel no revulsion. I only feel agreement because it does feel cruel that I had to find her as a sinner, to know her through her trials, to want her this profoundly while she seeks absolution with her certain death looming. My resolve is weakening with each breath she takes, with each pain that she encounters. I fall deeper into her madness with each new misery she endures.

She may be possessed by demons, and they may afflict me the same now, but I'm not sure it matters to me anymore. I know that it should, yet here I am, tempting my lust once again with my mouth only inches from her parted lips.

Stop.

Pull back.

Confess your secrets in penance of your desire.

"I'm slated to become an Elder one day," I blurt out the truth, which seems less like an honor and more like a curse as moments pass—a punishment for sinning with her to get what I always wanted, yet forced to spend a lifetime without her.

"What?" She jerks her head back and I release, letting her pull away.

"It's what the Elders told us when they asked me, Owen, and Killian to remain behind. They're watching us in these trials to determine whether we've shown ourselves worthy to be the next generation of Elders."

"I…I don't know what to say." She blinks, turning her head away and gazing off at the wall, at nothing.

"It's something I've always wanted."

Her head snaps to look at me. "To become an Elder? Why?"

"To serve God by interpreting the Impulse Edict for the sake of all men in Ember Glen." I reach out to tuck her hair behind her ear. "I've always dreamt of it, of holding that power, of being one of the three highest members of authority in our community."

Her face twists with a mixture of disgust and sadness, and I can't stand it. I can't take the way she looks at me with horror in her haunted eyes. It makes my gut clench with an unpleasant ache—a feeling of sickness I only get when I know in my soul that something just isn't quite right.

So what isn't right?

Is it the way she feels about my words?

Or is it the way I feel about them?

"So you always dreamt of it," she repeats my words slowly, "but do you still dream of it now? Is that the future you desire, Warden Rainn?" There's a sharp pang in my gut at her return to the formal address. "To end my life in the trials and go on with your life as you'd planned it?"

No.

The word echoes loudly in my mind, reverberating and sending a shudder down my spine.

What do I say?

What can I tell her?

How do I find the truth in my muddled mind?

Sorrow finds its way into my soul at the reality of the situation, setting it on fire to burn me torturously in a blaze of crackling misery. I reach around her to grip the back of her head in my palm and drag her forward, forcing her to bring her forehead to touch mine.

"My life will never go on as I planned it," I tell her, letting words I haven't revised escape me freely. "I didn't plan for this. I didn't plan to find you as anything other than a sinner. I didn't plan to find your heart."

Her lashes flutter as she closes her eyes, her hand gripping my wrist where I hold her head, not to pull my hand away, but to keep me in place. "Is there any part of you that believes it's God's plan? That maybe the God you pray to wanted us to find each other…to find a better life?"

"It doesn't matter to you what the God I pray to intends for us. You're asking whether I'm willing to see a different future than the one we've been assigned."

Her head nods against mine and her eyes flicker open to meet mine, to look for the truth within my gaze, and that's all she'll find there.

"I don't believe that God could have planned to make my heart beat the way it does whenever I see you, to make my soul vibrate at the sound of your voice…" her thumb gently caresses across my wrist, "to make the ground tremor beneath my feet whenever you touch me like that, with softness and unearned compassion."

"You must believe it's the demons which plague me, then." I see her sad smile, muscles twitching at the corners of her lips.

"Maybe it's mine. Maybe I have my own demons which plague me—make me lie to my brothers, make me want to sin with you… over and over again."

I tilt my chin forward to kiss her, quickly pushing my tongue past her teeth to devour her, letting our tongues speak silently to share our fears and longing without words. The kiss breaks naturally in a moment of beautiful tension, a shared desire for more, though we both know this isn't the time or place for more.

"I'm starting to believe the whole of Ember Glen is plagued by demons, Mercy. That maybe we're all on the brink of sin."

She looks at me sweetly, a touch of concern wrinkling her forehead. "I think you're plagued by confusion, Arlo."

My forehead creases to match hers as I watch her with a serious expression. "I am." I let out a breath, finding some strange relief in the admission. "I'm so confused about everything, and I don't think I've ever felt so lost."

She nods as my hand drops to wrap around the side of her neck, my thumb absently stroking her throat. She reaches a hand forward and draws her fingers through my hair at the side of my head, tangling through the strands and rubbing my scalp in a circular motion that has my eyes fluttering shut.

"I understand you, Arlo. I've felt that confusion before, and I know it's painful. I know, and I'm sorry."

I force my eyes to open, to look at her gorgeous face and see her for what she is in this very moment—not as a sinner, and not as a woman on trial seeking absolution for a wretched soul.

How could her soul be wretched when it resonates so clearly with mine? Is mine wretched, too? Or is the lens of our judgment so smudged that we can no longer see the truth?

"The only solution is to seek the truth," she whispers, responding as though she could read my mind. "The confusion only ends when you seek truth through the madness, when you seek truth above all else."

My heart drops like a lead ball in my gut.

Right now, the only truth I know is that her last day is coming… and when she perishes, I may not survive it, either.

LATER, WHEN I'M alone, I write the truth that springs from my madness for Mercy, my hopeless longing, my ardent passion.

Will I miss her when she's gone?

Would the sky miss the stars?
Would heaven miss an angel?
Would the wildflowers in the meadow miss the rain?

Can the moon glow without the sun?
Can the snow fall without the clouds?
Can a man purge without a willing servant?

Will my lungs burn when she takes her last breath?
Will my blood refuse to flow through my veins?
Will my limbs stiffen when she becomes forever still?

Will I miss her when she's gone?

With all the brightness of her starlight hair.

Will she remember me in her damnation?
I'll never have to wonder.
I'll wreck my soul to meet her in hell...
and she'll never know the ache of missing me.

chapter eleven

Mercy

I WEAR BLACK tonight.

It's the night of service beneath the full moon, and instead of wearing red, as trial participants are meant to, I've chosen to show solidarity with my sisters, regardless of what they think of me now. I found my black servants' clothes, which had been left in my room—the outfit I'd worn the day Arlo first brought me to the Homestead—and washed them in the tub so I could wear them tonight.

The long-sleeve, form-fitting black top is more modest than the black corsets my sisters will wear, though it does bare the top of my chest with its sweetheart neckline. I brush my hands over the mid-length skirt, feeling an unexpected wave of emotion as I look down at the asymmetric tiers of black lace and the black boots I've refused to stop wearing.

It's strange to feel as though I'm traveling back in time—wearing the clothes of the servant I'd been for four years. And though I've only been wearing the elegant crimson gowns of a trial participant for a few weeks, it may as well have been decades for how different the world feels now. It's not that the world feels different so much as I feel bolder living in it, braver, more willing to take a daring stand and make my rebellious thoughts known loudly and clearly—the end of my life is quickly approaching and I have nothing left to fear.

Coming into that fearlessness is bewildering, remarkable, and at times, perplexing. It's unsettling to realize that I've accepted the fact that I'm going to die, that my days are numbered, and there's nothing I can do to change that. Sometimes it makes me feel uneasy that I've accepted it, but other times, like tonight, it makes me feel empowered.

I smile to myself, pleased with the decision to wear this, as the small act of defiance fuels me with a burst of energy. Though my sisters have turned against me, they're my sisters, nonetheless. I don't fault them for believing all the things they've been told to believe since birth. If anything, it makes me feel all the more settled in my decision to wear this tonight—to show the Control that I am still one of them, and perhaps, someday, more of them will rise against our oppression.

I open my bedroom door and step into the hallway, heading for Delle's room. Before I reach it, her door clicks open and she slowly steps out into the hallway, anxious hands running down her skirt.

Her *black* skirt.

My grin broadens as she turns to see me and lets a nervous smile touch her cheeks. I'd told her my plans to wear this tonight as my small act of rebellion and solidarity, as I didn't want to surprise her with my choice not to wear what I was meant to. But I hadn't expected that she'd choose to do the same. Truly, I *should* have expected it, with the way she's grown bolder and has begun to find her voice.

She's dressed as a servant from head to toe—a role she'd only had to fulfill once before she chose to participate in the Trials of Dissension. She looks stunning and strong in her black corset top, with thin strips of lace that drape off-shoulder. Her layered skirt is similar to mine, and of course, she has on her black boots.

I'm sure she feels relief to wear the comfortable boots since she's been wearing those awful shoes with the tall heels, provided by the Control, until now. I'm convinced those shoes were supplied for us to wear only to slow us down if we tried to run.

"Look at you," I say as she stops in front of me. "A stunning little rebel in the making."

"I like to consider myself a mini-Mercy. Just taking notes from the woman who paved the way for my sins."

We laugh together, and it feels good to smile, to joke, to share pride in our small defiance, even if the joy will only last for a few moments.

"Thank you for doing this, for wearing that," I say to her.

"I couldn't let you do it alone. I just…I want to be brave. I'm trying to be as brave as you are."

My head tilts as I sigh. "Delle, you are the bravest person I know."

"I wouldn't have been brave enough to do this," she gestures her hands down in front of her outfit, her eyes flicking down, "without you telling me you were doing it. I wouldn't have even thought of it. And I wouldn't be here at all if it weren't for you…if you hadn't chosen to run at the last service and get the attention of the Control. They brought the trials back because of you, Mercy, and it gave me a way out."

I want to remind her that she was the one who ran first that night, that if it hadn't been her first service—and if I hadn't already been labeled a rebel, chosen to run, and drawn their attention—it might have been *her* actions that spurred them to bring back the trials.

She's so much stronger and braver than she gives herself credit for. But I don't tell her that, and not because I don't want her to credit herself for her strength. I think she needs to work that out for herself to become the woman I know she'll be…even if she'll only be that woman for moments before she dies.

I'm so proud of her for choosing to fight for something better than the life she was assigned, but I feel equally broken-hearted that the Trials of Dissension are the only choice she was ever given.

Serve or die.

Malo fucking mori…

I pull her in for a quick hug, silently thanking her for seeing me as more than just a woman who sinned—more than the woman who was too scared to serve when it meant being lit on fire, who ran from a duty she never wanted nor asked for. We smile at each other as I pull back, but as moments pass, joy and pride fade.

"I wish we didn't have to watch the service tonight," she says on a sigh.

"I know. It nearly feels worse to have to watch them endure."

The faces of Ellary and Cambria come to mind. I see Ellary's bright, kind smile and her striking green eyes, her features framed so beautifully by her shiny, straight brown tresses. And Cambria, with her dark eyes and hair, her sensual pout that she liked to paint with burgundy lipstick, which always looked so stunning on her medium-brown complexion.

The sight of them in my mind lifts anxiety through my center, stress floating up from behind my ribcage and causing an ache in my chest. It was bad enough having to witness what was happening all around me on nights of service—to see my sisters hurting and in pain, and not be able to do anything about it. Yet somehow, sitting and watching it unfold on a screen seems worse.

We wait in the hallway until Arlo's door clicks open, and he appears. His foot has barely crossed the threshold when my heart starts pounding, my body turning to face his. My eyes lift, searching to lock on his, but instead, his gaze traces me from bottom to top, taking in my clothing with a frown and a wrinkled brow.

"What are you wearing?" he asks.

I pull back my shoulders. "The uniform of servants."

"You're no longer a servant." His gaze flits over to Delle, then comes back to me, once again tracing my figure, lingering at the curve of my hip. He blinks and shakes his head. "It doesn't matter.

There's no time to change, anyway." He waves his hand down the hallway behind us. "Just go."

"Where's Theo?" Delle asks as we turn and walk toward the stairs.

"Setting up camp for service. He'll be back soon."

"Will you be purging tonight?" I ask, though I'm not entirely certain I want his answer.

"All men must purge beneath the full moon," he says, though I don't feel like that answers my question.

His hand closes around my wrist, halting me with a sharp tug. His body collides with my backside as he steps forward to close the distance, and he holds me in place as Delle continues on, oblivious.

He speaks against my ear, and I feel the heat of his breath across my skin. "You tempt me dressed this way, like a servant. I have only one desire to purge, and it's with you, starlight."

My stomach flips and my pulse speeds at his words, at the way his hand loosens from around my wrist and his fingers trace up my arm, leaving a trail of goosebumps in their wake.

"And if I were still a servant," I whisper, "then purging with me tonight would not be a sin."

What am I saying?

Why did I say that to him?

"Sweet sin," he mutters breathlessly. "If only I had your service—"

"Coming?" Delle reaches the staircase and turns to glance at us before descending the steps.

"Yes." Arlo quickly releases me and steps back. "Get moving, Mercy."

A shudder travels down my spine. Some vicious, wanton part of me hopes he'll grab my wrist again, pull me into a room, shut me in behind a closed door, and kiss me the way only he can. Yet, the truer part of me knows that I must keep this night in reverence. I must focus on what my sisters are about to endure, because feeling their pain emboldens and empowers me…

And frankly, I need all the boldness and power I can get.

I rush ahead, dragging myself from Arlo's inexplicable hold on me, and jog down the steps to get away from the distraction of him. In my haste, I pass Delle about halfway down the stairs. I step down to the foyer where the sunburst pattern on the tile lays mockingly, an instant reminder of my day of torture during the first trial. Then I stop and wait, turning my back to the staircase to avoid gazing at Arlo as he descends behind us.

I can no longer look that man in the eyes without giving away the obvious manner in which he makes my body sway, intoxicated by his very presence.

"We'll be down the hall," his voice echoes as he descends, "in the room where Delle's trial was held."

"Why?" Delle asks sharply. "Why in that room?" She crosses her arms over her chest, her hands coming up to rub her bare biceps.

"They couldn't have set it up somewhere else?"

"No." Arlo is terse with the single syllable.

He steps down to the main floor, circling around us and moving toward the hall. Delle and I follow him to the room where she served her first trial. The door is open and Arlo gestures for us to go inside. I move past Delle as she takes a deep breath, entering the room slowly, hoping to give her a few moments to steel herself before entering the space where she endured her own torturous trial.

The room is roughly the same size as the bedrooms upstairs, except it has no bed, no furniture to speak of, really. It's been emptied out to create a dark, enclosed space for us to sit and watch the horror.

There's nothing to look at aside from the large white screen setup along the far wall—no mirrors, no artwork hung on the walls, not even wallpaper or a lovely shade painted on the walls to draw our eyes away from the screen. There are windows behind it, but they only look out to the open village square beyond. There's nothing of comfort in here at all. Just four walls, dim lighting, and two simple wooden chairs, placed side-by-side and facing the screen.

"Take a seat," Arlo commands.

As Delle comes in beside me, we pause to share a glance. I give her a reassuring nod before I move deeper into the cold, stark room. We circle the chairs, and Delle gradually lowers to her seat, shifting uncomfortably to settle into the hard wood.

I stand beside the other chair, placing my hand on the backrest as I stare down at the seat. My nerves prickle and my pulse quickens as I'm overcome by intense and unexpected anxiety. It's not quite the same kind of anxiety I would feel just before serving, though it strikes me abruptly and harshly all the same. And it feels different— too intense for knowing that I'm not serving tonight.

Not anxiety.

A knowing feeling…A stab of instinct…

It feels as though the energy all around me is shifting and changing; as though the earth might crack open beneath my feet and swallow me whole; as though the sky might crumble and fall, raining its remnants down to destroy the world.

It feels as though everything is about to change.

"Take a seat, sinner." Arlo's voice is firm.

I look back at him, still firmly planted in the doorway. He leans his shoulder against the frame, with his arms crossed, one leather-clad finger tapping his bicep. The look of him there takes me back to the day he brought me to the Homestead, when he took me to my room, ordering me to undress and take a bath.

I remember thinking how disarmingly beautiful he was then, and I think it now, as well. His thick, wavy strands of tawny brown hair are disheveled in an intentional manner. The slightly ginger hue through his russet tresses carries through his short beard, and even through the lighter strands from his chest, hinted through the open collar of his button-down shirt.

The buttoned waistcoat serves to emphasize his stunning frame—lean and strong but not overly broad with muscle. My eyes are drawn to the silver chain that runs from one button to the small pocket stitched across the side—my fingers twitch to grab hold of it and draw him against me.

I press my eyes shut and shake my head, blinking away the image of pulling him close, his warm arms encircling me, his soft lips kissing my cheek, whispering against my ear that he'll miss me when I'm gone, that he aches for me, that he must have me now…

"Mercy," he snaps. "*Sit.*"

My eyes pop open to meet his, narrowed and strikingly blue, the intensity of his stare emphasizing the wrinkle of his brow as he watches me with a serious expression.

Confusion.

Just as I'd concluded the other day when we spoke in the courtroom, Arlo Rainn is confused, conflicted. I can see it now in the way he tries to maintain his authority, though his muscles twitch to loosen, to lengthen, to relax in my presence. In a way, it's humbling to know how conflicted he truly is. Internal conflict rises from dissonance, from seeing what doesn't make sense and seeking the truth that lies somewhere beyond.

It gives me hope for him.

I have no hope that my future will change, but it's comforting to know there may be hope for Arlo. And if there's hope for Arlo Rainn, then perhaps there's hope for Ember Glen, too.

He looks so troubled by his inner conflict that I can't help but ask, "Are you okay?"

Delle spins sideways in her seat to glare at me, curious about why I asked, perhaps surprised that I should care at all whether he's okay.

"I'm fine, sinner. Just sit." He turns his head to avoid looking me in the eyes, but I see the muscles in his throat work as he swallows nervously.

I understand why he's calling me a sinner, why he's speaking to me so curtly and keeping his distance. He can't hold me and speak to me the way he did in the courtroom a few days ago—though I long for him to do that again. The understanding of it does nothing to relieve the emotional whiplash it causes, and it's giving me a headache.

It brings about a tense frustration that burns in my chest, striking up annoyance for the way I struggle to keep up with his ever-changing manner of being. With exasperation, I turn and plop in my seat, turning my back on him and facing the screen.

"The live stream should begin in about ten minutes."

Delle is still turned sideways in her seat, looking back at Arlo in the doorway. "And we just have to sit here and watch it? For how long?"

"How long is a night of service? *That* long."

"The entire night?"

"We'll allow you breaks if needed."

I scoff, "That's more than I was ever granted in service."

Arlo chuckles. "Didn't you elect to take your own break from service when you ran, sinner?"

His tone has oddly changed, sounding so similar to the way it did during the first trial. It was forced, clipped, cold, and emotionally disingenuous in the calculation of his words. It was how he spoke to me in front of his brothers; when he needed them to know he was with them, that he felt the same outright hatred for me as they did… even when I know in my heart that he doesn't hate me.

Still, he doesn't need to speak to me so harshly in front of Delle—he didn't when we worked with Delle and Theo to prepare for the first trial.

So why is he speaking that way now?

Is someone listening?

I whip my head over my shoulder as I spin in my seat, turning sideways like Delle so I can look at him. "Are we being watched?"

His eyes find mine and widen ever so slightly, imperceptibly to someone who wasn't watching carefully. "You're not being watched tonight, sinner. You're the ones doing the watching." He turns his head slowly to hide his single nod, dragging his eyes away to look off distantly into the corner.

Of course, we're being watched.

Maybe the Elders are watching us via camera from their hiding place—wherever that may be—or perhaps we're simply being recorded as a safety measure given that it's a night of purging. The men of the Control are meant to purge, just as all the men in Ember Glen. There will be chaos outside in the forest, and perhaps they worry we might cause our own brand of chaos from within.

We are sinners, after all.

A few silent minutes pass, and then Theo arrives, his presence announced when he says, "Everything's set up. The live stream should come on in five minutes."

Delle whips her head, instantly seeking the location of his voice, finding him standing near Arlo, just inside the room. Theo gives her a tense smile and her cheeks pinken. Her obvious crush on him is still unsettling for me, though I know in the grand scheme of things, it doesn't matter. Delle's future and mine are the same.

"Where is the rest of the Control?" Delle asks.

"At camp in the forest, preparing to purge," Theo says, then tilts his head as his eyes narrow on her. "What are you wearing?"

The slight flush of her cheeks darkens. "Servants' clothes." She looks at the floor, grabbing hold of one of her long, ashen strands of hair with both hands, twisting it nervously. "For solidarity." She slowly turns back to face the screen.

I twist in my seat to look between Arlo and Theo. "Will you

two be joining your brothers in the forest tonight?"

"Our brothers will enjoy the service for now," Arlo says. "They'll return in shifts so we'll all have time to enjoy the purge."

His confirmation that he'll leave to purge the Impulse conjures sordid images in my mind.

Will he use another servant to ensure his brothers aren't suspicious of him?

Are his urges so strong that he'll want to purge?

Will he enjoy it?

I'm suddenly aware that this must be how the domestic women feel when they watch their husbands leave to purge every month under the full moon—those who actually care for their husbands, that is, because truthfully, not all of them do.

A painful lump rises in my throat at the thought of Arlo using another servant, and I swallow hard against it. I swivel in my seat to face the screen again, turning my back on him.

"Then I hope you find a suitable servant to meet your needs tonight, Warden Rainn." My words come out sharply to hide the angst in my tone.

Something burns inside my chest, something like heartache, though that doesn't feel like the right word to describe it. It feels something more like…jealousy, perhaps? I feel jealous at the thought of another servant being used by him.

"I'm certain I will…" he says, and I hope it's insincerity that I hear through his clipped tone, "someone who doesn't run."

I force a chuckle to hide the jealous ache that his words cause me. "Someone who hasn't yet learned why they should run from men like you."

Men like him…or men like them?

If I believed in God, I might pray for clarity. Arlo Rainn confuses me on an existential level. He fills my waking thoughts so thoroughly, yet those thoughts are constantly bouncing around my mind, flinging from one side to the other as I try to formulate a concrete opinion of him.

He's cruel, but considerate.

He's demanding, but accommodating.

He's blessed, but broken.

He's divinity and sin, heaven and hell, a god and a demon.

I hate him and I cherish him in equal measure, though I'm beginning to feel the scales tremor as I fight to keep them balanced—all while he adds weight to the side that begs for something deeper than simply cherishing him at a distance.

"Be quiet, Mercy," Arlo says with exasperation. "Just because you have a mouth doesn't mean you should be constantly running it."

I roll my eyes, annoyed with the way he goads me…though, at the same time, it tugs an unwanted twist of the corner of my lips in amusement, and it sets off a flurry of feeling in my stomach. I hate it and love it all at once, and there's only one word I can think of that explains it. *Passion.*

Love and hate.

Bliss and pain.

Desire and fear.

Serious talks and playful banter.

The dichotomy of our doomed connection is overflowing with passion, and I desire more of it. I want passion with him in all its forms, both good and bad, right and wrong, pleasure and sin. I want to let him show me heaven before I fall hard and fast, straight through to the depths of hell.

And I only hope that when I do fall for him entirely, he'll jump off the ledge to chase me into hellfire where I'll burn for him for eternity.

A TENSE SILENCE settles thickly through the room as we

wait for the service to begin. Though it's only a few minutes, time passes slowly. The empty room is unsettling, especially when every noise is amplified through our silent waiting. When I hear a click from somewhere behind us, Delle and I both jump.

The projector whirs—which tells me the click was the sound of it switching on—and the light from the projector shines from behind us. I hold my breath, waiting for the images to appear, wondering where they've placed the cameras and what horror we'll be forced to watch.

With a flash and a brief flicker, the live streaming of our sisters' night of terror appears on the screen, moving images filling it from corner to corner. I see the clearing in the forest where the bonfire is lit, where the servants and men will gather, where a prayer will be led, and where the events of the night will begin.

It's not quite from a birds-eye view that camp is filmed. The camera must be placed high up in the trees, such that I'm looking down upon camp from an angle, but I can't exactly see everything—some areas are obscured by the placement.

Service hasn't begun yet. I watch on bated breath as the servants of Ember Glen appear from the darkness of the trees surrounding the clearing, filtering into camp. I'm surprised that I feel more anxious than I've ever felt for a service, that nagging pang of instinct stabbing through my gut and stirring nausea.

The brightly burning bonfire appears with an eerie glow behind the scratches and tracking lines caused by the projector. The servants—all dressed in their black corsets and skirts—begin to circle the high flame, enough of them present to create two rings around it.

Wesley crosses the clearing, approaching the bonfire as the servants gather to form their circle around the flame. He almost always leads the incitement and prayer, probably because he has a pleasant yet commanding manner of speaking, that's both calm and engaging. He stops behind the outer ring of the circle of servants as they join hands, waiting with his palms folded in front of him as the remaining servants come from the darkness and move toward the light.

My nerves electrify, rushing a current of anxiety to prick beneath my skin, and my eyes pinch shut. This part of service was always the worst for me—though by all accounts, it was the easiest part for most. This is the part that required me to declare my faith and grant my consent to be used beyond my own limits and expectations. It required me to falsely declare my consent to the horror I had no choice but to endure, even when said horror meant meeting my own death. This part required me to chant our prayer and declare that I'd rather meet death than dishonor: *malo mori quam foedari.*

It always made me feel sick. It was the false declaration of my faith and honor that twisted my insides. Yet it was the waiting—the moments of standing in front of the scorching heat of the fire, the anticipation of my own desecration—that turned that sickness into outright fear.

"October ninth, twenty-one eighty-five," Wesley begins and the chattering voices fade to dutiful silence. "We gather tonight beneath the full moon to honor the Impulse. We welcome the men of our community to this night of service. We thank them all for the pain they've endured over the last month in suppressing their impulsive urges in anticipation of the right to purge tonight."

"Thank you for your endurance," the servants murmur in chorus.

When my fear would ramp up in these moments before the purging began, the rehearsed replies would sound so obnoxiously clear, so enthusiastic, reminding me of how different my thinking was from the other women. But now, in my separation from service, it sounds like a forced recitation of unwilling women. That's exactly what it *should* sound like, because that's exactly what it *is,* but I'm surprised at the clarity in which I hear it.

My fear gives way to anger, and I scoff, my eyes popping open to watch in rage as I cross my arms over my chest. A heavy hand lands on my shoulder so suddenly that it startles me, and I snap my head sideways to find Arlo at my side.

"Quiet," he commands, drawing his hand away from my shoulder, dragging it along the back rail of my chair while allowing his fingertips to graze my back.

I square off in my seat, facing forward as I swallow a mixture of swirling emotions.

"This is a night for purging," Wesley continues, and I find my heart fluttering, skittering around behind my ribcage as Arlo lowers to his haunches beside me, his gloved hand still resting on the rail near my shoulder. "Tonight, the men of Ember Glen are granted a reprieve by God's grace. As it is written in the Impulse Edict, the violent and sexual impulses of men must be satiated to allow the community to live in peace. Each month, beneath the full moon, when men are at their celestial worst, there will be a gathering of servants and men. No rules or laws shall be enforced against man in his use of servants who give themselves freely to God's will."

Give themselves freely to God's will...

If it's God's will, then how can they give themselves freely?

Yet another contradiction of faith.

Wesley begins to rattle off the expectations of service, which are simple, few, and enforced monthly. No man who's purged or woman who's served before needs a reminder, but the speech is always given for the benefit of those who are new to the ritual—that includes the sixteen-year-old girls on their first night of service, and the fourteen-year-old boys unleashing the Impulse during their first purge. They only need to know that the men can't do harm to other men, and because women must focus on effective service, they may only be used by one man at a time.

I feel Arlo shift at my side, leaning toward me, and he speaks so softly that I almost don't hear him. "I've spent a great deal of time lost in thought these past few days, and my thoughts are gray, muddied with contradictions. But I'm trying, Mercy. I'm trying to seek truth through the madness, like you said." The leather of his glove creaks over the wood where he grips the chair.

I turn my head to look at him in bewilderment. "What?"

"Face forward and lower your voice," he snaps.

I lower my arms from across my chest and press my palms against the seat of the chair beside my hips, gripping the edges while pushing myself back in the seat. I turn away and look forward at the screen as he commanded.

He's quiet for a moment, and my eyes turn to glance over at him, waiting for him to speak again. When he finally does, I have to strain my ears to hear.

"I've been thinking about the Impulse and what we've been told about it. That men have a natural inclination toward impulsivity and unpredictability, have uncontrollable urges for violence and lust."

Where is he going with this?

"As I spend time with you, I've seen you prove yourself to be impulsive and unpredictable. Delle, too. I can even remember a time when my sister was younger that she behaved the same. You've shown me your own rage and wishes for violence against those who have wronged you. More telling than all of that…you've shown your lust. You've shown me that you could lose yourself in desire as easily as I could. Perhaps it's the demons that plague you, or perhaps…"

I'm desperate for him to finish that sentence, eager for it. My breaths quicken in anticipation of his words as I quietly wait for him to finish.

"Perhaps women have the Impulse, too."

I sigh heavily, an odd relief washing through me at his train of thought for the mere fact that he's thinking…he's *been* thinking, because this couldn't be a new thought. He wouldn't share something he hadn't already mulled over.

"Perhaps we do," I whisper.

I choose not to tell him that I think the Impulse is a lie, that every urge and desire we have—man or woman—is human, and we all have the power to control ourselves through choice, without the need to purge. I choose not to say that now because I'm so in awe that he's spent time thinking about this, and I don't want to derail him from sharing more with me.

"If that's true…*If* it's true, Mercy, then servants are stronger than the men of Ember Glen." He drags in a heavy breath and forces it out. "My Impulse to have you right now is so strong that I can hardly think about anything else."

His hand moves slowly, slipping from the rail, trailing down the side of the chair back. His fingers graze secretly along my hip as they draw across the seat, coming to a stop at the heel of my hand.

Leather kisses my skin as he draws a finger across the back of my hand, and my fingers twitch where they grip the edge of the seat. He traces an invisible line over my knuckles and down the back of my index finger, which rises in response to greet him.

I can feel each of his breaths, steady and heavy, and I depend on each one to sustain me. It's as though each inhale steals all the air from the room, making me dizzy with need, and each exhale provides the oxygen that wakes me up and excites me.

"I feel you," I whisper back, and his hand clutches my fingers at the edge of the seat.

My eyes flutter shut, but then I open them again quickly, unsure of how we're being monitored—whether we're watched or listened to, whether we're recorded. His words are so faint, and his movements are so secretive that I realize the stakes.

"Be careful," I remind him.

I try to pull my hand away, but he squeezes, holding tighter. "I am. I'm trying."

"Try harder." I swallow, attempting to rid myself of the longing that rises and lodges in my throat. "You need to purge," I tell him, though I instantly regret the words.

I don't want Arlo to purge.

I don't ever want to think of him using another woman… touching her, tasting her, binding her, sinking inside her and coming undone. The ache of such a visual makes my heart pound in double time. I forcefully yank my hand from his and press it over my aching chest.

"You may be right," he mutters. "It's God's will."

There's a tense pause where I try to refocus my attention on the screen, try to listen to Wesley as he leads a prayer.

"It's God's will," he repeats again a few moments later, "but perhaps His will is no longer meant for me. Perhaps it's only meant for men who haven't tasted the holy water that drips between your thighs when you come."

I gasp, and I can't stop from turning my head as I seek his eyes. He shoves to his feet, and though I desperately try to connect with his gaze, he doesn't meet mine—he turns and walks away.

"*Malo mori quam foedari,*" Wesley recites on the screen, and the servants and men repeat, "*Malo mori quam foedari.*"

As I fight to catch my breath that Arlo stole from me, a bright white flare lights up the sky with a brilliant flash across the windows beyond the projector screen. A few moments pass, and then a resounding burst of thunder booms, causing Delle and I to jump in our seats as the vibrating sound rumbles through the walls.

I huff out a surprised breath as the crowd on screen recovers from the startling thunder with soft chattering and nervous laughter. A storm won't change anything. The service will still go on as planned in the forest, adding an extra layer of misery for the servants.

"Ladies, please," Killian shouts over the chatter. "Return to your circle so we can complete the incitement of service."

Silence among the women falls quickly at the command, and they rejoin hands in the circle around the bonfire.

Wesley clears his throat and speaks again. "Our dearest honored servants of Ember Glen. Do you enter this service with the understanding that tonight, the Impulse rules? Are you prepared to serve our men by any means necessary as they purge, such is the will of God and your duty to serve?"

"As God wills it, we give ourselves fully to serve the needs of men," they vow in unison.

They'll speak it whether they believe it or not. I repeated the same ritualized response at every service purely out of fear, knowing the outcome I'm facing right now was always a looming consequence.

They speak it because—whether they realize it or not—they have no choice.

I sense Delle's eyes on me, and it calls for my attention. I turn and meet her stare, sharing a beat of understanding for the shared pain of our sisters. I reach out my hand to her, and she places her palm in mine. In solidarity, we force our eyes to the screen, to watch the cruelty of service with wide open eyes. I give the women my attention, my acknowledgment, my reverence for the strength of their true endurance as they experience yet another night of torture at the hands of vicious men.

"As God wills it," Wesley says, "so shall we proceed. Let the service begin."

chapter twelve
Mercy

CHAOS ENSUES ON screen. Some men strip bare before quietly selecting a woman to use, while others run to grab the one they desire and drag her away from the fire. The sounds of their primal excitement are grotesque as they growl, roar, and howl at the full moon like a pack of wolves.

I'm horror-struck for the way it looks from the outside, like a festival of terror hosted by cruel men. I'm not sure whether it feels better or worse to watch it unfold from afar.

Not worse…nothing could ever be worse than serving under the full moon.

Watching it happen from a distance is certainly better than experiencing it firsthand, but it still brings me emotional pain. Distress clouds my mind, and the clouds rain down my insides with a sense of shame. I feel shame that I'm not enduring this torment with my sisters.

I know my shame is unwarranted—it's not as though my presence would lessen their suffering. This shame is born from a lifetime of indoctrination, which has taught me to believe that service is my one and only role; it's taught me to believe that service is the only means in which I provide value to my community, by which I can value myself.

And this shame is exactly what the Control and the Elders wish Delle and I will feel in watching this tonight.

I refuse.

I straighten in my seat and search my mind for pride.

I fix my eyes on the screen, turning my focus to a single dark spot in the corner where the trees appear like a black blur in the night from the hazy projection. I try to tune out the sound of pandemonium as I focus my attention on that single spot.

I'll stare at it all night if that's what I have to do.

But without warning, the spot moves.

The single rectangular block that shows us the clearing suddenly shifts on screen, shrinking and sliding to the top left corner. Then, three other rectangles materialize, and after a moment of blackness in each, new images appear. There's now a grid of four boxes, each camera showing a different angle, granting us an all-encompassing view of the debauchery in the clearing.

Overwhelmed by the movement, my eyes roam aimlessly, unable to find a spot to focus on.

Who is using Ellary and Cambria tonight?

The thought bursts in my mind, and my gaze shifts, frantically searching to find Ellary and Cambria in the chaos. I don't want to watch what they endure, but I have to lay eyes on them.

As my gaze travels across the four images on the screen, I realize I can't see into the forest beyond the tree line. We're not seeing the complete image of the depravity that occurs tonight, but that's no surprise—it would be too much to cover.

I watch for minutes before I spot Ellary, yet as soon as I find her, I almost wish I hadn't. She's not been claimed by either of the Higgins brothers as she is so often. Instead, I find her lowering to her knees before Hyatt Price…The man who set Ivy Jane on fire.

"Ellary…" I breathe out her name, fear gripping me and stopping my heart.

I turn in my seat, looking behind me for Arlo, seeking him out for comfort or reassurance—or something else, but I don't know what. I find his eyes fixed on the screen, staring, rubbing his hand down his short beard.

"Hyatt Price," I mutter, not knowing what else to say.

Arlo tears his eyes from the screen to meet mine. Slowly, he shakes his head, and I don't know what that means. I find no reassurance as he returns his gaze to the screen. I turn my frantic stare to Theo, and he shrugs, but turns away, stepping out of the room.

I turn my attention back to the screen, fixating on the box in the bottom right corner which shows Ellary kneeling before Hyatt. The glow of fire light flickers behind them, casting a dark, shadowed aura around the outline of their bodies. His fingers touch beneath her chin and lift, and she dutifully raises her head to look up at him. I can see his mouth moving as he speaks to her. I can see her nodding against his touch, a proud smile spreading across her cheeks.

And when his other hand moves, my heart finally starts again, beating wildly against my ribs in such a pounding rhythm that I worry they might break. He holds a knife, the metal blade glinting through the shadows as another strike of lightning illuminates the night. The flash on the screen is bright, temporarily washing out the images with its flare.

If I thought God existed, and that He was good and benevolent, I'd imagine that lightning strike was sent to bathe all of Ember Glen in light, to expose the true demons and bring them from the shadows. But I know the only demons in Ember Glen are men, and Hyatt is the darkest of them all—a truly evil force, a demonic darkness looming above my bright and beautiful friend, Ellary, who has been blinded against the truth.

I can see the truth…and it's horrifying.

It frightens me so much that I hardly hear the raucous thunder moments after the flash, which cracks and rumbles all around.

Delle's hand squeezes mine in an attempt at comfort. And

though I wish I could give her a reassuring smile, I can't. I can't give her anything while Ellary kneels before Hyatt Price.

How can I watch this happen to her?

Hyatt moves the knife closer to Ellary, and I hold my breath. I feel like I'm standing on the edge of that very blade, teetering on the verge of my sanity. I mentally prepare for the strike, waiting on bated breath to see him stab her, slice her, cut her open…and each moment of waiting brings a new torture.

But then he turns the knife, pinching the blade to offer the handle of it to Ellary.

What…

She nods, granting him the dignified smile she always holds, and wraps her palm around the handle. She looks down at it in her hand for a moment, then lifts her other arm, turning her palm up toward the thundering sky. I watch her chest rise as she takes in a deep breath, and then she draws the tip of the blade across her forearm, near the crease where her elbow bends.

"No!" I shout. My hands shoot up to cover my mouth as thick liquid—which appears black through the darkness on screen—quickly pools and flows from her arm. I leap from my seat, moving toward the screen without any conscious thought. I think I hear Arlo call my name, but it's muffled, far away. Ellary drags another line parallel to the first, drawing more blood from herself, her chest heaving as she lifts the blade and positions it to draw another line.

"Ellary, no!" I shout, my palm touching the screen as if I could reach through it to stop her.

No one's going to stop her.

No one's going to help her.

Hyatt's lips move, speaking words I can't hear, but I know he's encouraging her, commanding her to cut more lines, deeper, faster…

He wants to watch her bleed.

He wants to watch her die.

This man is a menace in every sense of the word.

"Help her," I mutter to no one.

I search the screen, desperately looking for Cambria. My eyes widen when I spot her in the box above Ellary's. Killian has her back pressed against a tree while he grinds against her body, but I see her looking past his shoulder, eyes widening, and I wonder if she sees Ellary, too. Judging by her expression, she must. Cambria isn't easily bothered, and she finds pride in service, so the fear I see in her widening eyes tells me that she must see Ellary and the violence she's enduring. It's the only thing I can think of that might upset her.

This type of violence is rare for Ellary; the woman was gifted with such innate sweetness to go with her tempting physique that the men of Ember Glen tend to adore *and* lust after her. It's kept her relatively safe for all these years. But now Hyatt has become unhinged and unpredictable...and he wants to unleash that on sweet Ellary.

"Help her," I whisper again, internally begging Cambria, the Control, *anyone* out at camp to go to her and to stop Hyatt Price from killing another servant—my *friend*.

No one cares.

No one is going to stop him.

This is a night of purging, and these men have been granted permission to ruin these women—my sisters—in whatever manner their urges see fit.

She's alone.

She's going to die alone, and no one can save her...

I can save her.

The thought shatters my rational mind, slicing through it with urgency, with empowerment, with insistence. If I'm quick enough, clever enough, maybe I can get to her and save her.

Nothing I do will change the fact that I'm fated to die.

So why can't I save Ellary before I meet my end?

My mind swirls, swiftly rolling through one idea and around to the next, whirling with options and possibilities. On the screen, I watch as Hyatt takes the knife from Ellary, nodding and stroking a hand down the side of her head, bringing a weak smile to her cheeks…weak, because she's bleeding.

He helps her rise to her feet, and he leads her away, taking her toward the tree line, beyond the view of the camera, into the dark forest…

Run.

Adrenaline floods my veins, and I welcome it, letting blind bravery take hold of me. Without a second thought, I turn…and I run.

"Mercy—" Arlo reaches for me as I sprint past him into the hallway.

He lunges to grab me, but I jerk my body sideways to avoid his capture, moving so suddenly that he stumbles as I escape his grasp. I won't let anyone stop me—*no one.* I'm not going to stand here and wait for Ellary to die.

Heading for the front door, I sprint down the hall, already seeing the fault in my careless plan. The large, wooden doors will be locked. But when Theo suddenly appears, coming toward me from the far hall on the opposite side of the sunburst, I immediately know what I'll do.

"Mercy!" Arlo shouts. A quick glance over my shoulder shows him righting himself and chasing after me.

I rush Theo as he steps into the foyer, crossing at a quickened pace, his eyes narrowing on me. "What are you doing?"

I slam to a stop right in front of him, and we meet with divinely perfect timing. I reach out and close my hand around his wrist, tug his arm and jerk him sideways. I catch him off-guard enough that he doesn't immediately pull back or use his brute strength to halt me. With a sharp motion, I yank him as close to the door as I can, trying to bring his wrist toward the spot where I believe the locking mechanism exists, hidden in the wood.

Please work.

Please, please work.

"Hey, what are you—"

The black band around his wrist engages the locking mechanism, which whirs and clicks, telling me that it worked, filling me with equal parts of fear, urgency, and excitement.

I drop his arm, grab the door handle, and pull.

"Stop!" Arlo shouts, and he's nearly right behind me.

I slip through a sliver's opening in the door—quickly stepping out onto the landing of the Homestead—then turn back to drag it shut behind me. I pull back hard on the handle, sitting on air as my body bends to hold it shut with all my weight. I need a beat to figure out my next move. I pant, not exactly breathless, but fueled by adrenaline, which makes every working function in my body quicken.

I feel Arlo pull on the handle from the other side of the door. He gives a sharp yank and my body lurches forward, the door opening a crack. I grit my teeth and use the full force of my body to jerk it shut again, groaning as I pull even harder. I need a moment to catch my breath, to reaffirm my decision, to find my strength again before I run…because I have to run faster than Arlo.

I can do this.

I can get to her before he gets to me.

My gaze travels up the door, skimming along the intricate design of wildflowers carved into the wood. It's so similar to the flowers tattooed on the forearm of every servant.

Perhaps we servants *are* wild, just like the flowers in the meadow. Perhaps the etchings on the door serve as a reminder of our fragile existence.

Individual flowers can be plucked easily, our lives so delicate that we're only one sharp tug away from death. The men of Ember Glen pluck us one by one, but no one cares about a single flower in the vast meadow, for it's filled as far as the eye can see with so many more.

I am only one wildflower, pulled from the earth, kept in a vase with only enough water to sustain me, though everyone knows I'm slowly wilting, slowly dying.

I've been plucked, and I'm withering.

But I will not die in vain.

I plant my feet in determination and set my mind on my sisters—on Ellary, on the beauty of those strong women who are simply trying to exist in this world. I set my sight on cutting off the hand that wishes to pluck them, for my sisters *will* greet the sunlight come morning.

I draw in a steeling breath and release the door handle, and then…

I run.

chapter thirteen

Mercy

AS I SPRINT down the stone steps outside the Homestead, I hear the door open behind me, quickly followed by the rush of Arlo's footfalls as he chases me. I don't look back when he calls my name, shouting for me to stop. I land on the gravel-covered square, turn east, and bolt toward the trees.

My layered skirt twists around my legs, but I pump my arms to aid my speed rather than hold up the fabric. Pebbles crunch beneath my boots, my feet pushing against the small stones as I run as hard and as fast as I can.

"Mercy, stop!" Arlo calls, his voice too close.

I can't let him catch me.

I let out a groan as I push myself harder, running faster than I ever have before. The world around us is silent, except for the rapid beat of our footfalls against loose stone. In the eerie quiet, another brilliant flash lights up the dark sky. This time, it's only seconds before the crashing thunder follows, the rumble vibrating through each stone beneath my feet, shaking me with urgency to push onward.

Faster.

The sound of a rushing waterfall crescendos. As I turn my eyes to the sky, I see lines of water descend. I have only a moment to realize the rain is coming before it crashes down upon us. The torrential downpour drenches me, instantly soaking my clothes and weighing me down.

I push harder, forcing myself faster as the tree line approaches. With a grunted sound of determination, I leap over the line dividing open sky from the welcome cover of lush, towering trees. The rain still pours, but the branches and the meager remains of autumn leaves ease its descent.

I trust my instincts to drive me forward, to direct my feet to camp, and find Ellary in the forest just beyond the clearing.

"Mercy Madness, *stop!*" Arlo shouts. His voice is farther away than I expected it to be.

I can do this.

I can outrun him.

I know this forest as well as anyone else. I have no fear of the dark or the trees, nor the obstacles across the forest floor that might make me stumble. If I fall, I'll roll onto my feet and keep running.

I push onward until I hear the familiar sounds of service— moaning, grunting, cries of pleasure and pain—mingling with the constant flow of rain pouring from the sky. I see the light of the bonfire through the trees, burning so bright and high that the rain hasn't taken it out yet.

I know Hyatt led Ellary away from the campfire, into the trees...

But in which direction?

I scan the clearing as I approach, and I spot bodies moving among the trees on the opposite side. Those bodies could belong to anyone. My gut tells me to turn left, to run around the edge of the clearing, so I turn, leap over a fallen branch, and push onward.

I'm nearly around to the other side when I hear the rustling ahead. Then I spot a kneeling silhouette in the dark, and instinctively, I know it's her.

There...she's there...Ellary.

Another figure towers above her, a looming shadow, a man-made monster by the name of Hyatt Price. They're farther from the clearing than I had anticipated, in a place where no one would easily find them…and his hands are on her throat.

She hardly moves, though his arms shake with the force of his grip. Her body is lax, breathless, arms loosely hanging at her sides—already unconscious. All at once, he releases her and steps back, and I watch in terror as her silhouette sways before toppling sideways.

"Ellary!" I scream, but she doesn't stir.

Hyatt's head twists at the sound of my voice, and I slam to a sudden stop, throwing my arms out to catch my balance as the toe of my boot catches in the mud.

"Mercy Madness," he croons with intrigue, turning and stepping toward me. "Is that you, sinner? Have you returned to service me and finally fulfill your duty?" He chuckles, reaching behind him, quickly drawing the knife from his back pocket—the same knife he made Ellary cut herself with.

I clench my fists as I widen my stance, mud squelching beneath my boots as I position myself for battle. Rain still spills from the sky, and I blink away the drops that catch on my eyelashes as I let the sound of the rushing rainfall embolden me. I'm prepared to welcome him, but not for service.

No. I'll welcome him with fury.

I'll meet him with all the rage of my sisters' suffering.

I'll show him the true meaning of misery.

I wait for him to come for me, but instead of stepping forward, he steps back, and an unexpected breeze sweeps past me. A force brushes against my arm and nearly knocks me sideways.

It's Arlo…and he's sprinting past me.

He didn't grab me, didn't tackle me, didn't stop me.

He didn't stop me…

He's bolting straight for Hyatt Price.

Hyatt lifts the knife as Arlo charges ahead, showing no signs of slowing or stopping.

I watch in shock, too stunned to move, as Arlo quickly closes the distance between them. Barreling toward Hyatt, Arlo reaches out to wrap his gloved hand around Hyatt's wrist, moving with such strength and speed that I can't quite say how he twisted Hyatt's arm around so smoothly. Hyatt cries out as Arlo shoves him to the ground, tumbling with him, and I can't tell where the knife is.

Did Hyatt drop it?

Is it on the ground?

Is it buried in Arlo's side?

Just then, Ellary stirs, and her sudden movement steals my attention. I dash past Arlo and Hyatt as they roll and struggle, and I rush to Ellary's side. I drop to my knees, reaching over to grip her bloody forearm, squeezing to try to stop the bleeding.

"Mercy?" Her forehead wrinkles in confusion.

"Ellary, I'm—"

"I'm okay," she says, then clears her throat against her hoarse tone.

She coughs, and the twitch of muscles in her throat draws my eyes down to the darkening spots that will surely become bruises—spots that wrap around her neck like a collar.

"The cuts aren't as deep as they look." She strains to speak after the way he choked her so violently, though I'm relieved to hear her strained voice all the same.

"There's so much blood."

She lifts her head, moving to sit up, and I help her rise slowly. "I cut carefully. The bleeding will stop..."

She was always the best among us when it came to caring for wounds, so it's a relief to hear her say that because I believe her. We'd learned how to care for each other's injuries as part of our anatomy lessons when we were younger because a servant's job was never done—we had to serve each other in healing after nights of purging.

"Mercy, I—"

"Drop it!" Arlo grunts, and my head whips over my shoulder at the reminder that he's still there, still battling Hyatt.

Why is he battling Hyatt? For Ellary? For me?

Arlo straddles him, fighting to keep his arms pinned to the ground. Hyatt flails, jerking and twisting, thrashing with violence that threatens to be a match for Arlo's strength. I watch in horror as Hyatt manages to wiggle his arm out from beneath Arlo's firm grip—and there, I see the knife. He pulls back his arm and plunges, aiming the sharp tip at Arlo's thigh.

"No!" I scream.

Arlo's head jerks sideways to look at me, and I clamp my lips shut, realizing my cry did nothing more than distract him. But just before Hyatt can sink the blade into his flesh, Arlo sees the knife. He clamps his hand around Hyatt's wrist just before the blade can slice into his flesh.

Their arms shake as they fight each other for control of the weapon. As strong as Arlo is, I distracted him, and that distraction caused him to grip Hyatt's wrist at an awkward angle. The blade lowers, inch by inch, and I'm frozen in stunned silence as I watch because I can't make sense of anything I'm seeing. The tip of the blade touches his thigh and slips, slicing through his slacks, drawing a line toward his knee that trails with crimson.

Arlo groans against the pain, against the struggle to keep the knife from sinking deeper, and his shadowed face contorts in rage. He twists, reaching over with his other hand, and though this move releases Hyatt's other arm from where it was pinned on the ground, it allows Arlo to leverage his weight.

He shoves the arm holding the knife and slams it to the ground. Just as I think Hyatt's going to flip him over, Arlo manages to wrestle the knife from his hand. Arlo flips it in his gloved palm, turns it sideways, and pushes the edge of the blade to Hyatt's throat.

Hyatt stills, chest heaving as he draws in one heavy breath after another. My chest heaves, too—from the run, from the chase…from trying to make sense of Arlo fighting this man when he should be capturing me and returning to the Homestead.

"Are you supposed to be here?" Ellary's voice startles me.

I'm quickly dragged into my own battle of shifting focus between her and Arlo.

"They're—" I stutter between the odd cadence of my breaths. "They're filming the service. I saw you with Hyatt, and I ran for you."

"You ran for me?"

"Of course." I help her move to rest her back against a nearby tree trunk. "I couldn't just sit there and watch him hurt you."

To my absolute surprise, she grants me a small smile, though it quickly fades as a familiar look of shame filters through her expression. I reach up to wipe the mud from her cheek, but her blood is all over my hands, and it only smears into the dirt that coats her face.

She speaks so quietly that I almost don't hear her through the waterfall crashing from the clouds. "Am I a sinner like you if I admit I was afraid of him?"

I no longer need to catch my breath; my lungs are filled with every molecule of meaning from her question.

"No. No, you're not. You're wonderful and good and everything God made you to be, Ellary Hill."

"What are you going to do?" Hyatt taunts Arlo from beneath the blade resting at his throat, and I look over my shoulder at the sound of his voice. "Are you going to slit my throat and kill me?" Hyatt grits. "You'll be condemned; you'll be a *sinner*."

Arlo's voice is a low rumble in the storm. "No good man would call me a sinner for ending you."

Hyatt laughs. "What are you even talking about, *no good man?* You and I are the same."

Arlo bends over Hyatt, and the blade digs into his flesh. "You and I are *not* the same," he snarls.

And he's right—they're not the same.

Arlo is not the same as he was before. Rather, he's showing what he has the potential to become. I don't know if I can withstand knowing about his potential to become more—so much more than he already is to my hopeful heart.

"Let me up!" Hyatt shrieks, bucking and twisting and kicking so madly beneath Arlo that he can hardly keep him pinned down.

Hyatt makes the choice to thrash against a man holding the edge of a blade against the hollow of his throat…and this choice is perhaps the last one he'll ever make.

Hyatt twists while thrusting his body upward, and Arlo begins to fall. As he tilts, falling sideways toward the ground, the hand which holds the blade moves with him.

Arlo slips, and so does his hand…so does the knife.

The blade slices across Hyatt's throat just before Arlo lands on his side, his hand still firmly gripping the knife that drew Hyatt's blood.

I stare in disbelief as Arlo rights himself, scrambling to his feet as his widened eyes dart frantically between Hyatt's bleeding throat and the knife held in his grip. He lifts his hand, studying the bloody blade, and then he drops it to the sodden ground.

Then, he leaps forward, bending over Hyatt, who's blood spurts from his throat, each pulse of his heart splashing with a new flood of crimson that spills down his neck, liquid racing like a river to coat the earth beneath him.

Arlo reaches over him, pressing both hands down to collar his neck, as if he could apply enough pressure to stop so much bleeding. He must know he can't. Hyatt's going to die, and if I live long enough to see him buried, I'll dance on his damn grave.

I turn to Ellary with a whip of my head, and I'm confused to find her eyes shut, her face calm, not wide-eyed with fear for what she witnessed or searching my expression for answers. I realize my kneeling body blocks her view of the scene behind me. She's tired from bleeding—which, thankfully, seems to be slowing to a stop— and from being choked to the point of unconsciousness.

"Is everything okay?" she mutters, sensing my attention on her. Her eyes flutter open and land on mine.

She didn't see Arlo slip.

She didn't see the blade slide across Hyatt's throat.

She doesn't know Arlo is the one who cut him.

A strange calmness washes over me, slowing my heart to a steady, thumping rhythm. Each beat pulses the formation of a plan—a plan that's aimed at saving Arlo from the same fate I'm facing.

He doesn't deserve to be saved...

But maybe, with time, he'll earn it?

He's just killed another man, and accidental or not, he'll be condemned for it. He'll be punished by death for this crime— perhaps burned at the stake. It doesn't matter that he's one of the Control; Hyatt did nothing in the eyes of the authority to warrant the attack. And if it comes to light that he fought Hyatt while I ran to save Ellary, then they'll say he did it for me, a sinner—and they'll call him a sinner the same.

Did he do it for me?

I look back at him, blood soaking his gloves and spattered across his shirt. Hyatt's gone still, and Arlo slowly sits back on his heels, lifting his hands from the dead man's throat. He raises his head, and our stare connects. My heart wasn't prepared to see the fear in his eyes; my soul wasn't prepared to feel such a sense of responsibility in this. I chose to run, and he chased me. He had no choice but to chase me.

It's not my fault that he chose to attack Hyatt, but I do feel responsibility for the situation I had put him in. Regardless of who is responsible for what, a much more significant and strange feeling overcomes me in this moment.

Gratitude.

I'm grateful that Hyatt is dead.

Arlo has my sudden, inexplicable gratitude for ending the man who murdered Ivy Jane, the man who came after me that fateful night—intent on setting me on fire—the man who made Ellary Hill slice into her flesh and bruised her neck while he strangled her to unconsciousness.

Hyatt Price was a menace, and he needed to be stopped. His death is a blessing to all, and Arlo delivered it. Arlo helped me save Ellary when all he had to do was catch me and drag me back to the Homestead.

I can't let him be punished for this—they'll kill him.

I can't live out the rest of my days without him.

I need him.

A quick plan forms in my mind. It's a terrible plan, a stupid plan that's likely going to backfire, but something deep within my soul begs me to carry through with it.

I turn back to give Ellary a quick once over, confirming the color is returning to her cheeks, that the flow of blood from her arm isn't heavy or worrying. "You're okay?" I ask to confirm.

She nods with a small smile. "Just need to rest a bit," she whispers, dropping her head back against the trunk and closing her eyes.

I lean in to kiss her forehead. "Stay here. And when they find you later, tell them it was me. Tell them I did it."

Her forehead creases in confusion but she doesn't open her eyes; she just nods, rolling her head to find a comfortable resting place.

I draw in one solid breath as I rise to my feet, turning and walking toward Arlo. He tilts his head sideways to look up at me as

I move beside him, thankful that the roar of rainfall masks the sound of my heavy breaths. Slowly, I crouch to my haunches at his side.

"Any God worth believing in would show you grace for this accident." I speak to keep his attention away from my hand, which secretly reaches for the knife he dropped. "Hyatt was out of control, and he had to be stopped. Your God won't condemn you for this."

A twinge of pain pinches my chest for the wish that Arlo—that *anyone* in Ember Glen—would show me grace as much as I show them.

My fingers graze the handle of the knife, and I stretch them around the grip, squeezing with a firm hold to keep it from slipping through my blood-soaked hand.

"Mercy—" Arlo begins, but I don't let him finish.

With a quick motion, I turn the blade in my hand, jam the tip against his forearm, and tear a quick, sharp slice through his shirt sleeve. The blade lightly catches his skin beneath, drawing a small trickle of blood along the line I cut, just as I'd intended.

He shouts, instinctively wrapping a hand around the cut, and his moment of surprise is enough to distract him, to keep him from stopping me in what I'm about to do.

I take half a second's pause to bring my fury for Hyatt Price to the front of my mind, and it's not hard to do. I only have to think about what he's done to my sisters—not just to Ivy before, and to Ellary tonight, but all the women he hurt in his gradually increasing sadistic behavior, which escalated with each service.

I find my fury for them, but for me, as well. Because he wanted to set me on fire that night, he led me to run, and in doing so, he took my life right along with Ivy's.

My rage boils, twists my features, and I let myself feel the way it burns. With the flames of anger licking beneath my skin, I lift my arm, raise it high, then drive the tip of the blade down into Hyatt's throat.

"Mercy!" Arlo's horrified scream echoes.

He reaches out to snatch my wrist, but I move too quickly for him to catch me. I pull the knife out and flinch as more blood sprays, splashing up like a tiny explosion that spatters blood all over me and Arlo. I spare Ellary a quick glance to see her just opening her eyes—probably at Arlo's scream—and they widen as she takes in the bloody scene.

"I did it. It was me," I remind Ellary as I turn on my heel.

I take off at a run, sprinting into the darkness.

And just as I hoped he would, Arlo chases after me.

chapter fourteen
ARLO

"MERCY!" I SCREAM as I chase her through the forest.

Tree trunks seem to jump out in front of me, shifting and closing around me as I run through blankets of rain. My shoulder slams against a dark tree, and I lift my hands just in time to push off another as adrenaline floods me.

I feel lost, confused; bouncing off one tree, then another, stumbling over twigs and branches as mud squelches and leaves crunch beneath my feet. I just keep moving, chasing, desperate to catch her. The rain still falls, and though the canopy of branches slows the descent, it still soaks me in delirium…yet it doesn't seem to wash away the blood that coats me.

So much blood.

Mercy chose to wear black tonight, to show solidarity with her sisters in service, yet she's covered in red all the same. She's drenched in the blood of a man who drove her to run, the man ultimately responsible for her placement in the Trials of Dissension. I should be horrified, nauseous, sick over watching her take that knife from the ground—the knife I accidentally slit his throat with—and stab him with intent. But I'm not. I find that I'm only curious about her choice to do it.

Surprisingly, I feel no concern for Hyatt Price. He's dead, and I don't feel mournful over it; I don't feel like we lost a man horrifically at the hands of a rebellious servant. I don't care that he's dead. I almost don't care whether it was the cut I made accidentally, or the final blow Mercy delivered that ultimately ended him.

All I care about is her…

Mercy fucking Madness.

I chase her dark silhouette, watching for the flashes of starlight hair each time lightning strikes and lights up the sky. My legs slow, colliding with grass that meets my knees, the forest floor disappearing as I stumble into weeds and wildflowers. She's lured me into the meadow.

The wildflowers—which look black in the night—all sway together in one direction, guided by the same wind which blows the storm through Ember Glen.

Three strides into the meadow, and I slam to a stop. A strike of lightning bursts so brightly that the entirety of the meadow, the sloping hills and valleys beyond it, and the dark mountains in the distance appear in a flash. It's a momentary image of the beauty surrounding Ember Glen, though it's instantly cast back into darkness.

Yet before that darkness falls, I see her in the flash of light—a star shining brighter than all the universe around her.

Mercy Madness stands in the center of the meadow, her stance wide and proud, chest-heaving from the chase. She's soaked in blood from head to toe. It stains her hair, coats her face, and drips from the bottom hem of her skirt. Arms held down by her sides, she still holds the knife in a firm grip. The wind-blown flowers and tall grass violently whip against her legs.

And the rain…

It spills from the sky, bending toward her with the whipping wind in a way that could make me believe she summoned it herself.

I see all of that—all of *her*—in the single flash of light.

I'm in awe.

Another flash lights up the sky, and this time, all I see is her.

Not the wildflowers that sway around her feet. Not the mountains at her back. Not the knife in her hand. All I see is Mercy, standing beautifully beneath the sheets of rain…rain that appears to cleanse her as it washes away the blood—perhaps as it washes away her sins.

Thunder crashes, rumbling through the wide-open valleys and hills beyond the meadow. I could nearly mistake the roar as a call from the heavens, from God himself, like a bursting message that His blessing circles this wild woman wielding a bloody knife beneath an electric sky.

"I killed him," Mercy shouts at me over the storm.

My feet carry me forward, slowly striding toward her dark silhouette.

"I ran, and you chased me," she says. "I ran to save Ellary, you chased me, and I fought Hyatt. I took his knife, and I stabbed him. You tried to stop me, but I cut you with the blade, sliced across your thigh, and cut your arm as we struggled."

I continue forward.

"You tried to stop his bleeding, but it was too late. He was already gone."

My heart beats faster as I listen to her spin this deceptive narrative.

"You left him behind because I ran, and you knew you had to catch me. Because it was me who killed him. You didn't attack him; you didn't slip with the knife. Do you hear me, Warden Rainn? *I* killed him, not you."

I stop two strides before meeting her, watching her blink against the droplets that catch on her eyelashes.

"That's a lie, Mercy. *I* killed him."

My words strike me as I hear them out loud, hitting me like a bolt of electricity that was meant for the sky, though it strikes my chest instead. I drop my head, scrubbing my hand over my face before I realize my leather gloves are ruined—they're soaked in blood that I've just smeared across my beard.

I look down at the red liquid, watching it streak the leather as the rain rinses it from my upturned palms. "His blood is on my hands…"

"It may be on your hands, but it's all over me," she says, and I sense her step closer. "I killed him. I did it. I won't allow anyone to believe otherwise, do you hear me?"

"Why are you doing this?"

"My fate is already sealed, but yours doesn't have to be."

My voice comes out harshly. "Why are you *doing* this, Mercy?" I step closer. "Why would you do this? Why would you *fucking* stab him and try to take the blame for an accident?"

"Accident or not, they would punish you by death. You know they would."

"And it would be my punishment to bear!"

"Well, now it's not."

"*Why?*" I shout at her.

"Because…" she looks toward the forest, staring into the dark for moments before bringing her eyes back to meet mine. "Because I finally know what I want from this life in the short time I have left. I finally know what I want."

There's a heavy pause as our breaths quicken between us.

"I want *you*," she confesses. "I want you at my side until I take my last breath. I want your strength, your comfort, the peace you give my mind in forbidden moments. I want you to take care of my needs—*all* my needs. I want you to be my true warden." She pauses and the air feels heavier, like it's harder to breathe. "I want you to sin with me until my days are done."

I fight the Impulse rising within me, the urge to grab hold of her right now and give her exactly what she wants from me. I lurch, aching to close the distance, but she raises her palm to halt me.

"And you will never, *ever* speak the truth of tonight. You keep this secret and always let them believe that it was me, that I was the horrid sinner who killed Hyatt Price. You let me take the blame and the punishment in kind, and you'll live the life they want you to lead. You'll do what you have to as a member of the Control so you can become one of the Elders, as you were meant to."

"*What?*"

"You'll become an Elder in exchange for me taking this blame for you. And when you do," another heavy, meaningful pause in her shouted words as she fights to be heard over the rush of rain, "you're going to change everything. You'll use your power to make women equals, to end these nights of service, to give everyone in Ember Glen a *choice* on how they live their lives. You'll fight for Ember Glen, for men to love women the way that you—"

She stops herself, lips parted in half-formation of the next word. Her eyes bore deep into my soul, imploring me to find the end of her sentence on my own. I don't have to search deeply for it. It's on the surface, etched into my skin, the only words that could ever describe the intense desperation and obsession I have for her.

The way that you love me.

I can't speak it because the words wouldn't be enough to show her the way I'm in awe of her. Words would never be enough to explain how she burns through my mind, sets fire to my old ways of thinking while sparking new ones to replace them. Words can't express the way she's clawed beneath my skin, seeped into my veins, altered my very soul.

In this moment, I can see her for exactly what she is…She's a brightly burning star, the kind that shoots quickly across the night sky, only existing for a short time before leaving our world entirely. Witnessing such an anomaly changes how you see the world, and it's exactly what she's done to me.

It's not demons that plague her, and it's not hell that she sprung from. She's born from the heavens, a gift from God, sent to change everything. And what an honor I will find in aiding His will. I've had her all wrong…so very wrong.

My head bobs, nodding in agreement with her plan—*His will.* I agree to her terms, her intention to burn bright and fast, to set fire to the world as it is, and ignite a new way of thinking through her death and the years that follow—years she means for me to lead. Years *God* means for me to lead.

"I'll do it. I'll do what you ask of me, Mercy Madness."

Her breath catches in her lungs, and she takes a small step back, as if she feels pushed away by the sincerity of my words.

I take a step closer. "From now until the day you die, I will worship between your legs as though you were sent to me by God Himself…because only an angel would take on such a burden to save the man meant to ensure her demise."

A strange heat and heaviness circle us in a way that makes it feel like the rain has stopped falling, though it continues to drench the world around us. I draw in the thick air between us with three shallow breaths, the last of which draws her a single step closer. It's as though she's the air I need to breathe, and my lungs beg her to come closer so they can be filled with her, can drown in her.

Her chest is only inches from my body, heaving as she takes in rapid breaths. She slowly lifts her head, blinking against the falling rain—which I can't even feel anymore—as she captures my gaze.

In her bewildering silvery-blue eyes, I can see everything she wants from me—everything she needs from me, everything she desires—and it's all a reflection of my own dark urges.

She tosses the knife with a quick lift of her arm, lets it fall, and it sinks into the tall grass. "Sin with me."

She doesn't have to say another word.

chapter fifteen
ARLO

I CHARGE FORWARD before she finishes the last syllable. I crash into her, throw my arms around her, and our bodies strike like lightning. A flash lights up the night as our lips slam together, the thunder quickly following. I feel the electricity from the sky ripple through us, and it's like a sign from heaven that this moment is divinely crafted—sacred, significant, transformative.

My hand splays across the small of her back, drawing her impossibly close as she arches against me. My other palm finds the back of her head, holding her in place so I can kiss her harder, hard enough to bruise our lips.

My hand slips over the curve of her bottom, fingers spread wide as I curl them into her fleshy cheek and grip her firmly. Arching back, I lift her from the ground, her feet dangling for a moment before she lifts them around me, climbing them up my sides. With my hand on her ass, I hoist her higher. She circles her legs around my waist, settling her weight against my hips.

Once our bodies are locked, feral need overthrows decency, a depraved manner of lust conquering our shared senses.

Mercy parts her lips to let her tongue seek mine with hunger, shoving the metallic taste of blood that smeared her cheeks into my mouth. We groan in unison, tasting the filth and fighting to lick it away faster with our battling tongues.

It's not enough to have my tongue inside her. I need to fill every open part of her, fill her so deeply that she can feel how thickly I need her…my twisted, dark, unholy need.

No, not unholy.

Twisted and dark, yes, but not unholy.

She's sent from God—it's so fucking clear to me now—and He must want me to indulge with her. If I'm to enact her will, then I should fulfill her every need, and in that way, my need for her could never be unholy.

The way I want her is destined, dark yet sacred.

Holding her tighter, I fall to my knees—a sinner kneeling in worship—surrendering to our carnal need. Her arms tighten around me as we crash to the earth. Our kiss breaks as she lands on my lap, her bottom bouncing off my tense thighs as I sit back on my heels.

The cut from Hyatt's blade burns and throbs as she drops her weight to sit on my lap, locking her legs around my middle. As she thrusts her hips forward over the cut, I imagine my blood slicking across the back of her thigh, soaking the fabric of her underwear.

My hand moves from her ass, pressing through the arch of her back as I lean forward. My gloves catch in her hair, fingers twisting through the strands as I devour her with another kiss. My skin is crawling, heart pounding, breaths swallowed up by her warm, luscious mouth.

I'm spiraling, losing control. I bare my teeth and bite her bottom lip, tugging harshly before releasing. My bite seeks the tender flesh of her neck, nipping, kissing, sucking along the curve. She pants as her hands roam my back, as her lips slip along my cheek, as she holds herself closer to align her curves perfectly with my body.

"Purge with me," she whispers. "Take me the way you wanted to the night you chased me in the forest."

Sweet sin.

I lower her, taking her to the ground as I bend over her, nestling us both in the overgrowth of grass and wildflowers.

Wildflowers and starlight…
This is the moment my poetry comes to life.

Celestial beauty and the scent of earth,
like the meadow and sweet mountain air.

Wildflowers and starlight.

I kneel between her legs, struggling to pull off my leather gloves—slippery from blood and the falling rain—and I toss them somewhere in the grass. Her bloody fingers scrape across her thighs as she gathers her skirt, hiking it up over her bent knees toward her hips.

I reach down with both hands to grab hold of the sloping neckline of her black top, which frames her breasts so perfectly. I tug the fabric sharply, yanking it down to expose her to the storm that swirls around us—the storm within us has already been raging for far too long.

She gasps as her back arches, pressing the peaks of her nipples toward the sky. The falling rain slickens her skin, painting her in a sheen of angels' tears that demand my desecration.

Slipping my arms around her, I run my tongue up the center of her chest between the thick mounds of flesh. I move one hand up her spine to grip the back of her neck as my tongue meets the hollow of her throat. I press a heavy kiss there as she swallows beneath my lips.

Tangling my fingers in her hair, I cradle her head against the ground as I kiss her deeply, devouring her entirely, consuming every bit of her.

Mercy's knees grip my hips as I grind my hard length between her legs. It strains behind my slacks and begs for the removal of all barriers.

I sit back abruptly, breaking our kiss, and she whimpers, reaching for me to cover her again. Sitting back on my heels, I pant with parted lips, staring down at her as I work my buckle, fingers twitching in the rush to free my cock from its prison.

She reaches down and pushes her underwear off her hips, raising her legs to shove them over her knees as my cock springs free. I shove my pants and underwear down my thighs and rush to help with her panties.

I lift one of her legs and stretch the elastic to get the loop over her boot. Then I let go, and her panties snap around her other ankle. I leave them hanging there, still hooked to one leg. I'm too lost to care about removing them entirely, too desperate to taste her.

I reach beneath her legs, sliding my hands up the backs of her thighs to grip at the crease where her knees bend. Lifting, I shove her knees back, forcing her body to curl as I bring her knees to her chest.

Her ass lifts from the ground as I press her legs back, her glorious cunt aiming skyward. I dip my head to kiss her pussy, licking and lapping as deeply as I kissed her mouth, tasting the darkest parts of her and willfully consuming them.

I'm in ecstasy for this moment where we can finally share our filth, our urges, our impulses. I now understand that she has the Impulse, too—the undeniable craving for sex and violence. Yet this shared craving is different from a man purging with a servant. It's different because it's mutual, delicious, *divine*.

Her hands fall to her breasts and knead while her eyes pinch shut in pleasure. I want to keep giving her that pleasure—*need* to give it—but for a moment, I have to pull back and just look at her. I keep her held in place, though I shift back so I can gaze down at her.

With the absence of my tongue, she opens her eyes and finds me watching her. I see the swirl of stars and galaxies in her eyes…

the entirety of the universe in her silvery-blue irises.

"Don't stop," she pants.

I drop my gaze, letting it land between her legs, curious to see how the falling rain splashes against her flesh. "Hold your leg," I tell her as I drop one to free my hand.

Her knee drops for a second, but she quickly lifts it back up for me, her hand reaching around to grip the back of her thigh to hold her knee against her chest.

I slide my free hand between her legs, then draw my fingers over her slick center. I graze the outer rim of her opening, dipping two fingers inside shallowly, then spread them in a V to open her wide. She gasps, her stomach jerking as it clenches in surprise.

Pushing through the leg I still hold, I fold her body further, angling her just right for a stream of water to pour down into that perfect opening. Rainwater pools in her cunt, and I let it fill her all the way up.

She gasps and whimpers, jerking beneath me, though she tries to hold still. With a snarl, I bend, place my rounded lips over the pool of water that fills her pussy, and suck. I drink from her, lapping the water that mixes with the flavor of her arousal.

Swirling the heady liquid through my mouth, I swallow half the elixir consecrated by her ardent flesh. I drop her leg without warning, and her boot lands on the ground with a thump. She lowers the other, hooking the heel of her boot around my ass as I move between her legs and bend over her.

I grip her face with one hand, pinching her cheeks between my fingers, digging in at the hinge of her jaw until the pressure forces her mouth to open. I dip low, stealing her gaze, and as she recognizes my intent, she opens wider.

Sweet sin.

I spit the remainder of the filthy mixture between her parted lips. Then I release her cheeks, clamp my hand over her mouth, and bend further, touching my nose to hers.

"Swallow," I demand.

Her eyes hood with lust. I let my other hand creep up her throat, and I feel it bob as she swallows. It's so filthy, yet so divine, to share that liquid lust. Reflexively, my hips thrust forward with the need to fill her, and my cock slips right inside her, *deep* inside her, burying to the hilt. She groans beneath my hand.

I lift my palm from her mouth and find her wrists instead. Gripping one in each palm, I lift them high and slam them to the ground, stretching her arms above her head. Her hips rise, thrusting up, urgently seeking movement.

"Please," she begs. "Arlo, please."

I drag out and slam back in, shifting her body along the ground, causing her to cry out from the force. The sound of her need is drowned by the rushing rain, but it echoes in my ears all the same. It's the only thing I can hear—the only thing I *want* to hear.

I thrust, fucking her hard with a steady rhythm. Shifting her wrists to hold them between just one of my hands, I bring my other to her chest, brush my thumb across her nipple, and swirl it around the peak.

"Yes," she breathes. "Yes, yes…"

I lift her breast, dipping my head to drag my tongue over the hardening bud, sucking until she's writhing beneath me.

"Make me come," she whimpers. "Make me come. Please, Arlo."

Tugging on her wrists, I lift them, scooping my head between the circle formed by her arms. She takes the hint and grips the back of my neck with one hand, the other trailing upward to sink her fingers into my hair. My eyes fall shut at the tug on my scalp, the curl of her fingers and the way they press into my skin.

I snake my arms around her, holding her tightly as I shift on my knees and sit back on my heels. I'm still inside her, my cock sinking deeper with the angle change as she's pulled onto my lap. She gasps, curling around her clenching stomach as I splay my hand over her back.

My lips are only a breath away from hers. "Use me. Let me serve you for this moment."

I might be as surprised as she is for what I just said. Her lips are parted—panting, gasping for reason where she'll find none. Her forehead wrinkles as her narrowed eyes dart around my face, searching, exploring…but I can't stand the waiting.

I need her to fuck me.

I capture her mouth in a desperate kiss before dropping onto my back, pulling her down on top of me. She sits up where she straddles my hips, cock still buried inside her. Her body convulses as she settles herself, shifting her knees on the muddy ground and squeezing my hips. She whimpers and sighs, twitching through small shocks that hint at the explosion to come.

And when she finally starts to move, my fucking soul leaves my body. She rocks her hips, settling her weight on me and grinding heavily. She keeps me buried to the hilt inside her as she fucks me.

Dear God, the way she fucks…How could she ever be wrong?

Her hands find my thighs as she leans back and takes from me, as she throws back her head and tilts her chin skyward. She moves recklessly, wildly, *freely*, and it's pure intoxication to watch her move. Her breasts bounce lightly with the movement of her grinding hips, her chest heaving with each panted breath. The rain still falls to drench her, slicking her skin so beautifully that it makes my cock twitch inside her.

I revel in laying beneath her, watching her move, letting her use my cock. I'm in awe watching her let go, my gaze locked on her face and the way her expression twists in filthy, desperate need.

I've spent so much time thinking about the Impulse in recent days, curious in my thought that perhaps women have it, too—not just men. It's in this moment, here and now, watching Mercy fuck me with a primal energy, that confirms the truth in my mind. She's lost to her urges, feral and hungry, using me to serve her carnal need.

Perhaps we all suffer the Impulse…and if that's true, then men are weak in comparison to women. I can't look at the sensual creature riding my cock with such urgent filth without drawing that conclusion.

If it's true, then everything I know has been a lie.

The sickness of dissonance punches my gut, begging to drag me into deeper thinking. There's so much my mind aches to consider—and I will consider it all—but right now, all I want to think about is Mercy and the way she blesses me with the thrusting of her hips.

I focus on the feeling, watching her fuck me harder, sensing the monumental build of her pleasure like a volcano on the verge of eruption. She pants out heated sounds of desperation, and I feel her cunt pulse around me, squeezing out my own pleasure and mingling it with hers.

"Come for me, starlight." I grit my teeth. "Fuck me and come for me."

The pulsing of her inner walls strengthens, tightens, then releases with a vengeance. She cries out into the night and calls for the thunder as a bolt of lightning streaks across the sky, lighting up the meadow…lighting up Mercy.

She comes undone beneath the electric sky, riding the waves of pouring rain as her thrusts turn to jerking twitches—the aftershocks of her pleasure. As the satiated smile spreads across her cheeks and she leans forward to lay her hands on my chest, I'm overcome with the need to fuck her breathless.

I flip her, slamming her down against the sodden earth. I collar her neck with my hand, shift my hips to the perfect angle, and fuck her hard. I pound into her flesh as she gasps for breath beneath me. Her hands shoot up a few seconds later to lightly grip my wrist, encouraging me to let up from my unintentional squeezing at the sides of her throat.

I jerk my hand away, slamming both palms to the ground at either side of her head. I bend and smother her mouth with mine, kissing her sloppily. Her palms greet my cheeks, smearing me with dirt and blood. She holds my face to hers to kiss me deeper as I thrust my way to release.

I feel myself swell inside her, pulsing, my body on the edge of release when her lips slip away from mine. I drop my forehead to meet hers, and our eyes lock.

A thousand silent words pass between us as she gazes deeply—it's some language I know could never be learned or spoken. There are no words to describe what passes between us, how we see each other, the flames that ignite between us every time we touch. Our connection is beyond reason, beyond language, beyond the guiding laws of the Impulse Edict…

Perhaps it's even beyond God Himself.

What we share is cosmic, toxic, fated, and forbidden.

I can't fight it, and I truly don't want to anymore.

As my release begs, the rain slows to a stop. I strain with the need to edge myself, to draw this out, to stave off my release so I can remain in this perfect desperation for just a little longer.

My body trembles over hers as the rain quietens and my heavy breaths and groans surround us. I don't know if I can hold myself back; I don't know if I can control myself with her.

I know I can't.

I never really could.

But the broken parts of me still need to try.

"I want to feel it," she pleads as the storm blows away, the roar of rain dying away to give space to the perfection of her voice. "Let me feel you come inside me." Her hips buck to meet mine as I still myself, and my face twists in the agony of delayed release.

"Not yet…" I tell her, and she doesn't look at me with judgment or frustration.

She nods her head against mine and licks her lips before parting them to take in a rasping breath.

I don't know what I'm waiting for, but I know I haven't reached the pinnacle of my tension yet, haven't found the perfect moment to let go and lose myself in her entirely.

She wiggles her hips, shifting me inside her, and I groan, tilting my chin to kiss her briefly, loving the way she makes me throb for her so relentlessly.

The sounds of our ragged breaths amplify as silence enshrines us, the clouds spent and completely spilled. My jealousy of the clouds peaks, and I can't help but thrust again, slowly pumping, swirling my hips to ensure my cock rubs along every inch of her pussy. In the quiet after the rainfall, our breaths and wetness create filthy songs to fill the night.

Sweet sin… I can feel her gathering around me again, squeezing, pulsing, hips bucking and rocking with mine.

Please God, let me hold this moment; let me edge until she comes with me.

Please.

Fuck.

I can't…

My movements hasten and frantic energy takes me. She whimpers against the growing need throbbing between her thighs. Her back arches to tilt her hips for me, head tilting back the same, lifting her eyes to the sky. She gazes beyond me, up toward the night sky, as she pulses her hips against me, eyes widening with some strange sense of wonder.

"Arlo," she quivers through my name, on the verge, barely controlling herself, "*please…*" she begs me to come with her.

She trembles as she blinks, as she fights her own relief in favor of finding mine. But then her body suddenly stills, and a peaceful smile tugs at the corner of her lips. "I can see the stars."

Sweet sin.

Starlight above us.

Wildflowers around us.

Everything about her brings me back to the words I wrote—to *wildflowers and starlight.*

I lose all control. I fuck her harder, driving us both toward that edge. I fuck until she finally releases, crying out into the night while coming hard around my cock. Her cunt squeezes me so perfectly, begging for my cum to spill inside her. A primal growl scrapes through my throat as I fuck her through my orgasm, the pleasure of it going on and on and *fucking* on.

I gaze deeply into her widened eyes. "I can see them, too. The stars."

She looks at me with such wonder and hope—hope that should evade her for a future she won't be a part of. I know right now that if I were ever asked to identify the moment my heart opened for this woman who I called a sinner, it would be this one.

Her voice is quiet, sad, yet still filled with that hopeful longing. "I want more of this, Arlo. More of you." She wraps her arms around me, pulling me down to hug her. "I want to live long enough to see the man you'll become."

I let her drag me down. I lasso my arms around her and roll us both to our sides to lay in the tall grass and wildflowers. Neither of us care that we're covered in blood and dirt. Her leg is around my hip, cock still buried between her legs. I hold her with more intimacy than I've ever held anyone. I've never been hugged this way, and it makes me feel more vulnerable than I did while I fucked her.

"You'll have so much more of me before the end," I choke out the words.

The end…

I tighten my grip on her, bury my face in the crook of her neck. This isn't the last time between us, but one day, we will have our last forbidden tryst. Mercy's days are numbered, and I'm powerless to stop it. She'll die, but I won't let her death be in vain.

I'll do what she asked of me. I'll cement my position in authority. I'll be whoever they want me to be in the Control until my time comes to serve as one of the Elders, and then I will use my power to influence the change God sent her to initiate.

I'll do it for Him, but more importantly, I'll do it for her...for Mercy Madness.

The life I knew before is done; I live mine for her now.

chapter sixteen

ONCE, I WAS told of a thing called magic—some supernatural force of spells, incantations, and dark rituals we were told to fear. Making magic meant making the impossible happen, and it was always explained as something tainted and filthy. Yet something magical has happened here tonight among the wildflowers, beneath the parting storm clouds in the night sky, and the stars peeking through as those black tufts roll away.

We made the impossible happen. We found mutual pleasure in our lust, and that would seem magical enough on its own, but the truly impossible thing is the understanding we seem to be finding in each other's arms. The longer he holds me, the tighter he squeezes, the more I feel him falling into me, coming to understand me, to care for me, perhaps even to appreciate me and the sacrifice I made for him.

I stabbed Hyatt Price.

My heartbeat finds an unsteady rhythm at the reminder, but guilt and shame don't wash over me as I expect them to. Instead, I'm met with something that feels like pride…like power.

I've never had pride or power in my life, and it feels *good*.

I tug my head back to look at Arlo, and we let our eyes roam each other, watching expressions, cataloging features. His gaze falls to my lips, and he licks his before drawing me into a spine-tingling kiss. His lips are soft and wet as they push against mine, encouraging them to part.

He twists us, rolling me onto my back as he deepens the kiss in such a sensual way that I never want it to end.

I never want him to stop.

Gradually, the kiss fades, but it feels natural in the way it ends. It doesn't linger with promises of pleasure that went unmet. It isn't tinged with hatred and rage. Now, there's satisfaction found in the touch of our lips.

Arlo sighs contentedly before laying his weight on me, nudging his face to settle against the crook of my neck. Nestled between Arlo and the steady ground beneath my back, I feel smothered, covered, perfectly protected, and safe for the first time in my life.

I smile as I look beyond his shoulder at the night sky. I marvel at how quickly the storm clouds sweep across the darkness. It's only then that I feel the chill of the wind blowing over us, heavy in its weight, rustling through the tall grass encircling our bodies.

The full moon creeps out from behind one of the clouds. It's only visible for moments as another cloud passes over it, but my grin broadens at the sight of it—bright and full and more beautiful than I've ever seen it.

I think I must have feared the full moon before, but in this moment, I don't know fear. I feel invincible, powerful, *magical.*

We don't speak, lying this way for minutes in the peaceful afterglow. I know that too soon we'll have to move, and the peace will be gone and the horror of my reality will return. I'm in no hurry for this to end.

And then the strangest thing happens.

I see a blinking star moving across the sky.

"Arlo, look…" I say with wonder.

He lifts from my body, twisting to look back and above him as I point my finger from my outstretched arm past his shoulder.

"There. That's a blinking star, isn't it?"

"Oh," he says with surprise. "I think it is. I haven't seen one in years…not since I was a child."

He shifts, pulling out of me regretfully, adjusting to buckle his pants. I hate the way I dragged him from the moment, so I focus on the red blinking light skating across the sky. I'm in awe of it. I don't think I've ever actually seen one myself—only heard about them.

He shifts beside me, laying on his back. I turn my head to look at him as he gazes up, watching the star with wide-eyed wonder, the same as me. His fingers reach out to graze mine beside my hip, and liquid fire runs through my veins. Slowly, he takes my hand in his, locking our fingers together. His touch sears my flesh, and I'll wear the scars of him forever.

He rolls his head to look over at me, catching me grinning at him. He returns the smile with a broad, wonderous grin, one that perfectly displays the long dimples that cut through his cheeks.

"I don't know that I've…" he pauses, "that I've ever actually seen you smile before."

I blink at him, the weight of that thought pressing down on my chest, making my heart feel heavy.

When was the last time I smiled so authentically?

When was the last time I didn't have to fake a tense grin while gritting my teeth?

When was the last time I felt happy?

I can't remember, and it makes my chest ache. If it's truly been so long since I've been happy—since I've genuinely smiled because I *felt* like smiling—then I don't want to let the feeling go. I'll have to, I know, but I don't want to…not just yet.

I turn my head and throw my gaze toward the moon before taking in a deep breath, drawing the joy back inside me. I let the feeling exist along with the pain and fear of my circumstance. It's the best I can do, and it will have to be enough.

I focus on the feeling of his fingers between mine, the warmth of his palm, the strength of his grip. Holding his bare hand feels more intimate than the sex we just had. I don't know how that could be, but that's how it feels.

It's a precious joining of the parts of us that do so much. Our hands touch, they feel, they create, and heal. They can also curl into fists that harm, fingers that scratch, palms that hit and hurt. But right now, our hands just exist together, intertwined, joining us as one through our shared touch.

I squeeze his hand a little tighter.

Quietly, I track the blinking red light of the special star moving along in the night, looking as if it's flying over the mountains.

"It almost looks close enough to reach out and touch," I whisper.

His fingers curl deeper around mine, and the tightening sends a shockwave of pleasure straight through me. It's like I want him inside me again. It's like I'll always want him inside me after the slightest touch.

"I can feel you," I say slowly, "dripping out of me."

He rasps out a heavy breath and rolls onto his side to face me, propping himself onto one elbow, close against my side. My lungs stutter when I look at him. He's drenched from the rain, his hair heavy and dripping. Water and blood mingle in his short, ginger-tinted beard, which looks nearly black in the dark. He places his palm on the center of my chest and drags his fingers down. My back arches in natural response to his touch.

He leans over me, pressing a kiss between my breasts as his hand skims down my stomach. "I'd like for you to always feel me dripping from your cunt."

"And will I?" My mouth suddenly feels dry.

His fingers play with the curls above my sex before dipping between my legs. He trails a line of kisses over my breast, stopping to tease my nipple, playfully scraping his teeth across the bud before soothing with his licking tongue. He brings his lips to hover over mine, and he steals my final breath.

"If I have anything to say about it, you will."

My eyes flutter shut as his fingers dip, swooping so lightly to catch the liquid remnants of his release as it pools between my legs. Too quickly, he takes his hand away. He brings his fingers to my lips, tapping lightly, and I feel the sticky fluid coat my dry, kiss-swollen bottom lip. With my eyes shut, I part my lips for him because I know exactly what he wants—he wants me to taste the mixture of us coating his fingertips.

Gently, he slips two fingers inside my mouth, pushing them forward along my tongue with aching slowness. I close my lips and swirl my tongue around his fingers, sucking and licking greedily. He pulls them out and gently grabs my throat. I open my eyes to find him staring at me with hunger.

"Don't swallow that. Let me taste it on your tongue."

He descends and kisses me deeply, the raw sweeping sensuality of his thick tongue intoxicating, bewildering, purely magical.

I've never felt so much emotion for such filth. I never would've imagined I could feel something painful and beautiful and raw tugging through the fibers of my soul from just tasting the flavor of each other's cum swirling between our kiss. It tightens my belly and makes me ache to have him all over again.

But the sound of voices drags us both abruptly and painfully from our lustful stupor. He pulls away with a snap, turning his head to gaze around the meadow. "We need to go," he urges, scrambling to his feet.

He reaches his hand down and my eyes fall upon his scars. I wish we'd had another moment where I could finally ask him about them. The voices grow louder, and they steal the moment from us. Our time of bliss for tonight has passed, and I don't know when the next will come.

Sadly, I lay my hand in his, and he pulls me to my feet. He grips the top of my shirt and pulls it up to cover my chest. Then he bends, reaching for the panties still looped around my ankle. He takes hold of them, and I lift my foot to let him pull them off. I reach out my hand to take them back, but he quickly folds them and slides them into his pocket.

I meet his eyes, and he gives me a beat of his remaining filth. "I'll be sleeping with those beneath my pillow."

My thighs twitch.

He grabs my hand and walks me toward the tree line as I smooth down my skirt.

"Are you really doing this, Mercy?"

He doesn't need to elaborate; I know exactly what he's asking— whether I'm really taking the fall for him and claiming responsibility for Hyatt's death. Though there's no way to say whether my stabbing or Arlo's accidental slit was the true cause of his death, I've already made up my mind.

I'm taking responsibility.

Arlo hasn't earned this from me yet, but he will. I know he will. He'll do what's right long after I'm gone when he has the power necessary to do it—when he becomes an Elder. I know I'll never live to see him earn my sacrifice, but I can only trust that he will.

The thought of Arlo growing older, alone, long after I'm dead and gone, stabs and twists inside me like a knife. I swallow a dry lump, feeling as though *I've* been stabbed in the throat.

I shift my hand, fingers clawing for that intimacy again as they reach between his and lock together. "Yes, I'm really doing this."

"It's stupid," he tells me. "Stupid, but brave."

We walk for a few paces, meeting the trees, and then he stops abruptly. Letting go of my hand, he grips my waist and pushes my back against the nearest trunk. His body molds to mine, pressing close. His hand comes up to cup my cheek, his thumb stroking my skin.

"I don't deserve this from you."

"No, you don't," I say breathlessly as he kisses the corner of my lips and along my cheek. "Neither of us deserve our fates. Mine was chosen for me, and now yours has been chosen for you. Shall we call it even?"

His thumb catches my bottom lip and tugs. "This will never be even."

I sigh, sinking against the tree. "It doesn't have to be. Not as long as you do what you promised me."

"Remind me exactly what it is I'm promising."

"That you'll live long enough to have real power here and find a way to change things once you become an Elder."

The corner of his mouth twists. "Oh, is that all?"

"Will you really do that for me?"

The smirk fades and he leans closer, the scruff of his beard brushing my cheek as his lips find my ear. His palms tighten around my waist. "If you survive, we can do it together." He pulls back to look at me, surely finding a confused expression on my face.

"What do you—"

Voices steal our attention before I can ask what he means, if he has an idea for how I might survive the trials, or if he's just living a fantasy in his head—one where I survive and he doesn't have to do it all alone. We both turn to look into the dark woods.

"I have to take you back to camp," he whispers. "I'll have to tell them what happened—that you ran and I chased you, that Hyatt attacked you and you fought back, and that you accidentally—"

"*No,*" I snap. "Not *accidentally.* You'll tell them I did it on purpose."

"Is this something you really want to be stubborn about? Your fate is sealed, yes, but things can get much, *much* worse for you before the end, Mercy. You're tempting punishment."

"I stabbed him in the throat, Arlo, and that was no accident.

I had intention, and they'll know it when they see him. I would've done it myself anyway, even if you hadn't slipped with the knife first."

"Maybe you would have, maybe you wouldn't…"

"I *would* have. It's why I ran from the Homestead, to save Ellary from meeting the same fate as Ivy Jane."

"Are you sure you want to—"

"Yes, stop asking. Now take hold of me and drag me back to camp."

His eyes flash with a familiar hunger at my demand, and though I meant it literally, I imagine the figurative vision of him chasing and catching me, dragging me away for my…*punishment.*

And I'm certain now that any punishment Arlo Rainn could dream up for me would be nothing short of divine.

chapter seventeen

Mercy

ARLO HESITATES TO do what he has to do, and though the hesitation warms my heart in knowing he's no longer eager to see me punished, we both know this has to be done. The more he hesitates, the more anxiety it gives me. If I'm to be punished, I want to get on with it so I don't have to fear it in anticipation.

After all, I have enough things to fear in anticipation of the remaining two trials.

I give him a beat to move, and when he doesn't, I take action. I push him away and stomp off into the forest. I only make it five paces before he comes back to life, rushing to catch up with me.

His bare hand closes tightly around my bicep, and he jerks me back. I nearly stumble as he twists me around violently, but his hold is firm enough to keep me on my feet as he drags me in the direction of camp. I glance at his face, seeing the way it's hardened with the mask of a man in control. He pulls me along with his lengthy strides as though I were truly his unruly ward.

I still am, aren't I?

Something deeply indecent twists through my stomach, spurring a depraved kind of excitement. It's like a game we're playing—deceiving the world through a shared mission—and obscene thoughts of forbidden moments wake me with a tingling thrill that prickles from head to toe.

I can hear his breaths as he pulls me along in the darkness, as our feet squelch in the mud, and I stumble over twigs and small branches. I can begin to see the campfire's glow in the distance, now just a low flickering light since the rain had drenched it.

Without warning, Arlo flings me around by his grip and I gasp when my back slams against a tree trunk. Before I can react, he dips to kiss me with a deep, fevered rush—mouths open, tongues lashing, silently swirling with the unspoken words of shared need.

He tries to pull back, and my hands shoot up to grip his face, holding him there so I can kiss him a little longer, so I can taste him a little deeper. Too soon, his hands wrap around my wrists, squeezing tightly so he can pull back and slip out of my grip. He lowers my hands and holds them between our chests, both of us panting with need as an aching growl rumbles through him.

"I don't know if it's the full moon, the Impulse, the fucking chase…but I feel as though I can't get enough of you, Mercy. I have to stop this and take you back, but sweet *fucking* sin, I want you."

"I want you, too."

He crushes me with his body, pressing closer to kiss along my jawline and down the side of my neck. "I have to stop."

"I know," I agree, but I feel myself sink into him all the same.

He releases my hands and grabs hold of my hips instead, moving so fast that I can't resist him as he twists my body to face the tree. My palms land on the rough bark, my cheek turning to press against it, and I don't even care if it scratches my skin raw. His fingers grapple along the back of my thigh as he inches my skirt higher, lifting it above my hip on one side. He flattens his palm, rubbing it over the curve of my ass.

"I want to purge with you again, just like this," he whispers.

The echo of voices carries toward us as someone draws nearer, though we're still hidden in the dark. I clamp my lips together to trap the sound of my heady breaths as I arch my back, pushing against his palm. He squeezes my flesh, and I stifle the moan that gathers in my chest.

His touch disappears, but it returns again with force. He smacks me with a thwack across the fleshy cheek, and it echoes. I cry out against the sting, and though I hate the pain, I don't hate the way it makes me feel like I belong to him, like he claims me. I feel like I'm the only woman he's ever wanted to touch, and in a very unexpected way, it's empowering.

"Get angry with me," I hear him whisper as he strikes me again. "Make it real."

He smacks me again, harder, then again and again in rapid succession. He hits me until it hurts so badly that I'm twisting, trying to get away. He smacks until I'm fighting him, though even in the fight, my belly clenches with desire for every touch.

I have to fight that pleasant need. I have to find my rage again. I need to make it real when he drags me back to camp. I have to make the Control believe that I killed Hyatt Price on my own, out of sheer hatred, or else Arlo will meet dire circumstances.

And I can't let that happen.

He's the only chance Ember Glen has at a better future. I know that future may only be a wishful dream, one that won't even come to pass for another twenty-three years—in a decade I will never see. But it's enough for me to hold out hope.

It's enough for me to take this punishment.

I would've killed Hyatt anyway if Arlo hadn't beaten me to it.

I let images of Hyatt fill my mind as Arlo strikes me. I see his silhouette looming over Ellary while choking her with both hands. I let the rage I felt when I found them build within me.

Before he can land the next strike, I whirl around, slap my palms to his chest, and shove to nudge him back. I try to slip away, but he lunges to grab me, trying to twist me around to smack me again.

I fight, trying to keep him from hitting me, but then I'm

distracted by two voices drawing nearer. A pulse of fear floods my veins, mingling with the arousal of his touch, and it makes me feel high—an overwhelming sensation that I have to pause and take a moment to revel in.

How can fear and desire exist in the same moment?

In my distraction, Arlo grabs hold of me, lassoing his arms around my waist from behind. He locks my arms beneath his and lifts me, kicking from the ground.

"Let go of me!" I shout from the fear, but secretly, I don't want him to as desire still pulses within me.

He marches me toward the glowing campfire, which gradually rises as its fed more kindling. I thrash in Arlo's arms, fully aware of the way his cock hardens against my bottom. I feel the vibration of his soul—the matching wavelengths of fear and desire—and it only strengthens my own. I can feel the way he fears bringing me to punishment as much as I fear taking it.

The shared dichotomy of our most primal fears and desires strengthens our connection in a way I never could've imagined possible. I wish I could halt time and simply exist with him, let ourselves feel the intensity of contradictions swirling endlessly between us. I can feel every emotion imaginable toward him in the span of seconds, and it satisfies every inch of my tarnished soul.

Something has awakened between us tonight—something magical has come to life beneath the rain and thunder, between the stars and the full moon. The magic is dark, but it doesn't feel wrong. The darkness of it feels so right that I wonder for a moment whether I do have demons playing in my mind—if perhaps I am born of hellfire and sent to reap destruction throughout Ember Glen.

It almost makes me want to laugh, but if that were the truth, I would welcome it, and I wouldn't deny it. It feels too good to deny. I find a twisted kind of eroticism in taking the roles given to us— the Control and the servant, the warden and his ward—and playing them out in partnership to bend the truth, to deceive so we can ultimately take what we want.

I thrash in his hold to play my part, jerking so violently that he's forced to lower my feet to the ground. The moment my boots touch the earth, I twist in his hold, breaking his arms away from my waist, and freeing myself. I whip around to face him, taking two quick steps backward before pausing, watching him for a heated beat.

And then, I run.

He chases me.

I want him to catch me…but I run faster.

I run until the light from camp shines bright enough to expose the shadows, and I sprint right past a man fucking a servant.

That used to be me.

The remembrance of being chased unwillingly strikes me like lightning, and it's instantly sobering. I slam to a stop as I'm brought back to reality with jarring force.

I may willingly play with Arlo now, but my sisters are still suffering. The small amount of power I've gained in earning his desire, his loyalty, his adoration must be used appropriately.

I must stay focused.

Arlo nearly slams into me from behind, bringing one arm around my waist as the other finds my hair, gripping and tugging back. "There you are, Mercy Madness."

"What's going on?" It's Owen's voice, I think, coming from somewhere behind us—the couple I passed who brought me back to the truth. "What are you doing out here?"

I hear the familiar sound of zippers and buckles as Arlo nudges me ahead, walking us together toward camp. Rushed footfalls pad across the ground, and in moments, Owen appears at our side.

"There's been an incident," Arlo grunts, trying to hold me steady as I fight against him. "Gather the Control."

"What kind of incident?" Owen asks.

We come through the trees, stepping into the clearing at camp. The fear in me peaks—judgment and punishment are coming, I know. The way I fight Arlo becomes genuine, because in this moment, I want to get away. I want to run, far and fast, from whatever I might face to spare Arlo.

Ahead of us, Park stands near the fire, drinking from a mug of ale. His face contorts in confusion as he spots us, and he begins to move, rushing toward our commotion.

"Let me go…" I beg quietly, and just like that, the begging is no longer a game.

I want him to let me go.

"What's going on?" Park asks.

"Mercy saw something she didn't like on camera and fled the Homestead," Arlo explains. "I chased her, but I didn't catch her in time."

"Didn't catch her in time for what?" Owen's dark eyebrows draw together.

"She saw Hyatt Price take Ellary Hill into the forest…with a knife. She ran to save Ellary, and in the process…" he trails off as I jerk against his hold. He latches his arm tighter around my waist and covers my mouth with his bare hand.

"And in the process…*what?*" My heart hammers, nausea rolling through my gut at the mere sound of Killian's voice.

He approaches from behind us, circling around into view. Stepping in close, Killian reaches out to grab my wrist. He tugs, attempting to drag me from Arlo's hold. I wanted Arlo to let me go just moments ago, but now, I fear it. I don't want to feel Killian's touch on my wrist; I don't want his arms around my waist or his voice against my ear.

Arlo's grip on me tightens. The hand covering my mouth crushes my lips as he draws me closer against him, forcing my head to tilt back onto his shoulder. "I've got her," he grits.

Killian yanks on my wrist, jerking me forward against Arlo's hold. Arlo doesn't let go, but my stomach crushes painfully against his rigid arm.

"Give her to me," Killian demands with narrowed eyes as Arlo pulls me back.

My heart flutters unwillingly at Arlo's reluctance to hand me over. It feels like protection, like care, like the love of a stubborn man who claims me at the risk of his own death. Yet, we both know he has to let me go. He has to play this wicked game as much as I do.

I stop fighting and relax in his hold. I hope he feels me relenting, giving in, and I hope that it's enough of a signal for him to know it's okay to let me go. I don't want him to ever let me go, but he *has* to right now.

My heartbeat quickens as his grip gradually loosens, and once he draws his arm away from my stomach, Killian pulls me with a sharp tug.

Being dragged from Arlo's arms feels like being pushed over a cliff's edge. It makes me think of the cavern where Arlo strung me up to prepare for the first trial. It's what I imagine it would've felt like being shoved into that dark abyss at the cavern's edge. It feels like falling into never-ending darkness, every nerve ending prickling with anticipatory fear of striking the bottom.

How far will I fall before I land?

Will it hurt?

Will I break?

Will the end meet me quicker than I anticipated?

The danger of this moment sends a deluge of adrenaline to flood my veins as Killian pulls me close. He brings me to stand in front of him, chest to chest, his hand crushing my wrist where he holds my arm down at my side. I stare up at him, meeting his scornful dark eyes with all the fear and fury that rumbles through me like thunder.

"Tell us what you did, sinner," Killian snarls.

"I killed Hyatt Price," I nearly shout, wanting the whole world to hear me. I want everyone to know that I took justice for my sisters into my own hands when they were so blinded by their faith that they couldn't do it themselves. "I took the knife he brought to service and slit his throat, then I stabbed him with it. You'll find him in the forest, along with Ellary Hill."

Killian's eyes are wild with fury, surprise, and disgust. I feel so satisfied with the look he gives me that it nearly brings a smile to my face, but I don't want to give him that.

He doesn't deserve my smile.

Not until I'm standing over him with a knife, ready to make him bleed the same.

"Go," Killian says to no one in particular. "Find him."

"You can thank me now or you can thank me later for the favor, Killian." He pinches my wrist, and I cringe against the pain, but I hold my stance and his stare. "Hyatt would've killed Ellary tonight, and then you would've lost two servants in the span of two months. Technically four, if you count me and Delle. I don't believe anyone else is coming of age to replace us in less than six months, isn't that right? How do you expect the men of Ember Glen will be served when all your servants are murdered?"

He chuckles darkly. "I could string you up again and let them all take from you to make up for the losses you've caused our village. Is that what you want, sinner? Are you such a wicked little bitch that you need to be used by all the men of Ember Glen to realize your place?"

I want to spit in his face, and I nearly do before a hand closes around my other wrist and jerks me backward, spinning me around to face the opposite direction. I slam into Arlo's chest as he pulls me close. I look up at him, brow furrowing at the way he stares down at me, lips parted like he's about to speak. But he's interrupted as Owen comes running back with shock written all over his face.

"It's true," Owen says in a rush, coming to stop beside us. "Hyatt Price is dead, just as she said."

"Fuck," Killian utters at my back.

I try to hold Arlo's gaze for comfort, but he drags it away, looking over the top of my head at Killian. "His body needs to be removed."

"He needs to be *honored*. This *fucking* whore!" Killian shouts, my shoulders jumping at the sound.

"*Stop it*," Arlo warns him with a near growl, turning us sideways so he can lean toward Killian. "Be quiet. We cannot halt service for this. Our men need to purge; it's their right, and it's our duty to protect it. We need to handle this quickly and quietly, and Hyatt can be honored another day."

"He's right," Owen agrees. "We can't halt service. It will only bring violence to the village if our men aren't given their monthly purge."

Killian looks nearly out of his mind, scrubbing a hand down his face, then smoothing both palms over the sides of his head before turning and pacing away. He turns abruptly and paces back. "Fine. *Fine*. You're right, I know you are."

"Is Ellary okay?" I ask Owen. "Did you find her?"

All eyes snap to me.

Killian charges toward us, crashing in so close against our sides that I feel his chest against my shoulder. "How *dare* you ask about the well-being of a servant in a time like this?"

Disregarding Killian's reaction, Owen answers anyway, "She's bleeding, but seems okay. She's with one of the Higgins now."

I feel some relief, hoping the Higgins brothers will take turns with her for the rest of the night, as they often do. She speaks with them sometimes outside of service, and they're kind to her then as well. Perhaps they'll have an urge to care for her rather than use her.

I won't hold my breath.

Rage darkens Killian's expression as he steps toward his brother. He places a hand on the center of Owen's chest and shoves so hard that he stumbles back. "This sinner doesn't deserve peace to know her friend's condition!"

With a quiet rage, Owen steps toward him, lowering his voice to a whisper. "We've already lost one man tonight…let's not lose ourselves in anger."

"Fuck you and your calmness, Owen; this situation *begs* for my anger."

"You need to step away from this, brother," Arlo speaks to Killian in a low, rumbling voice. "Go and purge. Your mind is clouded by the Impulse."

Killian's head snaps, eyes wide as his stare meets Arlo's. Arlo shifts me in his grip, trying to move me behind him, but the subtle movement backfires. Killian sees an opening, and he takes it. Lunging toward us, he grabs me harshly by the shoulders, jerking me back hard enough to drag me from Arlo's grip. I cry out as Killian's fingers dig into my skin, as he whips me around to face the fire, and with force, marches me toward it.

chapter eighteen

Mercy

"I SHOULD SET you on fire the way Hyatt meant to in last month's service," Killian hisses at my back, shoving me ahead toward the flames.

"No!" I shout.

I try to plant my feet, but they skid in the mud, and I stumble forward. I struggle to right myself, nearly falling, but Killian grips my hair and jerks me upright, steadying me before shoving me toward the flames again.

I will not meet my end tonight.

I will not welcome flames to swallow me.

With a scowl of determination, I try to plant my feet again, working with the mud and letting my boots sink into it—one, then the other. I firm up my stance, feet shoulder width apart, and though I brace myself for another shove, Killian's determination to hurt me matches my determination not to allow it.

He releases my hair without warning, and my weight pitches forward. Before I can steady myself, his hands strike my upper back, and he shoves me so hard that I fall. I drop to the ground, catching myself on my hands and knees. My palms dig into the pebbles and twigs as they press down upon the sodden patch of dirt that covers the clearing.

Then his hand is in my hair again, tangling so deeply between the short strands that his nails dig into my scalp. He jerks my head back so hard that it lifts me from the ground, and I rise to my knees. My dirty palms shoot back, reaching for the hand that grabs me.

My gaze lifts toward the sky, and for a moment, I can see a sliver of the bright, full moon peeking from behind a cloud. Yet the meager light from above is quickly blocked by Killian's dark expression as he bends over me, looking down with a tense jaw and gritted teeth.

"You should throw yourself on that fire for what you've done, for all the evil you've brought to Ember Glen. You're straight from hell, and I should send you back."

No.

No, no, no.

My heart races being so close to the fire with his threat to burn me. I know he could do it, that he *would*. Even if I hadn't killed one of their precious men, it's a night of service and if the Impulse urges him to do so, then he can without meeting a single consequence.

"Don't," I whisper, quietly pleading, and it makes me feel weak.

"What was that, sinner?" His head turns as he scrutinizes me, glee spreading across his cheeks at the meager hint that I might grovel and beg.

"Don't, please…" I feel instant shame for the begging words slipping from my lips.

Shameful or not, I'll beg if it might spare me. I'm afraid of Killian—afraid of the power he holds, the intensity of his hatred for me. I'm afraid of the fire and being burned like Ivy Jane was.

He releases my hair and violently tosses me forward, and I land on my hands once again.

"Crawl, Mercy Madness. Go to the flame."

I shake my head and my whole body trembles. He won't stop. He won't stop until he's hurt me, and on this night, he's allowed.

Except…

"I'm not a servant." I breathe deeply, drawing in the smokey air that wafts from the flames, and let it strengthen me, like a demon fortified by hellfire. I speak louder. "I'm not a servant; I'm a participant in the Trials of Dissension. I'm already sentenced to the ultimate acts of service in the trials, and it's not my duty nor obligation to serve your urges tonight, Killian."

"No, you're not a servant," Killian hisses. "you're a disgrace to every servant who ever lived in Ember Glen. And it may not be your duty to serve my urges tonight, but you do deserve punishment for what you've done. You deserve everything that's coming to you in the trials."

And then his voice is gone, and I feel his foreboding presence disappear. I feel him move away, and relief sinks through me. Slowly, I push back and sit on my heels. Wiping my dirty palms on my skirt, I look down at my black clothes, and the world blurs around me. Tears I refuse to shed burn behind my eyes as my mind takes me back to all my nights in service.

Four years of service.

Four years of misery and horror at the hands of men.

Four years of subjugation, and no closer to freedom.

My breath catches, and a small sob breaks free. I lower my head to try to hide it, but I can't. Legs appear at my side, and right away, I know they belong to Arlo. I can feel him there. I want to reach for him, wrap my arms around his knees and hug myself to him. I know I can't, certainly not right now.

Maybe later he'll hold me?

A few quiet moments pass, then Arlo mutters, "Fuck," and I feel the weight of the world crash onto my shoulders.

I glance up at him to see that he's looking off behind me, in the direction from which Killian left. With a sinking feeling, I turn my head to look in the direction of Arlo's gaze.

Killian returns, only he's not alone.

Cambria is at his side, holding his hand as he hurries her along. She rushes to keep up with his pace, though she still has a slight limp from the last service when Killian had broken the toes on her right foot. He brings her around to stand beside me, and I feel like I can't breathe. I lift my chin to look up at her, but she refuses to look at me—she's still upset with me for sinning, but her expression is neutral, impassive.

"Put your hand in the fire, Mercy, or Cambria will take the burn on your behalf."

My eyes snap to Cambria's, and surprisingly, hers meet mine the same way. It's brief, just a quick shared moment where I bear witness to a flash of fear so uncharacteristic of Cambria Miller that it strikes me with unease. She has always been fearless, but she's afraid of the fire, too.

Maybe all the servants are now that they witnessed what had happened to Ivy Jane. The memory of her black hair awash in flames continues to haunt me.

Cambria's throat works as she swallows, tearing her eyes away from me and casting them toward the flickering firelight. "I'm happy to serve," she says, though her voice sounds strained.

"And you always serve so well," Killian praises her. He speaks with an eerily calm voice, a doting manipulation he uses to keep Cambria under the spell of serving with pride. "It's such a shame your friend betrayed you so with her sins. Did you know she killed Hyatt Price tonight?"

Cambria gasps and her eyes find mine again, her dark judgmental gaze pummeling me with guilt I know I shouldn't feel. She always had a way of making me second-guess myself, though I don't think of it as a bad thing. When I spoke of thoughts I shouldn't, she was always quick to question me, to encourage me to question myself and to think about why I'm so stubbornly blasphemous when God's will is so clear.

As clear as mud.

She meant for the questioning to lead me back to faith, but

really, I think her encouragement is what led me to sin—because I *did* constantly question myself, and it led me to the truth. I found the truth because of her constant reminders to stop and think. Cambria never could have realized that stopping and thinking meant questioning the doctrine. She wanted me to challenge my thoughts, to find my purpose through God's will…and I did. I just don't think she ever imagined that God's will for me was to find a way to change everything.

"Ellary was doing her duty in serving Hyatt," Killian continues with Cambria. "Mercy witnessed it on camera and escaped the Homestead. She's so lost to her demons that she ran into the forest to end his life."

Cambria's eyes narrow on me at the mention of Ellary.

Are they narrowed in anger?

Does she hate me even more now?

Or do I see a hint of recognition there that Ellary's life was on the line? Does she understand how dangerous Hyatt was and that he would've killed Ellary tonight?

"What do you have to say to that, Cambria? What do you have to say to your friend about the treason she shows us in committing her sins?"

"I…I don't know what to say to that." Cambria's eyes leave mine for the fire again. "I don't know what to say."

"Speechless," Killian remarks. "See what you've done to your sisters, Mercy? You've hurt them beyond comprehension. Now pay them back with your pain, and put your hand in the *fucking* fire."

What do I do?

Heat ripples from the fire before me, so hot that beads of sweat coat my face as I gaze into the dancing orange light. The crackle and roar of the whipping flames seem to crescendo as all other sounds fade around me.

It's just me and the fire, and the decision that lingers: burn my hand or watch Cambria burn hers.

It's no choice for me at all.

I'd set myself on fire to spare my sisters.

Though the choice is simple, the execution of it is hard-won and horrifying. I don't know how to force my hand into the fire; I don't know how to fight the instincts already screaming at me to back away because I'm too close to the flames.

I glance at Cambria before refocusing, and somehow, I manage to move. I shuffle on my knees, scraping along dirt and stones until I'm so close to the fire that the heat threatens to suffocate me. I lift my hand, but I'm shaking, trembling, more afraid than I've ever been before.

Cambria yelps, and my head whips to see Killian grip her wrist and drag her toward the flame. "Do it, Mercy, or I burn her, and I will hold her hand in the flame until there's nothing left but bone."

"Don't!" I shout at him. "I'll do it! I'll do it…" I slowly reach toward the fire.

I feel frantic, out of my mind with fear. The sight of Ivy Jane's floating black hair as she ran, doused in flames and dancing across the night, comes into my mind, and the image won't leave me.

I have to do this.

I have to do it for Cambria.

I can do this.

I saved Ellary, and now I must save Cambria.

A nervous half-sob, half-chuckle shudders through my chest as I suddenly think of the second trial: Service by Sacrifice. It nearly feels like the trial now, choosing to burn myself in sacrifice for my friend. I don't suppose they'll let this moment count for my trial—I know this moment will be nothing compared to what my trial might be.

What sacrifice could they dream up that would be worse than this?

I want to scream, I want to cry; I want to laugh manically

through the storm of chaos in my head. I choose to sacrifice for Cambria—I *do*—but all my natural instincts prevent me from pushing my hand into the flames.

Instinct halts me, but it guides me all the same. It begs me to seek Arlo because I know he can help me. I know he *will* help me.

I turn my head and raise my chin, looking up to meet Arlo's steady gaze beside me. He's already watching me with guarded fear. With my stare, I beg him. I beg him to save me, to hurt me, to be my warden and inflict my punishment himself. I need him to help me make this sacrifice, and I just…

I just need him.

Arlo's brow furrows as he tilts his head. His blue eyes bore into mine, searching to understand the message I'm silently sharing. For moments, he looks at me with confusion, but when he receives the message, I *know* it.

His eyes widen, nostrils flare as he draws in a heavy breath, chest heaving as he fills his lungs. I nod, a brief, simple granting of my permission, telling of my need for him to help me fulfill my sacrifice.

Satisfied that he knows what I need, hoping on bated breath that he'll be brave enough to help me, I turn away and stare into the orange glow before me. My gaze tracks the small sparks of ember spewed from the crackling fire and floating away into the night. I catch on a single speck, stare at it as it flares with a small, white-hot glow. The way that it flickers and sparks steals my attention, and for a moment, my mind can drift, float away with the sparking ember until it's light dies out and it falls as ash to the ground.

I'm thankful for the moment I drift with it because it grants Arlo a moment to take me by surprise. All at once, his body presses to my side as his bare hand closes around my wrist.

Heat.

He's a different kind of heat beside me, the kind that offers warmth and peace. I feel it for a moment before he tugs, dragging me to the depths of hell.

With my arm stretched long and shoulder straining to keep myself back, he pushes my hand into the open flame. I scream as flames lick my hand, instantly searing my skin and ripping pain through my flesh like a thousand knives slicing around my hand all at once.

The pain is overwhelming, and it seems to last forever, even though my hand is dragged out of the fire just a moment after entering. A strangled scream claws up my throat as Arlo lowers beside me, falling to his knees. His fingers are still coiled tightly around my wrist. My entire arm trembles beyond control, shaking through my spine and amplifying my pain.

I need to see it.

I need to look.

I have to know how bad it is.

I dare look at my hand, and I can't stop my tears from falling. Blisters already form, but not just on my hand…they form on Arlo's fingers, too—they dipped into the flame where he held me.

He burned himself to help me.

A warped sense of gratitude for Arlo sweeps through me as powerfully as the flame licked across my skin.

I pant, trying to steady my panicked breathing, watching as Arlo slowly unwraps his hand from mine, one finger at a time. We both sigh in relief as his hand easily opens, thankful that our skin hasn't fused from the heat.

I look over at him, and he gives me a nod so imperceptible that I wonder if I saw it at all. He draws in a shuddering breath, and though his blue eyes are soft staring back at me, his voice is hard… as it needs to be.

"These scars will be yours to bear until you die, sinner," Arlo says. "Let them be a reminder of the pain you've caused our community with your sins…and as a preview of your pain to come for all you've done."

I have to turn away from him as he speaks. I know it's what he has to say, but it's still hard to know what's real. I turn my attention to Killian, looking up at him from my knees, waiting on bated breath for him to let my friend go.

Let her go.

Let Cambria go!

The seconds drag on like minutes—like hours—until finally, he lets go of her arm and releases her. Cambria rushes to step back, and my eyes widen in shock. I catch her gaze to find her eyes wide, surprised at herself for retreating—the very thing that landed me where I am right now. She comes forward as quickly as it happened, and no one else seems to have noticed. Their eyes are on me, but mine are on her. She looks horrified with herself, and I shake my head, trying to reassure her without words, though I know it doesn't work.

"You're lucky your warden is strong enough to do what's right, sinner," Killian says. "Cambria can finish serving tonight without burned flesh because your warden knows what you deserve." Killian lifts his gaze to Arlo. "Well done, brother. You did what was right."

Arlo shoves to his feet in a flash. "I'll return her to the Homestead."

"I can take her if you'd like to purge now," Owen offers.

Arlo's hand closes around the back of my elbow and he hoists me to my feet. "She's my responsibility," he says, whipping me around. "I'll return later when she's settled and secured."

Will he return?

Will he still purge tonight?

The thought plagues me, but the pain in my hand serves as a reminder of what could happen to him if our forbidden romance is discovered.

I'm lucky it was just my hand…lucky they didn't march me out into the village square and burn me to death on the spot. Maybe I was afforded the same leniency men are granted under the full moon—they still wanted their service, and they didn't want to be interrupted long enough to deliver me a swift and tormenting end. I'm spared for murder because these sordid men want to chase their lust. But spared tonight only means more to come. In the trials, they'll draw it out, the worst punishments of all.

Arlo leads me away from camp with his palm wrapped around my arm, and when we're nearly at the tree line, he whispers with urgency, "I'll take care of your hand at the Homestead. As soon as we're out of their sight, I need you to run with me. I'm sorry, Mercy."

I'll run with him, as far and as fast as he needs me to.

Who is this man?

What is he becoming?

Arlo Rainn was the hateful man who bound me, who shared me, who cut my hair, who used me.

But he's also the man who lied to his brothers, the man who held a knife to Hyatt's throat to save Ellary, who worshipped me beneath a thunderstorm in the meadow…The man who burned his own hand to help me burn mine.

He's capable of change, and that means that he's capable of changing Ember Glen.

chapter nineteen

ARLO

MERCY AND I run together through the forest and across the village square, surrounded only by the sounds of our footfalls and heavy breaths as we flee service. We turn and rush up the stone steps outside the Homestead, and she forgets for just a moment as she reaches down to lift her skirt so it doesn't catch on her feet. She hisses through her teeth as her burnt hand touches the fabric, but she shakes it off and continues onward, keeping pace with me.

We stop only long enough for me to unlock the front door, and I hurry her inside. I quickly brush off Delle and Theo when they try to stop us to ask about what they must have witnessed on camera. Mercy's hand is burnt and blistering, and taking care of it is my only immediate concern. We rush past them up the staircase, and I urge her down the hall faster, nudging her into the relative safety of her bedroom.

I slam the door shut behind us as she breezes past me with her hand wrapped tightly around her wrist, squeezing as though she fears her burnt hand might fall off if she doesn't hold on. Her face is twisted with pain, and she hisses through labored breaths.

I feel her pain, and it's so much worse than my own, but at least I know she still has feeling in her hand. I tried to pull her as high into the flame as I could—fire is fire, but I read once that flames are cooler at the top. The fact that she has pain is good. While her pain makes me shake with fury, it also means that the burns weren't deep enough to deaden her nerves.

If she's in pain, she'll heal.

It will hurt, but she will heal.

Striding past her, I head for the bathroom. "Come with me."

I head right for the vanity and turn on the faucet, adjusting the temperature until it's cool, but not cold. I pull the stopper for the drain and let the basin fill.

I turn and see her standing behind me, staring down at her pinkened, blistering flesh. She lifts her head to look at me—her face pale behind the dirt and dried blood, her expression distorted with pain.

"What do I do?" she asks with a whisper of worry under her breath.

"Come here," I tell her, though I go to her before she takes a single step.

Turning to stand beside her, I slip my arm around her, splay my palm against the small of her back, and press her forward as we move to the sink.

We stand side-by-side at the vanity, watching the basin fill, and when her head rises to look at her reflection in the mirror, I do the same. I'm surprised to find that we look…different. I suppose I shouldn't be surprised.

I *feel* different.

I feel like the world has shifted beneath my feet. Like heaven has drifted away to float somewhere among the stars, too far out of reach, and hell has risen to greet us here on Earth. And as for us… We look like the tortured souls who clawed their way up through the splintered ground.

We're both dressed all in black, hair flat but frizzy as the rain soak starts to dry. Mercy's starlight strands are flecked with mud, tangled from rolling in the meadow. Our clothes are crooked, clinging to us with remnants of dried blood and dirt coating our skin that didn't wash away from the storm.

Our eyes meet in the mirror, and I hold her stare. I allow myself to look at her—truly look at her—and in her eyes, I see everything I ever wanted. I see all the things I never knew I wanted, everything I could never have guessed wanting in my life until she was in it. My heart threatens to break my ribs as it tells me how I really feel about her fate.

How will I live when she's dead?

"Arlo?" She draws me from my thoughts.

I look down to see the sink is full, so I flip off the faucet. "Here." I gently wrap my burnt fingers around her wrist and guide her hand into the cool water—just as I had guided her to the flames.

She tenses, whimpering as I move her hand, but then she relaxes as the cool water soothes the burn. It soothes me, too. My fingertips are burnt from diving into the flame with her. It's a familiar pain for me—at least, it's one I can tolerate—but for her, it's new and undoubtedly overwhelming. Her entire hand is burnt from direct contact with a roaring flame, and I know it has to be excruciating.

"*Fuck*, this hurts," she mutters.

"I know. I'm sorry."

"It's not your fault." She turns her head to look at me, and I do the same.

There's a long pause, a moment of staring where we just look at each other. I take the time to study her features, to appreciate her beauty and commit the look of her right now to memory. She may resemble a tortured soul, but she's a tortured soul prepared for battle. She looks like a warrior—my fallen angel, like a soldier in the throes of battle, sent to save us.

She was sent to save me.

I let go of her hand so I can grab hold of her face with both of mine, unconcerned with the pain in my freshly burnt fingertips. She keeps her hand in the water as I hold her steady, bring my face closer until the tips of our noses touch.

"You're something more…so much more than I thought you were." I don't even know what I'm saying as my unstable emotions have the best of me, and they're taking control. I know that makes me vulnerable, unsafe, but I feel powerless to the way she's taken hold of me tonight.

My thumb strokes slowly across her cheek, dragging down the dried track of a tear, an imprint of the trail it made running through the patch of dirt there. Then, I kiss her slowly, taking my time to softly part her lips with mine, gently sweep my tongue between her teeth, and sensually taste her. The connection of our kiss ends naturally, gradually slowing to a stop, and I keep my eyes closed as our foreheads touch.

"Will you kiss me like that tomorrow?" she whispers.

My eyes open to find her already looking at me, our eyes so near that they're able to see straight through to our truest layer.

"Yes. And every day after until you take your last breath."

I swallow against a lump in my throat, suddenly struck by the morbid reality that the day of her last breath draws nearer with each passing second. I thought we'd both accepted that her death was coming, but now the thought of it vexes me.

Everything about her vexes me.

She's a sinner by our laws—which are meant to be the laws of God—but tonight, I knew she was more. She's an angel, a prophet, a sacrificial lamb. She's everything, yet she's nothing I can name. Whatever she is, she's mine, and I'm claiming her for eternity.

It takes too long for me to blink and drag myself from this moment of peace with her. Slowly, I lift my hands from her cheeks and sink my fingers into the cool water with hers.

"We need to soak the burn for fifteen minutes, let the skin cool," I instruct her. "Then we'll rinse it to make sure it's clean. You'll need to keep it covered to avoid infection. I'll have to go find bandages from our medical supplies…and something for the pain. It's gonna hurt like hell when we have to change the covering."

She stares at our hands in the water. "How do you know about healing a burn? Is that how…" Her head twists to look sideways at me. "Is that how you got the scars on your hands? Are they from burns?"

I hesitate. It's not something I ever planned to share with her before, but things are decidedly different now. Everything's different now, and I *want* to tell her. I want to share with her; I want her to know me, though the thought of her knowing me is terrifying.

"Yes."

"How? What happened?"

"It's not a very interesting story," I say evasively.

"I still want to hear it."

I sigh, slowly shifting my hand so my fingers come to rest above her wrist, careful to avoid her burns, though I'm eager to touch her.

"Before I came of age to purge, my urges were strong. I had to find a way to control myself, and my mental strength at the time was low. There was one night when our power had gone out," as it often does in the village, "and my mother lit candles and placed a few around the house. I was thirteen and in the quiet of night, my mind raced with thoughts from the Impulse—sexual thoughts that drove me mad with lust. It would be another year before I could purge under the full moon.

"At the time, I was still trying to understand what the Impulse was and how nights of service would help me satisfy those urges if I could just wait a little while longer to indulge. So I felt that I needed a way to control myself until then…some method to tame the urges until I was old enough to enact them.

"That night, I sat alone at the kitchen table, long after everyone else had gone to bed, and I watched the flame of a lone, lit candle dance. The firelight had me mesmerized. It captivated me, held my attention, and before long, it allowed my thoughts to drift away from impurity.

"I didn't burn myself that night. The first time was a few nights later when I had urges to defile myself. I felt so much shame that I would've done anything to make it stop."

The shame I felt back then over my sexual needs washes over me as I tell her this. It strikes me with adrenaline, making some part of me want to run from the room and pretend I never told her this, pretend it never happened. Yet something in my soul urges me to keep speaking.

"I went to the kitchen and found one of my mother's candles. I lit it with a match, took it to my room, and watched the flame, but watching wasn't enough when my needs were so strong. I wanted to touch it…so I did.

"I held my hand over the flame and let it dance across my skin. I'd nearly screamed that first time because I couldn't seem to draw my hand away, feeling as though I needed to let it burn, and burn deeply, so I let it.

"A few days later, it was a full moon, and I spied the servants leaving their homes in the village, all walking away as the sun was setting to head for the village square on their way to the forest. That was the first night I really saw the servants, recognized them as women, saw their beauty, and found lust in anticipation of purging with them in the next year.

"The lust made me sick, Mercy. It was unholy because I wasn't yet of age to have these urges, and I couldn't understand why God gave them to me if He didn't want me to purge yet." I turn my face to the mirror, seeing my brow furrowed with the internal dissonance I'm feeling over the memory.

Why would God give me urges before He meant for me to purge them? Why would He give men urges at all if it's so sinful for them to act on them outside of service?

Why haven't I questioned this all along?

Mercy meets my stare in our reflection.

I spit out the words in a rush. "I lit a fire in our backyard that night and stuck both hands into the rising flames."

She gasps, probably because she knows what that feels like now…excruciating.

"My mother treated my wounds that night." I pause. "She told me she was proud of me."

"What?"

"She was proud of me for finding a way to control myself, to suppress the Impulse until I became of age to purge. She encouraged it; she gave me candles and matches to keep in my bedroom." My gaze shifts, staring off at nothing as I hear my words out loud—how strange they sound. I've been setting myself on fire for years to combat the flames of desire sparking within me.

Why is it okay for me to burn the flesh God gave me, but not to use that flesh for pleasure outside of service?

I shake my head, blinking back to Mercy in the mirror. "That was normal for every boy my age, I suppose. We all had our vices and means of self-control when we were younger. Once I came of age and was able to purge, it lessened those urges on normal days. It made sense then, all of it. Purge monthly and the entire community benefits from our collective weakened Impulse for the rest of the month."

Silence greets me, and I let it hang until she speaks.

"I'm sorry, Arlo. You were only a child trying to do what you thought was right."

Her eyes are soft as she looks at me in the reflection, her expression compassionate, sinking a hook into my gut for the way it reels me in. She looks at me as though she were looking at a child, as though she somehow sees innocence within me, but there's none left.

"We've been told what was right and wrong every day of our lives. You were just a child and you—" She lets out a heavy sigh. "I'm so sorry you were made to feel that hurting yourself was praiseworthy. I never thought…I didn't think about the men of Ember Glen and how they were raised, how they were harmed."

I chuckle briefly and shake my head. "Why would you think of it? Why would anyone? It's just the way it is. It's the way things have always been, and it's worked. No one ever had any reason to think differently…" I pause, meeting her stare again to give her a meaningful look, "Except for you. What happened tonight was no accident. I think…I think God sent you to spark change."

Her lips fall open, her face loosening with relief at my words. She looks like I've told her everything she ever wanted to hear, and perhaps I have. Perhaps she only needed someone's acceptance and understanding to find her real strength, her true purpose.

She doesn't respond, and we let silence fill the space. I wonder what she's thinking, but I don't ask. I let her have the quiet because this day has been filled with so much damn noise. I shift closer, let our bodies touch as we soak our burnt hands—hands we burnt together in sacrifice for one another.

Sacrifice.

It's the theme of her next trial, and perhaps the entire meaning of our relationship. I'm risking everything in being so open with her, slicing open my chest and letting my heart bleed out for her. Yet at the risk of bleeding my veins dry, it's a sacrifice I choose to make for her—one I choose to make *with* her.

It's in this moment that I realize I'm going to break the promise I made her tonight—I'll be here for her through her trials, and I'll take care of her every need, be her true warden in every wholesome and depraved manner she demands. But I am not going to live my life as an honorable member of the Control so I can become an Elder and maybe effect some minor change decades in the future.

No.

I'll live honorably long enough to find a way out of this, to figure out how to take her safely away from Ember Glen, or burn the whole damn village down myself, even if it means she and I are the only two people left in existence.

And if I fail, then I'll die along with her because I can no longer fathom the thought of living without her.

chapter twenty

Mercy

THE NIGHT WAS long and painful.

Arlo cleaned my burns and wrapped my hand with sterile gauze. He covered his own with a fresh pair of leather gloves that he'd pulled from a store of them kept in his room. I was concerned about him wearing gloves over his burns, but he assured me they made a good covering to keep them clean, and that his injuries weren't nearly as bad as mine.

Once our injuries were tended to, I was forced to return to the room downstairs to watch the remainder of the service with Delle. Theo and Arlo each had to take a turn and leave us for a couple of hours— it was a night of service after all, and they were expected to purge.

Though there might have been doubt as recently as last night about whether he would purge with another servant, there's no doubt in my mind now that he didn't. Something changed between us, something powerful, as though we were struck by lightning in that thunderstorm and forever altered by the electricity.

When he told me about his scars last night, I made a decision, and it feels like one of the most significant choices I've ever made…

I chose to give him my trust.

I trust Arlo Rainn.

There's something freeing in giving him that, in choosing to assume he truly does care for me rather than fear him. It's freeing to make the choice to see the truth in him. And the truth is that he's a victim of Ember Glen as much as I am.

It broke my heart to hear how his mother praised him for harming himself to suppress his desire. I can't imagine how damaging that would be for the mind of a thirteen-year-old boy. He was just a child. He was preached in shame and guilt from the beginning, and his behavior as an adult is no wonder to me now.

It's not an excuse for all the ways he's harmed me—he's responsible for the choices he's made—but I now understand what shaped his mind in his youth, and I feel responsible for helping him see the truth. I *want* to be responsible for helping him heal, breaking down his walls, finding his compassion—not just for me, but for all the people of Ember Glen. I don't owe him that, but it's what I want for him. Before I'm dead and gone, I want him to see what I see, know what I know, feel what I feel.

The sun is rising as I stand beside Arlo in the village square. A long line is formed by the Control, the seven members stretched out across the open space and standing side-by-side. Their purpose is to thank the women for their service last night as they make their way across the gravel, heading for Sanctuary.

I bathed last night, and all the dirt and blood are scrubbed clean from my skin. I've been made to put on a red gown, as my black servant's clothes were insulting to the women who served. I've been asked to stand in line and thank my sisters for their service along with the Control because, as Killian put it, I should be showing my respect for their additional efforts to make up for the loss of me in service.

I don't want to thank them.

I want to tell them I'm sorry that they have to serve. I'm sorry they're hurting, that they're used and abused. I'm sorry that I can't save them, but I hope that one day, Arlo will become an Elder and make this place better for the generations to come.

I want to be defiant and snide, but I'm entirely too exhausted to do anything but stand here. And whatever medicine Arlo fed me a half an hour ago seems to be mingling with my system now. It's lovely because the pain in my hand is gradually dulling and fading, but it's also making me uneasy…My head is feeling lighter, freer, like my cares are slowly slipping away, and I'm looking at the world through rose-colored glasses.

What medicine is this, and why don't the servants have access to it?

We've suffered so many nights of pain, and the medicine we had was much weaker than this.

The world feels steady beneath my feet, though my body seems to lightly sway. I'm not sure whether the sway is real or it only feels as though it's happening as this powerful medicine takes hold. Either way, it's nice, like being soothed and rocked in the arms of a breeze that moves me slowly. Lulled into compliance, I quietly thank my sisters in service as they pass me and Arlo in small groups and clusters.

As more and more servants pass, my anxiety grows, creating a strange sense of nausea as it combats the calming effect of the medicine. I wait on bated breath to see Ellary and Cambria return. I stare at the forest, hoping with each new emergence of women dressed in black that I'll see them both there, walking on their own two feet.

It feels like hours have passed when I finally spot two figures emerge from the trees. As Arlo and I are so far down the line, I can't quite make out who it is yet. I lean forward, peeking around Arlo and straining my eyes because hope tells me it's them. The two women are walking side by side, and though they're slow, they're on their feet and moving independently. As they get closer, I recognize the bob in Cambria's steps, the slight limp in the cadence of her walk.

It's them.

Ellary and Cambria are okay.

I let out a heavy breath as relief washes over me. I watch their faces as they walk past the line of the Control, hoping for a moment of eye contact, a hint of recognition, some connection—however small—to acknowledge our years of friendship.

I know it's selfish, but a part of me wants their recognition of what I did for them both last night. I know it's unlikely that either of them truly understand why I ran for Ellary or why I sacrificed my hand to spare Cambria's. I know their gratitude shouldn't matter to me because I don't imagine they'll have any. I don't blame them for that—the beliefs they've fallen victim to aren't their fault.

It's just that I have so much love and appreciation for them, for all the times I spoke out of turn and they gently shushed me, for all the times I expressed my strong emotions over our fate and they calmly fought to bring me back to faith. They were gentle and kind with me for so many years when they didn't have to be.

Tears spring to my eyes as I realize how much danger I put them in, especially through my teenage years, yet they never dissociated with me. They stood by my side and tried to help me become a better servant.

Our beliefs were never aligned, but they cared for me regardless—they helped me unselfishly until they simply couldn't anymore. Perhaps I would have found my way to understand God in the way they see Him if Ember Glen had been rooted in kindness and love rather than pain and sacrifice and suffering.

"Thank you for your service, ladies," Ryker says to them from further down the line. One after the other, each man of the Control thanks my friends for suffering to their benefit as they make their way to Sanctuary.

As they come closer, my gaze drops at the hint of color in Ellary's hand, contrasting against her black clothes. She holds a plucked bundle of red and purple wildflowers from the meadow—

the crimson petals match the dried blood which encircles her arm. My pulse races at the memory of last night, finding her so weak and bleeding, so afraid that she would die by Hyatt's hand.

She didn't die.

She's okay.

And Cambria's hand isn't burnt because I spared her.

Arlo helped me spare her.

I glance at Arlo, giving him a silent thank you for being my strength, for pushing my hand into the flame when I couldn't do it myself…but he doesn't look at me. He stares straight ahead, distant, cut-off, unreachable in this moment. Strangely, I understand the disconnect, and somehow, I'm not upset by it.

"Thank you for your service," Arlo mutters as Ellary and Cambria approach.

"Thank you for your—"

My words cut short as Ellary's hand opens, and the wildflowers fall, floating to land on the ground at my feet. I stare down at the bundle of amethyst and ruby, with their emerald-green stems. I'm lost in them for a moment, but soon after, I lift my gaze and find them both looking at me. I meet their eyes, sharing a brief moment of connection I've been longing for with each of them. A nearly imperceptible smile touches Ellary's cheeks, and though I see no smile from Cambria's lips, I see it in her eyes.

Gratitude.

My chest sinks as all the air in my lungs leaves me in a rush. They still have love for me, and I hadn't realized how much I needed to know that until this very moment.

As they turn away, continuing past us toward Sanctuary, I drop my head to gaze at the wildflowers at my feet. I start to bend, reaching to pick them up, but a shiny black shoe blocks my path, startling me, causing me to sharply rise and jump back. The shoe slams down to stomp on the flowers, twisting and tearing apart the bundle, petals pulling away from the stems and grinding into the gravel. I already know it's Killian before my eyes rise from the ruined bundle to confirm.

When he meets my furious gaze, he cocks his head to the side. "I guess we'll be keeping a closer eye on Ellary and Cambria from now on."

I feel the weight of his words sink through my stomach, heavy and nauseating. Though I'm so grateful for their gesture—the connection, the love shared through those flowers—I'm so regretful that they chose to do that. A shared look would've been enough for me.

But also…I'm proud.

I'm proud because they knew extending such a gesture could bring a more watchful eye to them, and they did it anyway. Not only did they do it, but they did it right in front of the Control. It makes me sick that they'll be watched more closely, but at the same time, elation swells in my chest, puffing me up with pride and making me feel all the more powerful.

"I guess you will." I stare back at Killian, hardening my expression, though the medicine in my system tries to soften me.

I hold his eyes, unwilling to look away first, emboldened by the chemicals in my system. A few moments pass where I wonder if we'll remain locked in this stare all day because I'm stubbornly resolute to hold it until he walks away—and he probably feels the same. A few more servants begin to cross the square, and Killian is forced to look away first, drawing his gaze from mine with a sharp whip of his head before returning to his spot in line to thank the servants.

The second that he moves, I feel awash with relief, and joy over the flowers from Ellary's hand creeps in with it. I draw my lip between my teeth to try and hide my growing smile as I side-step closer to Arlo.

I don't dare look at him right now—I'm too afraid I'll grab him and kiss him in this medicated state, which is starting to feel like inebriation. But I dare to let my hand float sideways, inching closer and closer until the back of my hand bumps against his leather-clad knuckles.

He flinches and jerks his hand away, but I know I only have to wait. Soon, his hand returns to his side as he lets out a sigh. His arm floats toward mine this time, repeating my gesture such that our knuckles kiss.

Though his hands are covered, I can feel him the same as if we were touching skin-to-skin. The leather gloves are a part of him as much as his scars. It's a special thing to me when he removes them to touch me, to feel me, to deliver pleasure…

And even with the barrier of his gloves between our skin, I feel everything he's feeling through our simple touch: elation, pride, hope, and fear. All of it mingles, swirling around our barely touching hands like a lasso.

As the last of the servants return to Sanctuary, and Park declares that they're all accounted for, the Control move to gather inside the Homestead. Delle and I trail along as we must. The men begin to chat, each of them moving to gather around the sunburst tile in an almost unintentional manner. Arlo whispers that Delle and I should wait by the staircase, in his and Theo's line of sight where they stand opposite the steps. I wobble up three of them before whirling around and plopping my bottom on the step, while Delle lowers hesitantly to sit beside me.

"Are you okay?" she asks.

I nod and give her a quick smile.

"We need to make a plan regarding Hyatt Price," Wesley says. "Park and I moved his body when the sun rose. I suppose we can ask the coroner's wife to begin the embalmment since he'll be resting from the purge." He sighs. "The Elders won't be happy at this loss of life."

"Mercy should be executed immediately," Killian snarls with angered conviction.

A laugh bursts uncontrollably from my chest, and Delle's hand shoots out to latch around my wrist in warning. I didn't mean to let it out—and I know the medication is to blame—but I need to control myself or they very well may execute me today.

Seven pairs of enraged eyes are upon me—even Arlo is angered with my outburst. I can't help but smile when I look at him, though. He's really quite handsome when he's angry.

"Mercy, stop…" Delle mutters under her breath, and I glance over to see the worry on her face.

The medication—I need to control myself.

I nod at her and clear my throat, forcing myself to remember the seriousness of my circumstances. Slowly, the men turn their attention away from me and back to each other.

"There's a reason she wasn't executed last night," Owen says. "As a participant in the Trials of Dissension, she's not a servant, and can't be considered as such."

Killian cocks his head. "And how should she be considered differently, Owen? She *murdered* a man in cold-blood."

"That's for the seven of us to decide together," Owen says. "Now that we've all purged and have clear minds, we can make that decision."

"I vote for immediate execution," Killian declares.

Park narrows his eyes in consideration. "But she's already a trial participant. Won't that make for a more meaningful example in her death?"

"So we're no longer pretending that one might pass the trials and survive, then?" My words fly from my mouth before I can stop them. "You're suddenly comfortable stating with abject certainty that death will meet us?"

All their heads turn in my direction, but I look at Arlo. He's fuming at me, staring me down with his bright blue eyes, surely wishing I would just keep my damn mouth shut. I nearly want to laugh, imagining the thoughts running through his head—surely, he regrets giving me a medicine which eases my pain while lowering my inhibitions.

I try to bring anger back to my mind. Shaking Delle's hand from my wrist, I cross my arms over my chest, and narrow my stare at Arlo. But everything just feels so laughable in my current state—the expression he wears is funny. He cocks an eyebrow, trying to command me with a look, but I think he knows what's happening here because I see the twitch of humor through the corners of his lips…those thick, kissable lips and the perfect tongue he hides behind them.

Stop thinking about his tongue…

Suddenly, nothing is funny, and the air around me is *hot*. Desire for him replaces inappropriate humor at my situation, and though I'd prefer not to feel heavy between my thighs right now, it's certainly preferable to laughing out loud every time they mention my looming death.

"At this point, yes," Killian grumbles. "Death is assured for you, Mercy Madness."

"And what about me?" Delle asks at my side, her voice anxious and weary all at once.

They all look at her, eyeing her cautiously, as if no one cares to confirm the truth for her. Without another word, they turn back to their little circle, effectively ignoring her.

If the trials are crafted to ensure my death, then Delle's death will come, too—and now the hopelessness of our situation has been confirmed for her. I hear the air leave her lungs, and it's sobering. I scoot closer to Delle and slide my arm across the small of her back to hug her to my side.

"The remaining trials will set an important example for the

other servants," Park continues. "It's why we chose them for Mercy in the first place. I say we allow the trials to deliver her punishment for Hyatt's death."

"If it brings about her death anyway, I agree," Wesley adds. "Today we should focus on planning to honor Hyatt. Mercy has her warden to keep watch over her and ensure she doesn't cause any more trouble." He nods at Arlo.

"Yet her warden couldn't stop her last night," Ryker snips, stealing an agitated glance at Arlo.

"That was a fluke," Theo says. "She surprised us both. She moved quickly."

"I did my best to stop her," Arlo mutters, gazing off into the distance. He defends himself, though it's clear to me he struggles with his words. I know it's hard for him to let me take the blame for this. "I lost sight of her in the storm and just didn't make it in time."

"It's okay, brother," Killian says, his voice so unusually calm and clear that it surprises me. "You did well once you caught her." Killian looks around the circle at each of the Control. "He pushed her hand into the fire to punish her when she refused to do it herself."

I didn't refuse...I chose to do it for Cambria!

I just needed Arlo's help.

"Just put it to a vote," Arlo snarls through his rising frustration. "Death today or death through the trials." His fingers curl into fists at his sides.

"Okay," Owen says. "Who wishes to move forward with the Trials of Dissension as the method of execution for Mercy Madness?"

The method of execution...

The way that phrase sucks the air from the room is striking. It's a definitive confirmation that there really never was any chance for me. It should cripple me, but I find it strengthens me instead. If death is assured for me, then the only thing I have left to lose is time.

Every man in the circle raises their hand to move forward with the trials—even Arlo does, though the lift of his arm is strained. He has to vote, and it only makes sense to vote for me to have more time.

In fact, all the men in the circle vote surprisingly to grant me more time in this life—everyone except for Killian, which was no surprise, either.

"I'm sorry," Owen says, looking at Killian. "Majority rules. We continue with the trials as planned."

"This is a mistake," Killian says, his voice remarkably steady. "I want it known that I don't support this decision."

"It's known," Arlo says.

"Don't forget that you'll have a say in how the trials are carried out," Owen reminds Killian. "Your voice will be important as we make those decisions."

"That's right," Killian says as the corners of his lips quirk into a half-smile. "Thank you for the reminder, Owen. That does make me feel better."

"Good," Owen says, "because we need to shift our focus to Hyatt Price."

"We'll need someone to go to the village and notify Hyatt's family," Wesley says. "Any volunteers?"

The room falls into silence.

"I'll go," Arlo says. "I'll take Mercy and make her explain what happened."

A few dark chuckles rumble through the room in appreciation of this idea.

"Yes, take the murderer herself to tell them of his death." Ryker laughs. "Let her know the full impact of the pain she's caused."

"I don't think it's wise to—"

"It's what she deserves," Killian says, cutting Owen off. "She must face his family's pain first-hand. Have her tell them everything she did. Have her tell his wife why she's now a widower, his children why they no longer have a father."

"I'm good with that," Theo agrees, though he casts a sideways glance at Arlo. "It will allow us to take the time we need to meet with the Elders and make arrangements to honor Hyatt. And let's not forget that today is a day of rest for *all* the men of Ember Glen. We, too, need to recover from this purge."

He's met with murmurs of agreement while I'm left confused. I don't understand why Arlo is volunteering to share the news of Hyatt's death, but more than that, why he would want me to be the one to deliver it.

It's not safe for me to go to the village, even with my warden. The people who hate me for my sins could riot, could seize me, could drag me from his side and take me to my execution—though I suppose it shouldn't worry me anymore, knowing that my execution is assured one way or another.

"Good." Leaving the circle, Arlo cuts across the sunburst and heads for me. "We'll go now." He reaches across the bottom steps and grips my elbow, tugging me forward.

"I don't want to—"

"You should've thought about that last night when you murdered a man, sinner."

I know he doesn't mean it with his nasty tone, but the act still hurts me. It wasn't that long ago that he thought of me as nothing more than a sinner to be condemned—it would be so easy for him to switch back in his thinking.

Regardless, I've chosen to trust him, so I don't resist as he pulls me through the front door.

chapter twenty-one
Mercy

ARLO'S PALM IS wrapped around my bicep as he leads me down the steps in front of the Homestead. I'm glad for his gentle hand there to steady me as the light-headed sway makes me feel a little uneven on my feet.

"I really don't think this is a good idea," I tell him as we land on the gravel-covered square. "I'm feeling a little…off."

"I'm well aware. I knew it was a risk giving you that medication, but I couldn't stand seeing you in pain any longer."

Our feet crunch over the pebbles as we walk forward, heading across the large open space toward the village.

"I don't think I can control my mouth. I'll say things I shouldn't to Hyatt's family."

He lets out a small chuckle. "Somehow, I don't think you'll say anything they weren't already thinking. I imagine Stefanie will find relief."

"Stefanie?"

"Hyatt's wife. She was a friend of my sister's when we were younger."

"Oh." I think I'm leaning because the world feels a little sideways.

Arlo stops too suddenly and turns to face me, gripping my arms in his hands and dipping to look at me squarely. "Are you okay? Did I give you too much?"

"How would I know? And anyway, I feel incredible for a woman whose death is currently being plotted by seven angry men." I grin, unable to feel upset about the truth when my mind is so fuzzy, when it makes everything seem so much funnier than it really is.

"How's the pain?"

"Gone."

"Good."

"Will it be gone forever now?"

"No. Just until the medication wears off."

"And how soon will that be? Can I have some more?"

He pushes back on my arms, and I realize it's because I'm leaning into him unconsciously, and he's trying to keep an appropriate distance. I know we're out in the open and could be watched. I'm capable of reasonable thought; I just seem to be a little beyond my means in controlling my spoken words and my movements.

"We'll see," he says. "I'm not sure it's such a good idea for you to be in this state for too long considering you and I have secrets to keep."

"I would never share our secrets, Warden Rainn." I pull my arms from his grip and raise my hands, showing him my palms. "See? I'm not even touching you right now," I appreciatively look him up and down, "even though I'd certainly like to be."

I take a small step back, then reluctantly drag my eyes away. I bend to gather my skirt at my thighs, hoisting it up to keep the length of it from catching on my black boots. I turn and shuffle off in the direction of the village. I force myself to continue onward, trying to ignore the insistent flutter of my heart which demands me to return to him at once and beg him to kiss me.

But then a thought I can't ignore bursts into my mind, and I stop abruptly, whipping around to face him.

"Mercy!" he calls out my name as he nearly crashes into me.

Arlo grabs hold of my arms again to keep me upright as I

stagger backward a step, gasping at his proximity. I hadn't expected him to follow me so quickly, let alone to be right behind me when I stopped.

Insistently, the words fly from my mouth, unbothered by our near collision. "Where do the medical supplies come from? Who makes them? How did you get the medicine you fed me, and why don't the servants have access to it?"

Why haven't I wondered about all this before?

"Slow down," he commands, his eyebrows knitting together with concern. "You're racing in every sense of the word, and it's beginning to worry me."

I make a show of taking a slow, deep breath before asking more calmly, "Where do the medical supplies come from?"

"From our medical supply store."

I huff. "Yes, I know, but where do they come from before that?"

His look of concern morphs into one of confusion—or more accurately, it's a look expressing internal conflict. "I don't know how to answer that."

"Try."

"The Elders send us everything we need in Ember Glen."

"But what does that mean? How do they send it? Where do they send it from? Where *are* they?"

"You're asking me for answers I don't have, Mercy."

"Yet they're reasonable questions that should be asked, aren't they?"

"They are…"

"Surely someone has asked them before."

"And surely no answers were given."

His hands tighten around my biceps as he takes a step closer. I'm so acutely aware of his presence, the minty smell of his breath as it breezes over my lips, the way my skin tingles beneath his touch, the way my body sways toward him so naturally. Perhaps it's some magic love potion he fed me instead of medicine which fills me with euphoric bliss.

No.

My feelings toward Arlo are natural in every sense. The things I feel for him could never be crafted or manufactured.

He lowers his voice to a whisper, though the square is entirely empty. "People don't ask questions as often as you, and most don't question anything at all. The Elders and the Control prefer it that way. There's a rule for everything, and when there isn't one that meets our needs…The Elders take time to review the Impulse Edict…and *always* return with an answer from God."

I can feel my face twist as I work through what he's telling me while combating my quickening pulse at his nearness.

"Are you saying that," I pause to gather my thoughts, trying to coordinate them with my speech, "that the Impulse Edict has an answer for everything…even when it doesn't?"

His eyes flicker as they narrow briefly, his forehead wrinkling as if speaking this to me now is the first time he's really thought of it. "Yes, I think that's what I'm saying."

"Do you think they're amending the word of God as they see fit?"

His eyes brighten with awareness and widen with epiphany, his expression softening with instant resignation to the truth. "Yes." He nods slowly. "Yes, it makes sense."

The medication is strong, but not strong enough to cloud the seriousness of this revelation. Still, I feel lighter at this heavy news because it's so telling of how willing Arlo is to change; it tells me that he must have considered these things before, that some small part of him must have wondered and questioned before I came along, and he simply prayed away his so-called blasphemous thoughts.

There is a natural goodness somewhere within Arlo Rainn's soul. It's only been buried too long, too deeply for it to find its way to the surface on its own. Maybe it's haughty to think this, but I wonder if he only needed me to find it and dig it out.

"Do you think anyone has questioned them on this before?"

"I think it's likely," he says, watching me with curiosity and consideration. "Someone must have noticed this happening before and said something about it. Or perhaps they just wondered in silence. I don't know anything for sure, but..." He looks off toward Sanctuary, getting lost in thought.

"But, what?"

His grip loosens and his hands fall away from my arms. "I've been reading your mother's journal, and—"

"You've been reading it?"

Anxiety swells. I'd nearly forgotten about my mother Mira's journal. I was reading it in the meadow the day the Control came to take me away and announced my forced participation in the Trials of Dissension. Arlo had taken the journal from me then, and we'd never spoken another word about it. My mind has been too preoccupied to think of it, but now that he's brought it up, I feel an ache in my heart for not having it through my final days.

"I want it back," I demand.

"Are you aware that there are pages missing?"

I blink at him. "What?"

"Three pages are missing. It's clear they've been torn out."

"I'm...I'm aware."

"Do you know where they are?"

"I don't understand how this has anything to do with—"

"Have you read it? Every word of it?"

"Mostly, yes, but I—"

"Do you remember the passage she wrote about her mother, and how she told her about the strange and untimely death of two members of the Control when she was a child?"

"Strange and untimely," I repeat, the two words striking my

memory and bringing the passage back to mind. "Yes, I remember that. She wrote that they died within days of each other, but their deaths were labeled…" I pause, trying to draw the words from the back corner of my mind. "They were labeled 'tragic mysteries.'"

"Doesn't that strike you as odd? It makes me wonder what information they discovered—"

"Before meeting a strange and untimely end…" I nod, understanding dawning on me.

"One of the torn-out pages was right after that passage. Mercy, I have to ask you…Did you tear out those pages?"

I shake my head. "No. They were already torn out when I found the journal."

"Where did you find it?"

"I was cleaning out my father's house in the village after he died a few months ago. It was in the drawer of the table beside his bed, though it was odd finding it there."

A wave of dizziness ripples, and I feel myself begin to sway.

Arlo reaches out to grip my shoulders and steady me. "Why was it odd?"

"Because it wasn't there before."

"Could the torn-out pages have been in that drawer?"

"No. There was nothing there but the journal. I cleared out the house."

"Is there a place you can think of where your mother might have hidden them?"

I feel my forehead wrinkle. "No, I don't think so. I'd imagine the pages were destroyed. There must have been something written on them that she didn't want seen." My eyes flutter shut as a peaceful exhaustion flows through me. "You smell too good to stand so close to me, Warden Rainn."

"But she was condemned for her sins," he murmurs, almost to himself. I blink open my eyes to find his narrowed in consideration.

"The Control would have confiscated her belongings." He looks at me. "Then how did you find her journal fourteen years after her death in a place where it wasn't before?"

"Hmm?"

"Do you think your father kept her journal all these years and left it for you when he got sick? He was ill for some time, wasn't he?"

I nod. "Yes, for a few years."

"I wonder who tore out the pages then…your father or your mother."

"Or someone else. Maybe someone else tore them out and kept them. Or destroyed them. There's really no way for us to know." I pause, and my head falls to the side. "Do you think those men who died knew something?"

"I think it's possible."

"And you think those three torn pages will have anything to say about it?"

"I don't know, but it makes me curious."

"The curiosity puts you at risk, doesn't it? Digging into Ember Glen's secrets. And sharing it with me is even riskier…"

I'm tempted—*so tempted*—to reach out to him, to place my uninjured hand on his chest, slip my fingers down to hook the chain that draws across from the button of his waistcoat to its pocket, and tug him closer. Remembering we're out in the open, I take a small, uneven step backward.

"It doesn't matter to me anymore. Not after…not after last night." He takes a step closer. "I don't expect I'll live long enough for it to matter anyway, and if I do, then it means I'm not held to our laws anymore."

He doesn't expect to live long enough?

"What do you mean by that? You and I had a deal, Arlo. You're going to obey and do what you have to do so you can live long enough to become an Elder and enact real change."

"Who's to say I'll have any more power as an Elder than I have now? Perhaps they're beholden to governance we know nothing about…I'm not sure of anything anymore, Mercy."

"That doesn't explain what you mean when you say you won't live long enough…What are you saying, Arlo?"

He sighs, moving closer still, though he doesn't reach out to touch me. Instead, he lets tension build between us, silently lingering in the way it has to out here in the open.

"I'm saying there are secrets being kept, and I intend to find out what they are. I intend to find out precisely what the Elders mean when they tell me that Ember Glen has been blessed by God with all the supplies and resources we need to sustain our way of life. I'm going to find out the truth and expose every secret."

He looks deep within me, catching hold of something in my soul that tugs me forward, and my body leans in his direction.

Squeezing my shoulder, he leans his head forward to speak close to my ear. "I'm going to find a way to save you, even if it kills me, because I won't live long enough to be an Elder without you. I never would've seen the truth without you."

"What did I do?"

"You questioned. You questioned everything, and it made me start to think. Because of you, Mercy, my eyes are open when they've always been closed."

I step backward, not because I want to get away from him, but because the meaning behind his words strikes me so hard that it overcomes me.

His expression hardens, and in a rush, he swoops forward, reaching out to snatch me by the wrist and tug me against his chest. "Would you *stop* backing away from me? It makes me want to chase you. Sweet sin, you're killing me."

I blink up at his blue eyes staring down at me. "Somehow I don't imagine it will be much of a chase in my current state."

A quiet growl rumbles through his chest. "That's what I'm afraid of."

"Then…you should probably release me and step back." I tell him what he *should* do, though it's not what I *want* him to do.

"Just tell me one thing before I do."

"Anything," I say too quickly.

"Is it as painful for you as it is for me?"

"What?"

"To want me now and know you can't have me until later?"

All the air leaves my lungs in a rush. "Does your question imply that I can have you later?"

He clicks his tongue. "If you can't answer my question, then I guess I don't have to answer yours."

"Yes," I blurt. "It hurts in unimaginable ways."

His eyes roam my body, narrowed in scrutiny as though he's studying me. "Does it ache between your thighs?"

I force out a whimpered breath as my body floats forward, and I sink through my weak knees trying to drag myself back.

For a moment, he draws me closer, his palms wrapping around the sides of my waist. He leans in to whisper against my ear, "I long to soothe all your aches, starlight. The ache of your hand, of your heart, of your swollen cunt—"

"You have to stop." I bring my palms quickly against his chest and try to push, but a sharp sting of pain shoots through my burnt hand. I hiss and pull it back as it cuts past the strength of this dizzying medication and the additional intoxication brought forth by his words, by his touch, by his very presence.

"You have to be careful with that hand, Mercy. It needs to heal."

"Then I need you to stop saying things that make me want to touch you."

"Oh, starlight, I doubt you'll ever stop wanting that." He smiles and those long dimples cut lines through his beard, and it sets a dangerous pace for my pounding heart.

I feel light-headed and weak again, overcome with that euphoric, pain-free bliss. My heart flutters, and my hand floats up to cover my chest as my feet stutter backward. "I think I need to lie down…"

"Not now. Come here." He turns sideways, facing the path that leads down to the village, holding out his arm for me. I slowly link my arm through his.

The tension transforms to comfortable silence as he leads me ahead, and though I imagine my mind should be swirling with questions and possibilities from this conversation, I find it to be unusually—and peacefully—quiet.

We cross the remainder of the square, and the gravel narrows to a pathway about fifteen feet wide. It gently slopes down a hill toward the center of the village, nestled in a valley below. Carefully, Arlo leads me down the path.

"Why did you volunteer to deliver the news to Hyatt's family?" I ask quietly. "And why did you bring me?"

He lets out a sigh as we walk. "To spare you, believe it or not."

"To spare me of what?"

"Of the likelihood that my brothers would come to the conclusion that all seven of us should bring you to deliver this news. It was a rash decision to volunteer, but it was a choice I made for you. I feared them dragging you through the village, parading you through town, calling people out of their homes to judge and belittle you, call you awful names and humiliate you."

I glance up at the sky. "Well, the day is still young."

I trip over my own feet and stumble forward, though I don't fall far. Arlo quickly lassoes his arm around my waist to balance me, and I can't help but laugh a little.

"I also didn't want my brothers realizing I gave you medicine that I shouldn't have, but in your current state, that nearly seems unavoidable now."

"The servants should have this…whatever it is." I have to fight the overwhelming urge to tilt my head and rest it upon his shoulder. "Why have something so potent and not give it to the people who need it most? Killian broke Cambria's toes the night I ran from service. Cut tiny marks all over her body with a knife, too. Did you know that? Can you imagine that suffering for days and weeks after service with painkillers as weak as what we're given?"

"You're meant to revel in the pain—"

"Oh, *fuck* off. You men know *nothing* of the pain we endure."

He's quiet for a few beats, but then he says, "I'm learning."

I'm learning.

The words fly straight from his mouth and strike me forcefully in the chest. They imprint on my heart in a way I wouldn't have expected them to.

I'm learning.

It's not an apology for what we've been through.

It's not an excuse for how he's contributed to our suffering.

It's nothing more than an acknowledgment that the suffering exists, yet it feels like so much more. Recognition of a problem must come before it can be addressed, and those two words express recognition in a powerful way.

I'm learning.

It's active, present, on-going.

Arlo is learning, and more importantly, willing to un-learn all the wrongs he's been taught.

As we follow the curve down the gentle slope, the village comes into view. It's a large, chaotic cluster of homes and shops built of dark hardwood. They're all crowded together in the center of a valley scooped out between large grassy hills.

We descend the slope and approach the outskirts of the village. We're not met with the usual noise and bustle of the people going about their daily business, but that's to be expected today. It's always quiet after a night of service. The men purged last night and will have the day to rest before returning to their work tomorrow, and because of the lack of ambient noise, Arlo lowers his voice before he speaks. "We'll be brief with Hyatt's family."

"What if they're angry? What if they demand my immediate execution? What if the villagers take it upon themselves to drag me away and burn me at the stake?"

"I won't allow that to happen."

"You can't control that."

"I can, and I will."

I look over at him as we continue onward, walking behind a row of houses toward the path that cuts through the center of the village. He shares a look with me, letting a smirk curl the corner of his lips.

How in the world does his arrogance twist through my stomach like that?

I'm fearful entering the village—there's a reason they've always kept trial participants separate from the people of Ember Glen. They may riot in their rage against me, gather to take my punishment into their own hands and end my life.

Strangely, the only sadness I have for the possibility of meeting my end today is the fact that I'll leave this earth so unsatisfied. I've yet to peel all my warden's layers and uncover the truest remains of his soul. I've yet to explore our forbidden cravings, my wicked thoughts and his depraved desires.

Before I die, I want all of him.

And that means I must give him all of me.

chapter twenty-two

ARLO

HYATT'S NEWLY WIDOWED wife Stefanie wraps a trembling hand around her cup of tea. She lifts it to her lips and takes a small sip before lowering it to the coaster on her small, round kitchen table. "You're sure that Hyatt's dead?"

"Yes, we're certain. I'm so sorry to bring the news of his loss this way," I tell her. "It's an unfortunate tragedy, and the Control will make arrangements for a service to honor him."

"Unfortunate." Stefanie's dark eyebrows, which match her deep brown hair, lift for a moment before she raises her cup and takes another sip of tea.

I watch her face carefully as she lifts her teacup higher, tilting her head down as she hides a twitch at the corner of her lips. My gaze narrows in scrutiny as long-held judgments fight for recognition in my mind.

Those judgments would tell me she should be weeping, sobbing, crumbling in shock before my eyes. They would tell me to take note of the way she seems to lack concern over the loss of her husband, and that we should keep a careful watch over her, perhaps reassign her to a new husband—a devout and God-fearing man who blindly follows the Edict and can lead her to a spiritual release.

Yet, as I told Mercy, I'm learning, so I fight the reflexive thoughts.

I find some strength in her at my side to help combat these

habitual thoughts—she's a darkly fallen angel whose mere presence guides me. If God sent her to change Ember Glen, then he sent her to change me as well. I must learn from her if I'm meant to carry out God's will as it's shown to me through her eyes.

Is it God's will or Mercy's?

Does it matter if I know she's right?

Stefanie's three children exist in the background, making small noises with their minimal movement, but they're awfully quiet playing in the living room behind her. Their faces seem strange, lacking expression, like they've buried their feelings deep inside. They looked that way from the moment we walked in, and it makes me wonder if they always behave this way.

I can see from here that the girl who seems to be the oldest of the three—maybe nine or ten years old—is marked for service; the tattoo of wildflowers split by two dark lines encircling her forearm is distinctive. The middle child doesn't bear the mark, which means she's destined for domestic bliss, and the youngest is still toddling, wobbly on her feet. Her fate won't be decided until she's five years old.

Three girls…Hyatt had three daughters.

It's striking how distant and closed-off the girls seem to be. We've kept our voices low, and I don't suspect they've overheard us speak about their father's death, so that news doesn't explain their somber presence.

It occurs to me that it must be difficult for a man like Hyatt—a man afflicted with the Impulse to such a violent degree—to transition from vileness to family after a night of service.

The purging is meant to be a release, to quell the Impulse, such that men can do their duty as leaders, husbands, fathers…But come to think of it, I don't know whether I can say with honesty that my own perverse sexual desires have ever been fully realized from a night of purging—they always linger throughout the month. And now that I've found my desire in Mercy, it seems I may never fully find satisfaction. Every hint of her presence makes me want her, and because my thoughts are consumed by her, it's a perpetual need.

It's an obsession, one I'm now convinced God instilled in my mind so I could enact His will by meeting Mercy's.

Studying Stefanie's expression, I see relief behind her eyes. It hadn't occurred to me before to expect relief, though it makes perfect sense now. If my sexual needs are never fully satisfied after purging, then perhaps Hyatt's violence remained too overwhelming for him to control after the full moon.

Perhaps his violence bled upon his family…

The mere thought of it sends a chill up my spine.

The entire purpose of purging is to keep our families safe.

And if it doesn't work, then what's the fucking point?

"How did it happen?" Stefanie tilts her head with curiosity. "Was it an accident," her eyes flick over to Mercy, "or was it intentional?"

She doesn't regard Mercy with disdain, with hatred for being a sinner, and it's surprising, to say the least. It was surprising that she'd let Mercy step foot inside her home as it is.

Mercy glances at me, as if seeking direction. Her eyes plead with me, and I can see that she wants to speak, that she wants to tell Stefanie the truth—as we crafted it—about what happened to Hyatt.

I give Mercy a nod. "Go on. Tell her."

Straightening in her seat, Mercy gives Stefanie full eye contact. She pulls back her shoulders, and my eyes are drawn to her chest, to the dip between her breasts where the V-neck of her long-sleeved crimson gown stops.

I recall kissing that very spot last night in the meadow as the rain poured down on us, and my mind drifts at the way it stirs longing within me. I long for her, though she's right beside me.

She asked me to indulge in pleasure with her for the rest of her short days, and I will, gladly. I long to indulge *now*. Yet each time I think about her in my arms, it triggers the agonizing reminder that our days spent in each other's arms are limited. My chest tightens, my heartbeat quickens, my veins burn with misery at the thought of a future without her.

I won't have a future without her.

If I can't find a way to prolong her days, then I will lose myself in depravity and chase her into hell if that's where God means to send her.

But is she still destined for eternal damnation if God means for her to spark change?

Confusion and conflict remain ripe within me, but I feel that true clarity is near, hovering around my soul, just waiting for me to discover the truth about everything.

"I did it." Mercy's clear but quiet voice draws me from my reverie. "He was hurting my friend, and I was afraid he would kill her, so I ran from the Homestead and I stabbed him with his own knife."

Stefanie's eyes widen, then her gaze drops to the liquid in her cup. Clearing her throat, she picks up a small spoon from the table and stirs her drink—for the third time since we arrived.

"It's so…" Her eyebrows knit together as she struggles with her words. "How tragic for my husband." She taps the spoon on the lip of her teacup and places it back on the table. "You'll have to forgive me…I'm in a bit of a shock over this news."

Stefanie is doing a miserable job at concealing her obvious relief. If I were the same man I was a month ago, I would immediately call for my brothers in the Control and insist we pray for her soul before swiftly reassigning her to another family unit.

There's a twinge of pain in my gut to think about how easily I could take her from her children, give them a new mother from another family unit, and force Stefanie to care for a new husband

and new children. I shouldn't feel glad that my hand slipped, accidentally slitting her husband's throat. I shouldn't feel pride in Mercy for taking the knife from me and giving him the bloody ending he deserved.

Yet, I do…because he did deserve it.

I shift in my seat at the thought I'd never expect to have for accidentally murdering a man.

Was it truly accidental?

Didn't I press down with the blade the moment I realized my hand was slipping?

"Would you like me to inform the rest of your family?" I ask. "I'm happy to relieve you of that burden."

Stefanie shakes her head. "No, Arlo, you don't need to do that. His family will be over for a visit tonight after the men have rested and recovered from their purge, so I'll tell them then. No need to disturb them now." She pushes to her feet and we follow suit with the understanding that our welcome is worn out. "I appreciate you coming by."

Such a casual thing to say after learning of your husband's death. I have a quickly passing thought of Mercy standing before me instead of Stefanie, of her as my wife, learning about my death in our home, in front of our children.

Would Mercy feel so unfazed?

Would she weep for the loss of me?

Would she suffer in grief?

I hate the thought of Mercy's pain, and it wrecks me as the image of her crumbling and crying forces its way into my thoughts. My shoulders tense and my neck strains at the image. But then my mind breaks, giving way to the image of her in a home that belongs to us, existing there as my wife, my partner, my companion—a woman meant to care for me and my needs—and I feel a warming sensation through my chest.

Yet, that's a life that could never have been.

The Control aren't assigned wives until they retire, and never if they become an Elder. And even if our fates had collided differently—if I had been a man allowed a wife and they'd assigned me Mercy—that life with her would be as unbearable as the future we face now.

I'd be unable to touch her, hold her, kiss her, devour her in passion, and grant us both pleasure through indulgence. Those carnal indulgences are only allowed for men, and only with servants beneath the full moon.

How could I spend a lifetime with Mercy without touching her?
I couldn't.

I've been thinking so much about the Impulse recently, about my lust and urges, and the way Mercy seems to crave me daily all the same. If women have the Impulse, too, then at least some of the domestics are living their entire lives suffering an itch they can never scratch.

Unless…

Unless they indulge in secret through forbidden trysts such as Mercy and I do.

Mercy's mother, Mira, was a domestic, and as I read it in her journal, she indulged her lust—and with another woman, no less. She wanted and had desire, and her thirst was so strong that she chose sin to indulge it…She had *died* for it.

I know with certainty that I would greet death with welcomed arms to quench my thirst for Mercy.

I clench my fists at my sides against the unbelievable tension coursing through me. "If anything changes," I say to Stefanie, "please let us know. Any of my brothers in God would be happy to care for you and your family in this time of tragedy."

"Thank you for delivering the news," she says politely, walking us to the door.

She pulls it open for us and stands beside it. I cross the threshold, stepping out onto the single stone step, then down to the gravel path that cuts through the middle of their front lawn. I turn to hold out my hand for Mercy to take as she steps down, but instead, I find Stefanie's hand on Mercy's wrist, halting her.

Panic grips me as I suddenly fear that I've misinterpreted the entirety of our interaction with Stefanie. She could be angry at what Mercy did, just waiting for me to leave so she could drag her back inside, lock the door, and harm her.

I place one foot back on the step and begin to rise when Stefanie whispers, "*Malo mori quam foedari.*"

The prayer halts me with confusion.

They're locked in a stare, Stefanie's eyes holding Mercy's with a significant look. There's no malice, no ill-intent, no hatred, or judgment; instead, there's peace. Peace and relief and gratitude. The prayer is intended to remind servants of their purpose, but I think Stefanie means it differently.

With a small nod, Mercy returns the prayer that she's been punished for refusing to speak in the past. "*Malo mori quam foedari.*"

Death before dishonor.

She doesn't mean this for Mercy; she means it for Hyatt, for whatever she and her children have suffered by him in their domestic life—for whatever way he dishonored his duty to protect them from harm, to provide for them, to lead them in God's will.

It's Hyatt who has been dishonorable, and her prayer spoken to Mercy was an acknowledgment that God's will has been fulfilled by the person who brought the dishonorable man to his death.

Relief I didn't know I needed to feel washes over me, loosening my tightened muscles and granting my soul a much-needed reprieve. As though last night's storm still lingers above, lightning strikes me with God's grace for ending the life of a man unworthy of the family he was blessed with.

I'm met by Mercy's grace as she turns her eyes to meet mine, showing me something I've never seen in them before—hope. There's hope sparkling like starlight through the silver pigments that brighten her light blue eyes.

Is she made from the stars?

Was her soul forged from the burning white light of the stars that touch heaven?

Did God steal the rebellious and rousing nature of a demon and mix it with her purity to craft her so perfectly?

Was she crafted for me?

I see the power she holds within her as a vessel of God…and of demons. She possesses all the compassion of a heavenly being with all the defiant conviction of a willingly fallen angel.

She certainly holds power over me.

Mercy smiles slowly, softly, and Stefanie nearly returns it. Mercy reaches out to place her uninjured palm on top of mine as she steps out, and I hold her hand as she moves down to the gravel path beside me.

She turns back to Stefanie, and her lips part to speak, but she's interrupted by a voice—a voice I'm familiar with.

"Stefanie!"

Mercy and I both look over our shoulders to see who called out Stefanie's name. It's Luna—the woman who was once my younger sister.

LUNA WALKS TOWARD us with urgency, with fear in her expression. She lives two houses down, across the pebbled pathway drawn between the homes, but I hadn't expected I'd lay eyes on her today.

I'm a little surprised to find she's no longer pregnant. She has a baby secured to her front with a wrap, one of her hands cradling at the back of its head as she rushes in our direction. Her other three children must still be at home, along with her husband, who would be resting from his night of purging. She should be there as well, taking care of him.

Shouldn't she?

Even after he's been gone all night fucking other women?

I had to go back to the forest for a few hours last night to give the appearance that I was purging, and I recall spotting Luna's husband, Archer, using three different servants, one after the other. I could have purged—I had the Impulse and the desire to seek pleasure— but no servant will ever do now that I know Mercy intimately. I'm ruined entirely by her, and it's just one of the many reasons why I know I won't survive when she's gone.

I don't think I've ever thought about nights of service from the perspective of the domestics before, and I almost wish I hadn't. Last night, Luna's husband indulged and enjoyed intimate physical pleasures, and rests peacefully today. Before me now, the kind young woman rushes across the lawn with a newborn baby strapped to her chest, looking disheveled and exhausted.

But surely, she's happy raising her family…It's something I've never asked—I haven't had a real conversation with her in years. I've had to disconnect from the family I knew before when I joined the Control in order to remain objective. But learning as I am, the palette of my objectivity has smeared, blending my black and white world into a swirling shade of gray.

"What's going on?" Luna's voice sounds on the verge of tears. "Is he taking you away?"

She brushes right past Mercy and me as Stefanie steps out of her home, quickly moving ahead to meet Luna on the gravel path. They throw their arms around each other, holding steady through several beats as Stefanie whispers, "It's okay. I'm not in trouble. Everything's fine."

Not in trouble…

There are the habitual judgments again. My mind wanders in consideration at the choice of words, and it begs me to watch this situation closely.

Stefanie's hand slips up to Luna's light copper brown hair, a messy pile of it tied on top of her head, and subtly cradles the back of her head. It's a brief slip of her hand, a moment of touch that's just beyond friendly. It's the intent in the curl of Stefanie's fingers that begs for my attention.

I don't think I would've noticed the subtlety of it before my passion for Mercy began to affect me. The way I hold Mercy, the way my hands always ache to tangle in her hair, to cradle her head, to draw her nearer—that kind of passion is too obvious to hide from someone who knows the feeling personally. Their embrace is not one that two friendly women should share.

Stefanie grips Luna's shoulders, holding her in place as she takes a quick step backward. Her eyes steal a furtive glance at me, then quickly flit away, the tendons in her throat straining as she swallows hard.

"Arlo is here on representation of the Control." Stefanie turns cold and distant again, shutting something off inside herself as she releases Luna's shoulders. "I'm afraid they had some terrible news to share with me."

Luna whips her head back over her shoulder, and I think I spy a glassy sheen of tears over her eyes—blue eyes which always looked so much like mine. "What news?"

"Why don't you go back home, Luna?" Stefanie suggests. "We'll talk about it later. I'm sure you don't want Archer to be bothered by the children."

Luna turns back to look at Stefanie, and though I can't see her face, I watch a shift happen. Her shoulders pull back, her neck straightens, and she tucks a wayward strand of unruly hair behind her ear. When she came rushing over, she looked just like the child-like version of herself that I always remember her being. But now, right before my eyes, her demeanor flips like a switch, and she straightens into adulthood.

It's an unsettling shift for me.

If I really think about it, though, that's how she always looks when I see her in passing in the village: rigid, hardened, carefully controlled. Nothing like the little girl five years my junior, who was once carefree and joyful.

As Luna turns to face us, the unconstrained expression of fear is gone, replaced by a hard, emotionless mask that disconnects her from the world entirely. She blinks, reaching down to adjust the hem of her ivory, cable-knit sweater over her long, light blue skirt, which reaches down to the top of her brown, laced ankle boots.

"I apologize for my messy appearance," she says to me with a tight-lipped smile, though she doesn't make eye contact. "I was just getting ready for my day, and I spotted you leaving here from my kitchen window. Surely, you understand how that concerned me for Stefanie."

The Control doesn't make many house calls except for handling matters of the law, so the concern for her friend is understandable—particularly seeing me here with a sinner condemned.

"Of course," I respond tersely, feeling conflicted about how to communicate with her in this rigidity. "There's no trouble here. I only needed to deliver some news to Stefanie. I'll leave it to her to share it with you as she wishes."

Luna glances back at Stefanie, who still appears emotionally distant, though she gives Luna an encouraging smile.

"When did you have the baby?" Mercy asks, and all our heads snap to look at her, surprised by the dreamy quality of her voice in this strange conversation.

Luna cradles her palm around the back of the baby's head, stroking down its notably full head of dark hair. Neither Luna nor

Archer have such dark hair, though it isn't surprising that her baby does. She would've been made pregnant by artificial means, and perhaps it was another man's seed that took. Regardless, Luna can't hide the emotion in her smile as she gazes down at the tiny sleeping thing.

"I had her a week ago."

Her. A girl.

I think that's Luna's first girl, as her other three are boys.

"She's beautiful," Mercy offers softly. "What's her name?"

I'm curious why Mercy is asking, but she's fully captured my attention with the kindness she offers in her voice, the way she seems to calm my sister in showing interest. As I watch Mercy, I realize she's swaying lightly. Whatever high she's feeling from the medication I gave her seems to be peaking.

She held it together so well in Stefanie's home that I'd nearly forgotten about the way it seems to have affected her. I side-step closer, my arm tense, preparing to reach around her if she wobbles too far.

"Her name is Soleil," Luna says.

"Oh, that's a beautiful name." Mercy smiles. "Soleil…like the sun?"

Luna grins and nods.

"You and your baby are the moon and the sun," Mercy remarks with joy.

Luna and Soleil.

The moon and the sun.

A small chuckle escapes me. The choice of name is so fitting of the Luna I remember as a child—whimsical, cheerful, and light. The moon, the sun, and my starlight are all orbiting me, and the gravitational force of each affects me deeply, stretching the fibers of my soul. The way they all tug at my spirit makes the details of this moment seem significant.

It's as though this meeting is celestial, divinely crafted.

"I'd heard it as a word, but I read that it was someone's name before in a book Stefanie and I had found—"

"Luna," Stefanie bites, sharply cutting her off.

A book they found?

"What book?" I press.

All the books in Ember Glen are carefully catalogued and accounted for.

Luna's eyes briefly widen and her joyful expression falters. "I should be going. Archer and the children will be wondering where I am." She marches past us, along the path that cuts through the lawn.

"Luna," I call out as I march in her direction. This is the most I've spoken to her in two years, and I'm hesitant to let the conversation end.

She stops, hesitating in place for a few beats before she slowly turns to look at me standing just behind her. "Yes?"

"Soleil…She's lovely. Congratulations."

"Thank you."

"Are you happy?"

She jerks her head up sharply to look at me with a furrowed brow. "What?"

"Are you happy in the life you've been given? Truthfully?"

Her cheeks twitch as she forces a fake smile, lifting her eyes to look beyond me. "Of course. I'm doing God's will as a domestic, raising a family, taking care of the house and my husband. Why wouldn't I be happy?"

"Because you're not free," Mercy says, and the rest of us are struck silent.

There's a gentle touch against my back, and I tense as Mercy moves to stand at my side, splaying her uninjured palm at the small of my back. My eyes widen at the momentary shock of knowing we're out here in the village, standing in the open, and she's far too close, touching me too freely. I need to get her out of the village before she starts spilling secrets.

"Can I hold the baby?" Mercy asks dreamily, her head falling over onto my shoulder.

Sweet sin.

The way my body responds to her closeness against my good damn judgment is infuriating. Every muscle in my body hesitates to push her away, but my mind knows that a moment's hesitation could be the difference between life and death for the both of us.

I reach behind me and snatch her wrist, sharply shoving her arm away and holding it up between us, making a show of aggression with harsh movements and my hardened expression.

"Don't touch me, sinner."

Mercy's eyebrows flatten into a straight line as she narrows her eyes. "You're supposed to call me starlight."

Fuck.

Bringing her here in this state—bringing her here at all—was stupid.

My eyes snap to Luna to see her reaction, but her gaze is on Mercy's wrist where I hold it in my grasp. Bewilderment washes through her features before she finally looks at me, and when she does, her eyes widen slowly. She's connecting the dots that she shouldn't be able to see.

I never could keep secrets from her.

"I-I have to go," Luna mutters.

With that, I expect her to turn immediately and walk away, but instead, she hesitates, then takes a tentative step closer to Mercy. As I let go of Mercy's wrist, Luna reaches out to grasp the other, circling her hand around the tattoo on Mercy's forearm above her burned hand.

"It's a vicious circle," Luna whispers.

Then, she sways forward, leaning in close to Mercy, twisting sideways around the baby to bring her mouth closer to Mercy's ear. She whispers something I can't hear, and my heart hammers as I watch Mercy's expression twist and morph while she listens.

A vicious circle?

What could she possibly be saying to Mercy?

And will Mercy even remember it after the medication has worn off?

Mercy grins and nods politely, turning her head to catch my stare. And as she smiles at me, giving no indication whatsoever as to what was said to her, Luna turns and rushes away.

I could chase after her and demand answers on the authority of the Control. I could command her to tell me what she whispered to Mercy, press her about this book she and Stefanie had found— and what it even means that they *found* it. I could call her in for questioning regarding her friendship with Stefanie and the extent of their...closeness.

Sadly, I think the man I was before Mercy seeped into my pores would have done just that. I think he would have sold out his sister in the name of God, in the name of maintaining status and power in Ember Glen.

It's bizarre to feel relief wash over me when I realize I am no longer that man. I'm not the same as I was before. And it's all because of the rebel standing at my side—the lightly swaying woman so high off the pain medication I gave her that she's bound to collapse into a lengthy slumber at any moment.

"Come on." I grip Mercy's bicep and drag her along with me. Truthfully, I'd scoop her up and carry her if it weren't for the prying eyes of the domestic wives assuredly watching from their kitchen windows.

I briefly glance over my shoulder to see Luna disappear through the front door of her humble home. It was as clear as day that Luna is unhappy. There's something lost behind her eyes, which were once a brighter shade of blue, but have seemed to have slowly dulled over the years.

Luna's unhappiness and Stefanie's lack of concern for her husband's tragic passing are telling. It makes me wonder; it makes me think. As Mercy so wisely told me to search for truth through the madness, I see a sliver of it now…

Ember Glen isn't what I thought it was.

It's not a perfect community of harmony and balance.

It's terribly out of tune, and someone needs to fix it.

chapter twenty-three
Mercy

A WEEK HAS gone by since the last service and the day that Arlo took me to the village. I've mostly been in my room, sleeping or daydreaming through a drug-induced stupor. Arlo kept bringing me the medication, and I kept taking it. When it started to wear off, the pain in my hand was so unbearable that all I could do was cry. So, I chose to lose time in a medicated trance rather than endure it.

I would have preferred to lose time in Arlo's arms. He did hold me some, curled up behind me in my bed, stroking my hair until I fell asleep. But he wouldn't touch me more than that, not even when I stripped myself bare and begged him.

He politely refused.

He said I wasn't truly present, and it wouldn't feel like us.

It's a rather romantic thought now that I can clearly think back on it. No one has ever really cared before about my mental and emotional presence in sex, so long as my body was available for use.

Though there's still pain in my healing hand, it's gradually becoming more and more bearable. Yesterday, I decided not to take the medication he brought me. I haven't taken it today, either, and my mind nearly feels back to normal. I took care of myself today, bathed and dressed, and as I head for my bedroom door to go and find Arlo, I hear a perfectly timed knock from the other side.

It's him.

I always know it's him by the way he knocks—heavy-handed,

sharp, insistent.

I pull open the door, and seeing him there before me lights me up from the inside. My feelings for him have grown immensely over these past days as he's taken care of me. It's his job as my warden, but it's also telling of his commitment to fulfilling the promises he made me. He promised me in the meadow, beneath the thunder and lightning, to take care of all of my needs, and he has been—save for one.

I step aside, holding the door open wide. "You can come in."

His eyes scan my body, taking me in with heat in his gaze that tugs some invisible string connected to my desire. "You must be feeling better," he says. "I haven't seen you out of a nightgown and robe for days."

"I'm much better, thanks to your care. I haven't taken the medication since the day before yesterday."

His eyes flash with recognition that my mind is clear and my body is free from influence. There's something heart-warming about the fact that he refrained from taking advantage of me in a delicate state, even though I wanted him to at the time.

"I can change the dressing on your hand—"

"No need." I shake my head and hold up my burnt hand to show him it's wrapped in a fresh layer of sterile gauze. "I did it myself. It actually wasn't all that painful this time. I think it's healing well."

He smiles, and the way his dimples cut through the scruff of his beard melts my insides. The hair seems to have grown out a touch while his focus has been on caring for me. It's just a little less perfectly manicured and a little more unruly—a physical change that reflects what I believe I see happening within his heart.

He's changing.

I sigh. Every moment that passes without being in his arms feels like torture in my limited days.

"Will you come in? Please?" I plead with him with my eyes,

desperate to bring him behind a closed door.

His eyes skate across my face, then dip down to my chest where my skin is exposed from the V-neck of my wrap-around satin gown. His gaze trails down the dip between my breasts, drawing past the red tie that fastens the gown at my waist. He tilts his head to regard the curve of my hip appreciatively.

The gown flatters me, but it's also comfortable. The sleeves are long, but cinched around my wrists, allowing the soft fabric to puff out and hang loosely over my arms without slipping down to irritate the healing burns on my hand. I've worn this particular dress on a few occasions, and he always looks at me the same way when it's on—which is why I chose to wear it today.

"Believe me, Mercy…" His voice is low and quiet. "If I had the time right now to rip that dress off you and make up for every moment lost this past week, you would already be naked and writhing beneath me."

His words suck all the air from my lungs.

"And I promise you," he steps forward into the open doorway, enticing me to step closer, daring to bring my chest only inches from his, "I *will* make up for that lost time soon." He sighs, and the heat of his breath warms my skin. "But for now, I just wanted to give you this." He lifts his hand at our side, holding up a brown leather journal…my *mother's* journal.

I'd asked to have it back, and he remembered. Seeing it again rushes a wave of emotion through me that I hadn't expected. It's almost like seeing her again—like having her with me to comfort me through the remainder of my arduous trials.

"Thank you, Arlo." My eyes press shut for a moment, then open again to fully meet his. "I can't tell you how much it means for me to have this back."

"You understand that you must keep it hidden, yes?"

I nod. "Of course."

I reach out to take it from him and our fingers graze in the transfer. He huffs out a sharp, heated breath at the touch, the soft connection sparking immediate pleasure in anticipated release. His tongue sneaks across his lip as he pulls his hand back and knots of desire twist inside my stomach.

"I can't stay right now," he insists, "but sweet sin, Mercy…I can't think straight when I'm with you. When I'm with you, I can't think about anything but the way you make me feel."

"Come in and shut the door. Let me help you give your mind a rest."

"The way you tempt me…"

"Please, Arlo."

He drifts forward, his body swaying impossibly closer, drawing mine toward him like a magnet. He's so achingly close that my breasts graze his chest, sending a shockwave of delicious need right through me.

And then he steps back.

"I can't. Not right now. I have to meet with the rest of the Control and the Elders in fifteen minutes about your next trial. I need a clear mind."

I turn sideways to clear a path for him. "So come in for fourteen minutes and let me give you a clear mind."

He pinches his eyes shut and his fists clench at his side. "Mercy…"

"Warden Rainn."

His eyes snap open and his blue stare is brimming with passion. I draw in a hopeful, shaky breath as his gaze falters in desire. I hold his stare, challenging him to come forward, to meet me with his need and use me to satisfy it…to satisfy us both.

He tugs on my arm and draws me close, wrapping his arm around my waist to embrace me as he gazes down at me. The way he looks so deeply into my eyes makes my breaths quicken. I want him to kiss me right here, in the doorway of my bedroom. I want him to sneak it away from me in a passionate rush before someone sees us.

I lean in, hoping he'll mirror me. But then he jerks back, closes his hand around my wrist, and drags me behind him into the hallway.

Still clinging to the journal, I rush to keep up with his quick steps. He slams to a stop in front of his bedroom door, unlocks it, and shoves it open. He whips me through the doorway, flinging me forward across the threshold.

I stumble in and whirl around to face him, smiling from ear to ear in anticipation of a few lustful moments with him. If mere minutes is all he has right now, then I'll gladly take them.

He slams his door shut, but instead of coming to me, he turns and goes to the set of drawers near the door.

My smile falters as he pulls open a drawer, unsure of what he's doing or why. But then he pulls out a length of rope, and my breath gets caught in my lungs. My heart stops for a moment, then starts again in a rush, pounding heat and lust through my veins.

Yes, I want him to bind me.

He's after me in a hurry, meeting me quickly as I step toward him. He reaches down to grip my wrist as he storms past me, dragging me behind him to the bed. "Sit," he orders, stopping beside it.

I plop down on the edge of the mattress without question. He starts to wrap the coarse rope around my uninjured right wrist, knotting it expertly before drawing out the length of it, attaching it to the post at the head of the bed.

Once I'm secured, he moves in front of me, coming in so close that I have to spread my legs to make room for him, that I have to tilt my head skyward to look at him. His knuckle swoops beneath my chin to hold me there.

"Fifteen minutes isn't nearly enough time to begin all the things I wish to do to you, starlight. If you truly want to give me a reprieve from the torturous thoughts I have muddling my mind, then you'll wait right here for me in agonizing anticipation. Tell me you'll think of me while I'm gone."

"You know I will, Warden Rainn."

A smirk brightens his expression as he groans. "Volunteering to be your warden was the best decision I ever made."

"It was." I nod.

My chest is heaving from the desire, from the heat of his proximity.

Slowly, he bends, his body folding forward at a creeping pace, lowering his lips to meet mine. Even more slowly, he kisses me, a soft press of our lips that would ordinarily seem so chaste, though it feels profane in its simplicity. Too quickly, he pulls away and leaves me there, sitting on the bed, my right arm bound to the bedpost. With a last glance, he shuts the door and locks it behind him, leaving me breathless and wanting...*waiting.*

I lift my arm and pull it away from the bedpost, dragging it across my body to test the slack. He's left several feet of slack so I can move my arm freely, which I appreciate since my other hand remains useless in its healing.

As I test the rope, I see I still have my mother's journal clutched in my bound hand. I loosen my grip as I realize just how tightly I was clinging to it.

Relief to have it back washes over me again, and I smile at the leather-bound journal as if it could smile back. I don't know how long Arlo will be gone—it could be ages if they're working on the details of the second trial. A lump rises in my throat and I swallow hard against it.

I can't just sit here doing nothing while waiting for him to return. I'll go mad—either from the dreaded anticipation of learning how I'll soon be tormented, or obsessively wondering about Arlo's plans for me now that he has me bound to his bed.

I've been wanting to go back and read some of what my mother wrote, so I decide to entertain myself by flipping back through the journal. I turn and raise my legs onto the mattress before scooting all the way back, straightening my spine against the headboard.

I open the journal and lay it on my lap, using one hand to flip to the very first page. For a few moments, I simply look at it, tracing the lines of my mother's handwriting with my gaze, memorizing the way her letters swoop and dance with each other. She had beautiful handwriting, and while I think mine is similar, it's not exactly the same. I can see the difference in the notes I scribbled in the margins.

I spend some time flipping through the pages and re-reading all the passages I've read before. It's my second time through, and I'm spotting new details, things I don't remember seeing the first time. It's just bits and pieces of her life—so much of it that happened before I was even born—and it brings a smile to my face to read about some of the joyful moments she had.

At the end of the passage I'm reading, I flip the page to find rough edges of parchment peeking out of the spine, remnants of a page that was torn from the journal. Arlo mentioned the three torn pages before. Truthfully, I have no idea what might have been written on them. I don't know whether they still exist, hidden away somewhere strange, or if they've been destroyed. It seems most likely that those pages are long gone.

I find it surprising that I recall Arlo mentioning it to me. I was on the medication then, and I'm struggling to remember all the details—except for the moment I stripped myself and begged him to fuck me, as that embarrassing moment is crystal-clear in my mind.

The other details are muddy...details like *vicious circle.*

I remember Luna saying those two words to me outside of Stefanie's house, and I wish I could remember the context. I know she whispered something to me, and I remember it made me feel like I wasn't alone. Yet I can't place the feeling with context because

I don't remember exactly what she told me. I know Arlo's curious about it—he's asked me twice, but I have nothing to tell him other than *vicious circle.*

There's something else here, covering the text of my mother's next journal passage. Folded pieces of parchment have been tucked in and laid to rest together here, either as a placeholder or...as something for me to find.

Did he find the missing pages?

My heart nearly stops.

But then my shoulders slump as I realize the folded pages are a different shade of parchment and couldn't have come from this journal. I tug the folded pages from where they're nestled in the spine, setting them in a pile on the bed beside my hip. Then, I pick up the first one and open it.

It's handwriting I don't recognize, yet I know at first glance who it belongs to.

Arlo.

A nervous flutter of curiosity ripples beneath my skin.

What has he written inside these pages?

Did he place them here intentionally, or was it an accident?

Of course, I know it wasn't an accident. Arlo would never be so careless. He meant for me to find them, but I nearly feel sick to my stomach to think of what they might say. My hand twitches and begins to shake as I thumb open the first page.

Breathing you in is sweet sin,
transgression worthy of fire and brimstone.

You are heat.
You are flame.
You are smoking ash which floods my lungs with each delicious breath I take.

Burn, sweet sinner, and I'll bathe in flames with you.

I will disintegrate to ash at your feet.
And my remnants will beg for your grace, your sin…your mercy.

Mercy.
Sweet, sweet Mercy.

Send me to hell, you demon of delight.
Burn with me.

It's poetry, a string of beautiful words all tied together with such elegance.
And the words are about me…

Mercy.
Sweet, sweet Mercy.

My heart thuds, sending a rush of emotions to flood my veins. A prickling, electric feeling shudders beneath my skin. I want to read the words a thousand times over, but I want to read what's on the next folded page even more. I reach for it and open it.

Light of the universe,
starlight in human form.

Celestial beauty and the scent of earth,
like the meadow and sweet mountain air.

Wildflowers and starlight.

Stunned at his words, I gasp.

Wildflowers and starlight.

He'd used those words to describe the scent of my hair, the nearly white shade of the strands that remind him of the stars in the night sky.

Wildflowers and starlight.

Those words belong to us.

I read them and think of the meadow, the way thunder rumbled through the mountains and lightning struck us with moments of bright light that kept the darkness at bay. I think about our promises we made to each other.

I think about the way he kissed me, the way he touched me, the way he gave me more pleasure than I've ever known as we lost control together among the wildflowers whipping in the wind.

I take my time to read each delicious word on the page, and then my fingers are scrambling to set it aside and move onto the next. Unfolding the third page, I read slowly, letting each word seep inside me and melt in the simmering blood rushing through my veins. I feel something unexplainable flowing through me...and by the time I finish the third page, tears spring to my eyes.

Your life will be taken.
Your light will be extinguished.
Your madness will fade into history...
but it will never be snuffed from my memory.

I pray my memory will be enough to sustain...to endure a lifetime without your madness.

A sob breaks through my chest as the warm tears which flood my eyes begin to spill down my cheeks. There's a fire burning inside me, flames encircling my heart, and his words only make it burn brighter, hotter, faster.

The pain of it awakens me to the truth, to the somber reality that I have so little time left. It awakens my soul to recognize that I would selfishly squander my last days alive in blissful denial of the world around me if it meant I could spend all my days and nights wrapped in his arms.

Like flowers need the rain, I need this man.

I'm desperate for him, foolish for him, selfish for him.

More than that, my heart is broken for him.

I'll be gone, and he'll have to live without me.

I want to push the pages aside and sob into the pillow, but instead, I pick up the last page and read the words to myself out loud.

My dark angel...
crafted in the sky,
the only light in a vast obsidian void.

A stellar explosion...
ashes of light,
she was speckled stardust over an onyx canvas.

An envious God...
stolen cinders from the sky,
heaven forged from the embers of her starlight corpse.

A demon's delight...
annihilator of bliss,
set fire to paradise, and her ashes fell.

Her light darkened...
the will of a demon,
starlight trapped in human form.

Her celestial embers…
the universe within,
the heaven I strive for contained in her flesh.

My suffering found…
untouchable divinity,
flesh of my dark angel formed by her demons.

Her outspoken rebellion…
mistaken for evil,
the truth of her origin hidden in her warmth.

Nirvana thrives inside…
sweet, parting thighs,
spread like the gates of heaven to beckon me home.

My spiritual awakening…
where holy water flows,
my thirst is sated in the kindling of her arousal.

A celestial roar…
her truth ignites,
the universe exists within her cresting pleasure.

Clarity is found…
my eternity in bliss,
she and heaven are one in the same.

My beloved starlight…
my mortal universe,
her death will bring the end of all things.

Yet…
my love for her is immortal,

and suffering will haunt my mortal flesh eternally.

She is paradise.
She is endless.
She is mine.

This man…He's everything to me.

I've felt every possible emotion toward him, and the most painful of all is love. Deeply, truly, unexpectedly, and profoundly, I've found so much love in my heart for Arlo Rainn.

There is no other way to describe what I feel for him.

I love him.

I love him in a way I've never loved anyone before, and I didn't even know that was possible. I love him intimately, passionately, with the kind of desperation that begs for me to give him all that's left of me.

The love I feel for him is the kind that's seen as rare and precious in Ember Glen—something found by luck or miracle or divine intervention because no domestic woman chooses the husband they receive. And yet, our rare and precious love doesn't feel lucky or miraculous or divinely conceived. It feels like punishment because I'm destined to die, and he's sentenced to live with a broken heart.

I sniff back my tears as I neatly fold the pages, piling them beside me again. Then, strangely, I hear my mother's voice in my mind, softly saying, "I'm glad I loved." It's not a memory of her saying that to me, but I do remember reading those words in her journal.

I'm glad I loved.

They seem to have stuck with me, and I feel compelled to find them. I flip to the back to re-read her last few passages, somehow recalling that I had read the words that day in the meadow, when Arlo took me as his ward for the trials. It's a passage where she wrote about the woman she loved in secret.

I'm glad I loved that incredible woman while I could. My hand shakes as I write this—the words are blasphemous, I know. But what does it matter now that I'm sentenced to death and my soul is already damned?

As I read the words, I notice something…something scribbled in the margin. I wrote many notes in the margins, but this one isn't mine. I never had a chance to write anything on these last pages before Arlo took the journal from me. It's the same handwriting as the poetry—the scribbled notes are from Arlo.

If Mercy's soul is damned, then so is mine.
Our souls are tethered eternally.

There's another note from Arlo further down the entry, but before I read his scribbled words, I read the passage from my mother beside them.

I regret everything.
I regret our stolen fates.
I regret our carelessness.
I regret that we didn't spend more of our numbered days together, sinning in secret.

And then I read Arlo's thoughts.

We could sin in secret daily, and it still wouldn't grant me enough memories to survive without Mercy. I would still regret that I couldn't save her. I don't know if I can go on without her.

My heart stops and starts chaotically at the acknowledgment

of the memories he wants to create with me and the regret he'll hold after my death.

I don't want him to regret that he can't save me.

I know he can't.

I thought I had accepted my fate, and I had—for myself.

How could I ever accept the way he might hurt when I'm gone?

I know he wants to try to save me, but I don't believe it's possible. I hold some hope, but it's not strong. The reality of my timed existence and the weight of his words bring fresh tears to my eyes.

I love Arlo Rainn, and his pain belongs to me.

I want our remaining days to be filled with memories for him to hold on to when I'm gone. It's all I can give him, and I resolve to do just that.

I fold the pages neatly and tuck them back into my mother's journal, closing it and setting it on the nightstand. And then I wait, remaining tethered to his bed, bound to him through my numbered days, ready to grant him memories of us that will last.

chapter twenty-four
ARLO

I'M DRAINED, EMOTIONALLY wrecked in a way I didn't know was possible. I'm physically exhausted from the drawn-out meeting and the mental whiplash I've suffered in all the back-and-forth discussions about the second trial. The entire ordeal was chaotic, frustrating, and for me—a man whose heart is bound to the participant meant to endure—it was torturous.

I thought the discussion of the second trial would be straightforward. Yet the moment we rested in our seats in the courtroom, Killian decided to throw in a wrench. He questioned the integrity of the trial if the wardens were aware of what would take place and able to share it with their wards. I was immediately confused by his questioning because we were told by the Elders that trial wardens were always meant to provide some preparation to the participants.

The Elders confirmed that yes, that's what they had told us before, but they were open to making a change. More and more, I'm coming to recognize the ambivalence when it comes to the Elders' rulings. They alternate between rigidity and flexibility in God's word, and their only consistency is in their support of tormenting women.

I'm beginning to think that divinity is absent entirely from these Trials of Dissension, that perhaps absolution can't be found for participants through these ultimate acts of service. With the way rules and circumstances are constantly changing, it makes me wonder which parts of it were in the original Impulse Edict.

Which parts came from God and which parts came from men?

Owen and Park argued against keeping the trial a secret, debating alternatively that it seemed unnecessarily cruel to make the participants wonder and fear—the trials themselves are punishment enough for sinners. Of course, Theo and I both argued the same. I need to know what Mercy is meant to face. If I can't figure out how to avoid putting her through the second trial, then I need to prepare her for it fully. I need to know what she'll be asked to do so I can prepare her to survive.

After some debate, a compromise was reached—one I'm not happy about, but one I'll have to accept. The compromise is for wardens to be told one detail, one single aspect of the trial for which the participants could prepare. But without the details, I could never fully prepare Mercy. I know how psychologically tormenting Service by Sacrifice is meant to be.

To think of it makes me sick to my stomach, and not knowing the details makes it feel even worse. I can imagine a thousand ways to punish a sinner. It wasn't all that long ago that I dreamed of ways to punish Mercy for her sins—though I can admit so many of those punishments in my mind led her from pain to teeter on the edge of pleasure.

The meeting stretched on for two hours, during which Theo and I were ushered in and out of the courtroom as they worked out the details of the next trial and decided what they would share with us.

And I only know one detail.

One horrifying detail.

My nerves are shot just thinking about it and all the ways in which this could play out. My mind is trained for debauchery, and I can imagine so many wretched scenes they might lay out before her. Adrenaline-fueled tremors tear through me as it floods my veins.

I don't know how I'll tell her, how I'll prepare her, but I'll think of all that tomorrow…or maybe the next day. The trial is set for ten days from now, and I could lose her then.

I could lose her.

I fight against my fear, struggling to push it from my mind as I jog up the staircase and race down the hall, knowing the only thing I can do for her right now—the only thing I can do for myself—is to sin with her in pleasure as I had promised her.

For all I care, God can damn us both to hell if this is the fate He's chosen for us. I'll sell my soul to demons and burn for eternity, so long as she and I stand together in the same flame.

Regardless of everything that weighs on us so heavily, I realize I've left her tied to my bed for two hours, and I feel bad for it. I didn't expect to be this long. I quickly reach my door and rush inside.

"I'm sorry I was gone so—"

My words cut short as my eyes land on her, still on the bed where I left her, curled on her side, quiet…asleep.

Sweet sin.

She is the most divine angel and the most wicked temptress. She's an agent of God and demons, the human representation of all that's good and all that's forbidden, and she's bound, waiting for me in my bed, finally unhindered by the medication that muddied her mind and slurred her speech.

I want her eyes open, her lips parted, her chest heaving as she pants through the pleasure I give her. I want her moans, her gasps, her sweet begging voice in the way she says, "please," and asks me for release.

I undress, stripping myself bare in the physical sense, but each item of clothing I remove feels like shedding a piece of the man I was before. Each discarded item casts off a part of the man who prided himself as an authority figure, as a future Elder, as a man who blindly followed the laws of God without any physical proof of the words He meant for us to adhere to.

I bare myself in every sense as an offering to her.

Though habit momentarily guilts my mind into believing her a false idol, everything else within me tells me she's worthy of all the ways I wish to worship her. I feel it instinctually, pounding through my heart, rushing through my veins, tugging at my soul, and prickling across my skin.

I walk softly across the carpet, each peaceful breath she takes drawing me nearer. I approach her at the side of the bed where she's curled up on her left side, facing away from me. Her right arm, which is still coiled in rope and bound to the bedpost, rests comfortably in front of her with the several feet of slack I gave it. Her fingers are curled loosely into fists, and her porcelain cheeks hold no tension at all. She appears so unusually calm, so relaxed, so peaceful.

I reach down with my bare hand to brush my knuckle down her cheek with a gentle touch. She doesn't stir, doesn't move, doesn't wake. She's as peaceful as I've ever seen her sleeping here in my bed.

The blisters on my fingers that I burnt in the fire with her were surprisingly mostly superficial and have all but healed—it's almost as though her skin touching mine when I thrust her hand into the flame offered some sort of miraculous protection. I kept my hands covered from her all last week while we both were healing, so touching her now, skin to skin, feels electric, shocking me with a jolt of pleasure that makes my cock twitch.

I draw my knuckle up her cheek again, turning my hand to catch her hair in my finger and tuck it behind her ear. A small moan escapes her as she shifts on the pillow. I should pull my hand away and step back, leave her to sleep. But I can't look at this woman without feeling the overwhelming need to touch her. I stroke my palm down the side of her head, and though it makes her stir, I don't regret it. If she wakes up, I'll wear her out enough for this peaceful slumber to find her again later.

She sighs out a heavy breath and her fingers twitch before she shifts her hand, drawing my attention to the knotted rope around her wrist.

Sweet sin.

The sight of her bound in my bed twists my insides, dragging out every sordid desire of the flesh I have for this woman. One moment, my eyes are tracing the slackened line of rope between her right wrist and the bedpost, and the next, the end of the rope is untied from the bed and knotted around my own right wrist. I hadn't made a conscious effort to bind my hand to hers, yet it happened.

Reaching down with my tethered hand, I drag my palm down her shoulder. My fingers trail along the silk sleeve covering her arm as I watch her slowly rouse to my touch. I slip into bed behind her and press in close, curling my body around her backside. I prop my left elbow on the pillow, and lean my head against my hand, watching her slow, soft movements as sleep slips away from her.

My movements are slow and soft, too, but filled with indecent intent. If she's going to awaken to my touch, then I want her filled with pleasure in her awakening. I spread my palm over her belly, tugging her closer, and though she's still gripped by her slumber, her back is arching, intensifying the pressure of her ass against my steadily thickening cock. I sigh as her body subtly shifts as she grows more aware of my presence, naturally tilting to lean back against my frame.

Slowly, I run my hand up the center of her body, slipping through the valley between her breasts, flattening my palm over the bare skin of her chest exposed from the deep V of her gown. I feel her chest rise against my palm as she draws in a deep breath, back arching deeper with tension, and then she lets out a whimpered sigh—a sound that's so peaceful, it brings me an unexpected moment of sadness.

Has she ever felt such peace before?

Has she ever lived a moment of her life without fear?

The thoughts ache as they take up residence in my chest, laying heavily on my heart. But I don't let the sadness of such thoughts consume me; instead, I let them fuel me in pursuit of granting her continued peace through her numbered days.

I let my hand rest there for some time, feeling the rhythm of her heart, the way it's slow and steady at first. Then it crescendos, gradually quickening, pumping more insistently as sleep slips further from her grip.

I can see her face clearly now that I've tucked her hair behind her ear, and I watch as her lips faintly twist from peaceful to blissful. The look of her desire is becoming familiar. It's apparent in the faint flush of her cheeks, the tension of her body as it subtly squirms against mine, the slight parting of her pink lips as her lungs demand a deeper breath.

The beauty of her face in this rare moment where passion meets serenity is overwhelming. It begs my hand nearer, an unseen force tugging my hand to glide up her chest, my palm circling her throat gently as it slips up to her chin. My thumb reaches to brush across her bottom lip, gently tracing the subtle curve of her smile that curls more deeply with each sweep.

I watch as she blinks her eyes, batting away drowsiness with her lashes. My thumb begs to press between her lips, to feel her warm, wet tongue glide over my flesh. Her body curls deeper, the thick flesh of her bottom pressing against my cock with a slight wiggle of her hips, and it urges my hand to move, to touch her in all the places that will make her beg for me to slip inside her. My cock thickens at the thought of her begging, the way she says "please" when she's on the edge.

Drawing down the center of her chest, I turn my hand and slip it inside the deep V of her neckline, seeking her breast and groaning when I find it bare—no bra or corset—beneath the silk. Her eyes flutter shut again as I gently move my palm, softly touching her skin and trailing my fingers over her nipple.

The way the tiny peak hardens with each brush of my thumb is intoxicating. I keep at it, teasing with the gentle touch for what must be minutes, until it's clear that Mercy is fully awake, aroused and needy.

Her hand raises sharply and lands on my arm, her palm curling around the rope knotted to my wrist. "Wait," she says.

I can't stop myself from pinching the hard bud and rolling it quickly between my fingers. She gasps and tenses, tilting to lean back against me, and her head rolls against the pillow. She looks up at me as I stare down at her, my eyes narrowed with intensity.

The strength of my passion doesn't frighten her, even when I feel like it should—when I feel like I'm feral, barely holding on and teetering on the brink of losing control to the Impulse.

I've never felt the Impulse so strongly as I do when I'm with her. The way I feel it with Mercy makes me wonder if every time I thought I felt it before her was just a lightly passing urge. The real Impulse lives and dies with her.

And that's not the way it's supposed to be.

The Impulse is a faceless, nameless plague on men. An uncontrollable need for violence, sex, and depravity. But in this moment with Mercy Madness, I feel it more profoundly than I've ever felt it before…yet, I wait.

I pause.

I control it because she asked for me to.

Fuck. Is the Impulse a lie?

Is the Impulse an excuse for vicious indulgence with impunity?

Dormant shame stirs, shaking through my shoulders, pricking an urge beneath my skin to add new blisters and scars with a flame against my palm. With the shame comes a strange exhaustion and my propped arm drops onto her pillow. I slip it quickly beneath her head, settling my arm under her neck as I fall to lay my head down beside her.

She leans back heavier against me, craning her neck to look at me. When her bewitching silver-blue eyes steal my gaze, guilt halts me, and I start to pull my hand away.

But she surprises me…she's always surprising me.

Her arm moves and her hand shifts, turning to slip beneath mine. At first, I think she's only creating a barrier against access to that sweet, hard peak of pleasure. But then her fingers thread between mine. The moment I realize she's taking hold of my hand, I lock my fingers with hers, gripping so tightly that every inch of our palms kiss. Then, she turns, rolling to lie fully on her back. I stay tight against her side, molding myself to her curves.

I feel the way her eyes stay on mine, even when I glance to see our hands locked together above her chest. My heart stutters as I take in the absolutely stunning view of our fingers interlaced, the same strand of coarse brown rope wrapped around each of our wrists to tether us entirely.

Some unmeasurable amount of time passes this way in silent watching, as we grow in quiet understanding that regardless of whether it's painful, shameful, or filled with heat and desperate need, this moment is ours and ours alone.

Right now, she's mine and I'm hers.

My heart belongs to this woman, whether God wanted her to have it or not.

"I found the pages," Mercy says quietly.

She still holds my hand, and her thumb brushes my knuckles. The comforting touch tugs at my mind, insistent upon its full presence and awareness. The urge to burn my hand is still present as I live here on the edge of indulgence, but I tuck the thought away, shoving it far back in a dark corner of my mind, knowing I can always satisfy the insistence later.

"I read the poems." Her eyebrows knit together as her expression turns thoughtful.

"I meant for you to."

My words are true; I had meant for her to read them. But having confirmation of it now makes me nervous in a strange way I can't say I've ever really felt before. My poems were always for me, never meant for another soul to read, and I never shared a single word of them with anyone before. No one else even knows that I write them.

She squeezes my hand, dropping hers back to rest against her chest and pulling mine down with it. My eyes flutter shut in reverie of the way she affects me. I sigh, letting the tension held through every inch of me loosen all at once, and I relax into the mattress. Letting my head fall deeper onto the pillow, I brush her cheek with the tip of my nose, breathing in the wildflower scent of her hair as I nestle my face against the side of hers.

"I have so much to say to you, Arlo. I don't even know where to begin."

I'm struck by a wave of unease, suddenly fearful that she didn't like the poems, that the meaning of my words was mistaken, that she simply didn't like that I've spent time writing about her while being so cruel to her. Regardless, I have to know. I need to hear her words and know what's on her mind, what's in her heart.

I let out a sigh. "Then just speak and let the words come."

Though my eyes are still shut, I feel the rise and fall of her chest beneath our hands and how it quickens in pace and pitch. Her fingers tighten their grip between mine as she whispers, "I'm bound to you."

My eyes pop open at the words, darting down to look at our hands, tethered by rope. We're literally bound, but I know that's not what she's saying. The deep expressiveness in her tone tells me her words mean so much more.

A few seconds pass as she silently fights through her panted breaths. I'm not sure if she's on the brink of shedding tears or if she's growing so heavy in lust that the desperation steals her breath.

"My heart is bound to yours, Arlo."

Now my breath is stolen by her words. It rushes out of me all at once, my body sinking into hers. I squeeze her hand and kiss her cheek, turning my head to draw the tip of my nose along her face, nuzzling into her hair, inhaling deeply.

Wildflowers and starlight.

"Against all odds, I've fallen in love with you," she continues, "and I don't want to waste another moment of my finite existence trying to fight it or trying to pretend that I don't love you."

Her voice becomes a heady drug, stirring new affections, rousing my every desire for her with the vibration of her words alone.

"The poetry…your words were everything to me. I know who you are beyond what you've been told to believe. I know who you were before you were broken. I know who you're meant to become, and I'm watching you become that man slowly, bit by bit, growing closer to everything you could be with each passing day.

"I'll love you when you become that man, but I love you just as well now. I think I even loved you before, even in your cruelty. Because I think you were right…that our souls are tethered. We're cosmically bound by a tether that can never be broken. I want to give you memories to last your lifetime if you can't—"

Jerking my head up from the pillow, I lean over her to cut her off with a kiss. I need her to physically feel the way her words resonate within me…but also, I can't bear to hear her finish that sentence.

I kiss her with rough sensuality, with pressure but not force. I sweep my tongue across the seam of her lips and she opens eagerly, seeking a taste of my tongue with a sweet brush of hers. I worship her mouth with mine, giving praise to the way her spirit grips me, overwhelms me with divinity and light, with sacrilegious pleasure.

The kiss becomes our unspoken words, a tangible exchange of

everything we feel for each other existing in a space that's beyond words. Our kiss becomes the discussion of our indecipherable needs and unexplainable emotions. Yet the kiss alone isn't enough to express it all. I need to use every part of her, and I need her to use every part of me.

With agony, I drag my mouth from hers, pulling my head back to look at her. The skin around her parted lips is flushed pink, soft and wet from our kiss, and it makes me wonder if the flesh between her legs is flushed and wet, too. Desire floods my veins, rushing blood to my center, hardening my cock, which pulses with the insistent demand to fuck her.

She shakes her hand from my grip and pushes it down her body, the rope that binds us trailing her hand. Her fingers grapple at the silk fabric over her thighs, bunching and gathering until it's lifted above her hips.

There's no barrier against her perfect pussy, no underwear to be removed. She was ready for me hours ago, and the evidence of it is clear in the slick sheen that coats her flesh. Her right knee bends slightly, pressing against my thigh at her side as she parts that heavenly gate, opening up for me so freely and insistently.

Yet, before I can reach for the divinity between her thighs, she stretches her arm and reaches for it herself.

My eyes are glued to her nimble, delicate fingers as they rub down her flesh, gently circling her clit before dipping lower and curling inside her. She moans as they sink, shifting her hips to sink them deeper. At the sound of her enjoyment, my gaze is drawn to her face, eager to see the expression of pleasure painted across her features.

Her eyes are already fixed on me, dancing across my face as if it brings her even greater pleasure to watch me.

"You were gone for so long," she whispers. "I read your words over and over..." Her fingers move, and I can hear the wet stroking of her digits over drenched flesh. "I needed you…I needed relief."

My hand snaps down, my palm instantly clamping over her knuckles as I halt her movement. "Did you touch yourself, starlight?"

The man I was only weeks ago would be horrified at the thought of a woman stroking herself in pleasure. Women aren't meant to satisfy that unholy need—the only exception occurring beneath a full moon when a man's Impulse demands it of a servant. Yet the man I am today finds it unbelievably arousing. Everything we do with each other is forbidden, wrong, sinful…and I want to commit every sin imaginable in her presence.

She nods. "I did."

"Did you find relief?"

She rolls her head against my arm, turning her face to press a soft kiss to my shoulder. "No."

"Did you try?"

She kisses my shoulder again before meeting my gaze, letting the corners of her lips curl ever so slightly. "No."

"Why?"

"It wasn't worth it to me without you."

I snap my fingers down between hers, reaching through her hand to lightly brush against her slick folds, a teasing brush that makes us both force out a heavy breath at the same time.

"Tell me what you did." I bend to sweep my lips over hers. "Were you on your back? On your knees? Which of these fingers brought you the closest?" I tighten my grip, bending my roped wrist deeper over her hand, rubbing all our fingers through her wetness.

Her eyes hood and she pants through her words. "Don't you wish to tell me what a sinner I am?"

I kiss her, a quick, heavy press of my lips to hers, followed by a quick drag of my tongue across her bottom lip. "You do enjoy being wicked, don't you?"

"I'm a wicked woman, Warden Rainn. It's what they all say."

"A wicked woman, indeed." I let go of her hand just so I can smack it away, and I spank her swollen cunt with my hand. "*My wicked woman. My sinner.*" I kiss the corner of her lips and along the line of her jaw until I reach her ear. "My fallen, forbidden angel."

I spear two fingers inside her, burying them as deeply as they'll go before the rest of my hand strikes the barrier. A rough moan claws out from her throat and her hips thrust up to greet my touch. The sound strikes me with impatient hunger for her pleas. I stroke my fingers inside her, pressing up to rub hard and fast over a ridged spot of flesh inside her.

I bend my arm beneath her neck to tug her closer to me, locking her head against my shoulder to ensure she can't escape me. Her face turns toward my shoulder as she pants, as her hips buck and writhe against my hand. I clamp my thumb over her clit, and press my fingers harder, stroking faster.

She lets out a sharp cry and I tighten my grip around her head, encouraging her to fully press her face into my shoulder. I feel her teeth grazing, like she needs to bite, but she's holding back.

"Do it," I growl as my fingers work harshly inside her. "Sink your teeth into my flesh. Let me know how good it hurts."

She whimpers, but then her bite closes, and her teeth clamp hard around the curve of my shoulder.

"*Fuck,*" I hiss at the burn, then groan at the ache that follows, but my fingers never falter.

"Arlo," she pants my name, "I need…" Her thought trails off as her body rolls toward me onto its side. Her hips rock, fucking my hand while she licks the flat of her tongue over the bite mark on my shoulder. I shudder beneath the drag of her tongue, wondering if she likes the way I taste.

I live for the way she tastes.

I'm hungry for it, suddenly feral with the urge to tear my fingers from inside her and lick them clean, but that won't do. I want to taste all the subtle flavors of her wetness through each moment of her rising pleasure, through the peak of her climax and the blissful fall that follows.

I'm thirsty, and the only thing that will sate me is the divinely unholy nectar between her thighs.

chapter twenty-five
ARLO

I TEAR MY hand from Mercy's cunt to the dreadful sound of her disappointed whimper, though I won't leave her disappointed for long. I grab her hand and quickly thread my fingers through hers to secure my grip. I stretch our tethered hands above our heads, and as I roll on top of her, I slam them down hard to the pillow.

She gasps as I settle my weight on her, as my hips roll and my cock teases between her thighs. The warmth, the wetness, the way she parts her legs and bends her knees, bringing them up to grip my hips…Every sensation vibrates through my soul and insists that this is where I belong.

I dip to kiss her with heavy lips and a thirsty tongue, coaxing a moan from her chest, and swallowing it whole. Her breasts crush to my chest as her back arches from the bed. By the time I manage to tear myself from her delicious lips, we're both beyond desperate, heated, and needy.

Mercy's half-hooded eyes lock on mine, and the look she gives me is so intoxicating that I get stuck there, watching her watching me as her hips writhe beneath me in heat.

Sweet fucking sin.

I need to taste her…I need the flavor of our forbidden craving to coat my tongue and drip down my throat.

I tighten my grip between her fingers as I bring my other hand to the curve of her waist. With a quick flip, I roll us both, twisting onto my back while I bring her on top of me, causing her to gasp at the sudden change of position.

Eagerly, she pushes through our locked fingers to rise on her knees, settling her weight against my heavy, thickening cock. She carefully holds her healing hand near her waist, and it strikes me with pain when I realize how careless I was in rolling her over on it.

With my free hand, I reach out to wrap my fingers gently around her forearm, covering the tattoo of wildflowers she's had since she was a child. My gaze narrows as I turn to meet her eyes, silently asking if she's okay. She answers with a bob of her head as she sits down heavily over my cock.

Fuck.

I groan as she moves, pressing down, gliding her hips forward and back to rub her wet pussy along the length of it. Her crimson gown cascades around us, spreading the silk over our bodies and spilling onto the mattress. It hides the filthy way she slickens my cock.

Red is the color of blood and sacrifice, and its why the trial participants are made to wear it—because they have to sacrifice pieces of themselves through the ultimate acts of service.

I could almost be fooled into thinking Mercy has willingly cut herself open for me, dousing me in her blood and painting it across my cock with her raging, righteous cunt. She demands her pleasure fulfilled, regardless of my own...and she deserves it.

She deserves to take from me.

I would sacrifice my pleasure for eternity if it meant she could have hers. Yet she tells me with her eyes that she wants my pleasure as much as she wants her own. My heart hammers at the way she wants to give me things I don't deserve. As she slickens me further with each glide of her hips, I feel anointed in her righteous blood.

I slip my untied hand from her waist, around to her back, and tug her down to bend over me. With only one hand able to hold herself up—and those fingers locked firmly with mine beside my head—she's forced to settle her weight on me, and the pressure against my chest feels fucking incredible. Her short strands of starlight hair fall forward around her face, tickling against my cheeks as her face drops close to mine.

"I want to taste you, starlight."

"Please…" she hums.

"I want you to lay on me just like this, but turn around so I can fuck you with my tongue. Bury me beneath this red silk and smother me with your delicious cunt."

Her mouth descends and she kisses me with a rumbling moan, tasting me as though she's showing me with her tongue how she wants her pussy to be kissed.

She doesn't need to show me.

I already know what she wants.

She sits up and releases my hand so she can maneuver. She brings her right leg over me to kneel at my side, then twists toward me, spinning her body in such a way that the rope draws across the front of her rather than hanging behind her.

I'm about to correct her, to sit up and help her turn from the other direction to untangle the rope before she straddles me. Yet again, as she always does, she surprises me. She lowers her arm to settle the slack against my chest, so when she climbs over to straddle me, she straddles the rope, as well.

The tether connecting our hands now runs between her legs, and I can't think of a more perfect place for it to be.

I have a perfect view of her ass and pussy as she scoots backward, her skin shadowed in red as the silk fabric of her gown shrouds my head. Before she settles, I twist my hand around the slack in the rope, and tug. She yelps as it jerks her hand down between her parted thighs and I tug until I can see her fingers wiggling beneath her sex.

"Move back," I command. "Give me your cunt. Let me devour

you, starlight."

"Arlo," she breathes.

Her hips wiggle, but she doesn't move back. Instead, I feel the rope tug sharply where it's coiled around my grip, and my hand shoots forward toward her ass. Still hovering, I watch as she drags the rope over her flesh, angled to glide over her clit, and she groans as the harsh fibers roughly rub over her sensitive flesh.

"Sweet sin, Mercy…"

I pull back on the rope, tugging up to drag it over her again. Mercy gasps, tensing at the sensation, the pain of the coarse rope mingling with her wet, desperate desire. She pulls it forward; I drag it back. We fuck her needy flesh together with the tether that binds us until she's shuddering, tensing, needy for my tongue to lick away the ache.

I uncoil the slack and let go of the rope, letting her pull it all the way forward through her legs. With a gentle hand on her back, I push her forward, encouraging her to bend and lay down on me. Her hair tickles my stomach, causing a jolt of tension through my muscles. Then I feel her lips kiss a trail down my stomach, making me shiver when I feel them press just inches from the base of my cock.

I groan, grip both her ass cheeks in my palms, and squeeze as I swipe my tongue up the length of her pussy.

She whimpers and loosens all at once, knees spreading further to lower fully against my face, her body falling to lay on me with her full weight. The way she sinks to our depravity sends shockwaves of bliss through my body. I feel the softness of her cheek rest on my stomach, her bound hand coming to rest at the same spot on the opposite side of my jutting erection.

I'm suffocated in her heady, delicious scent, and my face is slickened by her arousal. And the way she lightly thumps her hips up and down against my tongue threatens to undo me entirely. I feel beads of pre-cum at the tip of my cock, and she hasn't even touched it yet.

Her hair drags across my skin as I feel her head lift, and without any warning, I feel her tongue lick across the tip of my cock.

"Sweet sin," I growl against her cunt.

Her fingers wrap around the base, and my hips jerk off the bed, rising to meet her perfect lips as she opens to draw me into her mouth. She envelops me in warmth, slowly taking me in along the flat expanse of her tongue. I falter, a full body tremor shuddering through me as I tense against the premature eruption that threatens from her slightest touch.

I close my eyes to revel in the power she holds over me, the celestial energy she exudes which calls for my satisfaction. I've never felt anything like her in all the years I've indulged my urges with servants on purging nights. The simplicity of Mercy sucking my cock while I lick her pussy is the most spectacularly erotic moment of my existence, which is nearly unfathomable given the breadth of my sexual experience.

She takes me deeper, then gradually begins to work me in and out with a slow, steady rhythm. I almost wish I could see her starlight hair bouncing with her bobbing head, but the view I have, nestled tightly between her luscious thighs, is more than enough to satiate my visual cravings.

She moans and it vibrates around my length, making my muscles twitch and my hips buck beneath her. Only Mercy could ever make me feel this lustfully insane, this wickedly sinful, this demonically divine. I could spend an eternity right here beneath her, finding all the sustenance I need. She sates my thirst with her arousal. She nourishes me with her ethereal energy. She grants me spiritual salvation as I serve her every need.

I want to serve her.

I want to serve this woman until I take my last breath.

I can't fathom ever denying her again.

With a long sweep of my tongue, I lick her from end to end and back again before swirling around her clit. I tighten my grip on her perfectly curved bottom and shake my head side to side, rubbing my entire face through her folds, washing my beard in her sweet nectar.

"Move, starlight," I mutter against her opening. "Fuck my tongue until you come."

She shudders, her hips sinking as the heft of pleasure weighs her down. I hold my tongue out—long and flat—and let her slide her pussy across it. She squirms at first, shifting her hips side to side as she plays against my mouth to test the sensation, but soon, she finds her rhythm, dancing forward and back as she presses herself down onto my tongue.

She manages to keep pace for a minute or two, bobbing her head to match the rhythm of her hips. But it's not long before she falters, finding such overwhelming sensation in riding my tongue. Her lips smack as they pop off the tip, and she pants warm breaths against my erection, beginning to move at a brutal, insistent pace.

Her forehead taps lightly against my stomach before she rolls her head with a moan, then turns to rest her cheek there instead. Her breaths turn to short, panting whimpers as her hips work. Then she's working her bound hand between our bodies, shoving it down until I feel her fingers brush the tip of my tongue at her clit.

"Arlo…" she whispers, and it's the sweetest sound.

Soon, she's writhing, twitching, and fucking toward her rushing orgasm. Her fingers curl, pressing hard against her clit. Her hips press down, angling in a way that nestles my nose snuggly between her cheeks. I groan in pure delight. If I should suffocate here through the force of her climax, I would die a happy man.

I want it.

I *need* it.

I have to taste the way she comes undone for me.

Give it to me, Mercy.
Use me and take your pleasure.
Let me be your servant.

These are all words I want her to hear, sentiments I want her to know, feelings that would grant her strength and comfort in knowing where she stands with me. She stands on a pedestal that rises high above me, and I'll gladly kiss her feet if that's all I can reach.

Mercy gives me her precious flesh freely, lets me taste her, lets me be the conduit for whatever spell this is that she weaves through my mind.

Not a spell...it's only her madness.
Madness I'm glad to be afflicted with.

"I'm...I..." she stutters through her speech as her body does the same, jerking against the same spot on my tongue as she presses down, as her fingers work frantically against her clit.

I dig my nails into her fleshy cheeks to spur her onward, encouraging her movements, her moans, her desperation. I tell her with a deep rumbling groan to come for me. Her body twists and jerks while fucking my face and her fingers.

And when she comes, she breaks apart—all the pieces of her shattering and bursting outward into the universe. It's as though I can feel her bursting into flames, burning to ashes, her stardust embers floating in the dark night sky as the remnants of a stellar explosion. It's like the words of my last poem come to life.

My dark angel...
crafted in the sky,
the only light in a vast, obsidian void.

A stellar explosion...
ashes of light,
she was speckled stardust over an onyx canvas.

I can't see beyond where my face is buried, but I feel the beauty of her entire being through such a powerful climax. She stifles the sound of it, pressing her lips to my stomach, gasping and moaning as she crests.

And then she falls.

Her body collapses onto mine, lax and spent.

Smoothly, I flip her onto her back, quickly twisting myself around to face her. She places her burnt hand above her head to rest on the mattress, and I watch as she pants, eyes fluttering shut though she tries to keep them open. As I rise to my knees, she spreads her legs for me, and I shift to settle between them.

She blinks her eyes open as pure satisfaction etches itself across her cheeks. She watches me as I swipe my hand across my face, intentionally gathering her wetness onto my fingers and bringing them in front of me to watch the way it shines as it glides between my fingers.

She lifts her knotted hand, drawing my attention to it, and I watch as she twists, coiling the rope around her palm to quickly shorten the slack. She yanks, and I fall for her.

I fall for her over and over again.

My hands land on either side of her on the mattress, but she continues to coil, further shortening the slack. She keeps pulling, tugging at my wrist until I relent. I drop to lean on my left elbow so I can lift my right hand and let her pull. She tugs at the rope, bringing my hand in front of her face, guiding my fingers to her mouth.

She wants a taste.

Understanding what she wants, I push two fingers past her pink lips. She closes her eyes as she sucks them in, taking in a deep breath through her nose in appreciation of the shared lust between us.

"Mercy."

Her eyes flutter open and meet mine as I slowly drag my hand away, catching my fingertips on her bottom lip. I trail my fingers down her chin, over the hollow of her throat, making her back arch as they draw a line down the center of her chest.

I sweep my hand right, pushing away silk to expose her breast, then sweep left to do the same with the other. Still leaning on my elbow, I dip my head to lick her nipple, to swirl my tongue around it as it hardens, to suck it into my mouth. I play until she's squirming again, arching her back and begging.

"Please," she pleads, and I think I might come from the sound of that word alone. "I need you inside me. Please."

My hand snaps to latch around her throat, pressing against her chin to tilt her head back. "Do you need me, starlight? Do you need me desperately, the same way I need you?"

"Yes."

"Tell me again that you love me."

Tension finds me with a sudden fear that maybe she didn't mean it when she said it before—that maybe she changed her mind now that I've given her some relief from the overwhelming urge to come.

Her eyes flicker, narrowing for a moment, as if she senses my fear. Then her gaze softens, and I feel her compassion slip between my ribs, blanket my heart, and comfort me in a way I didn't think was possible from a single look.

"I could say that I love you again, and you would hear the words," she says softly, "but if you need to feel that it's true, you only need to kiss me. Put your lips on mine, Arlo."

Put your lips on mine.

It's a command I don't hesitate to fulfill. My lips are on hers in a flash, pressing with bruising need. She lets out a whimper beneath my rough kiss that begs me to ease and let her lead this connection. Easing back, I lighten my pressure to a feather-light brush.

Gradually, she guides me by feeling alone with subtle movements of her lips against mine. Slowly, she coaxes me to deepen the kiss, drawing us both into a slow burning heat that simmers between us.

She parts my lips with hers, gently slips her tongue between my teeth, and sweeps across mine with unspoken words. Her silent words intensify, mingling with my own as our tongues tangle. I can hardly breathe with the way she devours me so sweetly.

She kisses me in the same way that I fell in love with her—languidly, imperceptibly, intensely, and entirely. I didn't know what love was, and I certainly didn't know it could be felt through a kiss, yet I feel it. I feel it from her so spectacularly.

My forehead drops to rest against hers as the need to catch my breath ends our kiss. "I felt it, Mercy," I admit. "Did you feel it from me, too? The way I love you beyond reason?"

Air catches in her lungs, and she stutters through a breath, nodding her head against mine. "Yes."

I need her. Now.

I shift my hips as my hand comes down from her throat to grip my cock. I line myself up against her, and with a steady thrust, I sink deep, nearly faltering to the sound of her gasping whimper. With my forehead still pressed to hers, I hold her stare as I bring my hand up to cup her cheek, to brush her lip with my thumb.

I fuck her slowly, deeply, ensuring she feels every inch of me inside her. Every movement is electric, hot, and sparking with fire I want to ignite. Each thrust is a strike against flint, sparking hotter, burning brighter. Soon we're panting and frantic, bodies jerking and writhing, seeking more, harder, faster.

"Fuck," I mutter as I rush toward the edge, and I know there's no use in trying to stay there when the sparks are flying so intensely.

"Come inside me," Mercy pants. "Please, Arlo."

The flames ignite, blazing through every inch of my body as I spill inside her. As if the universe celebrates our union, she comes with me, my release spurring hers. She starts to cry out, and I kiss her hard to silence her.

I would scream for her if I could; I would let the fucking world know how good it feels between her thighs. I would claim her away from any other man for all of eternity.

I collapse against her, spent and fighting to catch my breath. I shift to press my ear to her chest, listening to the beat of her heart. With each breath she takes, her chest rises and falls, lifting and lowering my head in a gentle rhythm.

Her breaths are heavy at first, but they gradually slow. Though I wish I could let them lull me to sleep while I'm buried inside her, they drag me back to reality. The reality is that soon, a day will come that I might lay my head upon her chest and find it cold and still, with no heartbeat, no breath, no life.

Ten days.

That day could be just ten forbidden nights away.

With each of her breaths, I'm struck with an ounce more dread for the second trial and what she'll endure…whether she'll survive.

She has to survive.

Time is fighting against me.

We need these moments together, but we have so little time to waste, and I need to prepare her for the next trial.

Minutes pass this way as we hold each other in the quiet. Yet gradually, I feel her tension rising, increasing with my own as my mind leaves bliss behind to formulate a plan.

"I've lost you now, haven't I?" she whispers.

I raise myself from her chest, propping my elbow on the mattress and leaning toward her side. I cup her cheek, rubbing my thumb along her jawline to soothe her.

"You haven't lost me."

She smiles, but it's tinged with sadness. "You're thinking about the end now, aren't you?"

My eyes fall shut, but I force myself to open them again, giving her a subtle nod.

"What…what did you find out about the second trial?"

I sigh. "The Control and the Elders decided it was best for you and Delle to enter blindly. I don't know what your trial will be, and neither will you."

"You don't know anything at all? Nothing to prepare us?"

"I do know one thing. They agreed to share one detail so we can do something to prepare you, but…I haven't figured out how to prepare you yet. It's more of a hint than a detail, really."

"Tell me." I see fear flicker behind her eyes, but it's quickly washed away, fading into determination. "Tell me what you know."

I'm hesitant to tell her—not wanting to cause her fear or worry until I have a plan—but she looks at me so expectantly, so insistently, that I know I can't deny her. Still, I fear saying the words out loud, knowing it will firmly end our blissful moment, and we'll be dropped head-first into the terrifying reality we're about to face.

My eyes narrow, studying her features, hating that I own responsibility for the anxiety that creeps into her expression. The question I ask next effectively sweeps away the anxiety to make room for outright dread.

"How long do you think you can hold your breath?"

chapter twenty-six

Mercy

A FEW DAYS ago, Arlo asked me how long I could hold my breath. Today, he and Theo lead me and Delle down the stone steps through the hidden passage from the courtroom.

"I don't recognize this path," I say to Arlo in front of me, leading the way with a burning torch in hand. "Where are we going?"

"Watch your head," he says. We turn left and he leads us through a narrowed passageway cut naturally through the stone. The arched ceiling hangs lower through this tunnel, forcing us all to trudge ahead with our heads dipped to avoid striking it. "I'm taking us to a place where you can practice holding your breath."

Those words alone steal my breath from me.

A surge of adrenaline pulses through my veins to think of what the second trial might be. I'm honestly a little frightened to think of where Arlo is leading us and what his plan is for preparation.

I don't know how we could ever fully be prepared when we don't know what's going to happen during the trial. There's any number of methods of torment that could steal away my breath—and every horrid scenario that comes to mind adds to my daily growing anxiety. Part of me is itching to retreat, to run back to the Homestead, crawl into bed, and slip into my nightmares, because at least I know I would eventually awaken from those.

I think I would rather know nothing about the trial than to have this tease of knowledge. Knowing I might not be able to breathe is frightening, but if I knew what to expect, then I could at least prepare my mind. Instead, I'm overcome by stress from the questions that plague my thoughts.

In what manner will I be asked to sacrifice myself?

How will they steal my breath? And for how long?

Will I be trapped somewhere? Drowned? Mouth and nose covered? Is it a false clue to induce anxiety?

Delle's voice trembles as she speaks from behind me. "You really don't know anything at all? Nothing more than the fact that we…that we might be breathless?"

"That's all we know," Theo grumbles from the back of our line.

Theo's been rather sullen since the meeting that decided our second trial, and he's put up an obvious wall against his interactions with Delle. It's noticeable, and I can feel the tension it creates with her. Though I wished for him to put up those walls before—against her obvious crush on him—I hate that he's putting them up now because she needs him. I see how near the end is, and I don't want her to be alone.

A twinge of guilt twists my stomach. I haven't been there for her. I've been sinning with Arlo, indulging with him as often as we can manage, knowing my final days are coming. I've been distracted by lust—he and I both have. We've lost sight of the fight, of trying to seek the truth, because we've been lost together in our passion. Delle deserves a better friend than I've been.

Still, the reality of death looms, and every passing moment feels wasted if I'm not spending it with him. Every day, I think to myself, "What if this moment were my last?" And every time I ask myself that question, my answer is the same—I'd choose to spend my remaining time in his arms.

My last moments, my final breaths belong to him.

"Almost there," Arlo says.

He leads us ahead through an opening into a taller passage on our right, and I'm thankful to be able to straighten to my full height as we pass through it. Then we make another turn and head through a tunnel that gradually widens.

At the end of it is a broad, circular opening, and I can see the cavern bathed in light—sunlight, not just from the glow of Arlo's torch. The stagnant scent of rock mingles with a new, gradually thickening aroma—the fresh, clean smell of mountain air after a rainstorm. I realize that the air feels thicker here, too, like when the clouds are full of rain and ready to burst.

There's water nearby…I can feel it.

I can see it, too. Not that I can see the water itself, but rather, I can see ripples of sunlight dancing along the rock walls of the open cavern ahead, reflections of gently flowing water.

I hesitate as Arlo continues forward, passing through the rounded opening cut with jagged edges through the rock. Delle moves around me, continuing ahead to follow him, and Theo pauses at my side.

"Go ahead," he urges with a tilt of his head.

I look over at him, his face visible in the light streaming in from the opening, though the flames of the torch held in his hand make shadows dance across his expression, darkening his features.

"Is Delle okay?" I ask him quietly, careful to keep my voice low enough that it doesn't echo.

"Are you?" His eyebrows draw into a straight line. "Are any of us?"

My expression mirrors his. I can't quite formulate a verbal response to that, so I shake my head slowly.

"Yeah, well…" he turns his head, looking through the opening where Delle and Arlo have their backs turned to us, "at least you and your warden have a distraction."

He knows…

I'm struck solidly in the chest by fear, my eyes widening with my stare locked on his face. Every muscle is rigid with worry as my mind races to formulate an appropriate response.

Do I deny it?

Do I admit it?

Do I beg him not to tell?

Does he know because we've been too obvious? And if we have, who else has figured it out?

His head turns back slowly, and he meets my eyes. We stare through a few beats as fear continues to pulse through my veins.

What do I say?

"I'm more observant than my brothers, Mercy. You don't need to worry."

"Please don't—"

"Your secret's safe. You're already a sinner condemned, so what does it matter to me if you sin through your final days?"

"I don't care what happens to me if our secret is found out. It's Arlo…He needs to be okay. I need to know he'll be okay when I'm gone—" My voice cracks with sadness, and the sound echoes. I clamp my hand over my mouth to silence myself before unexpected tears fall.

Theo grabs my wrist and gently pulls my hand from my face. "I can't promise you he'll be okay because I know he won't be. But it won't be because of me. You've kept the secret for me that I didn't participate in using Delle in the first trial, and I owe you, keeping this secret in exchange. I just…" He sighs and lets go of my wrist, and I let my arm drop to my side. He blinks, shakes his head, tries to smile, but it falters into a frown as he shrugs. "Sometimes I wish I could have the same with Delle."

"You've never—"

"I've never, Mercy. Not even the night she ran and I chased her. I did hurt her…" his gaze turns, looking off into the cavern through the opening, "the lashings on her back. She's just too…" He seems lost for the right word.

"Young." I fill in for him.

He bobs his head. "Innocent. Or at least, she was before the trial."

"She's still innocent. She's still young. And now she'll never have a chance to grow—"

"Don't say it, Mercy." His head snaps to give me one final look, and though his tone is firm, his expression is filled with pain. "I know what she'll never have a chance to be." He turns and stalks through the opening, heading into the cavern after Delle and Arlo.

My heart aches for him. Theo is like Arlo in many ways—a man with goodness buried deep, hidden beneath layers of trauma and shame and a lifetime of brainwashing.

Our exchange is too much for me to process right now. I need to focus. I need to try to prepare myself for this trial, not because I think I'll survive them all—I know it will be rigged against me. I just have hope that I might survive this one, hope that I might extend my limited days with Arlo for just a little longer.

So, I take a steadying breath, and force my feet to move, refocusing my thoughts on the preparation ahead.

Passing through the round opening, my gaze traces the flat expanse of solid rock beneath my feet, finding that the slab of bedrock stretches out to my left maybe twenty feet or so along a wall of rock. At the end of it, water pours from a dark opening about halfway up the rock wall, filling a basin that stretches out in front of me from left to right, parallel to the rock wall at my back. The basin is the size of a small pond, the cavern wall at the opposite side encasing it.

I'm mesmerized by the gentle but steadily pouring waterfall that glistens in the sunlight, which shines through an opening at the ceiling of the cavern, at least two stories above us. My gaze traces the rays of light shining down over the pool of crystal blue water that fills the basin. It's so beautiful here that I can almost ignore the autumn chill.

"How on earth did you find this place?" I ask in awe.

"Lots of exploring," Arlo replies.

I turn toward his voice, watching as he takes Theo's torch and places it on a black bracket fixed on the rock wall. I notice his own torch is still burning brightly from another bracket, and the messenger bag he brought with him rests on the slab beneath it.

I have to assume he placed the brackets himself—he'd done all the rigging in the other dark cavern where he'd strung me up and prepared me for the first trial. A shudder tears through my spine at the memory, which was equally good and bad. He'd hurt me that day, but I also recognize that my pain had driven a wedge through his version of the truth, and it had started to splinter then.

"Are you going to—" Delle starts, her arms crossed over her chest, hands rubbing over her biceps. "Are you thinking of having us go in there, under the water? I can't swim…" She backs away, her path curving toward the broad circular opening in retreat.

Theo rushes in front of her, blocking her from my view. I see him cover one of her hands with his. "I can swim, and you know I would never let anything happen to you."

"Well, that's a lie, isn't it?" Delle's voice rises in pitch, tension creeping into her words. "It's your job to ensure I make it to the trial where terrible things will happen to me. You've let all kinds of awful things happen to me already!"

Theo's hand drops away and he takes a step back. It's an immediate cue for me to step in, to share some strength for her, especially as I've been so absent as of late.

I rush to her before she even finishes speaking, slipping between her and Theo. She starts to move away from me, but I halt her, reaching out to grip her cheeks, though she doesn't immediately give me her attention—her eyes fixate beyond me toward the water.

"Look at me, Delle." I wait until she lifts her worried eyes to meet mine. "I know this is frightening…I'm frightened, too. But Theo isn't going to hurt you here. He's trying to help you. If you don't want to prepare, that's fine. No one is forcing you to do anything today. But you *will* be forced to face the second trial, and preparing your mind to endure panic now will only help you later."

I sigh, loosening my grip. I keep one hand on her cheek, while the other strokes over her hair, down the side of her head. "You can choose to do as much or as little as you want to prepare for your next trial. If you want to sit over there with your back against the wall and watch me prepare alone, you can. If you want to go back to the Homestead and do nothing at all, you can. Right now, you still have control."

Her eyes flicker around my face as I speak, fear etched into every twitch of her expression.

"Remember that you chose this, Delle. And it's still your choice how much you want to fight for survival. I wish you would fight with everything you have. If any woman would be the first to survive the Trials of Dissension, it would be *you*." I know neither of us will survive, but it doesn't matter. Delle needs hope to fight, and I'll say whatever I have to say to give that to her.

She deserves to have hope, even if mine is lost.

I pull my hands away and step backward, giving her space to choose whether she'll move forward or retreat. "Theo wants to help you, and I hope you'll let him. Don't forget what he and Arlo did for you in the first trial. They couldn't spare you from all pain, but they did everything in their power to protect you as much as they could. They mean us no harm; they're as bound by duty as we are by service in these trials. Don't forget that, Delle."

I watch as a single, silent tear slips from the corner of her eye, tracking down her cheek. "I'm so…I'm terrified, Mercy."

"I know." I nod slowly. "I am, too. You're not alone in fearing this, but we still have to fight, Delle. We can't give up just yet." I reach out and wipe the tear from her cheek with my knuckle. "The more you expose yourself to your fears now, the more prepared your mind will be for whatever we'll face in the next trial. And who knows? Maybe it won't be so bad as what we imagine. Maybe whatever Arlo and Theo have planned for us here will be worse, and the trial will feel easier."

She scoffs, crossing her arms in protective defiance, and sniffing back her tears. "I doubt that," she says, rolling her eyes.

A grin twists at the corner of my lips. "You stood before the Control and the Elders not so long ago and despite your fear, you spoke your mind freely. You can do anything, Delle. And you can do this."

"*You* can do anything; *I* can't."

"If only you knew just how weak I was, you'd know that you're so much stronger and more capable than you give yourself credit for."

She huffs out a heavy breath, forcing agitation to the sound of it, though her fear is masked behind it. "Okay. Fine. I hear you. I'll try whatever they have planned today, but I'm not promising I'll do it again."

"That's good enough for me." I smile and nod in acceptance before turning to look at Arlo and Theo behind me. "So, what's the plan? How will you prepare us?"

Arlo's arms are crossed over his chest as he takes a step forward. "Service by Sacrifice is meant to test your willingness to sacrifice yourself for another. Sacrifice is one of the ultimate acts of service because servants must give parts of themselves to satisfy the needs of men."

I quickly fall into fascination listening to him speak and watching his body language as he tells us of the second trial. It's fascinating because I can see the way he's changing—I can hear it in his voice, in the way he says the words he once would've recited without feeling. He says them now with a hint of disdain and disbelief, and it gives me such hope for the man he'll become, for the changes he could make in Ember Glen long after I'm gone.

"This trial could be designed in any number of ways," Arlo continues. "It's impossible to predict exactly what our brothers have planned, but since we have this one hint, this morsel of knowledge that it might in some way require you to hold your breath or be deprived of oxygen, then we can at least exercise your lungs and work on extending the time in which you can hold your breath. It's something…

"Beyond that, we also know that the trial will hold a psychological component. It's meant to involve a difficult choice… one where you'll have to choose to sacrifice yourself, but the choice isn't meant to be an easy one, so I don't think that practicing holding your breath alone is going to cut it. The next two trials are meant to be arduous, brutal. An element of fear will likely be involved, so conditioning your mind will help prepare you, as well."

"So, we are going in the water, then?" I ask.

Arlo nods. "That's my plan, yes." His throat bobs as he swallows nervously, and it strikes anxiety within me, as well. "Theo and I will go in with you to ensure you're safe, but also to ensure we're preparing you well. You'll fight being underwater for too long, and you may need to be subdued."

That's the moment it hits me, a punch of adrenaline racing so fast through my veins that I can feel it tingling in my toes and through the tips of my fingers in mere seconds. "You're going to subdue us underwater…" I say to clarify my understanding of the events about to unfold.

"Yes, for however many times you want to try. We'll slowly increase how long you're under, both to prepare your mind and your lungs." Arlo drops his arms and takes a step toward us. "I know this trial won't be easy. Most participants lose their lives by the end of the second trial, and I'm not going to mince words about it. This trial will be dangerous and likely terrifying. If some form of oxygen deprivation is involved, then panic will bring you to a swift end, so figuring out how to calm your mind through your fear will be crucial. And now is the time to figure that out."

My head bobs slowly in understanding and agreement, though my mind tries to disconnect from the raging fear that pulses through me. My eyes lose focus, shifting to look somewhere beyond him as I fight to bring myself back to the present, to keep myself fully aware and in the moment so I can do what has to be done to prepare.

I'm terrified, but determined.

I need to pass this trial.

I need more time with Arlo.

I blink and take a deep breath, then turn my head to look at Delle. "Are you ready to do this?"

She looks at me, fear widening her hazel eyes. She straightens to her full height and pulls her shoulders back, though her jaw tenses from fear.

"Okay." She nods. "I'm ready."

chapter twenty-seven
Mercy

I'M BURIED BENEATH the surface, entombed in a water-filled coffin. Arlo's fingers dig into my shoulders as he presses down, holding me under the water while I struggle against him.

I need air.

I need to breathe.

The edges of my vision are blackening from the deprivation of oxygen and panic is taking control.

Don't panic. Be still.

No matter how many times I repeat those four words in my mind, I can't help but lose myself in a frenzy of fear, wildly thrashing for the surface. I fought so hard the last time I went under that I asked Arlo to bind me and force me still. I needed him to tie my legs to stop me from kicking at him and thrusting myself away, but he couldn't bring himself to do that. At least he was willing to bind my wrists this time.

Still, my frantic thrashing continues, and it almost feels like it's worse now than it was when my hands were free. I can't grab him, I can't pull his hands from my shoulders, I can't squeeze his palm, or give him a physical signal that I've reached my breaking point. With my hands tied in front of me, panic rises faster and sharper than it did before.

Let go of me!

Let me up!

I scream inside my mind as my muscles twitch, instinct telling me to open my mouth and take in a deep breath. I have to fight through the urgency in my mind that begs my body to take over.

I made Arlo promise to hold me down for ten seconds longer, no matter how much I fight. I can keep fighting the unavoidable and make this harder on myself, or I can focus my energy into finding some pathway in my mind that leads to peace and calm.

Don't panic. Be still.

Don't panic. Be still.

I can't! I need to breathe…

Just as my panic peaks, Arlo's hands fall from my shoulders and slip beneath my elbows. He yanks me up, and I crash through the surface, water splashing and rippling away from me as I break into open air. I gulp in a desperate breath as he moves to hold me up, snaking his arms around my waist.

Seconds later, there's another splash beside me, and I turn to watch Delle break from the surface. Delle gasps for air with her mouth open wide, fear dousing her expression.

I blink the water from my eyes as I look away from her while panting to catch my breath. She's above the surface again, and that's all I have the capacity to concern myself with at the moment. My head feels light and wispy. We've done this over and over, and it's starting to drain me. My muscles feel listless from the repetitive oxygen-deprivation exercises. It's only been short bursts beneath the surface, but we've done it so many times that it's starting to catch up.

My hands are pinned between my body and Arlo's, and I have to fight the urge to lift them, loop them over his head, and lean my cheek against his to rest. Instead, I ask him, "How long?"

"Forty-five seconds," he says.

"Forty…forty-five? That's it?" I draw in a deep breath to fill my lungs fully, then blow it out slowly. "I told you to keep me down for fifty."

He shakes his head. "I couldn't."

"I need you to be stronger than me—" I start, but Delle's shaking voice cuts through.

"I can't! *I can't.* I can't do this anymore!" Her fingers have a death grip on Theo's shoulders. "Take me out. Now!"

Arlo and Theo are both able to stand on the rocky bottom of the pool. The surface comes up across their chests, nearly drawing a line across their shoulders. I could strain on the tips of my toes and tilt my chin high to keep my face out of the water, but I wouldn't be able to do it for long. Instead, I rely on Arlo to keep me up because I don't know how to swim, and neither does Delle. So, when she demands for Theo to take her out, she has to wait for him to move, which he does right away.

He takes her to the edge, and she reaches out to place her palms on the stone, which is level with the top of the pooled water. Her hands are unbound because she was too panicked at the thought of being tied, so she's a little bit braver in letting go of Theo than I think I would be in letting go of Arlo.

She struggles as she works to pull herself out, still panting and fatigued, but she doesn't struggle for long. Theo grips her waist and hoists her up, twisting her around to sit her on the edge.

Her eyes widen as she looks at him, quickly reaching down to tug her gown across her bare legs. There's a strange, tense pause between them, but then she blinks, huffs in frustration, and drags her legs over the edge. She maneuvers to her feet and takes a few heavy breaths as we all remain still, waiting.

"I can't do anymore of this today. I'm done," she says.

"Fair enough," Theo replies easily, and lifts himself out of the water.

He shakes his hair, flipping the wet strands from his face before stalking across the stone slab toward Arlo's messenger bag. He pulls a dry gown from it and takes it over to her, holding it out. "Here.

Go back through the entrance to change." He indicates the broad circular opening we entered the cavern through at her back. "I'll wait here while you dress."

Delle gives him another look that makes me feel sad for her. I don't know what she feels about him. She has a crush, that's certain, but I had many of those when I was around her age—though that was all before I began service.

It brings to memory the way we were encouraged to develop these little crushes and attractions for the men in Ember Glen while we trained to be servants. It was regularly discussed in school when I was fourteen and fifteen-years-old, on the brink of age to serve. We were taught that men like to be longed for, adored, pursued.

Domestic wives are forced into celibacy, so men certainly aren't allowed such longing from them. Yet it was no harm at all for servants to look, to long, to even go so far as to innocently and appropriately let a man know that she would find honor in serving him under the next full moon.

It was all a ruse, though. It was a part of their control. They had us convinced that we would enjoy our nights of service, that under the full moon, we would be able to seek out and serve the men we longed for…as if it would be romantic. Service could never have been romantic in the way they wanted us to believe. It was never enjoyable and it was never consensual.

Delle peeks around Theo to look at me, still held up in the water with Arlo's arms around my waist. "Are you staying?"

I nod. "I'm going to try a few more times. You don't need to wait."

I hope she doesn't wait.

I do want to practice again, but I'm also eager for time alone with Arlo. Though what we're practicing here is anxiety-inducing, the beauty of this cavern—the sunlight, the waterfall, the gentle bobbing of the water that blankets us in our embrace—calls for a memory to be made here.

Delle nods and rushes out through the entrance, turning to move out of sight so she can change.

"You want to try again?" Arlo asks.

I look at him squarely, seeing in his eyes that he also feels the call for memory-making. His palm splays, fingers stretching wide across the small of my back, subtly encouraging me closer.

"I do," I tell him. "But give me a minute to catch my breath."

I lower my hands between us, curling my fingers into fists, pushing lightly. I get that Theo knows, but it makes me uneasy, and I don't want to risk it all falling apart with so little time left. The trial is just a week away and that could be the end.

We wait in the pool as Delle returns in a dry dress, waiting while Theo steps out to change. I make a show of deep breathing, trying to make it obvious that I'm only waiting to catch my breath and ready my mind, and not just waiting for them to leave.

This forbidden love has turned me into a liar. We've all become liars because so much of what we want and need is forbidden. Perhaps that's why it's so difficult to find the truth.

Theo returns in dry clothes and takes one of the torches from the rock wall. "Be mindful of your time," he says to Arlo. "It looks suspicious when you're both gone for too long."

Delle's eyebrows knit together as she looks at Theo, trying to decipher his words. I don't dare look her in the eye for fear she'll figure it out, too. I think somewhere deep down she probably knows, but as I said to Theo, she's still innocent in her thinking, and I only hope she hasn't connected the dots.

I don't know how she would react.

Arlo gives a nod in response.

Delle and Theo disappear through the tunnels, leaving me and Arlo alone in the water beneath the shining sun. We wait in stillness until we can no longer hear the echoes of their voices, until the last hint of light from Theo's torch fades into shadow.

At the same time, our heads turn and we look at one another. Our eyes meet, and an involuntary flash of heat sparks between us. A breath passes, then Arlo's eyes fall to my lips. He lurches forward to capture them in a kiss, but I stop him with my fists against his chest. Before we lose ourselves, I need to try, just one more time.

"Keep me down for sixty seconds, no matter what." I take a deep breath, pinch my eyes shut, and sink beneath the surface.

The muffled roar of water fills my ears as he lets me go, his arms drifting away from me as I fall under. I'm calm for the moment. His hands aren't on my shoulders, gripping tight and forcing me down. He hasn't touched me at all yet, and I think he must be waiting until he sees me fighting for the surface.

Seconds pass before a hint of anxiety creeps in, and I know I need to get ahead of it. I bring the meadow to my mind and imagine I'm there, lying on my back in the sunshine.

In my mind, bright sunlight warms me.

Tall green grass tickles my skin.

My lungs are filled with the scent of wildflowers.

Shades of ruby and amethyst surround me with vibrancy.

My daytime dream is peaceful and calm, but conjuring an image of the meadow also reminds me of the heated night Arlo and I shared beneath the full moon.

The moon, round and bright white.

The flash of lightning and the rumble of thunder that vibrated across my skin.

The rush of pleasure that passed between us.

The starlight appearing behind the clouds.

And the rain—the unrelenting rain that drenched us, soaked us, drowned us...

No...it didn't drown us that night.

But I'm drowning now.

The images and memories I conjured to calm me disappear as panic rises, and I realize Arlo's hands still aren't on my shoulders. He's not holding me down, and I could get my face above the surface if I really wanted to.

But where is he?

A rush of fear concerns me that something's happened to him, and my eyes pop open at the worrying thought. And there I see his crystal-blue eyes blending so spectacularly with the crystal-blue water. He's right in front of me, sunk beneath the surface, and right here to feed my strength.

His hand moves slowly in the water, reaching out to grab hold of the rope that binds my wrists. He tugs lightly and our bodies are drawn nearer, floating together like two celestial bodies moving through space. His other hand floats up, and with two fingers, he points to my eyes, then turns his hand to point to his own, silently urging, "Watch me."

I nod slightly as I fight the urge to let out a bit of the air I'm holding in my lungs.

I fail.

Bubbles shoot out from my lips as I let go of my breath. Arlo drifts closer, his grip on the rope solid and unyielding. He has the same grip on my soul, meeting my eyes with the intensity and strength I can feed off of.

I'm not doing this alone.

Arlo's doing this with me, and it feels profound.

Moments pass as my lungs begin to ache, screaming for me to let go of the air inside so that I can draw in another breath. I let it escape with one small puff at a time, trying to hold it for just a little longer between each release, though the relief of letting go feels so good.

The tension builds within me, painful aching in my chest as my lungs beg for the movement of air. Pressure builds behind my nose and mouth as every single human instinct insists that I stop fighting the urge to take a breath. It becomes so painful that I squeeze my eyes shut, scrunching my face, trying to fight against the urge to breathe because it will only let the water into my lungs.

And then my arms rise.

I open my eyes to see Arlo lift them, ducking into the loop formed by my bound wrists. I let them fall around him, then I pull back on my hands until they catch around his neck. I tug him toward me as his hands find my waist and he pulls, our bodies drifting together with ease.

The urge to rise and breathe is etched across his face, but he fights it with his eyes on mine. His arms slip around my waist, and he holds himself against me, gripping as panic slips through his features. Slowly in the calm, clear water, he brings his face closer to mine until our foreheads touch, and we hold there, our eyes locked and determined.

We're both determined to fight through these last seconds, and I know if we share our strength, we can. He gives me his, and I think I give him mine, too. I have to give him mine when he starts to struggle, when he starts to let out too much air from the breath he's holding and a rush of bubbles trail from his nostrils.

He hasn't gone under once today and now he's trying, struggling to match the time I've been building up to. I feel the way his anxiety greets him, twitching through his body, causing him to jerk and kick his legs as though he wants to leap for the surface.

I want to leap, too.

I can hardly hold on any longer, but I know the time is close.

So close.

Just a few more seconds.

His eyes shut as his face tightens, fighting against the need to breathe, and I know I have to bring him back to me. My chin tilts and I press my closed lips to his. His eyes don't open, but they don't have to. I see a fraction of the tension sneak away from his features. His arms hug me closer. And there's the way his head tilts so slightly, as though he wishes he could part his lips and deepen our kiss.

I lift my legs to wrap around his middle, settling my bottom against his thighs, crossing my ankles behind his back to tighten my hold. One of his hands slips down from my back to curve around my ass, holding me up and keeping me close.

A few more seconds…

Our embrace tightens, our lips press harder.

Almost there…

His palm curves, his fingers dig into my flesh.

Now!

As if Arlo can hear inside my mind, knowing the exact moment when I truly can't bear a second longer, his feet drop to the bottom of the basin, and he launches us toward the surface.

Our kiss breaks as we burst through the waterline, both of our mouths opening wide as we gulp for air in thick, heavy breaths.

But he doesn't let me go.

We're still tangled together.

I blink rapidly to rid my eyes of excess water as we battle to take ownership of the air between us. Our eyes meet as we gasp and pant, the rush of water from our break slowly fading to calm. His eyes dance around my face, narrowing with a scrutinizing gaze before settling on my lips.

And just as I think of how much I want him, how much I need this moment to become a memory of fierce passion, his head tilts and his mouth descends, lips crashing against mine. We share a breath between us as powerful relief strikes, as our lips eagerly part and tongues quickly slip. I sigh as my back arches, and I tighten my legs around him to pull myself closer.

I haven't fully caught my breath, and though my lungs are aching, I find the ache easy to ignore. Every cell inside my body vibrates with pleasure and passion, and it's more demanding than the need to breathe. Maybe it was the desperation of breathlessness that spurred such intensity, our pretend play at suffocation devolving us to our primal needs.

Breaking free from my lips, Arlo kisses across my cheek in a fevered rush, skimming over my jaw, pressing his lips to my neck. "I want you so much that I'd die for this." His large hands curve, fingers digging in to grip my bottom cheeks firmly. Keeping me snug against him, he steps forward, taking me backward to the edge of the pool until I feel the rock touch my spine. "I'd let you steal my last breath. I'd let you end me for a moment of warmth between your thighs."

I pant, letting my neck roll back against the ledge as his lips skate across my throat. "Then find warmth and meet your end, Warden Rainn."

A growl vibrates from his chest, and I feel his teeth scrape across my skin. He pins me to the rock wall with his weight, lowering his hands, fingers scrambling to reach beneath my skirt and hook the fabric of my underwear. He tugs them over my ass and down my thighs. I tighten my arms around his neck as I lower my legs, kicking to help him tug them off over my bare feet. He lets them float away in the water, and I don't care about getting them back.

In a rush, his hands find my waist, and he hoists me up out of the water. The unexpected lift makes me yelp in surprise as he seats me on the ledge in front of him. He grips my knees to spread my legs as his gaze drops, then his palms slowly slip up my thighs, taking my dress up with them. It's clear he's intent on devouring me.

I scoot closer to him as he slips his hands over my hips, reaching around to grip my ass and hold himself against me. I tilt my hips down to teeter on the brink, hanging off the edge and ready to fall for him.

He gives me a quick glance with his sultry blue eyes before his face disappears between my thighs, and he kisses me there as though he'll never taste me again. My bound hands land on the top of his head and my fingers tangle through his hair.

He inhales deeply, drawing in my scent, and the way he groans makes my stomach clench and wetness rush to my center. He licks and laps, curls his tongue to dip inside me, then swirls it around my clit. My head drops back as I revel in the way he makes me feel so alive, even while I'm living my last days so close to death.

I hum in appreciation at the way he worships me while I tighten my grip on his hair. "I love the way you taste me."

"And I love the way you taste," he groans against my skin.

I lower my head to look down at him as his eyes raise to meet mine. I see them light up from his sinful grin as he rubs his tongue over my clit. Then he closes his lips around the swollen spot and sucks with a light, pulsing rhythm.

"Arlo…" I breathe his name.

My back arches, my body twisting in beautiful tension. My eyelids flutter with the ecstasy he brings, but I don't want them to close…

I want to see him.

I need to watch him there between my thighs.

I need to see the way he tastes me so boldly.

I want to watch him give me power I was never granted before as he gives me pleasure absent his own—not entirely absent his own, but certainly, he gives it freely. His face is buried between my legs, fervently worshipping the part of me that was used and abused by the men of Ember Glen for so long. He adores the flesh that was meant for service, yet instead of serving him, my warden serves *me*.

He gives me power freely with each swipe of his tongue. And the more powerful I become, the more his need for me grows.

Arlo turns feral between my thighs, licking, sucking, pressing into me so deeply that his beard tickles and scratches my sensitive flesh. I squeeze my thighs against his ears as he works, tasting every inch of me for minutes or hours or however much time passes in pure ecstasy.

I'm swollen with need, aching pleasantly with the urgency to come. He holds his tongue against my clit, pressing hard, turning his head side-to-side to rub it with an insistent, heavy pressure.

"Arlo…please," I beg as my head falls back.

I'm so close, so heavy, so filled with need…I'm about to fall off the edge into a dark void of pleasure that never ends.

But just before I fall, he stops.

He reaches above his head to grip the rope between my wrists with one hand as the other curls around my waist. The backs of my thighs scrape painfully over the rock ledge as he jerks me forward. My body drops into the water with a splash, and a rush of panic hits me as he takes me off-guard. But the panic swiftly turns to excitement as his arms close around me.

My legs float instinctively to wrap around his waist, and I drag myself against him. He ducks his head into the loop of my arms, and I hold myself there as his hands slip between our bodies. His knuckles bump against my sex as he works to unbuckle his belt, unzip his pants, and bare his cock.

I shift my body with urgency as he juts his hips forward, the tip of him nudging my entrance. I whimper at the tease, but he eases my suffering as his arms wrap around me, grabbing my ass in one hand and splaying the other across the small of my back to hold me steady as he sinks deep with a sharp thrust.

We gasp together.

We sigh together.

We find a strangely frenzied sense of peace together.

I'm overwhelmed with pleasure from the way he tasted me, need lingering from the way he brought me to the edge. I'm desperate to jump from that cliff, to let myself quickly fall back into the dark pit where nothing matters except for the thrill he gives me. I dig my heels into him, thrust my hips, and ride his cock as he holds me in the water.

His lips part as his eyes darken, watching me as if it's the first time he's ever had a woman, and the look of it only intensifies the throbbing between my legs. His eyes dance across mine, delving deep, seeing something in me beneath the surface.

It must be something deeply erotic, feral, powerful, and needy, because that's how I feel. I feel strong; I feel like I own my sexuality in this moment, taking from him with my rocking hips. I feel like he would let me use him to find my own pleasure without seeking any for himself.

His forehead touches mine in the way he always does it, and it makes me sigh. "Use me," he says with a shuddering breath. "Take it from me, Mercy. Stake your claim in corrupting me. God only knows that corruption is my fucking salvation."

"Arlo…"

"Take it. Take it all from me. Make yourself come undone so spectacularly that I can sense no other god in existence but you." Each word he speaks is a match strike between my legs. "Fuck, Mercy. You've become a god to me. Let me be your only disciple, and I'll worship you forever. Sweet *fucking* sin," he growls the last three words, tightening his grip on me, thickening inside me.

I slow my hips to a sensual rhythm, rolling my body in waves that ripple the water around us. I lean in to kiss his cheek, to brush my lips across his skin and whisper against his ear, "Is this your prayer between my legs?"

He shudders, holding me tighter. "More than prayer, deeper than worship…This is my *service*."

Service—my only role in life, the torture I unwillingly endured at the hands of men, and he gives his service to me freely now.

"I'm your servant, Mercy." His voice shakes as he makes the admission, and it ripples through me. It shocks me with pleasure so consuming and joyful that my eyes burn hot with the threat of tears.

He tilts his chin and kisses me softly, wetly, sweetly. Then he nips my bottom lip between his teeth and gives it a playful tug before releasing it. "Promise me forever."

"I promise." The words rush out of me, and there's an instant shift, a jarring switch from desperate sex to an aggressive, feral, all-consuming need.

I need to feel every inch of him.

I need to fuck him harder.

I need to come so roughly that I feel the ache of my release for days.

My rocking thrusts become frantic pulses, my mouth dropping open in anticipation of my release as it builds. With each beat, my pleasure coils tighter in my center, twisting and turning me until I can't think of anything else.

Nothing exists in the world but our writhing bodies.

"How close are you?" he pants.

"Close…" I barely manage the word.

"You'll come for me?" One of his hands slips between us, sliding up my chest, over my throat, curling around to grip the back of my neck.

My head bobs.

His lips curl into a smirk. "Then, I need you to hold your breath one more time for me, starlight."

"What?"

"I'll let you up when you shatter around my cock. Now take a deep breath, Mercy." His grip on the back of my neck tightens. "*Now.*"

His lips fall on mine, pressing as hard as his fingers dig into the back of my neck. It nearly takes me too long to make sense of what he's saying, what he's about to do, but then I quickly take in a short, sharp breath through my nose. Then his hand on my ass squeezes to firm up his hold, and the way it shifts my hips strikes me at the perfect angle.

I cry out into his mouth at the shockwave that sparks my climax, and my deep breath is spent. My orgasm crests, but we descend. Arlo bends, laying me back on the water, sinking me beneath the surface with his lips attached to mine.

He buries us in a liquid coffin, sinking us toward a watery death I would welcome a thousand times over if I knew it would always feel this good. A jolt of adrenaline from being forced under floods my veins, and it drives my climax faster up the peak. My thighs squeeze as I continue to rut my hips breathlessly through my release.

The bliss shatters spectacularly, and my body twitches through aftershocks as he sinks us deeper, kneeling on the rock floor beneath our feet, lifting me upright in his lap.

I want to watch him come.

My eyes open against the water to see my hair floating around me in slow-moving waves. The pressure of water filling my ears is a low roar that dulls all other sounds, making it seem like we're in a world all our own. His wavy hair floats away from his scalp, and I imagine seeing him floating in space, surrounded by the light of the stars.

His beauty is otherworldly, and in my euphoria, I see him as an ethereal savior.

Could this man still save me?

Arlo moves his hands to hold my hips, and he thrusts, fucking me with short, shallow thrusts, fucking me quick and hard to take himself over the edge in a matter of moments.

I watch without breath as he comes undone. His pleasure meets me with a beautiful calmness. There's a perfect, serene bliss under the clear waves as we float together in the gentle sway with our spent bodies still joined.

How long have we been under?

Less than thirty seconds?

More than forty-five?

It doesn't matter. I know I would take the ache and fear of having my breath stolen if I knew it would save this man still sunk inside me. In truth, that's exactly what I have to do for him. I have to carry his secrets to my grave to save him.

I like to think there's some version of the world where Arlo and I could have been together, that some civilized place might still exist out there, somewhere beyond the mountains, where we could choose who we love and how we love them. Some place where partnerships weren't selected by those in power, but instead, by the people themselves. Some place where loving a servant like me wasn't forbidden. Some place where my mother could've been with the woman she loved. Some place where love was stronger than hate, and hate wasn't encouraged by a spiteful god.

Maybe that place exists somewhere.

Maybe it exists nowhere.

Maybe it can only ever exist in these stolen moments between us…and maybe it dies when the men of Ember Glen take my breath from me for the last time.

chapter twenty-eight

Mercy

RED.

I'm swathed in the color of blood, cloaked in the shade of sacrifice.

A crimson corset cinches my waist, and though the vertical boning is rigid—nearly too tight in the way it's fastened—the fabric is soft against my skin. A sheer tulle allows the porcelain shade of my skin to peek through the spaces between the lacy flower appliques across my waist. My chest is exposed above the sweetheart neckline, formed by the rigid cups which cage my breasts.

Sheer sleeves cling to my shoulders, sewn with elastic to keep them from slipping with the weight of the long sleeves which drape loosely down my arms, secured with more elastic that's uncomfortable around my wrists.

I gaze at my profile in the mirror from where I stand in the foyer of the Homestead, beneath the chandelier.

Red.

Sacrifice encases me and blood flows in waves of fabric all around me.

My eyes leave the mirror, tracing down the layers of the gown, sighing at the beauty of the dress that may be the last one I will ever wear. I suppose if I should die today, this would be the most fitting attire to wear while taking my last breath.

The dress is truly stunning. Layers of the same sheer fabric as the sleeves float down from where the skirt is secured with a red silk bow around my waist. A chilled autumn breeze sweeps in from the wide open front doors, rustling the layers and making the appliques of floral lace dance like the wildflowers in the meadow.

Red.

Everything is red.

Blood-red.

It's the color of a servant's ultimate sacrifice—blood spilled from the violence of purging.

My blood won't be spilled today—they'll save that for the next trial, Service from Bloodshed. But today, I will sacrifice. I will be tested emotionally, psychologically, asked to choose some form of torment for myself in exchange for…something. I don't know what I'll be asked to sacrifice myself for yet, but the fear of it is already torment enough.

I glance at my reflection again and lift my gaze from the dress, meeting my eyes in the mirror. One corner of my lips twitches in the direction of a smile, though the motion doesn't carry all the way through.

The Control had called a special meeting yesterday with me and Delle. They'd been firm and insistent that they wouldn't tolerate us wearing servants clothes like we'd both done when we were forced to watch the last night of service under the full moon.

They were very clear that the only color we were to adorn was red, because we were no longer worthy of wearing black like our sisters. I'd put on the red dress they wanted me to wear, but if they thought I'd so easily take to their demand, they were sorely mistaken.

I mixed all the colors in the palette of make-up in my room until the powders turned a hazy shade of black. Then I painted it across my eye lids, sweeping the dark shadow up to my eyebrows. I drew a thick outline of black liner around each eye, and the way it frames my gray-blue eyes reflects my world as light surrounded by darkness.

The recklessly applied onyx is my quiet defiance, a silent reminder of who I am—the rebel they can't control.

I've vowed to myself that I won't let this make-up run down my cheeks today. I won't shed a single tear; I think I shed them all last night with Arlo, anyway.

I close my eyes at the memory of the last words he spoke to me before I fell asleep…before I chaotically fell into a restless slumber that I'd fought for hours in his arms. His embrace had tightened before he whispered the words that chased me into my dreams, "Whatever happens tomorrow, I promise, I won't leave you alone. Alive or dead…I'll follow after you, starlight. I won't let you go."

His words gave me comfort in the moment, but now, they threaten to force tears from my eyes, and I promised myself I wouldn't cry today. I fear that if I die, he'll break his promise to me. I fear that if I die, he'll chase me into the afterlife instead of staying strong, learning to lead, growing older to become an Elder who could enact real change in Ember Glen.

There's a lonely part of me that selfishly hopes for just that. It hopes for him to follow me into death and chase me to hell, or heaven, or wherever our souls may find themselves. But if he did, then suffering might remain in Ember Glen forever, and I can't have hope for that. I have to hope for his strength to remain.

I force my gaze from the mirror and look out through the wide open front doors of the Homestead to the sound of feet padding down the staircase at my back. It's Arlo and Theo. I know it from the way the air has shifted, the way it feels like it's all swept away and pulled out the doors, sucking every last hint of oxygen from the room. I stifle a gasp at the feeling of change, knowing that it's all about to begin.

Or end.

I steal a quick glance at Delle at my side, but her eyes are downcast as her chest heaves, as she fights for each breath in her rising fear. I quickly look ahead because the sight of her struggling through her panic is too much for me to handle.

I hear their feet come down on the landing, and there's a pause, a beat of silence in not knowing exactly what's coming next. My breaths quicken, though I fight to remain steady and calm. I know this is only the beginning of this awful day, and I can't let panic get the best of me now.

A minute of anxious silence passes.

And then there's movement.

Arlo appears, walking along my side, and as he moves past me, he draws a long red veil over my head, holding it delicately in his gloved hands. A long, sheer layer of crimson tulle floats down in front of me as he drops the veil, cloaking my vision in red. The veil is speckled with the same flower appliques that appear on my corset and down the skirt of my gown. They line the hem of the veil, giving some weight to keep it down.

It's beautiful.

It's stifling.

It shrouds me in terror.

This is it…

This day could be my last.

My vision is obscured by the flower appliques, and everything I see is marred with red. Arlo appears as though he's tainted by my blood as he steps in front of me. My heart stops beating at the sight of him—his jaw set, his expression hardened to hide his emotions, though he can't hide them from me. His downcast eyes lift to meet mine beneath his lashes, and he falters, just for a moment, just long enough for me to see how broken and fearful he feels today.

This can't be the last day.

It can't be.

I have to survive this.

"I can't," Delle whispers from just a few feet away. Theo stands before her, lowering her veil. "I don't think I can do this…"

Internally, I scream, and every part of my soul screams with me against the horror of this moment.

I have no words for her now as I did before the first trial. There's nothing I can say to bring her comfort or give her strength, because I have neither today. We may face death, and there's no reassurance I can offer against it.

"You can do this," Theo whispers. "I know you can. Just stay calm, okay?"

Emotion overcomes her and she starts to cry. Theo jerks forward, almost as though he was going to hug her, but quickly stops himself. He grips her shoulders instead. "Okay, let it all out right now. You have ten seconds, Delle, and then you need to stop. You can't carry this emotion with you to the trial; it won't serve you."

I appreciate that he's trying, but I'm frustrated by his words. It's not possible to leave emotion behind. I'm carrying the weight of the strongest emotions I've ever felt with me to this trial.

I feel so heavy, yet I also feel the way I'm beginning to shut down inside. I feel the dial turning the intensity of my feelings down, gradually easing me into a state of numbness.

Arlo's bare hand touches mine and my attention snaps to him, wondering why he removed his glove. My gaze narrows on him as I feel him place something small in my palm.

"Hold on to it. Take it if you panic. It will calm your nerves and slow your breathing. You have to stay calm to survive."

His fingers slip away from mine as he drags his hand away and quickly puts his glove back on. My fingers curl to grip the small object in my hand, and I quickly realize what he's given me. It's a single pill—the medication he gave me when I burnt my hand and the pain was too great to bear.

"Does Delle—"

"No." He shakes his head. "There was only one left and I...I need you to have it."

I swallow a rising lump in my throat and give him a small nod before turning my gaze to look beyond him. I curl my fist around the pill to hold it tight, grateful that he wanted to try to help, but unsure of how I feel about using it.

Outside, Owen, Park, and Wesley stand side-by-side halfway down the stone steps leading up to the Homestead. They face out toward the village square where a row of four large projector screens are set up. There's a space between the middle two, allowing a wide gap at the bottom of the stone steps for us to pass through. The villagers are gathering to watch our processional as we leave for the trial, throngs of men, women, and children filtering across the large gravel-covered square to bear witness.

I feel the veil move as Arlo adjusts it. It doesn't need adjusting; he's just anxious and needs the distraction of busying his hands.

"You just couldn't help yourself, could you?" he asks, and a weak smirk tugs at the dimple in his cheek.

"What?"

"The black around your eyes, Mercy. You just had to do it, didn't you?" There's a hint of teasing amusement in his voice, and the sound of it gives me a moment's relief.

"I can't follow *all* the rules, now can I?"

"No. You can't." He sighs. "You look—"

"Wicked? Sinful?"

"Powerful...Otherworldly."

Words fail me at the way he looks at me, with awe and longing, though it's tinged with fear and heartache. Tears well in my eyes, and I fight feeling anything in favor of numbness.

I blink away from him, glancing around to see Park turning to walk up the steps toward where we stand just inside the Homestead. The processional to the site of the trial is about to begin. My heart kickstarts in a chaotic rhythm, and my gaze darts back to Arlo, seeking him with urgency.

"Warden Rainn, I—"

"Don't say it." He shakes his head sharply, silencing me. "No last words."

My breath catches in my lungs at the way his eyes narrow and flicker across my face, skimming down to take in the full sight of me. He draws in a deep breath and I see the way his shoulders shake. If he breaks, it will break me, too.

I have to look away.

Park steps across the threshold, stopping a few feet in front of us. "It's time."

I swallow hard, my throat suddenly dry. I don't suppose anyone would give me water if I asked for it.

Water.

Will I be under water today?

I've wracked my brain trying to think of all the methods of torture one might use to steal another's breath in a test of faith and sacrifice. Water is the best I could come up with on my own—it's how we practiced holding our breath and taming our fear.

Yet it seems too easy, too simple.

Whatever it will be, I'm afraid for it.

My head turns, tracking Arlo as he moves to stand beside me, my mind urging me to take a final look at him before fear takes hold of me and makes me forget the world around us.

The first thing I search for is the crystal-blue of his eyes. They're always so striking, enchanting, able to hold my attention through my darkest moments—even now. His thick hair is a little messier than usual, which matches the way his beard remains untrimmed and unruly. I like the way it looks on him compared to the perfectly trimmed and polished way he was before. It makes him seem a little more rugged, a little feral, less rigid, and more flexible...more like the man he needs to become.

Still, his attire is sleek in comparison. He wears perfectly pressed dark gray slacks beneath a black, knee-length overcoat. The black coat is unbuttoned, revealing the gray waistcoat he wears over a crisp, white button-down shirt. A familiar silver chain links from one of the fastened buttons of his waistcoat to the pocket stitched at the front of it.

With a final sweeping glance, I draw in the complete picture of the imperfect man I fell in love with.

I fell in love with him.

Beyond reason, beyond sense, beyond the will of God, the universe, demons, or men, I fell for a man who was impossible to love…and now I have to leave him.

Air rushes from my lungs in a huff of awareness.

This day might be our last together.

"Are you wearing the boots?"

I nearly leap out of my skin. Arlo whispers the words, but the silence in my mind is so loud that his voice is startling. He holds out the crook of his arm for me to take, side-stepping closer. Slowly, I hook my arm with his.

We look at each other, and he gives me a secret grin. "Well? Are you?"

Though fear shakes through us equally, I want this moment. I want to give him one last smile before we go, one last memory of my rebellion. I kick my foot out to the side as I reach down to lift my dress and show him that, of course, I'm wearing my black servant boots.

When our eyes meet again, I give him a small smile.

"Good. I would have been disappointed if you hadn't worn them." He briefly returns the smile, though it quickly falters with his shaking voice as he looks out toward the village square.

He subtly side-steps closer, tugging through our linked arms like he's afraid I'll let go.

"Alive or dead, I'll follow after you, starlight. I won't let you go."

"Alive or dead…" I mutter, and I feel the air move as his head whips to look at me. "I won't let you go."

His jaw twitches as he tenses. A glossy sheen appears over his eyes, making perfect oceans of blue that might just drown me in heartache.

I force a small smile against the overwhelming sadness that claws its way up from the depths of my soul. I fight my tears as I squeeze my eyes shut, shake my head, and turn away from him.

"Wildflowers and starlight," he whispers, and my heart shatters.

Those words mean more to me than any other three words he could ever speak. *I love you* isn't ours; it never really could be. I don't want *I love you* when we have *wildflowers and starlight*.

Park gives a nod, then turns away to lead us forward. I drop my hand to quickly link my fingers with Arlo's. I squeeze, and he squeezes back. I try to tug away so we won't be seen, but he holds me for a beat longer, a moment past reasonable risk.

How do I let go of him?

With a lurch in my stomach, we move, following Park through the open front doors as Arlo's grip slowly loosens, as we both have to fight to let go of one another. As I link my arm in his again, we take our first steps onto the stone staircase to begin this procession of our suffering.

chapter twenty-nine
Mercy

COOL AUTUMN AIR swirls around us as we descend the stone steps, sending a ripple of goosebumps up my arms. The long sleeves do nothing to protect me from the chill given that the fabric is sheer, and neither does the veil. I can feel the impressive length of it trailing behind me, flowing like blood down the staircase from the Homestead.

Arlo and I lead as Delle and Theo follow behind us. I hear Delle crying as Arlo guides me, but I don't look back. I can't look back. I can't let the last time I look at her be like this—dressed in that red gown, covered by that loathsome crimson veil, crying through her fear and heartache. She's breaking, and I can't bear to witness it.

I'm breaking, too, but I have no tears to shed. The well is dried up, every drop boiled and evaporated by the flames of suffering that flicker within me, a fire so hot that it threatens to burn all that's left of me in a painful blaze of misery.

Park meets Wesley and Owen ahead of us as he steps down to the gravel. The three of them proceed ahead between the gathering of villagers, a group of them on the left and another on the right, leaving a wide aisle for us to pass through as they watch.

"Where are Killian and Ryker?" I whisper, feeling the need to know so I'm not taken off-guard at their sudden appearance.

"At the site of the trial."

We reach the final step, and our feet land on the small pebbles that cover the square. Then, we pause.

I hate the pause.

It prolongs these dreadful moments, allowing tendrils of fear to coil around my veins, squeezing to intensify the looming panic.

Worse than my own panic is hearing Delle's as they stop behind us. She fights to get control of herself, whispering, "It's okay. It's okay. I can do this," as she sniffles, trying to find the strength to stop her tears.

I know she feels weak, but I wish she understood just how strong she is.

I wish they all understood how strong they are—my sisters in service. They don't even recognize the value of their worth beyond serving the men of Ember Glen, and no one can blame them for that. It's what they've been told since they were babies. But part of me wonders….

What if?

What if they knew their strength?

What if they knew their worth?

What if they knew there could be more than painful sex and unprompted violence?

What if I die today, never knowing what could be if they only knew?

My stomach lurches. I bend forward around the awful clench in my gut, the knowing of terror to come, the harrowing realization that I could be marching to my death at this very moment.

Arlo whispers beside me, "Don't give them this, Mercy. Don't let them have the satisfaction of your fear in this moment."

I'm too afraid to open my mouth to speak in fear that I'll spew the contents of my stomach and give them all such a glorious image of my final moments to laugh over when I'm gone. A tremor tears through me, breaking into a full body shiver that shakes through me uncontrollably.

But somehow, I force myself to stand.

I link my shaking arm with Arlo's, and together, we leave the dreadful pause. I lift my chin as we walk, my black boots—hidden beneath the length of my red gown—crunching over the small stones and pebbles beneath our feet.

My eyes scan the crowd as we walk, searching for Ellary and Cambria in hopes I can make one last connection, give them a silent goodbye. My stomach twists in knots as I search for them, my heart pounding out of control. As adrenaline rushes through me, I struggle to track individual faces in the crowd. They all blur together as I'm brought to walk before them in the shame and disgust they have for me.

"Malo mori quam foedari."

The prayer is spoken, words fleeing mouths and catching on the breeze, swirling all around me. They're not spoken in unison; they come from the individuals who wish to see me die for my sins, the people of Ember Glen who are so lost to their faith in God that they think I deserve death for fleeing that one night of service. It feels like so much time has passed since that night, and nothing in Ember Glen has changed.

Arlo will change it.

I have to keep my faith in him.

The prayer is spoken over and over as we proceed, following Owen, Park, and Wesley.

"Malo mori quam foedari."

Over and over and over again until…

"Circulus vitiosus."

The two words are spoken by a single, unsteady voice, and the procession comes to an abrupt halt. Owen turns to look at Arlo with a confused expression as Park and Wesley glance at each other the same.

Another voice cuts through the odd silence, *"Circulus vitiosus."*

I feel Arlo tense at my side in the confusion. The Control

in front of us scan the crowd, searching for the voices that spoke words I've never heard before. They don't have to search too hard; someone's arm shoots straight up from the center of the crowd at our right, drawing everyone's collective attention to the sight of it.

It's a woman's arm, palm open wide with fingers splayed, and when the words are shouted again, it's clear they're coming from her. "*Circulus vitiosus!*" The words break through the quiet confusion, bursting loudly and clearly in such a way that I can feel it vibrate through my bones.

The blade of a knife rises sharply to the woman's bare arm, stretched high above the crowd, and we all watch in silence as she draws the tip of it straight across the back of her forearm, slicing through her flesh. A line of blood pools and drips, soaking her skin in crimson. All of Ember Glen watches in shock, frozen by the surprise of this moment.

For me, it's a moment of unexpected peace to witness this brutal action that feels so much like solidarity. For the Control, it's a clear act of protest—one that will need to be stopped immediately.

Circulus vitiosus…

What does it mean?

The crowd begins to shift, and voices rise, but the woman with the bleeding arm shouts one final time as Park and Wesley begin to move toward the crowd. "*Circulus vitiosus in aeternum!*"

"Sinner!"

"Stop her!"

"Someone take the knife."

The men in the crowd begin to turn on her as one of them reaches for her arm, circles his hand around the dripping line of blood. Wesley and Park drive their way through the crowd, and the people part to make way for them as they join four or five men from the village who've taken an active role in subduing this woman.

Someone takes her to the ground, pinning her arms behind

her back, but she's not fighting, not struggling, like she's already accepted this consequence because she knew it was coming…like she had planned for it. It's not until she turns her head, pressing her cheek to the ground, that I realize who it is.

Stefanie Price, Hyatt's newly widowed wife.

"Fuck. Where's Luna?" The words rush from Arlo's lips as a terrified whisper. I look over at him to find him scanning the crowd, tension tightening his features.

I search for her, too, wondering if she's part of this with Stefanie, worried as I'm sure Arlo is, that she may do something to get herself in trouble. If she does, I know Arlo will react, and selfishly, I don't want that. I need him. *I* need him because I know that nothing will stop this trial from happening today.

More than my selfish need for him, he's kept promises for the future of Ember Glen that require him to maintain control. I cannot allow him to lose focus, to lose control of himself. He has to become an Elder when it's time for the next Shift. So when I spot Luna ahead of us, standing beside her husband, with Soleil strapped to her chest and her other children beside her, I tell Arlo right away.

"She's there, up ahead. I see her."

"She's going to—"

"She's not going to do anything."

He fears she's going to act as Stefanie did, but I know she won't. I can see horror on her face, the surprise and utter shock. Tears stream down her cheeks as she watches Park and Wesley lift Stefanie from the ground. Her palm cradles the back of her baby's head as her other hand tightens its grip around her son's palm where he stands at her side. She may be unhappy with her domestic life, but she clings to her children, and I know she won't risk leaving them.

It makes me wonder for a moment why Stefanie chose this, knowing it would take her from her children. Though I suppose now that Hyatt is gone, she doesn't need to be there to protect them from him. They'll be assigned to another domestic family unit, and any home they're placed in would surely be better than the one Hyatt ruled.

Owen appears in front of us. "Move, *now*," he tells Arlo as I watch Park quickly bind Stefanie's wrists with rope behind her back. He takes hold of her arm and drags her toward the aisle where we stand. "Keep the processional moving, we can't draw further attention to this."

Owen abruptly turns on his heel and marches ahead, expecting Arlo to follow…but he doesn't move.

Arlo's frozen, rooted to the spot, his eyes fixed on Luna, watching with blue blazing fear. He's afraid for her, afraid she'll follow Stefanie and speak those words that seem to be blasphemous, words of protest or solidarity…something I don't know or understand.

Circulus vitiosus…

Circulus…Does that mean circle?

Are they saying vicious circle?

Those are the two words I remember Luna saying to me, but I have no idea what they mean or whether that's really how *circulus vitiosus* translates—I can only guess. Yet, even in my confusion over what's happening and the meaning of the words, my heart flutters with wonder and a strangely optimistic flurry of hope. Whatever the words mean, it's clear to everyone that these are words spoken only by sinners. And in Ember Glen, sin is our only weapon in the fight for freedom.

If there are murmurs of rebellion among the women, if there's a chance that my sins have sparked a war, then my death may just set it ablaze. Arlo must survive the loss of me to stoke those flames, to guide the so-called sinners to the corrupt so they can burn them to ashes. He needs to remain strong, in control, an influential member of the authority. He has to survive, regardless of whether I do or not.

I take a step forward while he remains frozen, and my arm

tugs against his, pulling until he moves with me. "You promised me, Warden Rainn."

I stare straight ahead, but from the corner of my eye, I see his head turn in my direction. I can feel the intensity of his eyes as they fix on me, but I don't turn to meet his stare. I focus on what must be done for Ember Glen, following as Wesley rejoins Owen ahead of us and they lead us through the crowd.

"You promised you would maintain control, that you would solidify your place as an Elder so you can bring change to Ember Glen. You promised me you would do what it takes to set sinners free and end the corruption and violence." I grit my teeth against the rising indignation that settles with a heavy weight in my chest. "You will *not* break that promise to me now, not ever. Whether I survive this day or not."

His gaze leaves me, but I feel the unease ripple through him, humming from his aura, mingling with my righteous anger in a way that makes me tremble.

"Luna…What if she—"

"You can't control her any more than you can control me. You will *not* break your promise to me, Warden Rainn—" My voice cracks and I fight to steady my emotions as we reach the end of the aisle between the gathered villagers. We follow as Owen and Wesley turn, leading us east toward the forest. "When this trial is done, regardless of what happens to me, you have to talk to Luna and ask her about vicious circle. If it's the start of an uprising, they'll need your power, your influence…they'll need your guidance. Do you understand me? Promise me right now that you'll do right by me. That you'll fight for my sisters and make this a place where choice and love and freedom can exist." When he doesn't respond right away, my voice trembles through the word, "Please."

He whispers so faintly, I can hardly hear him, "A place where you and I could have loved freely forever…"

He sighs, and I feel his understanding in that release of breath. I feel acknowledgment shiver through him. I feel his promise in the way he drops his head, staring at the ground in resignation.

Silence cages us together with our shared sorrow as we enter the forest…and not a single word is spoken between us for miles.

OWEN AND WESLEY lead the way, maneuvering around tree trunks and stepping over fallen logs as we march through the forest. The day is overcast and dreary, and we're surrounded by chilly air that only makes my shivering that much worse.

We proceed this way through the forest for what feels like an eternity. We're approaching the second hour of walking this rough terrain, and I'm exhausted.

During the first fifteen minutes of our trek, our veils continually snagged on twigs and leaf stems as they dragged across the ground. It was slowing us down, so Owen insisted they be removed, and he carries both of our veils now. It makes me wonder whether there was a point to having us wear them at all, or whether they were just meant to be the shroud that draped us in terror, knowing our trial was about to begin.

My arm is no longer linked with Arlo's. Instead, I hold the front of my dress up with the heels of my hands resting against my thighs, fighting my way through each step of this endless processional.

I glance behind me to check on Delle as she walks side-by-side with her warden. Theo carries a pair of red shoes in one hand—shoes with tall heels they expected us to wear on this hike through the forest. I'm glad I didn't, but I feel sorry for Delle because clearly, she's barefoot now. The ground is rough and cold, and it adds another layer of torment to the suffering in this trial.

Twenty minutes ago, the ground began to gently slope upward, and each uphill step becomes more tiresome than the last. The trudge up the incline slowly siphons air from my lungs. I'm already panting in my anxious state, and it makes me angry. I'm angry that I have to exert myself just to be tortured and tested.

Another twenty minutes pass as we travel up the never-ending slope, and I can feel the air is changing. It's growing colder, and I hear the gentle autumn breeze crescendo toward a vicious howl as a sharp incline approaches. A mass of greenery and wild overgrowth conceal the ascent, but looking up and beyond, I can see the bases of tree trunks jutting from the ground ahead, which is high above us.

Owen and Wesley shift, moving one behind the other as they come upon a narrow path beaten into the dirt, the end of which disappears between a cluster of tall bushes.

This is it…

The instinctive clench in my gut tells me we've reached the site of the trial.

I stop, loosening my grip to let my hiked-up skirt fall and skim the dried leaves beneath my feet. I quickly clench my fist again when the small white pill slips, reminding me of its presence in my palm. I'm not even sure how I've managed to hold on to it this entire time.

If the trial will begin beyond this path, I know now is the time to take the medication. Yet I've already decided that I won't. There are two of us participating in this trial, and only one pill. I can't take it for myself if there's none for Delle. She struggled far more than I had in preparation for this trial, and I'm truly terrified for her. Giving her this pill is the last thing I can do for her, my final parting gift, knowing that the odds of both of us surviving—of *either* of us surviving—are low.

Arlo stops to look at me, questioning me with a tilt of his head. I meet his eyes for a moment, then turn to look at Theo as he and Delle catch up to us. "Could I have a moment with Delle?"

Arlo and Theo glance at each other, but Arlo gives a small nod. He turns his head to look behind him and calls up the path, "Owen."

A few seconds pass before Owen appears from the overgrowth,

his eyes narrowed in confusion. "What is it?"

"Our participants would like a moment with each other before the trial."

Owen looks between us with a surprisingly severe expression. "Fine, but only a moment." He takes a step forward and crosses his arms over his chest, watching, waiting.

I hold out my empty hand to Delle. She drags her wide eyes away from where they were fixed on the narrow dirt path to look at my outstretched hand instead. It takes her a beat to blink away from her outright fear, but then she finally swings her arm forward and places her hand in mine.

I drag her a few steps away, staying close enough that Owen will feel secure in knowing that we're not trying to run, but far enough that none of the men will hear my whispers. I turn to face them and tug on Delle's hand to move her in front of me, making sure her back is turned squarely to them.

"Give me your hand," I whisper once she's facing me.

Her forehead creases with confusion, but she lifts her hands between us. I flatten my palm beneath hers—the one that holds the pill—before turning our hands over. Then, I slowly slip my fingers down to her wrist to keep her hand right there in front of her between our bodies, concealing it from the Control at her back. She looks down at the pill now resting on her palm.

"Take this," I whisper, "right now. But don't let them see. Swallow it down, quickly."

With trust I don't understand, she nods, and my fingers fall away from her arm. She pinches the pill between her finger and thumb, quickly and sneakily bringing it up to her lips, then popping it into her mouth.

I watch her throat bob as she harshly swallows it dry. "What is it?"

"It will calm your nerves, trick your mind into euphoria. It will help to ease your panic."

"You already took one?"

"Yes," I lie.

"Is this…" Her bottom lips trembles as she shivers against the chill while simultaneously fighting tears. "Is this it?"

I sigh, reaching out to tuck a strand of hair behind her ear, and tears threaten to well and fall—tears I promised myself I wouldn't shed today.

"This is it." I nod sadly, but I force a small smile for her. "I'm really proud of you, Delle. You've become the woman I always knew you could be."

"Mercy, I want you to know that—"

"Stay strong and fight for it, Delle." I had more to say to her, but the moment she said my name, I splintered. She said my name, and for whatever reason, that was the thing that drove a wedge into the crack, breaking through my remaining strength with force. I have to get away from her before it crumbles and falls to pieces on the cold, hard ground.

I lift the front of my skirt and rush around her, pushing past Owen, Arlo, and Theo, trudging ahead up the narrow dirt path. Just a few steps in and greenery surrounds me. My boots dig harshly against the ground as I push my way up the steep incline.

The howl of wind intensifies with each step, beckoning us forward with its ominous roar. Lifting my chin, I look ahead up the path, and in less than a minute, I can see the end of it opening up again to the forest.

Some part of me wants to stop, pause, and take a breath. That part wants me to turn back and run away. It wants me to leap into Arlo's arms and beg him to take me far, far away from here.

Yet I know I can't.

I can't run from this fate; I can't hide. The cowardice of fleeing won't inspire change, but my participation in this trial just might.

This path is steep and hard to climb, and though I hate it with every molecule of my existence, I cannot stop. This is a path that must be traveled to the end once the first step has been taken…and I took the first step the night I chose to run from service.

I push harder through the final inclined steps, and as I come out from the bushes, the ground levels out. I can finally take a full breath. Arlo's not far behind me; I feel his presence pulsing at my back as I slowly move forward between the trees, yet I don't turn back.

My eyes are fixed on the sight before me.

Twenty paces ahead of me, the forest comes to an end. The colors of autumn dissolve into bleak and desolate shades of gray; the brown soil, yellow and orange fallen leaves, the emerald- and hunter-green hues of the evergreen shrubbery all fade into solid, drab rock. The forest ends to give way to a gray slab of rock, which stretches from the tree line across a vast, semi-circular clearing.

And at the end of the clearing, the world ends, dropping off into nothingness at the edge of a cliff. Beyond is open air, empty space that's filled with dreary fog. I see the jagged outline of gray mountains in the distance, clustered together and rising menacingly toward the sky. My heart skips a beat before wildly thumping against my ribs.

I falter as I step back, instinctively wanting to put as much distance as possible between myself and the edge of that cliff. Arlo's palm wraps around my forearm, gripping tight and halting me. He spins me around to face him, dragging me closer, but I can't look at him with my panic rising—meeting his bright blue eyes will only make it worse. I turn my head away to avoid his stare, and my gaze drops to the forest floor.

I quickly find that looking at the ground is no better for my anxiety. My gaze follows a trail of flattened leaves beside us, the crunched and leveled remnants which show a path that someone has recently walked parallel to the tree line. My head gradually rises as I follow the trail to its end, and fear punches through me as broken leaves fade into disturbed soil.

Two large piles of soil rest as mounds behind two side-by-side trenches dug into the earth, nestled between the trees. The trenches are slightly longer and wider than the wooden boxes hovering on platforms above the empty, dug out pits—wooden boxes long enough and wide enough to fit a body.

Coffins.

Graves.

"No…" I gasp, the word sneaking out from between my lips.

Movement from beyond the graves steals my attention. I turn my head toward the motion and see people coming out from the forest, crossing the slab of stone, and making their way to the precipice.

Black skirts whip in the wind, and my heart drops into my stomach. Ellary and Cambria walk toward the cliff's edge with their hands bound in front of them by rope…and Killian leads them there to stand on the precipice.

My body jerks into action, twisting to run after them, but Arlo stops me with both of his hands painfully squeezing my biceps. It aches as he digs his fingers into my flesh, but he'll have to grip tighter if he wants to keep me away from them.

"You can't go to them." He struggles to keep hold of me as I fight against him, twisting and jerking. "Mercy, *stop!*" He shouts so loudly that his deep voice bounces off the trees, carries into the clearing, and echoes through the void beyond.

I freeze, going still at the harsh sound of it, gritting my teeth against the cold, the fear, and the anger, which all make me shudder. My lips fight a snarl, a primal urge to hurt the man in front of me to avoid feeling the hurt within me.

He didn't do this.

Arlo didn't choose this for me.

He huffs, tilting his face closer to mine. "The only way you can save them is by sacrifice. It's your trial, Mercy. It's your friends who you have to sacrifice yourself for."

My eyes dart madly about his face before finally settling on the blue of his irises. He grabs hold of me with a look that encircles me. It feels as though he coils his rope around my body, twists and knots it, tightens it to force me into calmness, stillness. Slowly, I nod, coming to understand that Ellary and Cambria will be okay; they won't be harmed today because I'm going to make the choice to sacrifice myself to save them.

And just as I begin to steady myself, Delle's scream tears through my soul, vibrates so harshly through my bones that they rattle and threaten to break.

She saw the graves…

Arlo's grip loosens, and I turn just in time to see her take off toward the clearing. I lurch, but Theo is already moving, already chasing. He swiftly closes the distance, throwing his arm to bring it around her, his forearm crossing her chest so he can drag her back against him.

As Theo pulls her back, I see what she was running for. In the clearing beyond the forest, Ryker moves with two others, walking them out to stand beside Ellary and Cambria, who are far too close to the edge.

Don't fall. Please, don't fall, don't fall, don't fall.

Four people—two for me and two for Delle—are brought to stand shoulder-to-shoulder on the edge of the cliff. Each pair of wrists are bound with rope and all of their faces are etched with fear. Ellary and Cambria are brought to be the ones I sacrifice for, and I shouldn't be surprised by that.

But I'm shocked to see who stands for Delle.

I recognize them both, though I don't know either one well.

One of them is a servant in training—a fourteen-year-old girl, not even a woman of age to serve—who Delle had a close friendship with. And the other…the other is Delle's seven-year-old brother.

I clench my fists as fury takes me. I drag in a breath, and every particle of it bursts, exploding in my lungs and erupting from me with a vicious scream that slices through the trees, tears across the void, and makes the mountains quiver. My fists punch down toward the earth as the scream draws every ounce of energy from my body, tensing every muscle and vibrating through every bone.

How dare they bring an innocent child into this?!

The flames of rage engulf me, setting me ablaze with righteous indignation. These men know no bounds, no decency; they show no respect for the same innocence and purity they pretend to treasure for their domestic women and children. They know nothing of sacrifice, yet claim that women should dutifully and unquestionably sacrifice for them.

What have the men of Ember Glen ever sacrificed for us?

I turn back to Arlo, stepping closer, letting him see the flames burning behind my eyes. "I have a vow to make, Warden Rainn. Today is *not* the day my life will end. I will survive this trial," I promise through gritted teeth. "I'll survive this, and you'll no longer be held to the promise you made to me."

"Mercy—"

"We're not going to save this place; there's no redemption for the vileness of these men. We're going to destroy it. You and I are going to burn Ember Glen to the ground."

chapter thirty
ARLO

MERCY SCREAMS, AND the power of it makes the mountains tremble. The image of her stuns me. Sheathed in red with her mouth dropped open wide, the dark sweep of eye shadow across her lids and the thick black liner, which frames her ethereal silver-blue eyes, makes her appear otherworldly, like a furious fallen angel shouting her disgust of the way the world has turned.

She leans forward to project her anger. Her fists are clenched as she powerfully slams them down at her sides, and I swear I feel the ground shift beneath my feet, as though the force of her fury shot out from her fists and punched through the earth.

Watching her lose herself in this moment is horrifying, troubling, yet inspiring. Her rage is a thing of beauty.

All I can manage to do is stare at her when she moves in front of me. "We're going to destroy it. You and I are going to burn Ember Glen to the ground."

I know I can't kiss her, but oh, how I want to. The strength she found in the blink of an eye—horrified one moment and coldly determined the next—has my heart beating wildly, making the ache in my chest that's existed all day feel more profound.

I can't speak.

I'm so in awe of her that I'm lost in her stare, so humbled by her power that my words refuse to share space with hers. Slowly, I nod, telling her with my eyes that *yes*, she will survive this, and *yes*, we will burn it all to the ground.

We'll do it together.

I won't have to do it alone because she's not going to die.

She can't die today.

"Wesley, let's get started," Killian calls from across the clearing, and Wesley moves, walking out of the forest and into the open space beyond.

I grab hold of Mercy's shoulders as she fumes with fury, her shallow breaths rapidly lifting and lowering her chest. Mercy and I share a final look—a beat of acknowledgment that we suffer the same anger, that we both want the same war. There's a child standing out there at the edge of a cliff, his life threatened for the sake of asserting our power over sinners.

No, they aren't sinners.

Mercy didn't sin.

It's for the sake of asserting our power over *women.*

I tell her silently that I'm with her, yet I turn her to face the clearing and nudge her forward to her potential death.

I can't stop these events in motion.

I can't spare her from this trial.

But I know she'll fight hard for each and every breath; she'll fight harder than I ever could to survive this, because her work in this life is not done yet. The people of Ember Glen need her...

I need her.

Wesley stops about halfway between the tree line and the cliff's edge, turning to face us as we move among the trees. He rubs his palms together, blowing a huff of breath between them to generate heat. "Wardens, please bring your trial participants forward."

I loosen my grip on Mercy's shoulders and move to walk beside her, lowering one hand to the center of her back to urge her forward as we move between the trees. She marches gracefully, powerfully toward the clearing, her anger carrying her toward the danger faced by the innocent ones standing at the ledge.

She vibrates with the hum of willing sacrifice—a low, eerie sound that ripples through me and tells of her willingness to face death for the lives of those being threatened.

The lives of innocent women and children.

Wind whirls around us as we step from the tree line, coming to a stop before Wesley in the center of the clearing, where he readies himself to begin the trial with the incitement and prayer.

We wait for Delle and Theo to come and stand beside us, and the waiting is dreadful. It takes them minutes, which pass with excruciating slowness. Delle cries and protests the start of her trial. It's not just the cold that makes me shiver, but the sound of her fear, her misery, her distress. It's the tension from Mercy at my side as she fights to ignore Delle's pain that makes it even worse.

Gradually, Delle calms. It happens so evenly that it's almost like she's falling asleep. When Theo is finally able to bring her to stand beside us, I glance over and notice that Delle is loosening, relaxing, almost in a way that seems…artificially forced.

I look over at Mercy and find her eyes on Delle. She looks relieved at Delle's state as she seems to calm, loosely hanging onto Theo's arm. Mercy sighs before she looks at me, telling me without words what she did, and that she's not sorry that she gave Delle the little white pill.

Though I had grappled with the choice, I wasn't able to bring myself to give the only pill to Delle. In hindsight, I probably should have. Mercy seems to have found some peace in her fury, though Delle found none on her own, and I should have anticipated that. Without thinking of it consciously, maybe I knew deep down that Mercy wouldn't have kept the only pill for herself when she was able to give it to Delle. She sacrifices daily for the benefit of others.

"October twenty-seventh, twenty-one eighty-five," Wesley begins, lifting his chin as if he's speaking to the treetops, where

I assume at least one camera is placed. "We gather on this day to bear witness to Service by Sacrifice, the second of the three Trials of Dissension for sinners Mercy Madness and Delle Carter of Ember Glen. We welcome all who belong to the community of Ember Glen to bear witness to this trial, such that it brings awareness to the hardships that await those who sin.

"It has been decided by the authority of Ember Glen that this trial shall be conducted in a means representative of the severity of the sins committed. This community cannot thrive without our nights of purging beneath the full moon, and our servants must be committed to making the ultimate sacrifice in God's name, such that our community will remain a safe place for all. Mercy Madness chose to flee death, and as a result, one of her sisters in service lost her life."

Who does he mean…Ivy Jane?

Hyatt would have set a servant on fire that night whether Mercy had fled or not. It's taken me a long time to see this, but I understand it now…It wasn't Mercy's choice to flee that resulted in Ivy Jane's death; it was Hyatt's choice to set her on fire that ended her life. Hyatt alone is responsible.

"Delle Carter teeters on the brink of corruption. She chose to participate freely in these Trials of Dissension when she was under no such obligation, even though she, too, fled during a night of service. Though we hold hope that she'll find absolution through these trials, her actions must also be met with consequences representative of the severity of her sins."

Wesley pauses, adding tension to the moment as we wait to hear exactly what this trial will entail, as the wind whips around us all, making hair and skirts dance sidelong to the current of air.

"This Service by Sacrifice will be achieved through the live burial of each of our trial participants."

"What?" Mercy snaps.

"No, I can't—" Delle starts, but Theo silences her.

I don't look at Mercy, I can't. If I look at her right now, I'll fall apart entirely. She needs me strong. She needs to see me strong so she can find her own strength in this.

Buried alive?

How long can someone survive being buried alive?

Our training was pointless. She doesn't need to hold her breath…she'll slowly suffocate.

Fuck.

Fuck!

I falter, my head dropping low as I take in a trembling breath. I struggle to lift it again, but I do. Pulling back my shoulders, my pointed gaze rests firmly on Wesley.

"In a symbolic gesture, the participants will volunteer to sacrifice their own life to save the lives of two others. Standing behind me are Ellary Hill, Cambria Miller, Juniper Holly, and Adam Carter, the dearly beloved of our trial participants. We've brought them here to stand on the precipice of death, a touch away from toppling over the edge. We put their lives in the hands of our trial participants today."

Wesley looks between Mercy and Delle. "Participants, you each have a choice, and it is yours to make freely. Your first option is to walk to your grave, climb into your coffin, and close the lid. If you make that choice, your coffin will be lowered into the ground, and you will be buried alive. You'll remain inside for an amount of time to be drawn at random. When that time has expired, you'll be exhumed, which may or may not be before you suffocate and die. If you choose this, the lives of your beloved will be spared. The moment the lid of your coffin is closed, their hands will be untied and they'll be sent home, unharmed.

"Your second option is to spare yourself. Walk to the edge and stand before your loved ones. Tell them you choose your life over theirs, and then you must push them over the edge. Perhaps the fall will kill them, perhaps it won't. But that's certainly something to consider in making your choice. Could you stand before them if they survived and look them in the eye, satisfied with the choice you made?

"Both options involve facing the uncertainty of death. Either choice is a sacrifice…for others or for yourself."

There's no choice in this and they know it. Even if Mercy or Delle were cruel enough to push their friends over the edge to save themselves, what would happen then? It wouldn't be enough to pass the trial, which by the very definition, requires the sacrifice of *oneself* in the service of *others*. It's intentional by design. Mercy and Delle have no choice; they must climb into their coffins and allow my brothers to bury them alive.

My stomach lurches and I fight the urge to double over as nausea takes hold of me.

"Arlo Rainn and Theo Hughes, as the selected wardens of these trial participants, please present them for this Service by Sacrifice."

A full body shiver moves through me, rattling my nerves and shaking away my strength.

How do I do this?

Just as I begin to fear losing myself—just as my knees weaken and threaten to give way, bringing me to kneel in sorrow—Mercy's voice cuts through the madness of it all, and her enigmatic strength helps me find mine.

"I present *myself*," she grits. "I will sacrifice myself for every woman and child standing in this clearing. I will sacrifice myself for all of Ember Glen." We each turn our heads to look at each other at the same time. "Take me to my grave, Warden Rainn. I'm done with this. I won't allow the fear of those innocent people standing at the edge to be prolonged any further."

She holds my gaze for beats longer than I should allow, but I'm stuck there in her gaze, in the knowing that she is something so much more than I ever expected her to be. And though I feel like my insides are melting—like my organs are liquefying and creeping slowly through the cage of my bones to drip toward the earth—something in her eyes gives me the strength I need to speak. To say my rehearsed part and move forward through this nightmare…

The only way out is through.

"I present—" I falter, then pause, clear my throat, and begin again, "I present Mercy Madness for the second of these three Trials of Dissension. Mercy, do you enter this trial with the understanding of your sins and the means by which you are required to serve?"

"Yes," she replies, with no hesitation, no fear…only fury.

Theo speaks, but his voice is weak, sad, and broken. "I present Delle Carter for the second of these three Trials of Dissension. Delle, do you enter this trial with the understanding of your sins and the means by which you are required to serve?"

"Okay. Yes," she murmurs softly, though it's hard to hear her with the whipping wind rushing through the empty space beyond the cliff's edge.

It's the medication that calms her, that makes her more complacent. It seems to be taking hold of her much more quickly and stronger than it had with Mercy, and I fear for a moment that maybe it's because her body hasn't matured enough to handle it, that maybe she can't withstand the strength of it, and it will do damage.

But what does it matter when she's about to step into her own coffin?

Fuck.

I hope it's strong enough to give her courage, to keep her relaxed, to bring her into a quick sleep so she doesn't suffer.

No.

They're not going to die.

They're strong; they will survive this.

"Let us share a prayer before we begin," Wesley says, and I sharply turn my head to watch as he bows his head. "Our celestial creator and divine spirit, we come to You in this hour of trials and tribulations, seeking good favor in honor of our righteous choices. We bring these sinners before You, offering the sacrifice of their service in honor of the Impulse Edict, to the sanctity of Your divine word. We ask for Your righteous judgment of the souls of these sinners. Should they serve appropriately through these trials and prove themselves to be truly sacrificial servants, we ask for absolution of their wretched souls. Should these sinners choose selfishly, we ask for You to grant the innocent ones with quick and peaceful passages into the afterlife such that You may welcome them with Your eternal grace."

The boy, Delle's brother Adam, begins to cry, and the echo of it carries through the void beyond the cliff to echo against the mountains in the distance. "I'm scared," he whimpers.

"No." The single syllable from Delle is strained, crawling out of her throat along with the sob she tries to subdue. "Don't cry, love. Don't cry. I won't let anyone hurt you." Her head twists and rises to look up at Theo. "Take me to the coffin. I'll get in." She looks back to Wesley, who still has his head bowed through the unfinished prayer. "Bring him away from the edge…Please…"

Wesley continues, "Please grant me and my brothers of the Control the strength and peace of mind to carry out this trial with the uncertainty of whether lives will be lost today, such that we may present these sinners with a fair and exhaustive trial for their souls. *Malo mori quam foedari.*"

"*Malo mori quam foedari,*" I hear my brothers repeat, but I don't hear the words come from my mouth…I don't think I hear them come from Theo, either.

Wesley lifts his head and looks at Delle. "Delle Carter, we've selected you to choose first." Strangely, Wesley seems to falter, shifting his eyes away for a fraction of a second, his throat bobbing as he swallows hard, before digging deep and bringing his gaze back to Delle. "Tell us of your choice. In this trial of Service by Sacrifice, do you choose to sacrifice yourself or do you choose to sacrifice the lives of your innocent loved ones?"

"Myself…" Delle whispers. "I choose to sacrifice myself."

"Very well." Wesley turns, holding out his hand as Ryker approaches, carrying a small black fabric bag. He hands it to Wesley, who tugs the drawstring to open it before holding it out to Delle. "There are ten pieces of parchment inside this bag, each with a different duration for your live burial before you are exhumed. Reach inside and draw your time."

I look away, gazing out into the distance at the gray backdrop of this living nightmare. I don't want to watch as Delle reaches inside that bag. I hold my breath to hear how long she'll be buried beneath the earth, trapped in her own grave, slowly suffocating. I hear her hand rustle through the pieces of parchment in the bag, and my gaze is drawn back to Wesley as she hands her selected page to him.

Slowly, he unfolds the small piece and reads aloud, "You've selected one hour."

He turns the page around to show us in confirmation, and my chest sinks with relief. Delle could survive an hour, especially with the medication to keep her calmer than I know she would've been without it. The relief I feel is visceral, but the nightmare isn't over yet.

Wesley looks at Mercy. "Mercy Madness, tell us of your choice. In this trial of Service by Sacrifice, do you choose to sacrifice yourself or do you choose to sacrifice the lives of your innocent beloved ones?"

"Myself," she fumes.

"Very well," Wesley replies, holding out the bag to her. "Reach inside and draw your time."

She doesn't hesitate and she doesn't take her time. With rushed and forceful movement, she reaches into the bag and quickly selects a piece of parchment, handing it to Wesley. He unfolds it and reads, and it happens so quickly, that I'm not sure whether I heard him correctly at first. But when he turns the page around to show us, my eyes confirm the truth.

Four hours.

Four hours, in a coffin, buried beneath the soil.

My brain stutters, stalling as it tries to wrap around that measure of time and whether there would be enough oxygen buried with her in that coffin to last for four hours…and truthfully, I don't know.

I don't know if she'll survive.

Voices speak around me, but I can't hear what they're saying. They all blend with the wind circling around us as faded echoes, whispers of spoken sounds without discernible words. The sound fades into an empty howl behind my ears. Space and time warp, stretching me apart into oblivion, making everything appear as though it's happening in slow-motion.

I'm unaware of how Mercy's arm has come to be linked with mine, how I've managed to unconsciously put one foot in front of the other, how the distance is closing rapidly between us and the two graves nestled in the trees.

At some point, we stop moving, and I'm still lost to the dull roar created by every sound in existence blending into one. It obscures the world in such a way that Mercy has to turn to face me, move into my space, and dig her fingernails into my bicep just to get my attention.

My eyes shift through the haze to find her giving me a stern look, but the moment I meet her eyes, the world harshly falls into focus. Sounds separate, my vision sharpens, and emotions flood my veins from my rapidly beating heart.

"Do you hear me?" she snaps, her eyes narrowed on me.

My head tilts in confusion because I hadn't heard a word.

"Mercy, I can't—"

"You can, and you will. The moment I'm inside, you will close the lid, lower that damn coffin, and bury me yourself. I will *not* allow you to let my friends die because you're too weak to do your duty."

"If wanting you to live makes me weak, then I am the weakest man who has ever walked this earth." I have no conscious thought of my words—they simply slip out.

Her eyes remain narrowed on me, but the harsh line of her eyebrows twists and softens. "This must be done, Warden Rainn. It must. And you have to ensure it. If I'm not buried, they will kill Ellary and Cambria. You know they will, even if I refuse to push them myself. You have to do this." Mercy's nails dig deeper into my flesh, and I savor the pain of it. If it's the last touch we ever share, I'll revel in the pain of it forever.

But suddenly, the beautiful ache is gone. Her hand has fallen away, and she no longer stands in front of me. She moves to her grave, and as I watch her walk, I have no awareness of anything else happening around me. I'm frozen in time as I watch her reach to lift the lid of her coffin. I'm stuck in place as the layers of her red gown shift and move, as she lifts her leg over the side of the coffin and climbs to stand inside it.

My chin lifts to look up at her eyes, finding her face etched with a myriad of expressions all at once. She straightens, pulling her shoulders back to stand tall and proud as she faces the clearing.

"I sacrifice myself for all the women in Ember Glen," she shouts, and the world around us falls silent. There's no roaring wind, no rustling leaves, no voices or footsteps…only silence and the piercing sound of Mercy's powerful voice. "I sacrifice myself in the name of all things deemed unholy. I sacrifice myself as a willing catalyst for *war*." Her jaw sets and she grits her teeth, spitting the last words with fury. "May the women of Ember Glen cut out the heart of every hateful man and deliver his soul to demons…And may those demons show no mercy in delivering their penance for our suffering."

She lowers. She sits. She closes her eyes.

"Warden Rainn," she calls out to me as she starts to lay back, "do your duty. Shut me in and bury me. Let it be done."

I suddenly find myself at her side, not knowing when I moved or how I got here. I lean over to see her laying in her coffin, her eyes squeezed shut, her black-painted lids appearing as eyeless voids. Her red dress takes up so much space in the coffin—space that oxygen might have filled.

Red.

The color of her sacrifice...

The time for it has arrived.

"Please," she whispers, as if she can sense how near my presence is without looking. "Before I lose my nerve, shut the lid, Warden Rainn. Shut the fucking lid..." her voice trembles, "and make sure they're all okay."

This woman, this warrior, this goddess or mystical being... Whatever she is, I'm in awe of her, bound to her, tethered to her for eternity. She gives her life so others may live. And her speech— her incitement of *war*, her declaration of her willingness to die in hopes it will spur others to rebel in the name of their freedom to live as they wish—gave me strength. It gave me power. It gave me the determination I needed to fight through this moment of true horror with my eyes set on the future and what must be done.

Rebellion.

An uprising.

An unholy war.

I will lead that war in her honor if she can't lead it herself.

She will *lead it herself.*

She'll survive this.

I reach over her to grip the lid, the leather of my glove creaking as I fold my hand around the edge. Then, I bend, dipping close enough to whisper, "Steady breaths. Don't panic. Be still."

"Arlo." Her eyes twitch to open but she fights it, and I imagine it's because she knows as well as I do that if our gazes meet, fear and sorrow will grip us both. She slowly lets out a breath, relaxing her features, trying to bring herself to calmness before she whispers, "Wildflowers and starlight."

My pulse speeds, racing through my veins with equal parts anguish and elation.

The last words are for me.

Her last thought is of me.

It's humbling and gut-wrenching, and the only thing I can do to survive this is to act.

I tug on the lid, preparing to lower it swiftly, but before I do, I tell her what she needs to hear in plain and simple terms—no holding back, no secret phrases or substitutions of words to hide their meaning from others.

"I love you, Mercy Madness," I whisper. "I love everything you were, everything you are, and everything you will become when you survive this. And you *will* survive this. You and I have a rebellion to lead."

A strained smile tugs at the corners of her lips, and that's it. That has to be enough. I open my hand to drop the lid, and it slams shut with a thump that bounces off the trees and echoes into the clearing. I step back, moving quickly to the head of her coffin, and press the button at the side of the platform. The mechanism whirs as the coffin begins to lower.

I have to hold the button down to keep it running, and my hand trembles with the urge to let go, but I can't. The moment that lid closed was the moment I trapped her with all the oxygen she'll get to take with her into her grave. The sooner she's buried, the sooner her time will start, and the more likely she'll be to survive.

She'll survive.

She'll fucking survive.

I lift my head and look out into the clearing, needing to focus on something other than the whir of the machine that sinks my

Mercy—my love, my wildflowers and starlight—into the earth. I can't look as I force her descent into her grave.

I look at Delle's loved ones at the edge of the cliff, watching as Ryker unties their hands. Her brother Adam runs for the trees the moment his hands are freed. If they're being freed, then it means Delle's coffin is closed, but I can't bring myself to look over. If I see that Theo's expression mirrors my agony, it might just break me.

I watch Killian carefully as he moves, first untying Cambria's hands. She steps away from the edge and waits for Ellary, turning to watch as Killian moves in front of her. I assume he's untying Ellary's hands, but the way he stands blocks my view of what's happening between them.

It's why confusion washes over me when Cambria screams, "No!" and lurches forward.

Abruptly, Killian whirls around and looks at me, but my eyes are quickly drawn away. I can only sense the curling of his lips in a vicious smile because all I can see is the widening of Ellary's eyes— the moment of panic in her expression—as she tilts backward, black boots teetering on the edge as she fights to maintain her balance and step forward.

Mercy's coffin lands at the bottom of her grave.

The whirring stops as the machine cuts off.

And I watch helplessly as Ellary falls.

Mercy and Arlo's story
concludes in book three...

brynn's books

The Four Families Trilogy
Counts of Eight
Dance with Death
Pas de Trois

The Four Families Spin-Off
King of Masters

Ember Glen
Spark of Madness
Blaze of Misery
Embers of Mercy

Senseless
Unheard
Unseen

Lawless
(Coming Soon!)
The Darkness We Hide

Standalones
Jagged Line Paradise
Sugar Wood
The Alter

connect with brynn

Author Newsletter
brynnford.com/connect

Goodreads
goodreads.com/brynnfordauthor

BookBub
bookbub.com/profile/brynn-ford

Instagram
@brynnfordauthor
instagram.com/brynnfordauthor

TikTok
@brynnfordauthor
tiktok.com/@brynnfordauthor

Facebook Page
facebook.com/brynnfordauthor

Facebook Reader's Group
Brynn's Daring Darlings
bit.ly/brynnsdarlings

acknowledgments

I have completely fallen in love with Mercy and Arlo's story, and I feel so grateful that I'm able to tell it. Though writing is a solitary process, I wouldn't have the time, energy, confidence, or perseverance to put words on the page without some amazing people who—for some unknown reason—want to see me succeed.

Chris, your patience and encouragement keep me going. Every time I think about giving up, you remind me why I started writing the words in the first place. I literally couldn't do this without you. *Wildflowers and starlight.*

To the woman who took a chance on reading a debut novel from someone she'd never heard of before and ended up becoming an incredible friend, consistent supporter, die-hard fan, and personal assistant, thank you for being you, Danielle! I've told you before, but I'll tell you again, I might have given up on this long ago if it weren't for you, and I'm so grateful that you keep me going. You really are the best!

I have the most amazing beta readers! You lovely ladies cheer me on, give me life, help me find and fix my mistakes, and just generally make me a better writer. You're also amazing people, and I'm so glad we connected through my stories. Danielle, Mary, Echo, Brandy, and Amanda, you are incredible. I can't thank you enough for the countless hours spent reading my chapters that I send to you in agonizing bits and pieces with terrible cliffhangers. I appreciate you so, so much!

I'm so grateful for my Street and ARC team and for everyone who has read, reviewed, or posted about this series. Seriously, *thank you.* I don't know if you understand how much you mean to me for taking the time to read this story and share your thoughts about it. Truly, I appreciate you more than I can say!

Najla, Nada, and the team at Qamber Designs, thank you so much for making my book look beautiful! I adore your team and the work you do is always spectacular. I can always count on you to create gorgeous covers and stunning interior design for my stories. You all are amazing!

Silvia. Let's chat for a minute about how awesome you are. Not only do you somehow manage to make my words sparkle and shine, but you put up with my crazy schedule when this book got the best of me. Your flexibility was literally my saving grace as I fought through writing this book. Thank you so much for making my words the best they can be!

My final thank you goes directly to you, reader. You picked up this book, you read the words I wrote, and for that alone, I am grateful. If you connected with the characters or the story and enjoyed this read, just know that you and I have met through these words, and I'm forever thankful you took the journey with me.

about the author

Brynn Ford is a USA Today Bestselling Author of dark romance for daring readers. She writes emotionally heavy love stories that will twist your soul and shatter your heart before pulling you back together with a hopeful happily-ever-after.

Brynn's books are dark, sometimes disturbing, and often overwhelming. But they're always brightened by an insistent, spicy romance that will live rent-free in your head long after you've turned the final page.

When Brynn isn't obsessively writing, you may find her binge-watching favorite shows while eating far too much junk food or fanatically reading, always seeking to lose herself in the emotional roller coaster of a damn good story. She's a firm believer that her characters continue to live outside the pages in the minds of her readers. Stories don't end just because there aren't any more pages to turn.